D0638748

DATE DUE

LIGHTNING STRIKES

Published by POCKET BOOKS

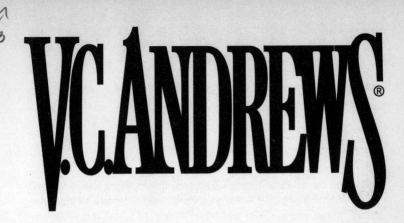

V.C. ANDREWS®

LIGHTNING STRIKES

POCKET **STAR** BOOKS

New York   London   Toronto   Sydney   Singapore

An *Original* Publication of POCKET BOOKS

A Pocket Star Book published by
POCKET BOOKS, a division of Simon & Schuster Inc.
1230 Avenue of the Americas, New York, NY 10020

ISBN: 0-7394-1166-7

V.C. ANDREWS and VIRGINIA ANDREWS are registered
trademarks of the Vanda General Partnership.

POCKET STAR BOOKS and colophon are registered
trademarks of Simon & Schuster Inc.

Cover design by Jim Lebbad
Back jacket illustration by Lisa Falkenstern
Printed in the U.S.A.

LIGHTNING STRIKES

Prologue

Sometimes in the early evening when the shadows deepened and thickened in the corners of rooms within Grandmother Hudson's mansion, I would hear soft whispering. It wasn't something I heard when I first arrived, but it was something I was hearing more and more now. The whispers sounded like voices warning me, but about what, I wondered. What?

Back in Washington, D.C., Mama had finally revealed the truth of my birth: my real mother was a rich white woman who had gotten pregnant with me in college. Her boyfriend at the time was a black man named Larry Ward, and after I was born my real mother's father had made the arrangements for me to live with Ken and Latisha Arnold. Ken had been paid well for it. I grew up thinking Beni Arnold was my younger sister and Roy Arnold was my older brother.

After Beni had been murdered by gang members and Mama had told me the truth about myself, she forced my white mother Megan Randolph to meet with us and then pleaded with her to help her get me out of the ghetto world. I thought Mama was trying to get me to live with my real family because she was worried more than ever about the drugs and the gang violence, but there was another reason, one I wouldn't learn until much later. Mama was dying from cancer and she wanted to be sure I was safe and had the opportunities she would never be able to give me.

My real mother was reluctant. She simply wanted to give Mama more money. She said it was the worst time for all this because her husband was being considered for political office. Finally, as a compromise which would still keep my true identity a secret, my real mother arranged for me to come here and live with her widowed mother, Frances Hudson. As far as the rest of the world was concerned, it was supposed to be an act of charity: taking in a poor girl who showed academic promise. Rich people had so many charitable causes and organizations to list under their names that adding one more, fictional or otherwise, was no problem.

In the beginning I thought I wouldn't last long in this rich, rural Virginia world attending Dogwood, a private school populated mostly by wealthy kids, but not because I wasn't up to the academic challenge. I had, despite my poor school, always been a good student, a reader. And I wasn't worried about being treated badly. None of these snobby kids could stare me down or make me feel bad with their remarks and looks. I had been through far worse.

No, what worried me was my real grandmother. She was a stern elderly woman who liked to lecture and rail at her doctor, her lawyers and accountants, and especially my mother's younger sister Victoria who had taken over management of the family businesses. Grandmother Hudson and I confronted each other like two prize fighters during those early days and weeks. I refused to permit her to get away with even a single innuendo, a single nasty remark about my life with Mama, Roy, Beni and even my adoptive father Ken Arnold.

Although we had lived in the projects of Washington, D.C., Mama had never given up her high hopes for all of us. She wanted me to have an education and become something. I was no slum girl, no ghetto bad girl, and Grandmother Hudson wasn't going to be allowed to paint me into that stereotyped picture.

She realized it soon enough, and soon enough we agreed to a truce and then, after time, we even developed a warm affection for each other. One day I learned she had even included me in her will. It enraged her younger daughter Victoria who didn't find out the truth about me until I was nearly finished with my school year at Dogwood. She wanted to blackmail my mother and force her to help get me out of the will.

I suspected this was the real reason I was given the opportunity to attend a prestigious drama school in London. It was just a way to get rid of me, a sort of compromise. However, Grandmother Hudson insisted that wasn't so.

"Do you think I would ever let my daughter dictate an important decision to me?" she bellowed at me when I so much as suggested it.

"No," I said.

"You're right about that. Not as long as there is still breath in these old lungs, she won't, so don't go feeling sorry for yourself or for me," she warned. "People who accept pity have thrown in the towel. On my tombstone, I want it written that here lies a woman who never accepted pity. Understand?"

"Yes," I said, laughing at her. She muttered and fumed but kept a smile under that mask of outrage, a smile only I could see.

Now, with the school year over, I was days away from leaving for England. Mama had died. Ken was in prison where he belonged. Roy was in the army, and poor Beni was gone. I really had no one but myself, for my real mother had managed to keep intact the secret of who I was, and now it looked like she would be able to continue keeping me without a name just to maintain peace in her own precious, perfect world. Her excuse was always the same—that she had to protect her husband Grant who was trying to become a politician.

Her own children, Brody and Alison, had no idea they were my half brother and half sister. I really didn't want to be related to Alison anyway, but Brody had become too attentive and my mother was worried that he was developing a romantic attachment. Brody was a football star and an advanced-placement student. My grandmother worried about the way he took to me, too.

I suspected that was another reason she was so eager to have me go off to London. She made plans to accompany me on the initial journey, but her doctor, who had managed, with my help, to have a pacemaker implanted in her, strongly advised against her making the trip. The pacemaker wasn't quite right yet. Naturally, Grandmother Hudson threw a tantrum and vowed to defy her doctor. I had to stand up to her and tell her that I wouldn't go if she came along.

"I'm not going to be responsible for what might happen to you," I told her firmly. She could bluster and wave her hands at the air between us, and I wouldn't flinch.

"That's nonsense." She paced the room, gesticulating wildly. "And just whom do you think you're speaking to?"

"I was hoping a mature adult," I said. Her lips moved for a moment without a sound emerging. Her tongue was so eager to lash out her words.

"You know you are an infuriating young lady, don't you?" she finally managed.

"I wonder from whom I've inherited that," I replied.

"Not your mother, that's for sure," she said. "Give her a crisis and she'll go out and buy a new dress."

She flopped in the big chair in her bedroom and sat back with her arms over the cushioned sides.

"I'm warning you. My sister Leonora, who agreed to let you live with her, is not anything like me."

"That's a relief."

"Don't be rude," she snapped. She took a breath, looked out the window, and turned back to me. "She's very stuffy. She and her husband Richard are quintessentially English. Their lives are filled with codes of behavior that make the rules I live by look like chaos. On top of that, you'll be living like one of her domestics, fulfilling chores. You might not be able to face them alone. Every day they'll remind you of how lucky you are to be able to serve them."

I retorted, "Lucky. I wonder every day what I did to be this lucky."

"You are a sassy child. Well," she said with a sigh, "they can't expect that I purged you of all your willful ways in the short time you've been living here with me. There is only so much a person can accomplish, even someone like me."

"Why, Grandmother, you are admitting limits?"

"Do you want to give me a heart attack? Is that why you're being so impudent?"

I smiled.

She turned away to hide her own smile behind her hand and then shook her head.

"I just can't imagine you living with Leonora. It was a bad idea."

"I'm sure it will be nothing compared to where I lived in Washington, D.C., Grandmother. Are there people being shot on the street in front of her home? Does she have dope addicts in the hallways and gang members standing on the corner ready to terrorize me?"

"She has her own hurdles for you to jump," she countered. "She believes she belongs with English royalty. All right," she said, nodding, her eyes small. "You'll see for yourself." She sighed deeply. "You'll be spending most of your time at the school, anyway, I suppose. After my ogre of a doctor signs me off, I'll join you and see that you're not being exploited."

"I think I can see to that myself," I said.

"Don't be arrogant, Rain. It's not becoming, and it will only lead to trouble."

"I'm not being arrogant. I'm being…confident," I said. "Do you think it's easy for me to agree to pick up and go to another country?" I asked, holding my hands out.

She laughed.

"I suppose you have a point. All right, let's not beat a dead horse. Get me my pills, please," she said, gesturing toward the nightstand by her bed. I got one of her tablets out and gave it to her with a glass of water. "Your mother claims she will be here tomorrow to say good-bye. Don't hold your breath," she told me. "I'm sure she'll come up with some convenient excuse like she has to attend some political function with Grant."

"When it comes to my mother," I said, "I've grown accustomed to disappointment."

She nodded sadly.

"On the other hand," she said, suddenly smiling, "Victoria would be eager to help load your suitcases and see you off."

"I know."

Her smile softened and disappeared.

"Maybe you're the lucky one after all. I have to stay here with my children and grandchildren, not that they'll visit me much. I don't expect I'll see much of Brody with you gone," she added with a suspicious look in her eyes.

"He hasn't called or written to me if that's what you're asking, Grandmother."

"Good," she said. She shook her head. "Your mother has to face up to the truth one of these days."

"Why?" I asked dryly.

She stared at me. I wanted her to say because it was the right thing to do, despite the danger and the consequences. Blood used to be thicker than water.

When I first met my real mother, I had hoped we would become close. I had looked forward to having a mother-daughter relationship. However, she was still quite a stranger to me and the chance of that ever changing seemed unlikely.

"I'm taking a short nap," Grandmother said rather than continue the discussion.

I fetched a blanket and put it over her legs and she closed her eyes. I hated seeing her so weak and fatigued. In a strange turn of circumstances, she had become my only real family. Six months ago, she wouldn't have even noticed me on the street nor I her. How fate toyed with us, I thought as I left Grandmother Hudson's room.

When I walked through the house, I heard the whispers grow louder in the corners. Perhaps they came from the ghosts of Grandmother Hudson's ancestors, wondering what their world had become to have someone with my background living here. Maybe the warnings I imagined came from that. Here a girl with black blood, a girl who had an African-American for a father, was living like a true grandchild, given the best of everything and was even included in this old, distinguished white family's legacy. The ghosts of this family's past might think we were tempting fate with such behavior.

I left the house and went down to the lake. Two rather large crows were perched on a rock. They stared at me with cautious interest. I wondered if any other species but man made a thing of color. Did other birds look down at the crows because they were black? They were quite beautiful, more glossy ebony than black, and their eyes looked bejeweled in the twilight sun. Roy had beautiful dark eyes like that, I thought, remembering.

I wondered how he was doing in the army. He had already been transferred to Germany and we had talked about his coming to see me in England. Surely, I thought, Roy must feel like an orphan too, for he was never close to his father and now, with his father in prison and his mother gone, he had only the army. At least I had Grandmother Hudson.

The sound of a car's horn sent the crows skyward. They passed over me, their wings flapping simultaneously making them seem almost like one bird. With their beaks slightly open, they looked like they were laughing as they sailed over the lake toward the safety of the pockets of darkness in the woods.

"Good-bye," I whispered and turned to wave to Jake, my grandmother's chauffeur. He had picked up my airline ticket and was holding it up like the winning lottery ticket. I hurried up the path.

"You're all set," he said, handing me the packet. "You're leaving the day after tomorrow. England. Wow! I bet you're excited, huh?"

"Nervous, more than excited, Jake."

He smiled and nodded. Jake was tall, lean and balding, yet he had bushy eyebrows. I loved his happy-go-lucky personality. Nothing seemed to get to him. Just before the end of school year, he had taken me to see his horse, a newly born colt. He had named it after me.

Grandmother Hudson was lucky she had someone like Jake, I thought. He had been with her a long time and they had known each other even before he'd become an employee. In fact, his father had once owned this property. In some ways he felt more like family to me.

"You'll do just fine, Rain," he said. "Just send me some English toffee from time to time. Speaking of the English, how's our own queen?" he asked eyeing the house.

"Mrs. Hudson is still threatening to come along, if that's what you mean."

"Don't be surprised if she's on the plane," he warned, nodding.

"If she is, I'll jump out. I told her so."

He laughed and headed for his car.

"I'll be here bright and early."

"Don't expect me to be bright," I called. He waved, got in and drove off.

It seemed to get dark quickly. The great house loomed behind me, the lights burning in Grandmother Hudson's bedroom window. I had been here only a short time, but at least I had begun to understand what it meant to have a home again. Now I was to go off on an uncertain adventure. I had been a success in the school play and people who supposedly knew about these things thought I might have what it takes to become an actress.

Why shouldn't I have what it takes to pretend? I thought. Most of my life I had to do that: I had to pretend we had a safe home life, a father who cared about us, a future for myself and my family. Now, I was pretending to be an orphan when I knew I had a real mother who still denied me. Illusions were as much a part of me as anything.

How simple it should be to step off one stage and onto another, I thought.

If I have to live like this and be like this, isn't it better to have an audience applauding and to take curtain calls?

The moon looked like a spotlight being fired up. The world around me was a great theater.

A wave of whispering rose from my imaginary audience and reached me in the darkness behind the curtain.

"Don't be afraid," Mama was saying.

"Take your position, Rain," the director ordered.

"Everyone ready?"

"Mama...I can't help it. I'm frightened," I cried toward the dark wings.

"It's too late, baby," she whispered. "Look. The curtain's opening."

I nodded. It was too late.

"Let's begin," I told myself and stepped forward into the light, onto the stage, as if I expected to be reborn.

1

A Grand Adventure

Grandmother Hudson sat there with an I-told-you-so smile on her face at the breakfast table after I returned from speaking with my mother on the phone.

"Well?" she asked when I sat in silence. I knew she wanted to hear she had been right. Spitefully, I wanted to keep her waiting. Actually, my reluctance to speak was more out of my own pain. No matter how brave a face I put on, I was still disappointed.

"She's not coming," I said quickly, my eyes downcast. "She says the attorney general is having them over for dinner. I'm supposed to call her if you dare make plans to go with me to England."

"I should go just for that," Grandmother Hudson said like a petulant little girl. "Have you packed everything?"

"Yes."

She slid a long white envelope over the table to me.

"What's this?"

"Extra spending money. I don't expect my sister will

buy you anything you need. It's a bank draft, so soon after you arrive, ask Leonora to direct you to her bank and have it deposited. You know, of course, all the money will be changed to English pounds?"

"Yes."

"You'll have to learn the exchange rate so you understand what things will cost. Of course you'll speak the same language," she continued, "but there are many differences. My sister has become an Anglophile. She has an accent and all, although there were times even recently when I caught her sounding more like an American. It will take a little getting used to, but that will be part of the adventure." She paused, sat back and sighed. "I wish I was your age, going off somewhere. I feel like I've been chained to this chair and imprisoned by my own traitorous heart," she moaned.

"You've told me many times that you did a great deal of traveling and that you enjoy not having to drag off somewhere," I reminded her.

"Yes, we did travel quite often until Everett became ill." She paused, looking thoughtful for a moment and then smirked at me. "No one told you that you have to memorize every last word I utter in this house and then throw them back at me."

I laughed at her and she smiled, wagging her head. Then she grew serious again.

"I should tell you a little about my sister Leonora and her husband Richard," she said sitting forward. "You already know he is a barrister, and Leonora will be the first to tell you how important he is. They live in a fancy part of London, Holland Park. I've actually only been there twice, once for a visit and once...for a funeral."

"Funeral?"

"They lost their only child Heather. She was seven at the time."

"How horrible. How did she die?"

"She was born with a defective heart valve and corrective surgery didn't solve the problem. One morning, they found she'd died in her sleep. It was very sad."

"What did you tell your sister about me?" I asked.

"What everyone else believes. It's better for us to leave it that way. My sister isn't as liberal minded as I am. For now, she thinks you're going there to live and help with the domestic chores while you attend the drama school. Since they have a maid, a cook, a butler and a chauffeur, I'm sure there won't be all that much for you to do. She's certainly not going to give up her maid and assign her duties to you. Having a team of servants is too much of a status symbol to Leonora."

"I'm not afraid of hard work, Grandmother."

"I know." She smiled and then her face turned somber to add, "It's not the work that will be hard. However, I wouldn't have agreed to send you over if I didn't feel you would do well, Rain. Mr. MacWaine will take good care of you, and I do hope to get there myself someday soon, despite my oppressive physician."

I nodded. I really did hope she would.

Later in the day while I was writing a letter to Roy, I heard Victoria come into the house. I could always tell when it was Victoria. Her heels tapped down on the tile floor like tiny hammers when she walked. Her steps were deliberate, each one falling with a vengeance. I suppose I could say she didn't walk as much as she marched, her long legs striding forcefully as her bony shoulders turned.

I could hear her voice, barely muffled behind Grandmother Hudson's closed door.

"I just learned of the expense of this ridiculous trip to England you're sponsoring, Mother. On top of it all, you're sending her first class?"

"You always travel first class, Victoria," I heard Grandmother Hudson remind her.

"That's me. I'm your daughter. I run the affairs here. I should travel first class. That…girl is a family disgrace, someone to hide, not blatantly wave about as if we're all so proud my sister had an illegitimate child with a black man. Daddy would turn over in his grave. *He* didn't even travel first class!"

"Your father never took advantage of his money. I never understood the reason for making it if you don't enjoy it," Grandmother Hudson said calmly.

"Exactly my point. She didn't make it, did she?"

"When will you understand that what I do with my money is my business, Victoria? We've had this conversation ad nauseam. If you want to be thrifty, be so with your own money and leave me alone."

"I saw how much that school is costing, too," Victoria said, ignoring Grandmother Hudson's wishes. "It's ridiculous to assume she has any talent on the basis of a school play. Conor MacWaine is robbing us. He probably enjoys taking advantage of stupid Americans."

"Are you calling me stupid?"

"It's not very bright to spend forty thousand dollars on…on that girl becoming an actress."

"If you're quite finished…"

"I'm not finished. I want to know when you're calling your attorney about the will, Mother."

"I told you what I've done I will not undo. When you make up your own will, you can leave her out."

"What?" Victoria's laugh was more like a thin squeal. "You don't think I'll ever include her in my will, do you? Oh, what's the use? I'm wasting my breath."

"Finally, you say something intelligent."

"Everyone shouldn't depend on me keeping my mouth shut forever about this, Mother. One of these days..."

"You'll do nothing," Grandmother Hudson snapped. "If you so much as suggest..."

"It's not right and it's...unhealthy to be coddling her like this. Megan should be ashamed of what she has done to the rest of us."

It grew quiet and then a few moments later, Victoria emerged from the room and stomped out of the house. I hoped she had marched out of my life. She was so bitter, with her teeth clenched all the time and her eyebrows turned in like someone with a continuous headache. She seemed to take pleasure in nothing. I didn't think she even liked herself, much less me. I imagined she lived in a house without mirrors so she could avoid looking at herself.

When I saw Grandmother Hudson later in the day, I didn't mention hearing any of the conversation between her and Victoria. I was sure she wanted me to forget it as quickly as she apparently did. She enjoyed so little in the way of pleasure from her children and grandchildren. It made me reconsider what it means to be rich and to be poor.

Just as he had promised, Jake was there early the next morning. We had barely finished breakfast when he arrived. After he stepped into the dining room, I realized I rarely, if ever, had seen Jake in the house. Occasionally he would bring in groceries or whatever packages had to be carried, but usually he waited outside by the car. This morning he looked spiffy. His uniform was cleaned and pressed and the brim of his cap glittered in the light of the chandelier.

"Morning, ladies," he declared as he took a tiny bow. "I am here to fetch the princess and her things for her journey to the Old World."

"Don't make a fool of yourself this early in the morning, Jake Marvin," Grandmother Hudson warned. She glanced quickly at me and then straightened with a military posture in her chair. "Everything is waiting in her room."

"Thank you, ladies," he replied with a smile on his lips, pivoted and paraded off to get my luggage.

"I'll miss Jake," I said, looking after him with a soft smile on my face.

"Yes, well, when you get to London, you'll see the way a chauffeur is supposed to behave, I'm sure. My sister wears her servants like ribbons on her chest. They're all properly uniformed and trained. My brother-in-law runs his home as if it was a Swiss timepiece. They live their lives according to the tick of that grandfather's clock. The English and their high tea.

"When I think of what a dizzy, foolish little girl Leonora was before she went to finishing school and then to England, I marvel at what one's ego can accomplish," Grandmother Hudson said.

"Don't you like your sister?"

"Like her? Of course I don't like her. I love her as I should love a sister, but we never got along. Now that I think of it, your mother takes after Leonora more than she takes after me. Some gene must have jumped ship when I wasn't looking," she added.

"Are you sure your sister really wants me there?" I asked, still suspicious about everyone's motives.

"Leonora doesn't do anything she doesn't want to do, even though she owes me more than she can ever repay. I don't mean to make her seem unpleasant. I have no doubt you'll enjoy your stay there and she'll be able to brag about the great charitable thing she's doing, and for an American no less!"

We heard Jake carrying my bags down the stairs. Grandmother Hudson glanced at the small clock in her hutch and then looked at me.

"You should get yourself ready," she said in a softer voice.

My heart began to thump like a tire that had gone flat. I still couldn't believe I was going to be taken to the airport and flown across the ocean. Grandmother Hudson had seen to my passport. Everything had been done. There was nothing left to do but go. I stood up slowly.

"I'm not good at good-byes," she said, "but I'll walk out with you."

"I was hoping you would come along to the airport," I said.

"Oh, I hate that ride. Besides, you have to learn how to be on your own from the get-go," she added firmly.

I swallowed back my anxiety and started out. She was right behind me.

Jake stood by the Rolls holding the rear door open for me. His smile glimmered in the morning sunlight. I hesitated on the steps, took a deep breath and started toward the car. Grandmother Hudson followed. When I got to the car, I turned and we looked at each other. I had a sinking feeling in my chest. What if we never saw each other again? I had said good-bye to too many people this year, I thought.

"Are you going to take better care of yourself?" I asked her.

"Do I have a choice with all these doctors poking their noses in my business?"

"No," I replied.

"Then you've answered your own question. Stop worrying about me. I'm an old lady. Worry about yourself, about becoming someone of whom we would all be proud, including your mama," she added.

It brought a smile to my face.

"Thank you." I glanced at Jake. The way he looked at us made me wonder if he knew more than he pretended to know. Impulsively, I stepped forward and gave Grandmother Hudson a hug. She stiffened as if it was unwelcomed, but in her eyes I saw the softness and affection that had drawn me closer to her all these months.

"I was afraid there was nobody in my family with a sense of propriety and the grit to do the right things. Don't disappoint me," she said.

"I won't." I couldn't hide the tears in my eyes.

"Good-byes are simply ridiculous," she muttered, spun around and headed back into the house.

Jake winked at me.

I got into the vehicle and he closed the door. Grandmother Hudson paused at the front door and looked back. I rolled the window down and we just gazed at each other. Then I lifted my hand as Jake started the engine. I waved once. She waved back and we were on our way. She watched us leave and then turned and entered the house.

How lonely she was, I thought, despite her brave and blustery act. She should be the one who goes off to drama school, not me. She's a much better actress. Both her daughters were disappointing to her and she didn't enjoy her grandchildren. Her friends were all society ladies who used her for her charity contributions. Her house was full of echoes, empty voices, dark memories, heavy whispers and heavier music drifting out of windows and caught in the wind.

"Don't worry about our queen," Jake said. He had been watching me in the rearview mirror. "I'll see that she does the right things and gets over to see you in short order."

"You?" I started to laugh, but there was a look on Jake's face that told me not to underestimate him. "I hope so, Jake," I said.

As we rode to the airport, Jake told me stories of his own travels, filling them with little warnings about people, about scam artists.

"Be really careful about who you talk to and never show your money. Never show anyone where you're keeping it on you, Rain. Just take out a few bucks for gum and magazines and stash the rest safely, hear?"

"Yes, Jake."

"If you take your time and don't let anyone rush you along, you won't make mistakes. When you're in a strange place, it's always better to listen first and talk last."

"All right, Jake."

"Just go directly to your boarding gate and wait with your carry-on luggage right by you. If you leave it for a second, there'll be some creep ready to scoop it up. The airports are full of parasites who hang around just looking for someone like yourself who looks green."

"Me? Green?" I started to laugh, but Jake kept a serious expression.

"These people are experts, Rain. They know how to tell the difference between a seasoned traveler and an innocent young lady," he warned sternly.

"All right, Jake. I'll pay attention."

"Good."

"You should have had a dozen daughters," I told him.

He laughed, but I really meant it. Why was it people who didn't want children, who were too selfish to really care for them, were the ones who had them, and people like Jake who were generous and loving at heart went through life alone?

Mama used to live with the deep-set belief that ultimately fairness and right would win out at the end, that there was a good and just superior power taking care of us. Maybe it wasn't evident, but it was there.

Poor Mama, I thought. I wonder if she died still believing in good angels or if she had lost her faith in the end and died with disappointment blackening her pure heart.

It wasn't until the airport came into sight that I realized not only had I not flown overseas, I had never flown anywhere! I wondered if Jake knew that.

"It looks so busy," I commented seeing all the vehicles double-parking, people rushing about, skycaps rolling luggage, shuttle buses winding around cars, policemen screaming at drivers and waving on other cars. I thought it was pure chaos. "What a mess. How does anyone know where to go?"

"This isn't your first airplane ride, is it?" Jake finally asked.

"Yes."

"Oh man," he said. "All right. Don't worry about it.

You'll have to check your luggage inside and show them your passport with your ticket. They won't let me park here, Rain, so you'll be on your own from the time I let you out. Of course, I could park in the lot and wait with you if you like," he offered.

"I'll be all right, Jake. Mrs. Hudson told me to be on my own from the get-go."

"She would because she thinks everyone was born with the same steel in her bones," he muttered.

"Victoria was," I said, thinking that was the best part of Grandmother Hudson to inherit.

"Yeah, that she was," Jake said, concentrating on squeezing the vehicle into an opening. As soon as he did, he stopped and jumped out of the car. He opened my door and went around to the trunk, signaling for a skycap.

"She's going to London," he told him. He helped load my luggage onto the small wagon and then turned to me. "He'll take you to the counter, Rain. Everyone will be helpful from there. Just remember the things I told you."

"All right, Jake."

"Well, the queen is right about one thing," Jake said. "Good-byes suck."

He and I laughed. I hugged him.

"Don't forget to send me pictures of Rain," I said referring to his colt.

"I will. You'd better get going, Princess," he said nodding at the terminal.

I started away.

"Show them English how good you are," he called.

"Okay, Jake."

He held up his hand a moment and then got into the Rolls.

"This way, lady," the skycap told me. I followed him, but I looked back at Jake and the car one last time. I would miss him more than I had dreamed. He had a quiet confidence like someone who knew important things and just stood in the background waiting for you to catch up.

Jake had been right about people being helpful. I was told that since I had a first-class ticket, I could wait in the lounge. It was comfortable and the flight attendants were friendly and helpful. One came to tell me when it was time to board. I followed a couple to the gate and boarded the plane. The man sitting beside me was an English businessman. He barely muttered his name and then went back to his paperwork. After the meal and the movie, he fell asleep. I don't think we spoke more than a dozen words and finally I dozed off myself.

It wasn't until the pilot announced that our landing was imminent that my English businessman asked me where I was going in London. I told him about the Richard Burbage School of Drama. He raised his eyebrows and nodded softly, which was the extent of his reaction to anything, and then he returned to his paperwork. Were all Englishmen this reserved? I wondered. I'll be talking to myself most of the time.

After we landed and were herded through customs, I saw a stout man with a square jaw and dark, beady eyes holding up a small sign with my name printed in large block letters. He was in a dark blue chauffeur's uniform with little gold epaulets on his shoulders, which were as thick and wide as his neck. He looked like a wrestler who had been asked to don a servant's outfit. All of his facial features were harsh, especially his mouth because of the way his lower lip curled out a little.

"I'm Rain Arnold," I said stepping up to him.

He looked me over as if he was deciding whether or not to believe me. He didn't smile or even grimace, but his eyes darkened and he thrust his hand out as if his arm was a steel coil, grasping my carry-on.

"I'm Boggs," he finally said. "Mrs. Endfield will be waitin' in the car. Follow me to the luggage carousel," he ordered.

"All right," I said, but he didn't wait for my response. He pivoted and started away, expecting I would keep up with his quick pace. He walked with his head straight, eyes forward, never turning to see if I was following behind him.

I could barely keep my eyes in my head. Everywhere around me people were talking in foreign languages. I saw Arabs in their national dress, people from Africa with their heads wrapped in colorful turbans, people from India, and hundreds of Orientals as well as businessmen of all nationalities walking quickly and carrying briefcases.

Not in my wildest fantasies did I imagine that a girl like me, coming from where I came from, would have this opportunity. Maybe I really was caught up in the babbling brook of destiny, swept along by forces I couldn't begin to understand. Mama, I thought, wouldn't your eyes bulge too at the sounds and sights here.

When we arrived at the luggage carousel, Boggs put my carry-on down and finally turned to me.

"Point out yer pieces," he commanded.

"Pardon me?"

"Yer luggage. How many pieces?"

"Oh, three," I said. "There's one!" I cried pointing. He grabbed at it and picked it up with such ease, I thought someone might have emptied it and stolen my clothes.

After we retrieved the others, he gathered them under his arms and in his hands, nodding at my carry-on.

"You take that," he ordered.

Again, I practically had to jog to keep up with him. He led me down the walkway toward an older looking, but well-kept Rolls-Royce. Before he opened the trunk, he opened the rear door and I peered in.

There was my Great-aunt Leonora sitting in the far corner. She had a much thinner face than Grandmother Hudson, but I saw the similarity in her eyes and nose. Her dark brown hair was styled with a sweep over the left side of her forehead. Every strand looked pasted in place forever. She wore a gray tweed suit and pretty gold earrings spotted with tiny rubies. I saw she wore a great deal more makeup than Grandmother Hudson, especially the rouge on her cheeks.

"Welcome to London, dear," she said. "Get in quickly and while Boggs is putting your luggage in the boot, tell me how my sister is managing herself."

"Thank you," I said slipping into the car. Boggs closed the door and opened the car trunk.

As soon as I sat, my nostrils immediately filled with the scent of her pungently sweet perfume. I nearly choked on the overwhelming waves of it. In the semi-darkness I saw that my aunt had small brown spots on the right side of her jaw.

"Mrs. Hudson wanted me to tell you how sorry she was that she couldn't come over with me right now. Her doctors want to monitor her pacemaker a little longer."

"She must be furious. I know my sister Frances. You don't tell her not to go somewhere," Leonora said. "How was your trip?"

"It was fine."

"First time abroad, is it?" she asked.

"Yes, ma'am."

"And I bet you're all excited about attending the school of drama. What a wonderful opportunity. I never would have thought my sister capable of such an enormous altruistic act. I know she is involved in this charity and that, but becoming someone's guardian so late in life is quite a responsibility."

She tilted her head a bit to look at me.

"I wonder from where she got this sudden, new motherly impulse? What have you done to charm my sister so?" she asked. There was a strange note of suspicion in her voice as her eyes widened with the question.

"I don't know," I said. "Mrs. Hudson has been very kind. It's as simple as that."

"Really? How interesting," she continued, still gazing at me with those scrutinizing eyes. "How are my nieces?" she followed.

"Fine, I guess. I don't see all that much of them," I added quickly. I felt my voice shaking. I hadn't expected to be put under such a cross-examination so quickly.

"Victoria is still not romantically involved with anyone."

"I wouldn't know, ma'am."

"She's been around often enough, hasn't she?"

"Yes, but not that often," I said.

"Hmm." She nodded slowly and then smiled. "I bet you're ravishingly hungry. We can stop along the way and get you some warm food, if you like. I know a nice new French restaurant that's not far. Do you like French food, dear?"

"I haven't eaten all that much of it," I said.

"Oh?"

"I'm really not that hungry," I said. "I ate enough on the plane. I'm okay."

I wanted to be polite and look at her when she spoke, but I wanted to look out the window, too. Where were the places I had read about in my history books? The Tower of London, Big Ben, Parliament, the National Gallery?

"Just yesterday," she said, "at tea at Lady Bishop's, I told everyone I was getting an au pair from America. It's usually just the opposite," she bragged with a short laugh.

"Excuse me? Au pair?"

"A foreign girl exchanging housework for room and board," she explained.

"Oh." How strange it was to consider myself a foreign girl, but that's exactly who I am here, I thought.

"When we arrive at Endfield Place, I'll have Mary Margaret show you to your sleeping quarters, and then you'll meet Mrs. Chester, our cook. Boggs will describe your duties to you, however. My husband has made Boggs the staff manager.

"What do you think of my new hairstyle? It's the rage in Paris. See how this side looks like it's floating?" She patted the side of her hair softly.

"How old are you again?" she asked, before I could say anything.

"I'm eighteen," I said, smiling to myself at the way she flitted from topic to topic. She reminded me of a hummingbird, buzzing over one flower and then rushing off to the next. It was as if she was afraid of being tied down for even a moment. She was either someone pursued or someone in pursuit, I thought and wondered if I would ever discover which it was.

"Eighteen. Yes, it seems like yesterday," she said wistfully. "Oh, I do hope you don't smoke," she said with a firm face of warning. "Richard won't permit anyone to light a fag in our home and he can smell it a mile away, so don't try to sneak one."

"Fag?"

"Yes."

"I don't understand. What's a fag?" I asked.

"Oh, it's what you Americans call a cigarette," she said, laughing. "I always forget whom I'm speaking to."

"Aren't you still an American?" I asked.

"Goodness, no. Richard wouldn't tolerate the idea." She gazed out the window and then turned back to me. "You're so lucky. We're having a week without showers, if you believe what you hear on the telly."

"Telly?"

"The televison set, of course. Richard says Americans can't live a day without the telly. I don't suppose you're hooked on one of those dreadful soap things, are you?"

"Oh. Television. No, ma'am, I'm not," I said.

"Good. Just look there," she said pointing to a woman pushing a shopping cart full of cans and bottles. "I don't know what this country is coming to these days. I see more and more aluminum miners foraging for recyclables to get food. Dreadful."

"Homeless people," I said looking back at the woman with the cart. "It's the same back in the States."

"Richard just rages and rages about them. He thinks the government should get them off the streets. Just the other day, he met with the P.M., you know, and gave him a bloody what for."

"Is that the Prime Minister of England?"

"Of course, dear. Now I'll stop talking and you tell me

about yourself. Pretend you're telling the story of your life. Go on. Where were you born?" she asked, resting her arms on her lap and sitting back as if I was about to tell her a fairy tale.

I started, describing my life in Washington, D.C., and what it was like growing up there. She listened and then suddenly, she leaned forward and tapped emphatically on the back of the driver's seat.

"Go the long way, Boggs. I'd like her to see the Gardens."

"Very good, Mrs. Endfield," he muttered and made a quick turn.

"Life is very difficult for black people in America, I know," she said. "Frances hasn't told you that our great-great-great-grandfather owned slaves, has she?"

Before I could reply, she shouted, "There!" and stabbed her finger in front of my face, "Kensington Gardens. Everything is in bloom.

"Lady Billings and I are going to sponsor a picnic for the orphans next month. Oh, I believe my sister said you were an orphan now. You must forget all that, my dear. Think of us as your surrogate family until...until whatever," she said laughing.

"Everyone tells me I could have been an actress. I have the talent for it. Boggs, can you drive a little faster? I promised Lady Billings I would ring her up this afternoon."

"Very good, Mrs. Endfield," he said quietly.

"You were saying?" she said, turning back to me and smiling. "Something about your sister Beni, I think. What a quaint name, Beni? Short for Beneatha? I knew a Beneatha. Oh yes, that dreadful East Ender who came around with the chimney sweep. Boggs, remember them?"

"Yes, Mrs. Endfield. I do indeed."

"Well, what happened to them?"

"I wouldn't know, Mrs. Endfield," Boggs replied.

"No, I don't suppose you would, Boggs. Dreadful people. You could see the soot in the very pores on their faces." She shook herself as if she had gotten a bad chill. Then she looked at me again and shook her head. "I don't know why you're not hungry, my dear. The food they serve on planes is just dreadful. However, Mrs. Chester will have something for you, I'm sure, even if it's tea and a fig biscuit. We're almost home. Endfield Place," she said grandly as if it was Tara from *Gone with the Wind*.

My head was spinning. A little while ago she had asked me something, but I forgot what it was myself. I really began to wonder how Grandmother Hudson and Leonora could be sisters.

"This is Holland Park," she said, "one of the nicest areas of London. My throat's suddenly so dry. I'll have a cup of tea myself when we finally get home. Thank goodness, we don't make the trip to the airport all that much, right Boggs?"

"Yes, indeed, Mrs. Endfield," he said. He was like a statue—never turning his head once during the journey.

"Well, in any case, welcome to London, dear," she said as we turned into a cobblestone driveway toward a very large stone house.

As we circled toward the front entrance, I saw what looked like a quaint little cottage behind the house. Well-trimmed hedges lined the front of it with a small walkway in between. It looked like fresh flowers had been planted along the path. The cottage was different, sparkling like new. It was a wooden structure with Wedgwood blue cladding and pretty white shutters. I thought it looked more like a dollhouse.

"What a pretty cottage," I remarked. "Who lives in it?"

My Great-aunt Leonora turned slowly to me. Her face had changed, hardened so that her true age seeped out from under the makeup and deepened the crevices in her forehead and the lines at the corners of her mouth and eyes.

"No one lives there," she said. "And no one is ever to go there."

Her voice was deep, almost threatening.

Then she smiled and laughed. She was obviously someone who could hop from one emotion to another in an instant.

"Welcome to Endfield Place. Welcome to your new home, my dear."

I gazed at the grand house and beautiful grounds. Home, I thought, when will that word have any real meaning for me again?

2

Visitors in the Night

My Great-aunt Leonora's butler walked with a pronounced limp. It looked like his right leg was shorter than his left. When he stepped down on his left foot, his right leg rose and fell almost as if it was a loose appendage he had to swing around. He was a tall, thin man easily about six feet four with curly brown and gray hair like one of the Marx Brothers. His face was long with a narrow chin so far below his lip it looked like it was slowly dripping away as he grew older. He had delicate lips that were tucked down in the corners and eyes set deeply in his skull. I thought he resembled a man who had once been so terrified by something that fear seized his features and froze them in this look of habitual shock. He waited alongside the car for Boggs to come around and open the door for Great-aunt Leonora.

"Get the bags out of the boot," Boggs snapped at him. The butler bobbed his head like a horse and started around to the trunk of the car. Boggs helped Great-aunt Leonora out and then stood back as I emerged.

"This is Rain Arnold, Leo," Great-aunt Leonora told the butler. He poked his head around the trunk lid and struggled to produce a weak smile. When he glanced at Boggs, who glared at him so fiercely, Leo moved more quickly. No one seemed to care or even see how he struggled with it all. Boggs didn't make any attempt to help.

"There she is," Great-aunt Leonora cried when the maid appeared in the doorway. To me it seemed like the butler and the maid had been waiting at the front windows to watch for our arrival. "Mary Margaret will show you to your quarters, dear."

I looked at the petite young woman who stared at me with interest in her soft blue eyes. She looked childlike and stood no more than four feet eleven at most. Her facial features were as perfect as a doll's and as diminutive. Against her dark blue uniform blouse, her small bosom looked to be no more than a pair of preadolescent bumps. She was so fragile, her wrists so narrow, I wondered how she could be anyone's servant. I thought she began to smile, but when she glanced at Boggs, she stopped her lips from curving and an icy fear slid over her eyes. Instead, she did a small dip of a curtsey and stepped back.

Behind us, Leo groaned and squeezed one of my suitcases between his arm and the side of his body, adjusting his hip bone to keep the luggage in place. The weight of the other two pulled his shoulder down so that the lines in his neck became embossed against his pale white skin as he clenched his teeth with the effort to hold on to them. Still, Boggs didn't offer him any help, and I was afraid to say a word.

"Mary Margaret will find you a proper uniform after she shows you your quarters, dear, and then, Boggs will describe your duties to you. Well, don't just stand there like some waxwork, Mary Margaret. Say hello to her. She doesn't bite, you know," Great-aunt Leonora said.

Mary Margaret's eyes went from her to me.

"Hello," she said barely above a whisper.

"Hi." I gave her my best smile, but she looked down and waited.

We entered the house. I was immediately surprised at how dark the corridor was. The walls were a shade of burgundy. There were pictures everywhere, all dark oils hung in dark frames. A gray rug lined the entryway floor and a very dim chandelier hung from the ceiling. Ahead of us was a staircase that wound to the right. It had a mahogany balustrade but the steps looked like stone. When I drew closer, I saw they were actually covered in a thin silvery gray carpet.

Mary Margaret started into the house with Leo banging my luggage into the door frame behind us. He was really straining, yet still no one apparently cared. It seemed I was the only one who even noticed.

"Wait," Great-aunt Leonora cried as I started after Mary Margaret. "I've decided to show Rain the house first. That way it will be easier for her when Boggs describes her duties. As soon as you settle her in, Mary Margaret, you'll take her to see Mrs. Chester and get her some tea."

"Yes, mum," Mary Margaret said, followed by the dropping of her eyes as if Great-aunt Leonora was some royal person who wasn't supposed to be gazed at directly. She added a tiny curtsey like a punctuation mark after responding, again.

"Over here is the drawing room," Great-aunt Leonora said.

I gazed in without stepping through the doorway. There was a small fireplace with a white marble mantel. Around the room were a variety of Romantic paintings and some portraits of dour-looking women and stern-looking men in gray wigs. The windows were draped in cream silk curtains and every table, every available space in fact, was occupied with some artifact, bric-a-brac, vases, pewter figures, or miniatures. There were footstools in front of the chairs and the furniture was done in a dark brown chintz. Against the wall to my right was a tall, dark oak grandfather's clock with the hands stuck on twelve.

"All these pictures were collected by my husband's ancestors. The National Gallery would like to get their hands on them," she added with a small laugh.

"Here," she continued moving down the hallway, "is our dining room."

Again, I stood back like someone at a museum being given a lecture and shown precious antiques which were to be looked at only and never touched. I felt as if there was an invisible velvet rope between me and every piece of furniture, every work of art, every statue. Great-aunt Leonora was as knowledgeable as a museum guide.

"Our dining room is built around a mantel inspired by one that was brought to Buckingham Palace from Brighton. The wallpaper was painted with decorations based on an eighteenth-century pattern, you know. Our dining room chairs have been done in Bertram and Fils chair fabrics. They are all the rage these days. That chandelier," she said, nodding toward the ceiling at a crystal and green glass chandelier, "comes from Russia. We recently had those French doors installed so we can enjoy the spring and summer air while we dine."

The doors looked onto the garden which was in full bloom.

She showed me what she called the formal living room and told me the Bessarabian carpet was worth thousands and thousands of pounds. There was a baby grand piano with some sheet music opened on it as if someone had just played. All the furnishings were in dark patterns and the room itself looked as unused and as untouched as a showcase in a furniture store window.

I was truly impressed by the library. It was cluttered with art and valuable-looking objects just like the other rooms, but the library was literally filled to the brim with books in built-in bookcases on every wall. I didn't think one more volume of anything could be added. The shelves went to the ceiling and there was a ladder that could be pushed along to get access to any book.

"Richard is very proud of his rare book collection," Great-aunt Leonora said. "Most of what you see here are first editions, some going back as far as the early nineteenth century. He has original Dickens, Thackeray, Samuel Johnson, George Eliot. You name the author, Richard has something of his or hers," she added with a tiny laugh that sounded more like the tinkle of small bells.

The library windows were also draped in silk. There was a velvet sofa with a matching chair. At the far end of the library was a large oak desk. Everything on the top of it was well organized. Whatever wood showed through gleamed with fresh polish.

"This is the only sexist part of our home," Great-aunt Leonora declared as she presented the next room that contained a large pool table. "The billiards room is truly for men only. Who wants to come out smelling like a tobacco plant anyway?"

We glanced at it for a few seconds, but it was long enough for me to get a strong whiff of the cigars that were smoked in it recently.

As we moved through the house, looking in on each room, I wondered how someone as fragile and small as Mary Margaret could keep up with it all. What a feasting ground for dust, I thought, with all these pieces of art, little statuary, glass figurines, and pewter.

Trailing behind us during this tour was Leo with my suitcases and Mary Margaret at his side. Boggs remained in the entryway standing like a sentry. Suddenly, Great-aunt Leonora spun around and clapped her hands.

"I've decided to show you some of the upstairs. Everyone else can wait here," she declared. I glanced at Mary Margaret, but she wouldn't look directly at me either. Her eyes shifted so that she looked at a blank wall space between two oil paintings of country scenes.

I followed Great-aunt Leonora up the stairs. She paused at the double doors of her and her husband's bedroom.

"I know what you're thinking," she said suddenly, hesitating to open the doors. I raised my eyebrows. She knew what I was thinking? I hoped not. "You're thinking our rooms are so small compared to my sister's house. Americans always do things in a bigger way than anyone else," she continued, once again referring to Americans as foreigners even though she was one. "These older houses weren't built that way. Here, we had to think about heating them and the cost of that, among other things. However, this is a house with history. Do you know it was built nearly a hundred years before the house Frances lives in was built?" she asked. I shook my head. "This is a country with a past, where laws and art and literature began. But," she said with a small wag of her head, "you probably know all this, being a good student. Voila!" she cried and threw open her bedroom doors with a dramatic flair.

She immediately explained that her bed was a Georgian-style painted fourposter. On the side of the room where she had her vanity table hung an Indian ivory-and-ebony oval mirror she claimed Richard had bought at an auction, outbidding someone named Lord Flanders by five thousand pounds. There was a satinwood table where she wrote her notes and letters, long velvet drapes over the windows, lamps she claimed had been imported from Egypt as well as some original Tiffany designs. According to her all of her furnishings had historical meaning and all were refurbished antiques. On the wall to the right of the entryway was a large portrait of a man who she immediately told me was Sir Godfrey Rogers.

"It's actually a self-portrait. He dabbled in art. He never developed any sort of reputation, but…it's good," she said, nodding. She looked at me anticipating some sort of reaction.

"I'm afraid I don't know who he was," I said.

She laughed that thin jingle of a laugh again.

"Oh, of course, I forgot. He was the original owner of Endfield Place. And I want to tell you right away," she added with a serious face, "the stories about the spirit of his dead mistress wandering the hallways of this house are purely imaginative. Don't let Leo or Mary Margaret or Mrs. Chester or anyone else tell you otherwise."

"Dead mistress?"

"There is a ridiculous tale that he housed his mistress

in some secret room because she had become pregnant with his child and rather than have his reputation soiled, he brought her here to give birth without society knowing about it. Legend, and I stress it's legend, has it that his wife poisoned her and she wandered and haunted the house forever and ever afterward until his wife committed suicide."

"How horrible," I said.

"All poppycock," she declared with a wave of her hand, "but the stuff that makes for good teatime chat. Very well now. Let's get you settled in."

I gazed around the bedroom again and then followed her out. Something was gnawing at me as we descended the stairs. It was the sort of feeling you have when you know you have something to say, something to ask, but what it is exactly is just a little beyond your thinking because you've been so distracted or you're so tired. It's like a feather tickling at the back of your brain.

I glanced again in the rooms we had seen as we joined Mary Margaret and Leo who waited in anticipation. Boggs was still in the entryway, his hands behind his back, rocking up and down on his heels impatiently.

"Do show Rain her quarters now, Mary Margaret, and as I said, take her immediately afterward to meet Mrs. Chester," Great-aunt Leonora commanded. I noticed whenever she spoke to the servants, she tilted her head back so that the tip of her chin pointed at them.

Boggs cleared his throat rather emphatically.

"Oh," Great-aunt Leonora said, "but, of course, before you do that, bring her back here and let Boggs describe her duties." She turned to me. "Welcome again, my dear, and good luck with your studies."

She started back toward the stairway. My eyes followed and then drifted off to look at Boggs, who had turned to glare at me. There was still no sign of welcome in his face. I followed Mary Margaret down the hallway and as we turned to enter what they called the servants' quarters, I realized what it was that had been nudging at my thoughts.

In none of the rooms, not even their bedroom, did I see a picture of their dead child.

If Grandmother Hudson had not told me of her, I would never have known she had even existed. How odd, I thought. Was it something English to hide the members of the immediate family who were dead?

I've got a lot to learn about this place and the people, and quickly too, I thought.

My bedroom was only slightly longer and wider than Grandmother Hudson's walk-in closet. I had a creaky, groaning iron bed with a mattress so thin, it made my bed back at Grandmother Hudson's house seem like a cloud. There was a small window with a faded yellow shade over it, and the floor was uncovered hardwood so damp and dark and grainy that it looked like it might be the original floor of the house. Leo set my suitcases down with relief and immediately left us, hobbling away. Against the wall on my right was a mahogany wardrobe which served as the only closet. Beside it on the floor was a little wooden chest with shallow drawers. The room smelled like mothballs.

"Can we open that window?" I asked Mary Margaret.

She stared at it and shook her head.

"I dunno," she said with big eyes. "Never did."

I went to it and struggled with the rusted lock until I

had it unlatched. Then I pushed up with the heels of my palms. It didn't move.

"I won't have any air in here," I complained gazing around.

"I'll go fetch Boggs," she said and left before I could tell her I'd rather struggle with it myself. I tried again, but it didn't even squeak. It's probably been shut tight for a hundred years, I thought.

I put my suitcases on the bed and opened them to take out my clothes and get some of them hung in the wardrobe. Moments later Boggs appeared. He paused for a moment to look at me and then went directly to the window. With a closed fist, he hammered around the frame. Then he put the heels of his palm against it and pushed up. The window groaned and lifted.

"I'll get some oil on this later," he muttered with annoyance. "Hurry along now," he said before he left.

I looked at Mary Margaret.

"This wasn't the room Sir Godfrey Rogers's mistress died in, was it?" I asked, half kidding.

She paled to an even whiter shade, almost the color of snow.

"Who told you?"

"It is?" I asked more vehemently.

"No one is supposed to talk about that," she replied.

She walked away and a little while later returned with a uniform folded in her arms. She placed it on the bed without a word. I unfolded it and held it up against me. It was close to my size.

"The loo is just down the hall here," she said.

"The what?"

"The loo." She thought a moment. "The lavatory."

"Oh, you mean bathroom. Okay, thanks," I said. "I'd like to throw some cold water on my face. I feel like I'm still flying."

She didn't smile.

"Better get along," she advised. "Mr. Boggs is waitin' on us."

"Right," I said. "We don't want to keep him cooling his heels," I muttered.

She tilted her head as if I had said something totally beyond her. I just shook my head and headed down to what she called the loo. It wasn't much of a bathroom. There was no shower, just a tub and a sink and a toilet. Above the sink was a small mirror. Every part of the house had been modernized apparently, but not the servants' quarters. They better not complain about Americans being class conscious and prejudiced, I thought.

I put on the uniform and then followed Mary Margaret back to the front of the house where Boggs was waiting. He looked me over from head to foot.

"Pin your hair back," he ordered. He looked at Mary Margaret. "Why didn't you tell her that?"

She looked nervous and frightened.

"She didn't have time to," I said. "She was afraid to keep you waiting much longer."

"I'm not talking to you, am I?" he asked me with fury in his eyes. "I'm talking to 'er."

Mary Margaret dropped her gaze and lowered her head quickly. I took a deep breath to keep myself from exploding and waited.

"You'll help serve breakfast and dinner and then help clean up the dining room after supper. There'll be dusting and polishing on Saturday mornings with Mary Margaret.

Wash the floor in the billiards room, too. See that every loo has paper and keep the bathroom off the billiards room spotless. Mr. Endfield's guests use it. Mrs. Chester will show you what she wants done in the kitchen. Whenever she needs something from the greengrocer, she'll tell you or Mary Margaret to go fetch it."

"What's a greengrocer?"

"It's a fruit and vegetable store. Margaret can show you the way the first time."

"Anything else?" I asked dryly. Didn't Great-aunt Leonora tell him why I had come to London? I had school to attend and studies.

"Just know your place," he ordered. "Everyone who knows 'is place gets along fine. Step out of it and you'll have to answer to me."

"Are you kidding?" I asked him, now feeling myself growing furious.

"Mr. Endfield prides 'imself on how well 'is house is run. There's no kidding about that 'ere. Take 'er to Mrs. Chester," he ordered Mary Margaret.

She nodded.

"This way, please," she said.

I hesitated and glared back at him. Mama would have said someone stepped on his hand when he was a baby and formed his personality in an instant.

I trailed after Mary Margaret, suddenly feeling the jet lag that everyone at home had warned me about. I felt more like I was floating along, walking in my sleep. Why didn't they at least give me a chance to adjust? I wondered. If I complained, would I sound ungrateful?

I was beginning to wonder if I cared.

* * *

"So yer the Yank come ta study ta be an actress, are ya?" Mrs. Chester said after Mary Margaret brought me into the kitchen. She had her hands on her hips.

She was a stout little lady with rolling-pin arms and heavy hips and an ample bosom. Her hair was blue gray, pinned in a tight bun. Her cheeks were rosy on the crests, but her complexion was the shade of faded old paper with some age spots under her temples and a small mole on the right side of her neck.

She wiped her hands on her apron and looked at me.

"Well, yer a pretty bird. I'll say that, but can ya hold up ya end?"

"Hold up my what?"

"Do your part?"

"Oh yes," I said.

She nodded, looking at me with a tightness around the corners of her mouth. "We start preparin' breakfast at six-thirty. Mr. Endfield likes a cup of tea taken up ta 'im by seven. Who's ta do that now?" she asked looking from Mary Margaret to me.

"I do that," Mary Margaret said quickly, almost as if she was afraid I would volunteer and take the pleasure away from her.

Mary Margaret wasn't unintelligent. I couldn't help but wonder why she wouldn't want to do something more with her life. Was it just shyness? She acted like she was from some lower caste of people who were forbidden to address or confront their betters. She made me feel even more class conscious than I did back home with some of those rich girls at Dogwood.

"Good. I just don't want the two of ya confusin' yer duties and buggerin' up so that I gets the gov on me arse, hear?" she asked firmly. Mary Margaret nodded, her eyes wide.

"Who's the gov?" I asked.

"Who's the gov?" Mrs. Chester looked at Mary Margaret. "It's Mr. Boggs, it is. 'E's in charge. I thought ya was supposed ta be a smart one," she said. "Ya open yer mouth just once to 'im and you'll know who's the gov round 'ere, eh Mary Margaret?"

"Yes, mum."

"Yes, mum," Mrs. Chester mimicked. She turned to me again. "Ya don't want ta cross Mr. Boggs when 'e's got a cob on. Now as ta what you'll do 'ere," she said. "First, I don't want none of me dishes broke or me glasses or cups, 'ear? Ya carry them around with care and watch 'specially during the washin' up. I don't need no clod ta mess up me kitchen. We keep everything shipshape. See 'ow me cooker shines," she said nodding at the stove. "Mr. Endfield, 'e's a regular Captain Bligh when it comes to 'ow this 'ouse is run." She thought a moment and then added, "Ya better know right from the start, should 'e ask ya for a cup of tea, 'e's a mif, see?"

"Mif?"

"Milk in first, girl. I thought ya was supposed ta be smart," she said with more disdain this time.

"I just got here a few hours ago, Mrs. Chester. I don't think it's fair to expect me to have learned all of your funny expressions by now."

"Funny expressions?" She looked at Mary Margaret, who, of course, looked down. "Ain't she the sassy one?"

"Mrs. Endfield wanted you to give Rain a cup of tea and a tea biscuit," Mary Margaret practically whispered to Mrs. Chester.

"She did now?"

"I don't need it. I'll wait for dinner," I said sharply.

"Will ya? That's a relief. All right, Mary Margaret. Show 'er 'ow ta set the table. For yer information, we eat after we serve them their evenin' meal, so you'll be waitin' a while," she told me. She stared at me for a moment.

"What?" I asked.

"You and ya family on the dole in America, are ya?"

"The dole?" I looked at Mary Margaret.

"Government handouts," she whispered.

My back straightened instantly.

"What makes you think that?" I demanded.

"I hear all yer black folks in America is, is all."

"You hear wrong," I said. "I guess there's a lot I'll be able to teach you."

Her eyes seemed to wobble in her head a moment. Mary Margaret held her breath, and then Mrs. Chester let out a loud cackle and pressed her hands against her round stomach.

"Ain't no tellin' what'll come spuin' out of 'er gob. Mr. Boggs got 'is work cut out for 'im, he does. I'm goin' ta enjoy comin' ta work 'ere every day, as long as ya here, that is," she said with a wink. "Okay, dearies, let's get ta work. Set out two extra plates tonight, Mary Margaret. They got guests."

She laughed to herself and turned back to her dinner preparations. She was making Yorkshire pudding, which she explained was a popoverlike bread served with roast beef, made by baking a batter of eggs, flour, and milk in the drippings of the beef. I had to admit to myself that it did smell delicious. And for what Mary Margaret called

45

the afters, desserts, she had made custard to pour over a Madeira cake, a kind of pound cake.

"Mrs. Chester was born within the sound of Bow bells, but she's been a cook in the finest houses," Mary Margaret said as we prepared the dining room table.

"Bow bells?"

"That's what a Cockney is. An East Ender," she continued. I shook my head.

"Less jabberin' out there and more work, ya hear?" Mrs. Chester called from the kitchen.

Mary Margaret zipped her mouth shut and worked faster. This is a house of slaves, I thought, slaves who order slaves.

Mama, we didn't have it so bad, after all.

I laughed to myself and folded the linen napkins. Afterward, I had some time to go back to my closet of a room and finish unpacking. I thought I would just lie down for a moment or two and catch my breath, but unfortunately jet lag took hold and I fell into a deep sleep.

A hard thump on the side of my iron bed sent an electric vibration up my legs, into my spine to the back of my head. I woke with a jump and sat up quickly. Boggs was standing there with a broom handle clutched in his hand like a club. He looked like he was about to whack me with it next. For a moment I was so confused, I forgot where I was. I blinked and blinked until my garbled thoughts settled down and cleared the screen of my memory. Then, I got mad.

"What are you doing in my room?" I demanded. It just occurred to me that there was no way to lock the door, but I had closed it. I was sure of that.

"You're late for servin' dinner," he said.

"I fell asleep. I flew here all the way from the United

States today. Maybe you people call it a pond, but it's an ocean and there's a big time difference!"

"None of your excuses. I told you to fulfill your duties. That comes first. Now, get yourself to the kitchen. Mrs. Chester is waitin' on you and Mrs. Endfield asked after you," he said undaunted.

"You have no right to come into my room."

"This ain't your room," he said with a cold smile. "You're just sleepin' in it and only because Mr. Endfield is charitable." He walked to the doorway and turned, pointing his long thick forefinger at me. "If you miss another duty, I'll see to it you work on your Sunday."

He left, his footsteps pounding over the rust-colored floorboards. I scrubbed my face with my dry palms and then hurried to the bathroom to wash it with cold water. My hair was messy, but I remembered I had to have it pinned up anyway, so I did that quickly and then I went to the kitchen.

"Well, look who's gracin' us with 'er presence," Mrs. Chester cried as I came through the rear door. Mary Margaret looked up from the tray she was preparing. She looked frightened for me.

"I fell asleep. Big deal. I happen to have jet lag. There's quite a time difference, you know."

"Is that so? Maybe I'll come in late tomorrow and tell Mr. Endfield I got jet lag, too," she quipped. "Help Mary Margaret serve the Yorkshire puddin'."

I took the other tray and followed her into the dining room. Great-aunt Leonora clapped her hands together as soon as I appeared. There was an elderly looking woman to her right and a very short, plump bald man to her left. My Great-uncle Richard had his back to us, but turned when Great-aunt Leonora cried, "Here she is, Richard."

47

I looked into the face of a very distinguished looking, handsome man with hair as black as mine and almond-shaped green eyes that most women would envy. That certainly went for his long and thick lashes as well. Because of his rich hair color and his ruddy complexion, he looked younger than Great-aunt Leonora. He was a little over six feet tall, and trim and fit looking in his pinstriped suit. Besides his wedding band, he wore a gold pinky ring on his left hand. It had a small diamond in the center. His hands were long, but as graceful as I imagined an artist's might be.

What impressed me was his posture, the firm way he held his shoulders and his back straight with his head high and regal. He turned toward me slowly as if every move, every gesture, had great significance. He didn't smile. His eyes narrowed, darkening with thought, and he held his perfectly shaped lips tight. There was great discipline in his face, not a wrinkle, not a twitch or a movement giving his feelings away.

"This is Rain Arnold, the au pair my sister sent over from America," Great-aunt Leonora began. "She is here to study at the Burbage School of Drama. This is my husband Mr. Endfield, Rain," she continued.

"Hello," I said, still holding the tray filled with Yorkshire pudding. He didn't move his lips. He nodded slightly, still looking me over as closely as would a doctor.

"And this is Sir Isaac Dudley and Lady Dudley, Rain," she added.

A smile flickered on Sir Dudley's plump face, his thick, soft lips curling inward and over his teeth so completely, he looked toothless for a moment. His wife barely glanced at me. She looked down at the Yorkshire pudding Mary Margaret had placed before her instead.

"Rain just arrived today," Great-aunt Leonora announced.

Mary Margaret raised her eyes and indicated I should serve the Yorkshire pudding on my tray. Sir Dudley was eyeing it so covetously, he looked like he might reach up and take his serving himself if I didn't move. I quickly did.

"To the left," Great-uncle Richard muttered. My arm froze and I went around him to serve from the left. This close to him, I inhaled the mixed aroma of his rich aftershave and a recently smoked cigar. I could feel his gaze still locked on me. It made my hand shake as I put the dish down with a bit of a heavy clang.

As soon as I did, he looked up at me.

"I'm glad my sister-in-law had the good sense to choose a school in England for you over anything the colonies has to offer," he declared.

"Colonies?"

Sir Dudley chuckled. It sounded more like a cough.

"Pay no attention to him, Rain," Great-aunt Leonora said. "My husband thinks he is living in the past. He is still getting over the American Revolution."

"The world would have been much better off had there been none," he said. Everything he said seemed to be like some royal declaration. His voice was deep, his pronunciation so correct and sharp, you couldn't help but listen. "Your people certainly would have fared better," he added.

"My people?"

"Don't go on so the first time you've met her, Richard. You'll frighten the poor thing. She's just arrived."

"Here, here," Sir Dudley muttered.

Lady Dudley's eyes bored holes in me, but my Great-uncle Richard's gaze softened suddenly, his lips finally relaxing into almost a smile, his eyes taking on a more distant look. He was gazing directly at me, but I felt he was looking past me, focusing on some memory.

Then, he blinked and I could almost feel the click in his brain, the change in the direction of his thoughts. It was as if he woke up and realized I was still standing there. His gaze changed, his eyes drinking me in, moving from my head to my toes.

"Of course," he said. "I'm sorry. I welcome you to Endfield House and I hope your experience here and at the school will be enjoyable and beneficial."

"Here, here," Sir Dudley chanted. I wondered if he could think of anything else to say.

His wife turned to my great-aunt and asked her about the charity event to take place in Kensington Gardens. The subject of me was not very interesting to her any longer. I glanced once more at Great-uncle Richard who still had his gaze locked on my face, offered him a smile, and returned to the kitchen. I didn't realize until I entered it that I had been holding my breath the whole time. I blew out the air and took a deep breath.

"Well, well, she's made it through the first course," Mrs. Chester said with a chuckle.

When it was time, Mary Margaret and I returned to the dining room to clear dishes and serve the afters. Sir Dudley wanted coffee, but everyone else had tea, and I remembered Great-uncle Richard was a mif. He looked impressed when I poured his milk in first and again made me nervous with his long, deep looks.

After we cleared the table and helped Mrs. Chester with the washing up, I was almost too tired to eat dinner. Despite Mrs. Chester's sarcastic ways, I couldn't deny she was a very good cook. We ate in the kitchen. While we ate, I heard the piano and looked at Mary Margaret.

"Who plays?" I asked her.

"Mrs. Endfield," she replied, looking up quickly at Mrs. Chester to see if she had done something wrong by telling me. Why was talking about anyone in this house so forbidden? I wondered.

Mary Margaret said she would take care of our dishes. She knew how tired I was. I thanked her and headed for my room.

I was so tired, I barely had the strength to get undressed and into my nightgown. While I was brushing my teeth, I heard footsteps in the hallway and imagined it was Mary Margaret. I could still hear my great-aunt playing the piano. I returned to my room and closed the door. However, as soon as I lay down and closed my eyes, I thought about Boggs shattering my sleep with his broomstick and panicked. I had no alarm clock. I would surely oversleep. I'll have to ask Mary Margaret to wake me when she gets up, I thought. I slipped into my robe and peered down the corridor. Where did Mary Margaret sleep?

Great-aunt Leonora was still playing the piano. The hallway light was dim and the shadows deep and long. I walked past the bathroom, deeper into the servants' quarters. The music followed behind me. Just as I reached the first doorway, Boggs materialized in the dark portal. He was in an undershirt and his pants.

"Where are you going?" he demanded.

"I was looking for Mary Margaret. I wanted to ask her to wake me because I have no clock in my room," I explained quickly. In the gloomy dimness his eyes were slick as oil. He frightened me with his stone face and un-sympathetic voice.

"Don't worry about it. I'll rap on your door," he said.

"I'd rather have Mary Margaret do it," I said. "Where is she?" I looked toward the end of the corridor. I couldn't see any other rooms.

"She doesn't sleep 'ere," he said. "She lives with 'er mother. I'll wake you. Have no fear of that," he said. His face was all in shadows.

"What about Leo?" I asked. Anyone but you, I thought.

" 'e lives above the garage. I thought you was tired from your trip," he added.

"I am."

"Then go to sleep," he ordered. He stepped back and closed the door.

I stood there for a moment in the narrow corridor. It was just Boggs and me here? I shared the bathroom with him? It gave me a sick feeling in the base of my stomach to think he was so close. I returned to my room and closed my door. Tomorrow, I'll buy a clock, I thought, and then I'll ask Great-aunt Leonora to have a lock put on my bedroom door.

I crawled under the blanket and rested my head on the hard pillow. The night air helped diminish the strong smell of mothballs, but it was still there along with a rancid odor that reminded me of some apartments back in the projects in Washington, D.C. The piano music stopped and was soon replaced with the creaks and groans throughout the big house.

I didn't fall asleep so much as I passed out. It was as if I was still traveling, being swept along by planes and cars until I was spiraling downward through my jumbled thoughts, falling into a well of memories that ran into each other, confusing faces and voices. Mama was reaching down, trying to take hold of me and stop my descent, but she was always just a few inches too far away. There was Roy calling after me, my name echoing around me. I passed Beni who just smiled and did a little dance before evaporating. Grandmother Hudson flashed on the wall of my dream for a moment, her eyes full of worry. I was losing sight of everyone I loved, hurtling deeper and deeper toward the light until I burst out into the center of a blazing fire and woke to the soft sound of my door closing.

My heart was pounding. I sat up. It was hard to see in the darkness. I was frightened by a silhouette but quickly realized that it was just the wardrobe. No one was in my room, but had someone been here? I listened hard for sounds from the corridor and heard none. Then I let my head drop to the pillow.

I'm so tired, I thought.

I'm so tired.

Even too tired to care about ghosts.

3

The New Girl, Again

Boggs rapped so hard on my door the next morning, I thought it would splinter. There's a man who would enjoy pulling wings off flies, I thought.

"Are ya awake?" he growled from the hallway.

"Yes, yes!" I screamed back. Mama would say he could turn a graveyard into a crowd of Lazaruses.

"Get to the kitchen," he commanded and walked away.

"Yes sir," I called back and saluted. Then I groaned. It wasn't only jet lag now. I must have been doing flips in my sleep, I thought. It seemed like every muscle in my body ached and the blanket was twisted around my legs. Outside my little window, I could see it was gray and overcast and the air was much cooler than I had expected. It brought another delightful realization. There was nothing to provide any heat for this room, not a radiator, not even an electric heater. That fact was brought home dramatically when I put my bare feet on the wooden floor. It felt as if I had stepped into an icy cold puddle. I scurried to locate my slippers and get into something warmer than my nightgown. I would have appreciated the time to take a shower, but there wasn't any shower or any time. I'd have to take a bath but looking at my watch, I saw I had only fifteen minutes to get myself to the kitchen to help prepare and serve breakfast.

After putting on my panties and bra, I checked the hallway, saw it was clear, and, carrying my clothes in my arms, hurried to the bathroom where I would at least wash myself. Why wasn't I surprised to discover we had no hot water? The faucet ran and ran and the water didn't warm at all. I had no choice but to scrub up quickly, shivering as I put on my blouse and skirt. The only benefit to having to pin up my hair was I didn't have to spend any time on it, but boy did it need to be washed, I thought.

The house was very quiet. I heard a pan clank in the kitchen and entered to see Mary Margaret filling a teapot with hot water. She glanced at me, but didn't take her eyes from her work as if brewing a cup of tea for my great-uncle was similar to heart surgery. She started out of the kitchen, yet to say good morning to me.

"Don't forget, milk in first," I muttered. She glanced at me with astonishment, saw the smile on my face, and widened her eyes. Didn't anyone ever joke here?

"So yer up and about," Mrs. Chester declared, coming in from the pantry. "That's a surprise. I'm sure Mr. Boggs had somethin' ta do with it, eh dearie?"

"As a matter of fact, he did. He slept under my bed," I said and she cackled. "What is that?" I asked, looking at what she was preparing for breakfast.

"Black puddin'," she said. When I continued to squint, she added, "spiced blood sausage."

"Ugh," I muttered. She tilted her head.

"Mr. Endfield enjoys a full English breakfast on Tuesdays, thank you. We'll be serving fried eggs, fried tomatoes, and toast and marmalade as well. Slice up them tomatoes. You can do that without cuttin' yer fingers, can't ya?"

"Of course," I said and began. I noticed she watched me out of the corner of her eyes.

"Ya handle that knife right well," she commented.

"I cooked a lot for my family."

She nodded. I gazed at the marmalade.

"Go on. Ya can taste it," she said and I did. She laughed at the face I made. "It's made from bitter oranges. Mr. Endfield's right fond of that."

"Does anyone eat cold cereal?" I asked.

"Cold cereal?" She thought a moment. "Mr. Endfield eats porridge every Thursday, but not cold."

"Every Thursday? Is everything organized by the day here, even what they eat?"

"That it is," she said.

Mary Margaret returned. Mrs. Chester looked at her a moment, getting some message from the expression on her face, and then she nodded toward the dining room.

"Set the breakfast table," she commanded.

I didn't think Great-aunt Leonora would get up this early in the morning, but from the way she rattled on cataloguing a stream of responsibilities after she came down for breakfast, I realized she was just as busy with her charities and social organizations as her husband was with his law firm. She was very well put together, too, with her hair brushed, combed and sprayed. She wore a light-blue cotton suit with a silk blouse.

My great-uncle had his nose in the London *Times* during breakfast, coming up for air only to make a comment about something he had just read. I noticed my Great-aunt Leonora simply smiled after everything he said and either muttered a long "Oooh" or just nodded. Finally, he folded his paper and turned to me as I was helping Mary Margaret clear the table.

"Do you know how to get yourself to the drama school?" he asked.

I glanced nervously at Great-aunt Leonora. Should I tell the truth?

"Of course she doesn't, dear," she replied for me.

"I suspected so. I can't spare Boggs this morning. You'll have to navigate for yourself," he declared.

I wasn't very disappointed about that.

He slipped his hand into his inside jacket pocket and produced a small pad. "Pay attention," he ordered and I stepped closer to the table. Mary Margaret glanced at me and hurried into the kitchen as if what he was about to say was prohibited from entering her ears.

"Though London was for more than a century the most populous city on earth, it was also always a collection of villages," he began. "Each village used to have a unique quality unto itself and some still do."

When he spoke, he didn't look directly at me. He talked down at the table as if he was a professor in a classroom starting a lesson.

"For example," he continued, "the government is focused around Whitehall, with power derived from parliament in Westminster, incomplete without the Queen of course, whose royal and public life is still centered round St. James's Park."

He looked up at me.

"You understand so far?"

"Yes," I said even though I didn't know what this had to do with describing how to get to the school. Was it a requirement to know English history before you could travel through the city?

"Good. The best way for you to get around is to take the Underground system. We call it the tube. All the stations are clearly marked with this symbol," he said, drawing, "the circular London Transport symbol. You'd best buy a monthly travel card."

"Oh, I have to change my money into pounds," I said in a small panic.

He looked up at Great-aunt Lenora sharply.

"That hasn't been done yet, Leonora?"

"Of course not, dear. She just arrived yesterday."

"Well, why didn't you take her directly to our bank and have it done?"

"I just thought settling her in, having Boggs explain her duties was more important. There wasn't time." She shook her head.

"I have to be in charge of every little thing these days," he muttered.

He reached into his inside pocket again, produced a wallet, and extracted a bill.

"This is a tenner," he said holding it up and waving it in front of me, "a ten-pound note. You know the difference between English and American money?"

"Yes," I said.

"Good. This will do you for today, but you'll have to see to your needs immediately. London is divided into a number of zones. A travel card must be valid for all the zones through which you wish to travel. The cost of the ticket depends on the number of zones you want to travel though, understand?"

He was speaking too fast and it didn't make sense to me.

"You can't just buy one ticket?"

"Yes, of course, but it will depend on where you want to go?"

"But I don't know that yet," I moaned.

He shook his head.

"This isn't difficult. Children manage it on their own."

"Well, it's not this way in the States," I protested.

"The states," he muttered, "don't have half as good a system of public transport as we do. You'll see that for yourself in short order. When you get to the station today, the clerk will help you. Here," he said, jotting on his notepad, "is your itinerary.

"After you get to the station, you'll go to Notting Hill Gate and change to the Circle Line which will take you to Sloane Square, where your school is located. It's near the Royal Court Theatre. It shouldn't be very difficult, even for an American, I imagine."

He handed me the slip of paper and the ten-pound note.

"Thank you," I said.

"You'll go out front, make a right turn and go two streets west to the station."

"Isn't this exciting for you?" Great-aunt Leonora cried clapping her hands together.

"I'll let you know when I come back," I said. Out of the corner of my eye, I saw my great-uncle's eyes brighten with a smile.

"It's nowhere near as hard as it sounds now," he said, "and unlike people in the states, people here will be friendly and helpful. Still, mind whom you stop to speak with and don't take any side trips for a while," he advised. He folded his paper and rose, gazing down the table at Great-aunt Leonora as if she was at the other side of a long tunnel. "See to this money problem as soon as possible, Leonora."

"I shall, dear," she said.

"Well, have a good day," he added and left.

I told my Great-aunt Leonora about the certified bank check I had and she told me she would take care of it all personally.

"Now that Richard has turned it into a royal crisis," she added.

I helped Mary Margaret finish clearing the table. Then we had our breakfast and I went back to my hole in the wall to fix my hair and put on a little lipstick. Before I left I gave Great-aunt Leonora the check Grandmother Hudson had given me. She gazed at it, her eyes widening and her eyebrows lifting.

"This is a lot of spending money to give someone," she commented. "I never knew my sister to be so generous. I'm sure Victoria knows nothing about it," she added thoughtfully. Then she shook her head as if she was shaking off a bad thought and smiled. "Not to say you won't be needing it. London is an expensive place. I'll see to it that you start with a few hundred pounds. Have a good day, dear," she added.

With my heart bonging like that grandfather's clock in the drawing room, I left the house and began my journey to my new school.

My first mistake happened only a block from Endfield House. I was concentrating on all the things Great-uncle Richard had told me and I stepped off the curb, forgetting that the English drive their cars on the opposite side. When I looked to my left, I thought I was safe. Next thing I heard was a squeal of brakes and the sight of an enraged driver. I jumped back to the sidewalk, my heart pounding.

"Mind the traffic light," the driver screamed with wild eyes stretched into his temples as he drove past.

I closed my eyes, sucked in my breath and started across the street when it was safe. The sky was still quite gray and I noticed that just about every pedestrian was carrying an umbrella. I didn't have one and no one at the house had offered one to me before I left. The first drops began just before I reached the station. I couldn't run across the street because of the traffic, so I had to wait even though I was getting drenched. Finally, I charged into the station and shook myself. My blouse was soaked. What a horrible beginning.

People pushed by me, rushing to and fro. I didn't think it looked all that much different from the subway stations in the States. There was even someone playing a saxophone in front of a can set out for coins. The station clerk was helpful, however, and moments later, I was waiting alongside everyone else for my train. I heard an announcement every minute or so telling everyone to "Mind the gap." I couldn't imagine what that meant until the train pulled up and I saw there was a gap between it and the platform.

"Mind the gap," I muttered to myself with a laugh and got aboard my first subway train in London. I studied the map and watched for the stations Great-uncle Richard had written out for me. Not long after, I emerged and found myself searching for the school in a slow, steady drizzle. I panicked, thinking I had gone the wrong way, and stopped to catch my breath in a storefront. My damp clothes were sticking to my body. What an embarrassing way to present myself the first day, I thought, and wondered if I shouldn't just turn around and go back to Endfield Place.

"You all right, sweetie?" a small, elderly lady asked as she stepped out of the shop.

I guess embracing myself and squeezing myself against the wall made me look peculiar.

"No. I can't find where I have to go," I said.

"And where would that be, sweetie?"

She looked up at me and blinked her eyes. Her face was almost painted, she had so much makeup on.

"Here," I said thrusting the address in front of her. She glanced at it and looked up.

"Oh, you're not far, sweetie. Just go left here until you come to the Plowman's Pub and it's right around the corner. Matter of fact," she said opening her umbrella, "I'm headin' to visit a friend who lives nearby. Always have my cup of tea with her about now," she said. "Later, when the pub opens, we go down and have a shandy. Come on, now," she beckoned and I knelt to step under her umbrella. We had to make some funny sight walking down that sidewalk, I thought.

"What's a shandy?" I asked her.

"A shandy? Oh, just half beer and half lemonade. Ain't you never had a shandy?"

"No," I said laughing.

"My first husband and me, we would spend every afternoon together at the Plowman for the last five years. He passed on six months ago."

"I'm sorry," I said.

"Yeah, it don't pay to get old, sweetie. You stay young and keep dry now," she called as she turned into the doorway of a building next to the pub.

I hurried around the corner until I found the address. It looked more like a small office building than a school, but the name was written on the double glass doors. I entered just as two girls in black tights came bouncing down the stairs on my right, giggling loudly. They looked like sisters. They both had very dark brown hair but one girl's was cut short at the nape of her neck and the other's was longer and seemed unbrushed, but in a way very attractive. Both had pretty faces. Their complexions were almost as dark as mine.

"Bonjour," the short-haired one said. "Can we help you?" she asked.

"I'm looking for Mr. MacWaine." I wiped my hair with the palms of my hands.

"Ah, yes, Monsieur MacWaine is in his office, no, Leslie?" she asked the other girl.

"Mais oui. You come to be a student?" she asked me.

"Yes."

"You are the girl from America?"

"Yes," I said laughing to myself. The girl from America, I thought.

"Très bien. I am Catherine and this is my sister Leslie. Welcome," she said.

"Thank you."

"Are you living in the dormitory, too?" Catherine asked.

"No. I'm staying with the sister of a friend. Actually, I'm working for room and board, helping with the housework, the meals."

"An au pair," they both declared with laughter.

"Yes."

"Très bien," Leslie said. "You want to be what, a singer, a dancer, an actress?"

63

"I'm supposed to study acting, yes. Are you dancers?"

"Today we are," Catherine said. "Tomorrow we are singers."

They laughed again, first turning to each other and then giggling. Both had button noses, small mouths and pretty smiles.

"We are from Paris," Catherine said, extending her hand.

"My name is Rain Arnold. I'm from Virginia."

"Enchanté," Leslie said. "You speak any French?"

I shook my head.

"Well, you will learn something from every language and perhaps speak French by the time you go back to America, eh?" Catherine said. She looked at Leslie for confirmation, but Leslie just shrugged.

"Maybe, maybe not. Monsieur MacWaine's office is just through here," she said pointing at a door. "He's busy figuring his numbers."

"Numbers?"

"Monies, dollars, franks, pounds, lire, yen," Catherine rattled off. "He's Monsieur Moneybags, eh?"

"Oui. He will make you a star, *chérie,"* Leslie said. "For a price."

They laughed again.

"You see all these stars?" her sister declared, gesturing toward the framed photographs on the walls. "How do you say...graduate...graduates from here? Someday maybe your picture will hang here, too?"

I nodded. The wall of fame looked impressive.

"We are off to electrocution lessons. We see you later, perhaps, yes?" Catherine said.

"Electrocution?"

"Oui. Where you learn how to speak perfect."

"Oh, you mean *elocution* lessons."

"*Mais oui.* See you later."

"I guess," I said as they turned and went through the door on my right.

They had come and gone in a whirlwind of energy and laughter. I found the door to Mr. MacWaine's small office open. He was on the telephone. The moment he saw me, he ended his conversation and beckoned for me to come in as he rose and came around his desk. There were pictures of former students on the walls in here as well and pictures of what looked to be dramatic productions. On one wall were posters from musicals and plays.

"Rain, how delightful to see you. Was your trip all right? Are you settled in with Mrs. Hudson's sister?"

"Yes," I said to both questions.

"Please, have a seat. All of your paperwork was completed long before today," he explained as he sat back down behind his desk. "I'll take you for a tour of the school and you can start with your drama-speech class. It's scheduled to begin in a little less than a half hour. So, tell me, have you had a chance to see anything of London yet?"

"No sir. I only arrived yesterday and went right to work at the Endfields' and then came directly here this morning."

"You'll have plenty of time for sightseeing. Don't worry about that, and it's part of our curriculum for you to attend theater on the West End. I promise you. This will be a most rewarding experience in every way. I'm so happy for you. Well, let's not waste any time," he said, jumping up again. "Let me show you around."

I rose and followed him out of the office.

"Presently for the summer session, we have only forty students. They are here at different times doing different things, so at any one time you may be with only a dozen or so students. We pride ourselves on our individualized attention."

As we walked deeper into the building, I began to hear a beautiful male singing voice. He was singing something in Italian. Mr. MacWaine saw the interest in my face.

"That's Randall Glenn," he told me. "A real discovery. He's from Toronto, Canada."

We paused at a door that had a large window in it and looked into the room. I saw a nicely built boy about six feet one or two with thick chestnut brown hair framing a handsome face. His eyes were such a vivid cerulean blue that I could see them brighten as he reached high notes, turning his body slowly in our direction.

A short, plump, charcoal gray–haired man accompanied on the piano. His fingers were so thick they looked glued together, webbed like the hand of some amphibious creature. When he turned toward Randall Glenn, I saw his face was round with thick, soft features.

"No, no, no," he cried, lifting his hands from the piano keys. "Too much in the throat. Sing from here, from down here," he cried patting his own diaphragm. Randall lowered his head and closed his eyes as if he had just been whipped.

"That's Professor Wilheim from Vienna. He is a tough taskmaster, but he has turned sand into pearls. If he believes in you, you will quickly learn to believe in yourself."

I watched as Randall Glenn looked up and began again. His voice carried with such resonance, I couldn't imagine anyone complaining. His eyes which were directed toward the ceiling lowered until they met mine. Seeing me staring at him must have broken his concentration, for Professor Wilheim slammed his hands down on the piano keys. The professor paused to calm himself down, then he looked at Randall and saw where his eyes were, and he spun on his piano stool. Mr. MacWaine lifted his hand and then turned to me.

"Let's move on. The professor hates the slightest interruptions," he added.

He showed me a small cafeteria off a tiny kitchen. There was a cork bulletin board with all sorts of notes, advertising the sale of things, including show tickets.

"The students make their own lunches here. We keep a variety of meats and cheese, yogurt and other things in the refrigerators. There's a microwave and a cooker to prepare soups and tea, if you like. After a while you'll see that we're all a little family."

The next two rooms were classrooms with blackboards. In one a half dozen students were reading and studying *The Taming of the Shrew*. A tall, thin, light brown–haired woman of about thirty walked about the room with her eyes closed, listening to the recitation. Every once in a while, she would stop the reader and ask him or her to interpret what he had read, how it should be acted and what the reactions of the other performers on the stage at that time should be.

"Every student," Mr. MacWaine whispered, "becomes something of a director as well as an actor. Here we believe the two are intertwined. That's Mrs. Winecoup who also teaches the drama-speech class you will be entering in about fifteen minutes." He made it sound like the countdown to a rocket launching. I felt the butterflies circling my heart.

We followed the hallway to another stairway which brought us to the dance studio on the second landing. Mr.

MacWaine explained how they had knocked down walls to create it. A tall, muscular black boy was going through ballet exercises. We watched him for a while.

"That's Philip Roder," Mr. MacWaine said in a loud whisper. "He's already performed in a production of *The Student Prince* in Amsterdam. He's a home-grown boy from London. By the way, Mrs. Hudson arranged for me to have everything you need purchased ahead of time for you. When we return to my office, I'll give you your tights, dancing shoes, books and accessories."

"Oh. Thank you."

"You have quite a benefactor in Mrs. Hudson," he said raising his eyebrows.

"I know."

On the way down the stairs, we passed the elocution class. I saw Leslie and Catherine and two other girls, one very tall with strawberry blond hair and the other slim, about my height, with flaxen blond hair, repeating sentences as the teacher, a dark-haired man of about fifty, recited them. There were two younger-looking boys as well.

"How now brown cow," Mr. MacWaine kidded. "Words are our tools here," he explained.

When we returned to his office, he gave me my things and my class schedule. After the drama-speech class, I was to report to Professor Wilheim who would audition my voice and then after lunch I was to see a Mrs. Vandermark who would evaluate my dancing skills.

"That way we'll know exactly where to start with you," he explained. He welcomed me once again, checked his watch and told me it was time for me to go to my first class. "Good luck," he offered.

After seeing some of the students, I really wondered

what I was doing here. I felt like someone who would soon be tested and discovered to be a fraud. Tomorrow they would give me my walking papers and I'd be on a plane heading back to the States. I almost wished it would happen. That's how nervous I was. In schools for performing arts like this, I imagined people were always studying you, evaluating you, judging and measuring you. It was impossible in such small classes to disappear into the woodwork like so many students did in the public school I had attended. I knew students back in D.C. whose teachers didn't know their names after having them for months. What a difference between something like this and going to school in the ghetto, I thought.

Leslie and Catherine were already in the classroom when I arrived. The other two girls I had seen in the elocution class were seated behind them. They turned to look as I entered.

"Ah, *chérie*," Leslie cried, "we've been waiting for you. Meet Fiona and Sarah," she said. The strawberry blonde, named Fiona, smiled at me, but the girl with the flaxen blond hair looked unfriendly, suspicious.

"Hi, I'm Fiona Thomas." I took her thin, long hand into mine.

"Rain Arnold." I looked at the other girl.

"Hello," she said, barely moving her lips. "I guess you can figure it out that I'm Sarah, Sarah Broadhurst."

The French girls were still in their dancing tights, but both Fiona and Sarah wore long skirts and loose, frilly collared blouses.

"Hi," I said to Sarah. Her lips dipped in the corners.

"Are you the girl who was discovered on a school stage in America?" she asked.

"I guess so," I said. "Where were you discovered?"

"Under a rock," a male voice cried from behind me and I turned to look into the soft blue eyes of Randall Glenn. He roared at his own joke. Leslie and Catherine laughed as well, but Fiona looked shocked. "Hi," he said extending his hand. "I'm Randall Glenn. I figured you were the new student when I saw you looking through the window. Are you in the dormitory, too?"

"No, I'm living with a friend's sister," I said.

"Where?" Fiona asked.

"Holland Park," I said. She looked at Sarah who smirked.

"We're not far from you. I live on Notting Hill Gate and Sarah lives in South Kensington."

"Was that the only play you were in?" Sarah asked me. She looked worried that I might have more theatrical experience.

"Yes, the one and only."

"Discovered at your debut? That *is* impressive," Randall quipped. "Don't you think so, Sarah?"

"I'm not the one to ask," she said. "Ask Mr. MacWaine."

"Sarah's worried she might have competition for the part of Ophelia in our cut from *Hamlet* this month. The school has a showcase night every two months," Randall explained.

"I'm hardly worried," she remarked but she looked at me with narrowed eyes for a moment before turning around.

I sat and Randall chose a seat across from me just as Mrs. Winecoup entered the room.

"Good morning, everyone," she said and smiled at me. "Has everyone met our newest pupil, Rain Arnold?"

"Yes, Mrs. Winecoup," Randall said. "We were all properly introduced."

His silly grin brought a smile to my face. He winked at me and then he turned to our teacher.

"Lovely. Welcome, Rain. You have the textbook, I see. We've just begun an analysis of *Hamlet* in preparation for a night of theater, dance and song we'll be having in a fortnight. Did you ever have the chance to read it?" she asked.

"Yes," I said, "but not very closely."

Sarah finally smiled.

"Good," Mrs. Winecoup said to my surprise, "maybe we'll get some fresh interpretations."

Sarah's smile evaporated. Randall looked like the little boy who had just stolen cookies from the cookie jar, and the French girls were lit up with glee. Fiona gazed at me as if I had already made some significant statement, and I felt as if my tongue had just been glued to the top of my mouth.

They don't take long to put you in the spotlight here, I thought.

But after all, that's why I was sent.

I think.

After class, I had to report to Professor Wilheim for my vocal evaluation. I told Randall and he volunteered to accompany me.

"I can't go in with you," he said, "but I have nothing until stagecraft class and I can hang around for moral support, if you like. Then, we could have lunch. I haven't been here long myself, but I'll fill you in the best I can," he continued when I just listened without commenting. He looked around nervously now. "I haven't had a chance to make a lot of friends. If you don't want me to, I'll just…"

"No," I said smiling. "That's fine. Thank you."

He beamed. Did he know how handsome he was? I

71

wondered. I'd had my fill of boys who did and were just plain arrogant about it. He seemed quite nervous however and talked without taking much of a breath all the way to the vocal studio. I learned that his father was a stockbroker. Randall said he was the oldest of three. He had a younger brother and a sister who was the baby of the family.

I was so jittery when I sang for Professor Wilheim, I could hear my voice cracking when I just sang the scales. He wanted to know if I could read music. Of course, I couldn't, and that put a look of disgust on his face for a moment before he sighed like someone gathering strength to walk another ten blocks. Then he asked what song I knew. None of the ones I mentioned pleased him. Finally, he asked me simply to sing "Amazing Grace" while he accompanied on the piano.

"Very good, very good," Professor Wilheim said when I finished. "You'll attend my intermediate class every Tuesday and Thursday at nine. Any conflicts?" he demanded. I glanced at my schedule and shook my head.

"No."

"Good."

When I told Randall I was in the intermediate class, he reacted as though I had already been cast in a major show.

"He thinks you can carry a tune; otherwise, he would condemn you to the *do-re-mi-forever* class," he said. "Maybe we'll end up singing a duet one of these days."

"Please," I said, "spare me the false compliments."

He grimaced as if I had slapped him.

"Don't forget I heard you sing. I'm nowhere near as good as you."

His expression changed to an appreciative smile, and then he grew serious as we entered the cafeteria.

"I hope I can live up to everyone's expectations," he muttered.

That was a feeling I could understand. It had to be more painful to be chosen and to fail than not to be chosen at all. Look at all the disappointed relatives and friends who would learn about your failure, and then what did you do with yourself? Would that happen to me? Whom would I disappoint though? I thought. Grandmother Hudson, maybe, but certainly not my real mother and certainly not Roy. He wanted me to just give up on any thoughts of a career and marry him.

There's always yourself, Rain, I thought. You'll disappoint yourself.

Sarah and Fiona were already at the table eating sandwiches and drinking tea. Philip Roder, the ballet dancer I had seen practicing, was reading a biography of Isadora Duncan and eating a yogurt. He looked up when Sarah asked how I fared with Professor Wilheim.

"He put her in his intermediary class," Randall volunteered before I could respond. He seemed so determined to keep a smile off her face.

"Really?" she asked, her voice dripping with disappointment.

"That's very good," Philip Roder said. "He's practically forbidden me from entering his studio. Hi. I'm Philip Roder." He extended his hand.

"Rain Arnold," I said, shaking quickly. "I saw you dancing earlier. You're very good."

"Thank you," he said.

"Oh, and you know about ballet?" Sarah asked me.

"About as much as anyone from where I come from, I guess, but I don't think you have to know all that much to tell that he's good," I said sharply.

"All right," Philip said, beaming a wide smile. "Someone with spunk."

Sarah looked furious for a moment and bit into her sandwich.

"What would you like to eat?" Randall asked me. I went to the refrigerator with him and picked out some cheese. He made us some tea as I prepared the sandwiches. Before we sat down, Fiona and Sarah left.

"What's her problem?" I asked, nodding in their direction.

"Don't mind her. She's always got a chip on her shoulder," Philip Roder told me. "She's like that to everyone, especially new students."

I nodded and then shrugged.

"Where I come from, Philip, she wouldn't be more than an annoying fly. One swat and she's gone."

He laughed loudly.

"All right, yes," he said. He looked at Randall. "You better be prepared if you're going to make any sort of play for this girl, Randall boy," Philip said as he rose. "Gotta go. See you later, Rain Arnold."

I looked at Randall. His face was the color of fresh strawberries.

"Listen to him. You're a little friendly with someone here," he said, "and the next thing you know, they've got you engaged. I hope you're not offended."

He really looked nervous; his hand trembled as he raised his teacup to his lips.

"Don't worry about it," I said. "The last thing on my mind at the moment is romance."

"Me too," he said quickly as if that was what I would want him to say.

I couldn't keep my eyebrows from hoisting.

"Really?"

"Yeah, sure, I mean…I don't mean I wouldn't want to ask you out or anything, but…I have to be serious about my work and…"

"I don't know how we could get along anyway," I said gazing down at my tea.

"What? Why?"

"You went ahead and assumed I was a tif. I'm a mif."

"Huh?"

"You put my tea in first," I said.

He stared for a moment and then he laughed.

"Oh. Yeah. Sure. I'm sorry. I should have asked."

"I'm just kidding. I don't know the difference. I just arrived. I haven't even seen the city yet."

"Really? Oh. Well, maybe we could meet someday this week and tour a little. I've been here a few times, but I never really paid much attention to anything. I was always with my parents on those tour group things. Would you like that?"

"Sure," I said.

"Good."

He looked so relieved.

But just at that moment, Leslie and Catherine burst into the cafeteria and immediately went, "Oh, oh, oh."

Randall turned crimson again as Catherine sat beside him and rubbed her shoulder against his.

"I try for him all this week and you win him with one smile already, *chérie?*" she asked me.

75

"All right, Catherine, control yourself," Randall pleaded.

Leslie stepped up behind him and put her hand on his other shoulder.

"Maybe we share him, eh, Rain?"

"Will you two stop it!" Randall cried. He glanced at me and then shot up. "I have to get to stagecraft and do some preparation. See you all later," he said, looking at me once more before hurrying out.

The two French girls giggled.

I had to laugh with them. And then I looked after Randall.

A handsome but shy boy, I thought.

Maybe I will like it here, I thought. One thing I had felt already from the other students was the absence of any tension among us simply because of the differences in our skin color. Maybe it was because here we were all so unalike, some speaking an entirely different language and all having different backgrounds and cultures.

Perhaps in the theater you could be anyone you wanted to be and if you were good at what you did, people in the audience forgot everything else about you. Everyone shared the illusion.

Grandmother Hudson might have been a lot wiser than I had thought, I concluded. She might have known all this. She might have known I'd rather live in my imaginative world than the world of reality I had been given by Destiny.

She might have known this was the way I could frustrate Fate and find happiness.

Finally.

I would know soon enough.

4

The Forbidden Cottage

After a few more days of traveling through London, I became more confident and actually began to enjoy riding on the tube. I even had the courage to leave the set route I took every day so that I could go shopping to buy myself a simple alarm clock. No matter how shrill the alarm, I thought, it would be a lot more soothing on my ears and heart than Mr. Boggs's fist pounding my door. As soon as possible, I bought the travel card Great-uncle Richard had advised me to buy. That was about the only question he asked me. He was very busy with important cases and missed dinner twice during my first week, but even when he was there, he asked me very little. He and Great-aunt Leonora either had guests to entertain or he was in deep thought about his work.

On Tuesday, I got up enough nerve to tell my Great-aunt Leonora about the bathroom not having any hot water. I had managed to take a shower at the school after dance class, but I couldn't stand not being able to bathe and wash my hair at home in the evening.

"Oh, I'm sorry, dear. Why didn't you tell me immediately? I never realized that bathroom was so inadequate," she said. "I'm so rarely in that part of the house."

She called Boggs and told him to get it repaired. He insisted there was enough hot water, but it couldn't be wasted by running it wantonly. It was the first time I had a real chance to stand up to him in front of Great-aunt Leonora.

"I don't think running enough hot water to take a bath is running it wantonly," I said.

"Of course it isn't," Great-aunt Leonora agreed.

"It's always been warm enough for me whenever I need it," he claimed.

"Maybe you don't wash as frequently as I do," I muttered.

"Women do have more needs in that regard," Great-aunt Leonora said.

He didn't turn red so much as his hairline rose with his ears, and then his mouth whitened in the corners, deepening the lines in his face until they looked like bloodless slashes.

"It's a forty-gallon 'ot water heater," he insisted. "It should do fine."

"I haven't felt a drop of that forty gallons yet," I threw back at him.

"Oh, dear, dear," Great-aunt Leonora chanted. "Dear, dear, dear. Richard won't like this. Not at all."

"I'll see about it, Mrs. Endfield," Boggs finally relented. He marched away, the back of his neck so stiff, I thought his head might snap off if he turned too quickly in one direction or another.

"Thank you," I told my great-aunt. "I don't mean to be any trouble to anyone."

"Oh, I'm sure it's not very much trouble," she said.

"Not that I know much about the plumbing and such. I leave those things to Boggs and to Mr. Endfield. Don't trouble yourself about it," she concluded.

I returned to the kitchen. Both Mrs. Chester and Mary Margaret had overheard me complaining. I could see that the very thought of challenging Boggs was terrifying to them. They both avoided looking at me and worked without speaking. It was as if they thought Boggs might believe they were part of a conspiracy to overthrow him.

"Why is everyone so afraid of that man?" I cried in frustration. "He isn't the owner of the house, is he?"

"I'd like those potatoes peeled, if ya don't mind," Mrs. Chester said, ignoring my question and turning her back on me. Mary Margaret raised her eyes and then lowered them quickly.

"In case nobody told you, slavery is against the law, even here," I muttered, but I didn't pursue it. How they wanted to live and work was their own business, I supposed, but I wouldn't just fade into the woodwork whenever Boggs widened his eyes or raised his eyebrows.

On Friday night while Mary Margaret and I were serving Great-aunt Leonora her dinner, the phone rang and Leo appeared in the doorway to announce that my great-aunt had a call.

"It's Mrs. Hudson from America, madam," he said. I looked up excitedly.

"Well, well, well, my sister finally calls. You'd think she would know the dinner hour here," she said, wagging her head and wiping her lips with her napkin as she rose.

There was a telephone in the drawing room.

"You might as well take this back into the kitchen and keep it all warm, girls," she said nodding at her food.

I was disappointed because I had hoped to speak with my grandmother. Moments later, however, Leo appeared to tell me Mrs. Endfield wanted me to come to the phone. I hurried down the corridor.

"My sister insists on speaking with you, dear," Great-aunt Leonora said. "She wants to be sure we haven't done away with you." She held out the receiver.

"Thank you," I said. "Hello."

"Is she standing there over you?" Grandmother Hudson asked immediately. I laughed to myself.

"Yes."

"Are you having an absolutely miserable time living there?" she asked.

I knew if I told her the truth, she would get on the first plane to London or have me take the first one home. The truth was that despite the way I lived here, I was beginning to enjoy the school. I liked my teachers, even Professor Wilheim who treated smiles and compliments as if they were diamonds.

"No," I said.

"You have enough money?"

"Yes."

"And the school? Is it as good as Conor MacWaine bragged it was?"

"I'm enjoying my classes and my teachers are all very talented people. There are so many talented students there, too."

"Just remember that you're one of them," she told me. She hesitated and then added, "My idiot of a doctor had me back in the hospital for a few days, otherwise I would have phoned before," she said.

"Hospital? Why?"

"This contraption is not performing as well as they expected. They may actually have to replace it. I'm thinking of suing someone only I haven't yet decided who it will be. Maybe all of them," she said.

"Are you all right now?"

"I am, as Doctor Lewis puts it, under observation. Don't worry about it. I'll have their heads eventually," she told me and I laughed.

I glanced at Great-aunt Leonora who was gazing at me with her head tilted slightly, her eyes full of amazement and confusion.

"Your mother called to see how you were doing. I told her to call you to find out for herself, but she pointed out that if she did, it might create some suspicion. Any excuse that fits," Grandmother Hudson muttered. "Jake sends his regards," she added.

"Oh, thank him and tell him I miss him."

"I believe that feeling is mutual. Your name is on his lips so much these days, I feel like I should check to see if you're still here."

I laughed again, and again my Great-aunt Leonora's eyes widened.

"How is my brother-in-law treating you? Like one of the lowly unwashed?"

"Not so bad," I said. "I'll write you a letter," I promised, "and give you all the details about my school and my experiences in London."

"Very well," she said with her characteristic impatience. "Put her on. I'm sure she's breathing down your neck."

"Thank you for calling," I said and smiled at Great-aunt Leonora. "She would like to speak with you."

"I was wondering if she would ask," Great-aunt Leonora said taking the phone. She waited until I left the room before speaking.

Afterward, she returned to the dining room and took her seat quietly. Mary Margaret and I were standing by the door waiting for her. As soon as she appeared, Mary Margaret went into the kitchen quickly to retrieve her food.

"How long did you say you were living with my sister, dear?" Great-aunt Leonora inquired, her eyes narrowing.

"A little over six months," I replied.

"She is certainly very fond of you. You should feel terribly honored. I can't think of too many people Frances is fond of. She was always a stern judge of others and very unforgiving, which was something she inherited from our father. Anyway," she said turning back to her food, "I'm happy for you, my dear." She flashed me a weak smile. For a moment I had the strange feeling that she was actually jealous of the affection Grandmother Hudson showed toward me.

"I appreciate everything she's done for me."

"Yes, I'm sure you do. I've heard more from her about you than I have about her own grandchildren," she continued. "You've met Megan's children, I assume?"

"Yes," I said.

"I've invited them all here many times," she said sadly. "Megan and her husband actually came to England once without stopping by. They claimed they were on some whirlwind trip through Europe. I don't know why they couldn't stop in for a cup of tea at least. I know Victoria is so busy she hardly gets abroad. What about your family, dear?"

"I have a brother in the army. He's stationed in Germany now and may come to see me someday."

"I hope he does. It's nice to have some family about you," she said wistfully, her voice soft and low. She ate staring at an empty chair to her right and after a moment, it was as if she had forgotten I was there. I returned to the kitchen and didn't come out until Mary Margaret and I had to clear the table. We ate our dinners in the kitchen as usual and then Mary Margaret and Mrs. Chester both left to go home.

The house was unusually quiet. Randall Glenn had asked me to go sightseeing with him on Saturday afternoon. He was coming by to get me after I had completed the morning chores. I was excited about it because it would be my first opportunity to see the famous places like the Tower of London, Westminster Abbey, Buckingham Palace and the like. There were so many things to see and places to go that we knew we couldn't do much more than skim the surface during one afternoon.

For now I thought I would read some of the plays I had been assigned and then go to sleep early. The thought of sitting in that dingy little room was not very appetizing, however, so I fetched my books and went into the drawing room. I was so involved in the first play, entitled *A Doll's House* by Henrik Ibsen, that I didn't hear my Great-uncle Richard come home. Suddenly, I felt someone's eyes on me and looked up to see him standing in the drawing room doorway, staring. I had no idea how long he had been standing there.

"Oh," I said, nearly jumping up, "I didn't hear you come in. I hope it's all right for me to be in here."

"Of course it's all right," he said. "Why shouldn't it be?"

I wanted to say that from the way Boggs ran the house, I didn't know what was permitted and what wasn't. I could give him a list of ridiculous restrictions an arm long and I had been here barely a week.

"What are you reading?" he asked.

"A Doll's House, a play."

"Yes, I know it well. So then, you are enjoying your schooling?"

"Yes, I am," I said.

He nodded. He looked uncomfortable, standing there speaking with me alone.

"And you're getting around London all right?"

"I'm not doing much more than going to and from the school on the subway. Tube, I mean," I said.

He made a soft smile and nodded.

"Yes, well, I wish I wasn't so busy at the moment. I'd spend a little more time with you and help familiarize you with our country. However, I'm sure you'll do fine. Mrs. Endfield seems pleased with you. I hope it continues to be a successful experience for everyone involved," he said, "and my sister-in-law's investment will be one that was well made. Continue," he added, waving his hand toward me as if I was practicing on the piano.

He pivoted and continued into the house. Later, when I decided to go to bed, I passed the billiards room where he was sitting quietly, smoking a cigar, and looking out the window into the night. He had his back to the door, so he didn't see me pass.

How strangely alone everyone seemed to be in this house, I thought. Great-aunt Leonora was upstairs in her bedroom and probably didn't even know he was home. What sort of a life did Boggs lead working and living here? No one ever mentioned anyone in his family. I couldn't imagine any woman wanting to be his wife, and if he had a child, I could easily understand the child refusing to admit Boggs was his or her father. Leo was elderly and seemed content to retreat to his small apartment above the garage. Mary Margaret behaved like a snail or a turtle, pulling herself into a shell if I asked anything too personal. I didn't know if she had anything that even resembled a social life.

Was everyone who lived or worked on these grounds and in these buildings staring out their windows at the same darkness, their eyes empty, their minds turned off like lightbulbs? We had more laughter and smiles in our miserable apartment back in the projects in Washington, D.C., I thought.

I walked along quickly but as softly as I would if I had to cross a floor of eggs, afraid to break the heavy silence that filled the house and everyone's lives.

After I had complained about the hot water and my great-aunt had spoken to Boggs, he did have something done about it the next day. However, it was still erratic so that I never knew when it would be hot and when it wouldn't, but at least I had some. I tested the bath faucet and found it running hot enough for me to take a bath. No matter how I scrubbed the tub, it looked dirty to me. There were rust spots that had probably been there when Sir Godfrey Rogers's mistress lived in this house, I thought. The tub itself looked old enough.

Nevertheless, I filled it and took off my clothes. The water was soothing. I wanted to have my hair washed and nicely brushed out for my sightseeing date with Randall. I scrubbed in the shampoo and attacked my scalp, grinding my fingernails into it because I felt so unclean. Then I leaned back and dipped my head under the water, held it there and scrubbed my hair for a few seconds before sitting up.

At first I didn't notice anything and then I felt the cool breeze and turned to see that the bathroom door was wide open. My heart stopped and started. I just sat there staring at the doorway, waiting for signs of someone. It was quiet and no one appeared. I rose out of the tub and quickly wrapped a towel around my body. Then I practically tiptoed toward the doorway, my heart thumping. I paused and looked out.

There was no one in the hallway. Had the door simply opened itself?

Maybe it was the ghost of Sir Godfrey Rogers's dead mistress, I told myself and laughed.

Still, it seemed oddly quiet. Not a creak in the old house, nothing and no one moving. I watched and waited until I felt a chill run through me from the colder air in the hallway and then I shut the door, dried myself off, emptied the tub, got into my nightgown and returned to my room.

Maybe because of the little scare, I didn't feel tired enough to just close my eyes and go to sleep. I turned on the weak lamp and read some more of my play. After a few pages, something outside my window attracted my attention. I thought I heard footsteps. I closed the book and turned off the light. Then I went to the window and peered out.

It was a partly cloudy evening with the moon and some clouds playing peekaboo. The yellow light illuminated the pathway around the house and for a moment, I thought I saw the silhouette of someone walking slowly. It disappeared with the moonlight and then when the cloud moved away and the illumination fell from the night sky again, I saw a deep, dark shadow take the form of a man who entered the little cottage. Moments later, a light went on. I waited and watched. Was it Boggs? Leo?

Footsteps in the hallway spun me around. I kept myself perfectly still, listening. The steps stopped by my door for a moment and then continued on until the sound of them faded away. I heard another door slam and then it was quiet.

I turned back to the cottage. The moon went in and out of the clouds again. When there was some light, I thought I caught a glimpse of someone else moving toward the cottage. This person looked very small. I strained to see. It looked like a little girl. That was my last thought as the moon was turned off like a light by the heavier clouds that tumbled across the sky and settled the night into deep and thick darkness that would last until the morning.

Silhouettes appeared in the windows of the cottage, one shadowy figure so much smaller than the other. I saw them close to each other and than apart and then they disappeared deeper into the cottage. I waited and watched the window until my eyes grew tired and my lids felt heavy.

So someone is using the supposedly off-limits cottage, I thought. So what? I've got enough to think about without adding any additional problems and mysteries. I retreated from the window and went back to my bed, finally feeling myself drift off, but hearing what sounded like those soft footsteps outside again. They died away as I settled myself into the arms of sleep.

Boggs was up before my alarm went off. I heard his heavy footsteps outside my door. Didn't the man ever sleep? I wondered. How could anyone take his kind of work so seriously and with such commitment? He acted as if this was Buckingham Palace and my great-aunt and great-uncle were really the king and the queen of England. I had noticed how he walked through the house every day, sometimes twice a day, inspecting everything. He seemed to know exactly where each piece of furniture belonged. If so much as an ashtray was out of place, he stopped to set it right. When I mentioned that to Mrs. Chester and Mary Margaret Saturday morning at breakfast, Mrs. Chester nodded and then laughed and said, "Wait until you see the white glove."

The white glove? I wondered. I didn't have to wait long to learn the meaning of that.

Right after we had our breakfast, Mary Margaret and I went to work dusting and polishing. As we started out of the drawing room after completing it, Boggs stepped in front of us at the door. I was on my way to clean the bathroom by the billiards room as he had ordered.

"Just a moment," he said.

We paused and watched as he dug into his jacket pocket to produce a white glove. He slipped it on his right hand and entered the drawing room.

"What's he doing?" I asked Mary Margaret.

She just shook her head as if our speaking to each other while Boggs was present was another prohibition.

Boggs went to the tables and ran his gloved hand up and down the legs. He looked at the palm of the glove and then did the same with the chairs, the tops of tables and the sides of the furniture. He went behind a small table, wiped his hand over the rear of it and then turned to us, his white gloved hand open, a smudge of dust across the palm.

"Well?" he said.

Mary Margaret rushed back in and quickly dusted and polished behind the table. He stood by, his arms folded, watching her.

"You expect us to get every spot in the room?" I asked him.

"Mr. and Mrs. Endfield expect it. I simply make sure," he replied. He gazed around, nodded and left the room to wait at the door of the billiards room.

"My brother probably has it easier in the army," I told Mary Margaret.

I didn't need Boggs looking over my shoulder to clean a bathroom properly. I had done it enough times in my life, but he managed to find places I didn't get to, places I never imagined anyone would look at or care about anyway. He appeared to have a good supply of fresh white gloves. Every time he found some dirt or grime, he showed it to me or to Mary Margaret and then replaced his glove to inspect again and again.

With him snapping a whip like a slave master, it took much longer than I had anticipated to complete the morning chores. When I was finally finished, I had barely enough time to get back to my room and change my clothes, much less fix my hair the way I had wanted it before Randall arrived.

I rushed back to the front of the house only to confront Boggs once again.

"There's a young man waitin' on you," he said. "Anyone who comes to see a servant waits outside," he added. "Next time be here to greet 'im yourself."

"I would have if I hadn't had to locate every particle of dust in this house," I muttered.

"Just do your job properly and save your complaints," he returned.

I couldn't wait to get out of the house. Just being in the

same room with him made me choke and my lungs ache as if there was a lack of oxygen.

Randall was standing on the driveway, trying to look at ease. Who knew what Boggs had said to him? I thought.

"I'm sorry," I said. "I didn't mean to keep you waiting out here. I just found out that's one of the house rules, guests of servants aren't permitted to wait inside." I glared back at the front door. "I'm lucky he lets me breathe."

"That's all right. It's a nice enough day," he said and stood there gazing at me so intently, I couldn't help but be self-conscious about the way I looked.

He was wearing a light cotton turquoise sweater, a white shirt and jeans. The turquoise made his eyes even more radiantly blue. There was a soft breeze that made some thin strands of his brown hair lift and fall over his forehead.

"I probably look a mess," I said running my hand over my hair. "With that ogre standing over me, it took longer than I anticipated to finish the housework. I had to rush to get dressed."

I had put on a pair of jeans and a button-down short-sleeve blouse. On the way out of the room, I grabbed my light-blue leather jacket. Now, it felt too heavy, but I dreaded going back into the house. Boggs would probably be standing in the hallway, waiting to quote some rule about entering and leaving more than once a day, if you were a servant.

"You look great," Randall said, flashing his soft smile. He nodded to reassure me he meant it.

I did have the feeling that when he said something, he really meant it. There was a quality of freshness and innocence about him. I didn't sense that edge, that harder, wiser and even tougher outlook on life that I had seen in most of the boys I knew. He wasn't afraid or insecure enough to want to shade every remark, guard every look. He looked as if he was doing everything for the very first time, too.

He dug into his back pocket and brought out a brochure that he opened and held out for me to read.

"This lists the must-see attractions. We're here," he said pointing to the map. "We should go first to Buckingham Palace and then we can go up to Trafalgar Square and the National Gallery. What time do you have to be back?" he asked and suddenly a small alarm went off inside me.

Was I supposed to be back for dinner or did I get some time off? My great-aunt hadn't told me and I certainly didn't feel like asking Boggs.

"I don't know," I said.

His smile froze.

"What do you mean?"

"I never told Mrs. Endfield where I was going. I don't know if she expects me here later to help with the dinner. I'm sorry," I said. "I'll have to go back inside and see if I can find out."

"Oh. That's okay. I'll wait," he said.

"I'll be as quick as I can," I told him and hurried into the house.

I expected Boggs would pop out of a room or out from under some table as he usually did, but he wasn't anywhere in sight. With Mrs. Chester out and Mary Margaret doing some shopping for her at the greengrocer's, the house was quiet. I thought for a moment, wondering if I should just leave a note for my great-aunt. It didn't really answer the question, however, so I started up the stairs to see if Great-aunt Leonora was in her suite.

When I drew close to the bedroom door, I heard what sounded like someone humming a children's song. There was even a laugh, a laugh that resembled the laughter of a small girl. I stood there a moment longer and then I knocked.

"Mrs. Endfield? Mrs. Endfield, it's Rain. May I speak with you a moment, please?" I asked through the door.

The humming stopped. I waited and then I knocked softly again.

"Mrs. Endfield?"

The silence was confusing. I knew I had heard a voice on the other side of the door. I waited and then, I decided to knock once more, a little harder. When I did, the door opened a few inches.

"Mrs. Endfield?"

Again, I was greeted with silence. I leaned forward and peered into the room. My great-aunt was sitting in a rocking chair with her back to me. Her head was down, and she was holding something in her arms. I was about to call out her name, when I felt a large, strong hand grab my shoulder and spin me around.

It was Boggs. Before he spoke, he reached past me for the doorknob and closed the door sharply.

"How dare you go snooping around like this?" he asked in a hoarse whisper.

"I wasn't snooping. I knocked and I called for Mrs. Endfield. The door swung open so I looked in for her, that's all," I protested. Surely by now my great-aunt had heard the commotion and would come to the door, I thought. I hoped she would, for Boggs was towering over me with eyes that shot fire at my face.

"What do you want 'ere? I thought you were going out for the day," he said.

"First, if you must know, I wanted Mrs. Endfield to know I was going and second, I wanted to see if she wanted me back to help with dinner," I explained.

"You don't ask 'er that. You ask me. Don't you listen? You was told that already. I already told 'er you was goin' out for the day," he said. "And as for your services, if you were required to be 'ere, I'd a told you that, too. You don't 'afta worry about that."

"Fine," I said. "Then I'm going."

His eyes followed me closely as I walked around him and to the stairs. I didn't look back, but I knew he was standing right there, watching me descend. My heart was thumping and a cold sweat had broken out over my brow and down the back of my neck. I practically ran out of the house.

Randall, who was leaning against the garden wall, straightened up immediately. I hurried to him.

"Everything all right?" he asked.

"No. Let's just go," I said. "Quickly."

He was nearly jogging to keep up with me. Finally, he reached out and took me by the elbow.

"Hold on. You're beating the hell out of this street and you're not even going in the right direction."

"What? Oh? What is the right direction?" I asked, sounding frantic.

He nodded in the opposite direction.

"Did that guy yell at you or something? I hope I didn't cause any trouble."

"No. Forget it," I said. "It has nothing to do with you."

He shrugged.

"Okay. We could continue and walk through the Gardens," he said, "and then catch a taxi to Buckingham, unless you want to stop at Harrod's first and see the world's most famous department store."

"Let's take it a step at a time," I said. "We'll walk through the Gardens first. I'd like to just breathe some fresh air."

"Okay. You're right. We've got lots of time. We're going to be in London quite a while."

"Maybe," I said under my breath. "Maybe you will, but I won't."

"What do you mean?"

"Nothing. I'm just babbling. Don't pay any attention to me."

I looked back in the direction of the house. Why hadn't my Great-aunt Leonora acknowledged me? She had to have heard all that noise. I had knocked loud enough to wake the infamous ghost of Sir Rogers's mistress.

And where had Boggs come from so quickly? What did he do all day, wait in the shadows?

Why did he want to keep me from seeing and speaking to my great-aunt? More importantly, perhaps, what was she holding in her arms?

At the bottom of my stomach, a small trickle of ice water began to run into my veins. There was something here, something even my grandmother didn't know about, I thought, or she surely wouldn't have sent me.

5

Outcasts in London

As we walked through the park, Randall played the tour guide. He read and spoke in a thick British accent, pretending to be a stuffy English lord, or as Mrs. Chester would say, "a chinless wonder."

He pulled his head back so that he could talk down at me with a lot of nasality.

"Kensington Gardens, adjacent to Hyde Park, was originally Kensington Palace's front yard, yes? Kensington Palace was originally called Nottingham House. It passed into royal ownership in 1689 when it was acquired by William and Mary. The King's asthma dictated a move from Whitehall Palace to the healthier air of Kensington, yes?

"Go on, take deep breaths," he said, taking big ones himself. "There, you see? One breath and all the soot is gone from your lungs," he declared. "Go on," he urged me.

"I don't have any soot in my lungs, thank you," I said.

He continued to read from his guidebook.

"After William III's death in 1702 the palace became

the residence of Queen Anne. Christopher Wren designed the Orangery for her and a thirty-acre garden was laid out by Henry Wise.

"The last monarch to live at Kensington Palace was George II, whose consort, Caroline of Ansbach, influenced the development of Hyde Park and Kensington Gardens. Consort?"

He stopped and thought. Then he smiled.

"Do you realize if it wasn't for his lover, this might not be here?" he asked. "Thank heaven for little girls, eh?" he sang now in a French accent.

People on both sides of us stopped to look and listen, their faces filling with smiles. His voice could carry across the city, I thought. How quickly he took me out of my dark mood. We were both laughing by the time we reached the famous Round Pond where two little boys were sailing their toy boats. Randall suggested we stop and just sit on the grass and watch for a while. I sat, embracing my knees and gazing around at the beautiful flowers. Except for the laughter and shouts of the children, there was little noise. How far away my troubled world seemed now.

Randall had a wistful smile on his face as he watched the little boys run about the pond. He reminded me of an old man dreaming he was young again.

"What's it like where you come from?" I asked.

"Toronto? We live in a fashionable part of the city. I always attended private schools, just as my sister and brother do now. As I told you, Dad's a successful stockbroker with clients as far away as Hong Kong."

"And your mother?"

Mothers intrigued me far more than fathers at the moment, perhaps because my real one had turned out to be such a disappointment.

"My mother is an artist," he said playing with a blade of grass as if it was a paintbrush.

"Really?"

"Well, she wants to be. She has sold paintings and some small sculptures, but mostly to friends of the family. One of the galleries in Toronto featured her work a year ago." He smiled. "I think Dad had something to do with that. If my mother knew or even suspected, she would have pulled her work out in a New York minute."

"New York minute?"

"Don't you know that expression? Dad's always using it. I+ means faster than anywhere else, I suppose because New Yorkers are always in a rush." He tilted his head. "Haven't you ever been to New York and been banged around by people hurrying down the sidewalks?"

"No."

"No? You've come to London, England, but you've never been to New York?" he asked astounded.

"I didn't always have these opportunities," I said. "For me, going to New York was about as difficult as going to London."

"Huh? I don't understand."

He waited as I carefully constructed my words. I knew what he was thinking. If I was attending such an expensive school in England, why was I so underprivileged in America?

"I'm part of a program sponsored by wealthy people, a charity. You could say I won the lottery or something," I added.

"You mean you won a contest where the prize was going to school in London?"

"Something like that."

"So it's like a scholarship? Did you perform something? Sing something in order to win it?"

"I performed," I said, feeling bitterness like rot in an apple spread through me and my memories. "I'm still performing."

He looked even more confused.

"Something's being lost in the translation here," he said shaking his head.

I fixed my eyes on him. I could feel the heat in them myself, cooking up the memories I would have rather left on the shelf.

"I come from a very poor neighborhood in Washington, D.C. My family lived in government-subsidized housing, in apartments called the projects."

"What about your parents?"

"My father was a drunk and always lost his job or wasted his money. My mother worked in a supermarket."

He nodded, but I had a feeling that what I was describing was so far out of his experience, it was as if I was telling him the plot of a science fiction movie.

"Do you have any brothers or sisters?" he asked.

"I had a younger sister, Beni. She was killed, murdered by gang members."

"Really?" He sounded shocked.

"I wouldn't want to make any of this up, believe me," I said. "I have an older brother who is in the army. He's in Germany now."

Randall just stared at me for a moment as if a mask had dropped off my face and he was looking at the real me.

"Do your parents still live there?" he finally asked.

"My father's in jail and my mother died recently," I said. "Depressed enough?" I muttered and got up and started away.

"Hey!" he called and caught up with me. "I'm sorry. I didn't mean to put you in a bad mood."

"You didn't. I was born in a bad mood," I commented.

"I would never know it by talking to you. No, I mean it," he continued when I stopped to look at him skeptically. "When I first started to talk to you at the school, I just thought you were someone different," he added.

"Different? Yeah, Randall, I'm different," I said laughing coldly. "That's for sure. It didn't take you long to spot that."

"No, I didn't mean in a bad way. You're…I don't know…not like any girl I ever met."

"I'm not surprised." Suddenly his white-bread world annoyed me. His whole life looked like a soft slide downhill and he had been born with a wonderful talent too. Who decided all this? Was there some judge who considered you when you were about to be born and with a wave of his hand, he sent you to this family or that, this world or that? What could I or Beni or Roy have done to be given this destiny as opposed to the one Randall had been given?

"You were brought up with a silver spoon in your mouth. You just said so yourself," I told him. "Private schools, rich parents, beautiful home…art galleries and theaters. Your family took you on expensive vacations. You were shocked to learn I hadn't even been to New York City!"

"No, I just…"

"You know why I seem different? I'm as good as an alien to you. You wanted to talk to me because you thought I was different?

"I'm different, all right. Boy, am I different. Yeah, I'm black and white, too, and…lost," I moaned, hurrying away.

I didn't look back. I knew deep inside that it wasn't fair to take out my frustrations on him and jump on every word he said, but I wasn't in the mood to be fair. I dug my feet into the grass so hard, I could feel the earth move beneath my heels. I walked and walked, passing all sorts of tourists, couples holding hands, families, young men carrying backpacks, people from everywhere. A stream of foreign languages rushed by: Italian, French, Japanese, Russian…I really could be from outer space, I thought and finally, short of breath, flopped on a bench.

I sat there staring across the park at the street full of traffic: double-decker buses, sightseeing buses, English taxi cabs, foreign cars mixed with American cars, people everywhere waiting for the green man to appear at the crossing light. It felt like a carnival atmosphere, like the whole world was on holiday.

"Wow. I practically had to sprint to keep up with you," Randall said coming up behind me. "May I sit beside you?" he asked.

"It's a public bench," I replied.

You're so bad-tempered today, Rain, I heard a voice inside me say.

"I'm sorry if I insulted you in some way," Randall began. "Believe me, I didn't mean to."

"I'm just tired of thinking about myself as different," I said followed by a deep sigh. "For a while I'd like to be the same, boring and common."

"Different doesn't have to mean something bad. It could be good. Lots of people want to be different," he said softly, gingerly, like someone walking on thin ice.

"My mother's always talking about being different. She hates being thought of as just another middle-class wife. I know because she's often saying that. I think that's why she wants to be an artist so much. While the wives of my father's friends are attending charity luncheons, afternoon cocktail parties and such, she's in her studio getting paint on her face."

"On her face?"

"She always comes out looking messy. My dad accuses her of tasting the paint before she uses it," he said.

I looked away to smile with tears still in my eyes. How wonderful it must be to have parents who love and cherish each other and create a warm, happy world for their children, I thought.

"You were right," he admitted gazing down, "I don't know too many black kids. But," he added, turning to me, "I really don't know that many white ones either. I don't have all that many friends back home. I guess it's because I've been attending these special schools, working with voice coaches, spending all my spare time on developing my voice because my parents want me to be a star."

"Don't you?"

"Not all the time," he said. He leaned back, the soft strands of his hair falling over his forehead. His eyes filled with a warm glow as he gazed into his own thoughts. "When we were watching those little boys back at Round Pond, I was thinking about all the fun I missed out on. I was given piano lessons, not many toys. My parents were afraid to let me participate in sports as if building my wind for something other than singing might damage my voice.

"They let me learn to skate, but being part of the

hockey team was impossible because of the conflicts with my music practice.

"You know what, Rain," he said suddenly as if the realization had really just occurred, "I'm different, too. I was always different in the eyes of my fellow students. I guess I was freaky to most of them."

"I doubt that," I said. I really meant not to the girls, not someone with his good looks.

"Yeah, well, that's the way I felt now that I think about it."

"Are you going to sit there and tell me you didn't have a girlfriend or girlfriends?"

He laughed.

"I had a girlfriend named Nicolette Sabon. We were taking singing lessons from the same teacher, Mr. Wegman. He used to tap a ruler on the top of my head to keep me in rhythm. He had Nicolette and me singing duets, performing at the school's productions and going around the city singing for ladies' organizations and clubs. We were together a lot because of that, posed for pictures together, were seen everywhere together, and one day Nicolette told me I was her boyfriend and she was my girlfriend. I remember she made it sound as if I had no choice. Like it was ordained by a higher power."

"How old were you?" I asked.

"Twelve. She was eleven."

"Twelve? Eleven? That was your only love affair?"

He shrugged.

"I had a crush on a girl when I was fifteen, but I didn't smoke or drink beer and she thought I was some sort of dud, I guess, because all I asked her to do with me was listen to music or go to a show. She said my good looks were wasted on me. She really made me feel different, speaking of feeling different. It got around the school that I was a huge bore, and I felt like crawling into a hole."

"She was an idiot," I said, "and your good looks are not wasted on you. People will love to look at you as well as listen to you. Your good looks fit the quality of your voice, Randall. Don't ever regret that," I ordered.

His eyes widened.

"I can't tell if you like me or hate me," he said.

I had to smile.

"I don't hate you. Of course, I don't hate you. Maybe I hate myself," I said growing serious again. "No, there's no maybes about it. I do."

"You shouldn't. I know I don't have the right to give advice to you. I know I can't even begin to understand the world you come from or what you've gone through before getting here, but I've seen many so-called talented girls and I'm telling you, you're the cream of the crop."

"Oh, is that right?"

"Yes, it is," he insisted.

I stared into those blue eyes, eyes as pure and as innocent as a summer's sky.

"I'm sorry," I said. "I didn't mean to jump on what you said back there. I had a very strange and difficult morning and I guess I'm feeling a little homesick, too."

"Funny, isn't it?" he said, nodding, "that no matter how hard or unpleasant we think our home lives are when we're there, we miss it when we're far away."

"That's because we're among strangers in a strange place," I said.

He nodded and then brightened.

"Well, let's keep going and make it less strange. That's what we set out to do today, wasn't it?"

He dug into his pocket again and produced the tourist brochure.

"Buckingham Palace." He read to himself a moment and then looked at his watch and jumped up, grabbing my hand. "Come on," he cried, pulling me off the bench so hard I nearly fell forward on my face.

"Why? Where?"

I had to run along with him over the grass toward Knightsbridge Road.

"We need to catch a cab."

"Why?" I cried.

"If we don't hurry, we'll miss the changing of the guard!"

We shot onto the road and as luck would have it, there was a cab just coming.

"Buckingham Palace as quickly as you can," he told the driver as we got into the cab.

"All right, guv," the driver said, smiling.

Randall read as I caught my breath.

"Buckingham Palace is the sovereign's London home, named for the Duke of Buckingham and Chandos, who erected it in the eighteenth century, selling it to George III in 1761.

"Just think," Randall said lowering the brochure, "it was built and sold before the United States even existed."

I don't know whether it was simply being with Randall and feeling his excitement or whether it was because I was in a new place, a whole new world, but suddenly all the darkness was washed away and the light of new discoveries filled me with a renewed desire to rise above my past and revive my ambition to find myself and my true identity. Even here, even so far away from everything and everyone I'd ever known.

Watching the changing of the guard at Buckingham Palace and then touring the Royal Mews and the Queen's Gallery was interesting, but took a great deal longer than Randall had anticipated. Even so, we took another taxi to Trafalgar Square. It was jammed with people. I didn't know where to turn first. After we had walked by the fountains and then had taken in the scenic view along Whitehall to Big Ben and Parliament, Randall wanted us to retrace our steps and go into the National Gallery.

"I've been here twice with my mother," he said, "but you can never see it all. Come on."

I felt like I was in a race with time, trying to get everything in before some clock boomed and turned me back into poor Cinderella on her return to the hovel she lived in someplace in America. Randall was behaving as if he thought I would suddenly stop and say, "I don't want to see or do another thing with you." His object was to keep me moving, keep my eyes and ears full of sights and sounds and full of the history he was reading and showing me.

"The National Gallery hosts one of the world's best collections of Old Masters, but it is very strong on the French Impressionists as well," he explained. "Do you know a lot about painting?"

"No," I confessed.

"Then you should spend a lot of time here. You can educate yourself quickly. The range is from the thirteenth century through the nineteenth." He rattled off the names of the famous painters and scooted me about to show me as many examples of their works as possible. Finally, I had to stop and sit on a bench, pleading not only exhaustion in my body, but exhaustion in my mind.

"It's no good this way, Randall. Many small bites aren't as good as slow, big bites. I'm not absorbing it. We'll come back. I promise."

He laughed.

"Okay. Okay. Let's just go for a walk back again toward Big Ben and enjoy the beautiful fall day," he suggested. "I promise, I won't rush you. We'll take little steps."

We left the museum.

"When I'm walking around in my own country or in places I'm used to," I said as we crossed the square, "my eyes can fall asleep, even while they're open, but here or someplace as new as this, I can't see enough. It tires me out, Randall."

"Oh, I know. I just get a little too enthusiastic sometimes. Sorry," he said.

"I don't blame you. I suppose if our roles were switched and I had been here before and wanted to show it to someone who hadn't, I'd act the same way."

When we crossed a street, he took my hand and we didn't let go of each other for a long time as we walked up to Big Ben. Afterward, we crossed another street and just wandered down a smaller, narrower road until we saw a pub called the Hearty Sailor.

Randall checked his watch.

"Well, what do you know. It's time for tea," he said. "Would m'lady like a bit of shepherd's pie and a pint of stout?"

"Stout? You mean beer?"

"Well, you have to be eighteen to be served here," he said, "and I won't be for three months."

"I'm already eighteen," I said.

"Really? Great. Come on."

Above the door of the pub was a colorful metal sign with a robust-looking sailor holding a mug of beer. Randall caught the direction of my gaze.

"All British pubs have a painted sign on the outside because most people couldn't read until the beginning of this century, so when their mates said, 'Meet me at the Hearty Sailor,' they'd just look for the picture."

"How do you know so much about this city?" I asked him.

"I just spent my time reading about it when I knew I would be living here and going to school here," he replied.

"For me it all happened so fast, I barely had time to learn the difference between a pound and a dollar," I said.

"No harm done," he said opening the door. "You have me, the perfect guide and translator, and I come cheap."

I laughed at his happy smile and we entered the pub. It was somewhat darker inside than I anticipated, but somehow I felt a warm and cozy feeling the moment we entered. The people who were inside gazed at us with interest, but no resentment like people often did when I walked into a new place back home. They made me feel I had intruded on private property and that where I was did not welcome strangers.

"Here's a couple a real customers, Charlie," someone cried and everyone laughed, even the man behind the bar. A short, dark-haired woman with deep brown round eyes and a face like a marble cherub appeared with a plate of food in her hands. She placed it on the bar in front of an elderly man dressed in a suit and tie.

"Can I help you?" the bartender asked Randall. He looked up at the menu written in Gothic style on a board above the bar.

"Want to try the shepherd's pie?" he asked me.

"Sure," I said.

"We'll have two shepherd's pies and two shandies," he said and produced two ten-pound notes.

We heard people chuckling.

"Ya old enough for an ale, are ya?"

I handed him my student identification card. He glanced at it and nodded and looked at Randall.

"Forgot mine," Randall said.

"He looks old enough to me, Charlie," cried a tall, thin man with an Adam's apple so prominent, I thought it would bust out and roll over the counter.

"Never you mind, Mush," the bartender said and everyone laughed again.

"I can only give 'er one," he said.

Randall nodded.

"Just a lemonade then," he said.

He gave Randall his change and he and I sat at an empty table. I gazed around at all the signs on the walls, the old posters, farm implements, swords and helmets, everything looking like it belonged in some museum. The bartender put Randall's lemonade and my shandy on the counter and Randall fetched them.

Everyone returned to their conversations as if we weren't there.

"This is fun, huh?" Randall asked.

"Yes. Everyone seems...friendly."

"Most of the pubs are owned by one or the other of the major breweries. Ones that are privately owned are called freehouses. This one's a freehouse and they usually have a bigger selection of ale. Too bad I can't get served, too," he said in a lower voice. "Go on. Drink yours. The beer here is different from America. They serve it room temperature instead of cold."

"Really? Why?"

"It's supposed to taste better," he explained.

I sat back and studied him a moment.

"Why are you smiling at me like that?" he asked.

"For someone who supposedly didn't get around much, who was locked away in music suites, you sure seem...sophisticated."

"I told you. It's all from reading. I've always been a big reader. I'd have a book with me whenever I went to my lessons because sometimes I had to wait for the teacher to finish with someone else, and, when you don't socialize a lot, you get used to spending your free time with a book," he said, shrugging as if it was the most obvious thing.

He was quiet for a moment and then leaned forward.

"What about you? Do you spend your free time with books? Or do you have a boyfriend waiting for you back home?"

"No, no boyfriend."

"Did you have lots of boyfriends? You asked me so I can ask you," he followed quickly. It made me laugh.

"Not really, no," I said. "I was too busy helping Mama at home. She was so tired all the time."

"So we both have a lot of catching up to do," he said.

"Oh, we do? I don't know, Randall Glenn. Sometimes,

you sound more experienced than you claim you are."

"What?" He looked sincerely confused and turned so crimson, I thought he might burst. Maybe he wasn't coming on to me as strongly as I thought he was. It was difficult to believe a boy who looked like he did was so innocent after all.

I sipped my ale and shrugged.

When our shepherd's pies were ready, the dark-haired lady brought them to our table and asked us if we wanted anything else. They were so hot we had to wait for them to cool, but they were delicious.

Suddenly, at the other end of the pub, two men who looked about forty started to sing.

> *"Fill up the cider cup,*
> *Have another round.*
> *Of all the drinks in England,*
> *No better can be found."*

"I know that one, too," Randall declared, and as if his voice was something that had a life of its own and would emerge whenever it liked, he began to sing along. Being trained, he just normally projected and in moments, everyone in the pub was looking at us. I felt like crawling under the table.

But, to my surprise, no one resented his intrusion. More of the customers began to sing along and in moments, the whole place resounded with the tune. When it ended, they all applauded.

"Now there's a voice, Charlie. Keep that one comin'," a plump, jolly-looking woman at the bar declared. There were many seconds to her suggestion.

"Give the lad a bit of brew for that," someone shouted from the corner.

"Yeah, break ya heart, Charlie. Part with some of the precious nectar."

More laughter followed.

"I'll pay for it, Charlie," the slim man with the protruding Adam's apple declared and slapped some money on the bar. "He's got to be eighteen. Look at the size of 'im."

"Aye," the woman beside him said. "A young man with a voice like that shouldn't go dry, Charlie."

"All right, ya blokes. Shut yer gobs," the bartender said. Moments later he brought a pint of ale to our table. "A gift from yer fans, lad," he said.

Randall's eyes widened with glee when he looked at me. I didn't know what to do or say.

"Thanks," he said and took a sip of the ale.

I tasted it, too, to see what his was like. Randall finished it and mine before we finished our shepherd's pies.

When we got up to leave, there was a round of applause and a cheer. We burst out onto the street, laughing.

"I'm a professional singer," he announced loudly to the world. "I got paid! Maybe it was just a beer, but I got paid!"

"Right and we could go to jail here for it."

"We better get going then," he said with a laugh, and we hurried away. "That ale was good. I could drink another of those. I guess I could pass for eighteen."

"You don't have long to go, Randall," I reminded him.

He laughed.

"That's right."

He looked silly, like his smile was lopsided on his face.

As we walked along, Randall talked more about himself and his family. The ale he had drunk seemed to have opened the dam holding back his personal life even more. From what Randall told me about his parents, despite their emphasis on his talent and their expectations for it, they seemed to dote more on his younger brother, who was an athlete and a more all-around student. I sensed that Randall felt his parents treated him as if he was someone unusual whose eccentricities would be explained by his talent and therefore excused and ignored.

"Dad always says things like 'That's Randall. He's special.' I'm not so special. I don't like being treated as if I was odd, do you?"

I had to laugh at the question.

"Oh," he said, "I'm sorry." He paused. "I really don't think of you as being different, Rain. I know I did a poor job of explaining that before, but I don't. I mean, you're unique, but you're not weird. Oh, just forget about it," he said, frustrated with himself. "I don't know what I'm saying anymore. And," he said looking around, "I don't know why we're walking in this direction."

"We better return to Endfield Place," I said.

"Right."

Randall found a station and we took the tube back to Holland Park. During the ride, he closed his eyes and nearly fell asleep. So much for his ability to hold his ale, I thought with a smile. Once we arrived, however, he snapped back to life and walked me to my great-aunt and great-uncle's home.

"I hope you had fun," he said.

"Oh, the best," I said.

"Sure."

"No, really, Randall. Thank you for the day."

He beamed and pulled back his shoulders.

"Yeah, well, I guess a girl could have fun with me.

We've got to do it again. We didn't see very much of the city. What are you doing tomorrow?" he asked quickly.

"I have the day off but I have to be back here to help with dinner," I said.

"Why don't we take a boat ride on the Thames and stop at the Tower of London? It will be better if you can come to the dorm, since the boats leave from right around there. Just take the tube to the school as you always do. You know where the dorm is, right?"

"Yes."

"How about 9:30? Is that okay, because if you want to come later, that's fine, but…"

"Yes, yes," I said smiling at his enthusiasm, "I'll be there right after I help with breakfast. They eat early so there shouldn't be a problem."

"Great, great, great." He turned to walk away and then as if just remembering something, spun around, took a large stride toward me, and kissed me quickly on the lips. "Bye," he said again and hurried off as if he was afraid of what I would do.

I stood there feeling stunned, and for a moment I didn't know whether I should laugh or feel wonderful.

The sound of the front door opening and closing behind me startled me and I turned around to see Mary Margaret step out. She paused when she saw me and then she started away looking like she wanted desperately to avoid me.

"Mary Margaret, what are you doing here so late?" I called to her. "I thought you had the afternoon off, too."

Reluctantly, she paused, looked back at the house and then at me.

"I had a few more things to tidy up," she said. "I'll be back in the morning to serve breakfast."

"How far away do you live?" I asked, stepping closer to her.

"Only a half hour on the underground. I've got to get home," she added, stepping back as if talking to me was forbidden.

"Is Mrs. Endfield all right?" I asked quickly.

"Yes," she said but narrowed her eyes. "Why do you ask?"

"I tried to talk to her earlier today, but she wouldn't answer when I knocked on her bedroom door. I heard her humming, but she didn't seem to hear me even when I knocked harder and called out to her. I thought she might be sick."

"I don't know," Mary Margaret said, shaking her head. "I don't know about that." She backed away faster, pivoted and walked quickly down the cobblestone drive, not once pausing to glance back at me. I watched her hurry away and then I turned back to the house.

My eyes were drawn instantly to an upstairs window. The curtain was parted.

I thought it was a window in my great-aunt's and great-uncle's bedroom, but the woman standing there had longer, lighter hair than Great-aunt Leonora. She was back in the shadows and I just caught a glimpse of her before the curtain closed.

Who was she? I wondered. Sir Godfrey Rogers's mistress? I actually frightened myself and gave myself a chill. As soon as I entered the house, I listened for a moment and then headed down the corridor toward my room. I wanted to relax and read and write letters to Grandmother Hudson and to Roy.

The house was strangely quiet and the lights were low

or off in every room. Boggs didn't seem to be around and I wasn't going to look for him. Maybe the ogre *does* take time off, I thought. Good riddance.

When I got to my room, the sounds of my own footsteps lingered in my ears. Once I lived in a world full of danger where drug addicts lingered behind buildings waiting to pounce on people so they could get some money to support their addictions, where innocent pedestrians were killed or wounded in gang war cross fires, where parents trembled when their children were out of the house, where the night was filled with the shrill sound of sirens, sounds that made our hearts pound our blood and filled our minds with pictures of horror. I had every reason to be afraid there.

What reason did I have to be afraid here, living among rich people who had servants and ate off real silver platters? I heard no sirens in the night, and yet the silence was somehow more frightening.

I quickly shut the door behind me.

The door without any lock.

6

Joie de Vivre

Moments after my alarm clock shook me out of sleep, I heard Boggs walk by my bedroom door. The slats in the old wooden hallway floor groaned under the heels of his heavy boots. I imagined the whole house cringed when Boggs woke up. If there was really a ghost here, she probably curled up behind some old wall and waited for him to pass, too. At least by buying the alarm clock, I had denied him the pleasure of pounding on my door.

I needed something to wake me. I had stayed up late writing letters the night before. I hadn't intended to, but when I began to describe things to Grandmother Hudson, I couldn't help but add all the details about the school and the sights I had visited. My letter ran on for pages and pages, and I kept it all on a positive, happy note. My letter to Roy was the same. We had a great deal of catching up to do and I was full of questions about his new life, too. Finally bleary-eyed, I stuffed and licked the envelopes and went to sleep.

However, despite my exhaustion, I didn't fall asleep as

quickly as I had anticipated. Many different emotions had been blended throughout the day until I had woven a tight cord around my heart, a cord with strands of sadness and anger, strands of joy and love, excitement and depression, hope and despair. Randall's beautiful eyes flashed before mine and the faces of some of the troubled women depicted in the paintings I had seen at the National Gallery appeared as well, some of them making me think of myself.

There were also many things during the day which had reminded me of Mama and Beni: a black woman with her little daughter in the park, some black girls laughing and walking on the street, the sounds of hip-hop coming from a boom box, a black mannequin in a storefront window dressed in a pantsuit similar to the one Mama used to wear, all of it conspiring to make me melancholy.

That wasn't all that threw me back in time. When I held Randall's hand as we walked along the streets of London, I recalled holding Roy's hand, his fingers wrapped fully around mine, clutching me as if he thought I was a balloon that might float away should he lose his grip. Back in those days, Roy's hold on me filled me with a sense of safety. I never felt vulnerable and in danger as long as he was at my side, no matter where we were or who was nearby.

But a girl my age needed more than just a sense of security, I thought. I needed to cling to love as well as strength. There were other emotions to explore, other feelings to have travel over the wires that ran back to my heart. I wanted laughter to sound like music; I wanted every smile to brighten the day even more; and I wanted words to find comfortable places in which to settle and plant the seeds of memories that would grow forever and ever until I was too old to remember or too old to care.

Could Randall Glenn do all that? More important, did I want him to? Did I want anyone to, or was I afraid of the pain of disappointment? The questions rattled around in my head, keeping sleep waiting at the door until finally even my mind surrendered and shut off the light that kept these thoughts as bright as neon signs.

Now I grumbled like a woman four times my age when I got out of bed. I stretched and yawned, resembling a sleepwalker as I moved around my closet of a room, plucking clothes out of the wardrobe. Finding my sneakers, I plodded down the hallway to the bathroom to wash and dress, and of course, pin back my hair to satisfy Mr. Boggs.

Sunday was another big breakfast day, or as Mrs. Chester called it, a full English breakfast. Out came the sausage, bacon, eggs, scones, kidney, jams, biscuits and tea. She and Mary Margaret were scurrying about the kitchen as if we had twenty guests this morning. There were no greetings or good mornings when I joined them, just orders barked at me: "Get that pan, wash this dish, cut those biscuits, take out the tea and be careful with those cups."

Great-uncle Richard was at the table with his morning paper. He was dressed in his suit and tie, his hair brushed impeccably, looking like he had been up for hours. When does he relax? I wondered. It was Sunday. Did he always wear a business suit?

Even my great-aunt was formally dressed with her hair done and her makeup complete as well. At first I thought they were going to church, but picking up their chatter as I moved about the dining room, I learned they were going to the country right after breakfast to visit with some friends at their estate. It was good news for us, for Boggs came into the kitchen to announce they wouldn't be back for dinner and we had the night off as well.

Contrary to the odd way Great-aunt Leonora had been acting the day before when I had gone up to speak with her, she was bubbly and energetic this morning. My great-uncle didn't look like he was really paying attention to her, but she talked at him as if her words could cut right through the newspaper he held up in front of him. She thought it was a very important day because they were going to the country home of someone who had been recently knighted. There was even a chance the prince would appear, but in any case, according to Great-aunt Leonora, "the best of society would be there." She talked about these lords and ladies, royals, in a way that made me think of Greek deities, gods and goddesses who made occasional visits to earth and gave mere earthlings the opportunity to kiss their hands or stand in their shadows.

"I think it's so unfair that you haven't been knighted yet, Richard," she complained. "No one is more deserving of the honor than you."

"Patience, my dear," he said folding his paper. He glared at her a moment. "Patience and not letting everyone know how much you want it is the recipe," he warned.

He turned to me because I was just standing there listening to them. I was still fascinated with the way they spoke, not only to me and the other servants in the house, but to each other. It was as if they were on a stage performing before an audience.

However, he made me feel like I had been eavesdropping and I spun around quickly to return to the kitchen.

"Just a moment, Miss Arnold," he said.

I turned back slowly, expecting to be reprimanded.
"Yes?"

He reached into his inside jacket pocket and brought out a small envelope.

"In light of what you are mainly here to do, I thought you would appreciate this," he said.

"What is it?" I asked, surprised. I stepped forward to take the envelope. He waited while I opened it. "Play tickets?"

"Two tickets to tonight's performance of *Macbeth* at the Royal National Theater, the Old Vic. I thought you might want to take along a friend, perhaps someone else from the drama school."

"Isn't that nice?" Great-aunt Leonora said. "Very thoughtful of you, Richard."

"Yes. Thank you," I said, quite taken aback by the unexpected gift. I didn't think he thought that much about me. Sometimes, when he looked at me, he wore an expression of wonder, as if he hadn't known I was here or had forgotten. Maybe he didn't think I would stay.

"You don't have to dress formally, but you should dress decently," Great-uncle Richard instructed. "It's located on the South Bank of the Thames. I'm sure you'll have no trouble finding your way there, now that you are a seasoned London traveler," he added.

I smiled and thanked him again.

"It's nothing. I have some influence with theater people these days and those are very good seats," he said. "Let me know what you think of the performance. *Macbeth* is one of my favorites," he added. "Perhaps someday, Mrs. Endfield and I will attend a performance with you playing Lady Macbeth," he said with a wide smile. Then, as if he realized he was being warm and friendly, he reached for his paper, snapped it sharply, and started reading again.

I glanced at my Great-aunt Leonora whose face was frozen in a far-off look as she gazed right through me. Sometimes the two of them gave me the feeling they moved in and out of their own worlds, oblivious to each other and anyone else around them.

When I went into the kitchen, I knew from the way Mrs. Chester looked at me that she had overheard the conversation in the dining room.

"I guess yer doin' pretty nicely 'ere for a Yank," she commented and glanced at Mary Margaret before turning back to me. "No lazy streak in ya, that's for sure. Ya do yer chores as yer told and don't whine and moan about it."

"Thanks, I guess," I said. "Although Yanks aren't lazy. You can't be the greatest country in the world and be lazy."

"Oh, listen ta that now, Mary Margaret. All that pride and she ain't got a bloody bean."

"You don't have to be rich to have some self-pride," I remarked.

"Ya listening, Mary Margaret?" Mrs. Chester chimed. She turned back to me. "I been tellin' 'er not ta be mopin' about with a face down ta 'er feet or she'll never catch a bloke worth a bob, but she don't listen ta me. Maybe she'll take a lesson from the likes of you," Mrs. Chester said.

I glanced at Mary Margaret and saw how nervous Mrs. Chester was making her.

"Mary Margaret is a very pretty young woman," I said. "Intelligent too. I'm sure she doesn't need advice from me."

Mary Margaret looked at me as if I had just escaped from a nuthouse and went out quickly to clear the breakfast table.

"Never mind what ya think 'bout 'er good looks," Mrs. Chester insisted. "Ya oughta let 'er knock about with ya. All she does is go from 'ere ta home ta be with 'er old sick mum. She thinks she's still a li'l girl, but I'll wager when that one gets toffed up, she'd catch an eye or two," Mrs. Chester predicted. "She's got a sweet face. It almost breaks me heart." She paused for a moment before continuing.

"I just feel sorry fer 'er, is all," she finally said, turning back to her work. "If I could, I'd find 'er a good bloke, meself. A decent tumble would grow 'er up overnight."

That's one strange prescription for wisdom and maturity, I thought.

Mary Margaret returned with dishes in hand, glanced at me fearfully and went to the sink.

She does act like a girl half her age, I realized, but really, what could I do for her? I had trouble enough finding my own way, and it wasn't as though I hadn't tried to be friendly with her. She avoided personal talk and looked at me as if I was some kind of threat, but I couldn't help but feel sorry for her, too.

"Would you like to go to the play with me tonight, Mary Margaret?" I asked.

She kept rinsing the dishes.

"Well, don't just keep the girl waitin', answer 'er," Mrs. Chester said.

Mary Margaret looked at her and then at me. She hadn't heard a word. She was too deep in her own thoughts, crawling into herself like a snail.

"I have two tickets to a play tonight. Would you like to go with me?"

She shook her head vigorously.

"Oh, I can't," she said. "I got to be with me mum."

"That's stupid and ya know it," Mrs. Chester said.

"No, I can't," she insisted and then, maybe because we made her so nervous, she dropped a dish and it shattered in the sink.

Before anyone could say a word, she burst into tears and rushed from the kitchen.

"See?" Mrs. Chester said. "Ya'd never know that girl was in 'er twenties, the way she acts."

I started to pick up the broken dish when Boggs appeared in the doorway.

"What's goin' on in 'ere?" he demanded.

"What's it look like?" I fired back.

"You pay for what you break in this 'ouse, you know," he said, looking at the pieces of the dish.

"She didn't break it," Mrs. Chester told him.

"You payin' for it then?"

"Don't worry about it," I said. "I'll pay for it. Slip the bill under my door when you march by in the morning. And if you want, you could add the VAT tax," I said. The value-added tax, I had learned, was like a sales tax in America.

He glared at me, nodded and left the kitchen.

"I wouldn't rag that man, I wouldn't," Mrs. Chester warned.

"Why not?" I demanded more firmly.

"'E's got somethin' bad inside 'im, 'e does."

"Then why does Mr. Endfield keep him working here?"

"I don't know," Mrs. Chester said turning away from me quickly, "and it ain't me place ta ask."

I shook my head and returned to the dining room to finish clearing the breakfast table. The Endfields were already gone. Mary Margaret came in to help, her eyes bloodshot and downcast.

"It's all right, Mary Margaret," I said. "Maybe you can go out with me some other time."

She looked up at me with relief in her face as if I had freed her from some horrible obligation.

And all I had done was ask her to go to a play.

I would have been happy to take Mary Margaret to the play if she had wanted to go. Perhaps we could have become friendlier as a result. Now that she wasn't going, however, my mind settled on Randall. I called the dorm to tell him about it and he was very excited.

"When you come today, you might bring a change of clothes with you," he suggested. "We'll spend the day on the river and do some more sightseeing, and then you can freshen up here and we'll go directly to the Old Vic. I've been there before. It'll be fun," he said.

I thought he had made a good suggestion, so I chose what I would wear and put it neatly into a large bag. Then I headed out to take the underground and go to the dorm, which was really only a two-story house about three blocks from the school.

As the skies cleared, it was turning out to be the prettiest and warmest day since I had arrived in London. Perhaps because of all the rain the city got, the flowers were the brightest I had ever seen, and that included some of the magnificent gardens on the estates in Virginia where Grandmother Hudson lived. The brightness seemed to put more smiles on the faces of people around me, too, and I wondered if people blossomed like flowers. If so, Mary Margaret could certainly use more exposure to sunshine, I thought.

The residence hall was a gray stone building on a side

street. There wasn't a dorm mother or anything like what might be in a school in America. There was a caretaker for the building, but other than that, everyone who lived there had their own apartments. The building had no facilities for meals, but in the lounge there was a small electric stove for a teapot.

Randall was sitting there waiting for me when I arrived, and with him were the French sisters, Catherine and Leslie. They all looked up.

"Ah, but here she is, the American princess," Leslie said. They both wore jeans and pretty light blue sweatshirts with designer logos on the front. Catherine had a pearl barrette in her hair.

"After clearing dishes, washing the table, and scrubbing a sink, I don't feel very much like an American princess," I explained.

"I told them where we were going and they wanted to come along," Randall said in the tone of a confession. "I hope that's all right."

"Why shouldn't it be?" I replied.

"You can't have him all to yourself so soon, *chérie*," Catherine declared, threading her arm through Randall's. He blushed and rolled his eyes.

"Are those your things for later?" he asked, nodding at my bag.

"Yes."

"Let me take them to my room for you, and then we'll get going," he said. I handed him the bag as he rose and he went out and up the short stairway to the second floor.

Almost instantly, Leslie reached up and pulled me down to sit beside her and Catherine.

"So, you tell us how you win this handsome boy's

heart so quickly, eh? We have both been trying since we first gazed into those beautiful eyes."

"You practically threw yourself into his arms," Catherine said, nodding with a grouchy face at her sister. "You frightened him," she charged. "I told you not to be so aggressive. Canadian boys are like American boys, right, *chérie?* They don't like their women to be, how do you say, in their faces. Am I not right, *chérie?*"

Why was it, I wondered, that everyone I met here thought I was some kind of an expert when it came to romance and men? Was it the clothes I wore? The way I walked, some gesture? When Mama was in a fun mood, she would slide her eyes from side to side and say, "You're going to be some heartbreaker, honey."

"I don't know much about Canadian men," I said. "Randall is actually the first boy from Canada I have ever met, and as for American men, most of the ones I know want to take advantage of you as quickly as they can. They'd love to have you in their faces."

"So?" Leslie shrugged. "What is wrong with that?" she cried and they looked at each other and giggled.

"What is wrong with that? They don't respect you," I said. "That's what's wrong with that."

They both grew serious for a moment as if I had introduced a whole new idea.

"You mean you think a man will respect you only if you are frigid?" Catherine inquired.

"No, not frigid. I'm not saying you have to be the ice queen or anything, but you shouldn't just lay back like a piece of meat on a platter," I told her.

Again, they both laughed. They were beginning to annoy me.

"Why is that so funny?"

"We don't think of ourselves as pieces of meat, but perhaps we think that of some of the boys we've been with, eh, Catherine?"

"*Oui.* Big sausage, eh?"

They smiled licentiously and nodded.

"Maybe things are different for you and where you're from," I muttered dryly, looking toward the doorway for Randall to rescue me from this conversation.

"You are much too serious, *chérie,*" Leslie said. She put her hand on my hand. "Being in love, having a lover, this should be amusing, too?"

"Amusing?"

"Maybe that's not the right word. Catherine?"

"Joyful, pleasureful," Catherine explained. "If you moan and groan and sigh and cry over every little kiss and touch, you will miss the *raison d'être,* the reason to be. To be is to enjoy. *Joie de vivre,* no?"

I thought about the gloom back at Endfield Place: Boggs growling at everyone, Mary Margaret whimpering and shy, Mrs. Chester a work hog, and my formal and stiff great-uncle and -aunt barely showing any feeling for each other.

"Maybe you're right," I said as Randall returned.

"Right about what?" he asked.

"Making love," Leslie eagerly offered.

"What?"

"Shouldn't we get started?" I asked quickly.

"Making love?" Leslie teased.

"Making love to the sights of London," I countered and they laughed again.

"*Touché, chérie.* Come, show us your London, *Mon-*

sieur Glenn," Catherine declared, jumping up. She put her arm through Randall's and tugged him toward the front door. He looked back at me helplessly. Leslie and I followed and we all headed for the underground and our day on the Thames.

As Randall had planned, we took a sightseeing boat up the river and stopped at the Tower of London. Now that he had three of us in his party, Randall was even more of a guide, but he didn't fool around as he had with me. He remained as serious as a schoolteacher.

"William the Conqueror founded the Tower. It has served as a military citadel, a royal residence, a political prison, mint, observatory and repository of royal property from precious documents to jewels.

"Those men in the brilliant red, black and gold outfits are known as Yeoman Warders," he said.

"That one is very good looking," Leslie whispered.

Randall ignored her.

"The White Tower is the major building. It was home to a long line of medieval kings who lived on the top floor, but everyone is interested in the Bloody Tower."

"Why?" Catherine asked.

"It's where the ghoulish fifteenth-century royal murders occurred, the murder of the young princes, Edward V and the Duke of York."

"I want to see the jewels," Leslie cried. "Who wants to look at some dirty old prison house?"

"We can see it all," Randall said firmly.

The sisters smiled at each other, enjoying it when Randall took control. I started to laugh with them. Maybe they were right; maybe I was too serious about life. It was more fun to be carefree.

After our tour, the sisters wanted lunch so we bought bread and cheese and to my surprise, two bottles of wine. When I questioned it, they looked at me as if I had been locked away with the poor dead princes.

"How do you eat without wine?" Leslie wanted to know.

I explained that where I came from, wine was not something adults wanted younger people to drink.

"There are too many winos on our streets, guzzling some cheap wine out of paper bags."

They finally looked serious as I described some of the scenes I had witnessed where men were sprawled on sidewalks, homeless, living in cartons or in alleys, getting a cheap high from wine that would probably take paint off a car.

Like Randall, the sisters came from a privileged life. They lived in a château outside of Paris with land that bordered on the Seine. They, too, had gone only to private schools, and my stories and illustrations were as fascinating to them as some television drama.

"We have heard about such things in America, but you are the first one we know who lives in such a place," Catherine said.

Then, as if unpleasantness was nothing more than a bubble to be burst, they both clapped their hands and declared we should never talk about sad things.

"You will be a great actress and never go back to such a world anyway," Leslie declared.

Even Randall had to laugh.

"That's why we're all here, to become stars," he said.

I actually enjoyed our little picnic and the wine, too. I was surprised at how much Catherine and Leslie knew about good wine, how important it was to know from what area in France the grapes were grown, and how it all had an important effect on the taste. They taught me how to taste wine, how to hold it for a moment in your mouth and suck air over it to feel the burn. How they laughed at my confusion and surprise.

We really were having a fun day, but Randall wanted us to go back early so he and I had time to prepare for the theater. The sisters wanted to know where I had gotten the tickets and I told them about my great-uncle, referring to him as Mr. Endfield. They exchanged subtle smiles.

"What?" I asked while Randall went to throw away our bags and paper from lunch.

"An older man, *chérie?*"

"What? You don't think…"

"Why not? Leslie almost had an affair with a married man last year," Catherine said as if it was something about which to brag.

"You did?"

"He was really just married, but still, he was desperate to have me as his mistress. He swore he might even kill himself if I refused."

"What did you do?"

"Refused. Imagine, to have a man kill himself over you, eh, *chérie?*"

"You'd like that?" I looked at both of them and smiled. "You're making fun of me, telling me fantastic stories to see what I'll believe."

"No," Catherine said. "It's true."

They exchanged knowing glances again.

"What?" I demanded.

"Our papa has a mistress," Leslie revealed.

"He does? And you know about it?"

"Mais, oui. But of course," Catherine said.

"What about your mother? Does she know?"

"Oui."

"I like her," Leslie said.

"Who? Your father's mistress?"

She nodded.

"But he's having an extramarital affair, isn't he? How can you like her?"

She shrugged.

"She's nice. She buys us nice things, too. These earrings are from her," Leslie said indicating the tiny pearl earrings she wore.

"You took a gift from the woman who is cheating with your father?"

"You don't like them?"

I guess I had my mouth open in shock when Randall returned. He looked at me askance and asked if I was all right.

"Yes," I said. "I think."

On the way back to the residence, the sisters talked more about their love affairs. They prided themselves in being what they called *femmes fatales,* women who deliberately inflicted emotional pain on their lovers. They called it the agony of desire or some such expression Leslie had read in a romance novel. I was afraid to ask them how many times and with how many different men they had made love, but there was no doubt in my mind they would reply honestly—even in front of Randall.

Yet, I had to admit there was something about them that kept me from thinking of them as merely loose girls, like some of the girls Beni had been friendly with despite my and Roy's warnings. Catherine and Leslie still had a good image of themselves. I couldn't explain my feelings;

although I didn't approve of what they were telling me about themselves, I didn't disapprove of them either. It was as if the lives they were leading were good lives for them and should be left at that. I did keep coming back to what they called *joie de vivre,* wondering if there wasn't something for me to learn and something for me to imitate and accept.

Goodness knows, I wanted to throw off the chains of depression and sadness that the last year of my life had wrapped around me. Maybe throwing myself into a romantic fling or two was the way to do it.

"Remember," Grandmother Hudson had advised before I had left for England, "when in Rome, do as the Romans."

I wasn't exactly in Rome, but I wasn't back home either.

We parted in the lobby of the residence hall because Leslie and Catherine's room was downstairs. As we said good-bye, Leslie smiled softly at Randall and then leaned over to whisper in my ear.

"Make him long for you, *chérie,*" she said, "until he is in pain."

I started to laugh. Randall looked away quickly and then we went upstairs.

He had a comfortable, nice sized room, but I suppose anything would look good to me considering the closet I inhabited back at Endfield Place. I saw that he kept it very neat, everything in its place. There were two windows that looked out on the street and got the afternoon sun, each draped in white cotton curtains. A light brown oval area rug was under and around the bed so he didn't have to put his feet down on a cold wooden floor. The bed itself was a rich cherry wood. It had a headboard with an embossed crest that was designed around the head of a lion. The room had a large closet and a matching armoire as well as a dresser, a desk and chair and two nightstands with a standing lamp next to the desk. The room was lit mainly by an overhead fixture that washed the antique white ceiling in a warm glow.

"I share the bathroom with two other students," he told me, "but they're both away for the weekend."

I was happy to see the bathroom had a decent shower in the tub.

"Why don't you go first," he said. "I know how long girls take. I have a sister. Here," he added, reaching into his closet to come out with a terry-cloth robe, "use this."

"Thank you."

He gave me some towels and a fresh bar of soap and I went into the bathroom and took a long, hot shower. Living in the servants' quarters at Endfield Place after having been spoiled at Grandmother Hudson's was difficult, but it helped me appreciate things I had taken for granted.

After I showered, I brushed out my hair. Randall was waiting in another robe when I returned to his room, lying on his back and staring up at the ceiling, trying to be patient. He sat up quickly as soon as I appeared.

"I'll just be a few minutes," he said. His eyes lingered on me as if he was unable to stop them from staring.

"I miss my shower," I said. "I'm sorry I took longer than I should have."

"It's all right." He smiled. What a beautiful smile he has, always so fresh, I thought. His well-protected life had kept him so unscathed there wasn't a mark or a scar, not an ugly sight or thought souring what nature had given him at the start. The purity and innocence of his eyes made me feel young and fresh and full of hope.

As he started past me, we touched and the contact stopped him only inches from my lips. I could see the confusion in his eyes, the struggle within him between the forces that wanted him simply to reach out and seize me, and that part of him that demanded he be respectful and polite. At the moment, I hated that part and perhaps tempted him by moving my face closer.

"Rain," he whispered, and we kissed. It was a sharp, clean touch that put little sparks on my lips, tiny explosions sending a hot sensation down through my stomach. I was still naked beneath the soft terry-cloth robe and he was naked beneath his as well.

We kissed again. His hands undid my robe and mine undid his. His lips went to my neck, to my chin, to my nose and eyes as he leaned forward. I felt his hardness grow against me, but my robe remained partially closed.

He lifted his face away and gazed at me.

"Rain," he said, "I can't pull myself out of your eyes. I felt myself drawn to them as soon as we looked at each other."

He made it sound like a confession. It was as if he was a little boy admitting his mischief.

"It's all right," I said and he kissed me again as his hands moved under my robe and over my breasts.

I moaned, and my legs felt weak. I thought he would lift me into his arms and bring me to his bed, but he kissed me again and again and then he pulled himself back and closed his robe quickly, grimacing as if he was in terrible pain.

"We'd better stop," he said.

Before I could reach for him or even shake my head,

he turned and fled the room. I stood there, trembling. I had to sit on the bed and wait for my heart to stop pounding and the blood in my body to cool. I could hear the shower going. I would rather never have been brought to this point than brought here and left dangling, I thought. A surge of anger rushed through me and then I lay back and told myself he was only trying to do the right thing.

What was the right thing? Leslie and Catherine would have tackled him at the door and dragged him back to the bed, I imagined and laughed to myself. I sat up, gazing at myself in the mirror on the back of the armoire door. I looked flushed, my eyes still electric. Calm down, Rain Arnold, I told myself. Get some control.

I took deep breaths and then went to my things and started to dress. He came in while I was still in my bra and panties.

"Oh, I'm sorry," he said, starting to back out.

"Randall, after what just happened, I don't think you have to step out," I said.

He smiled, nodded and came in, going right to his closet.

"I didn't mean for it to happen like that," he said with his back to me. "I mean, I didn't intend…that wasn't why I suggested you come here and all. I don't want you to think that," he said.

"Stop worrying about it," I told him after I slipped on my dress.

He turned to me. He had his pants on, but no shirt.

"Really? You're not angry at me or anything?"

"There's no reason to be angry at you, or even myself," I said. "We're both adults, aren't we? If I didn't want to be here, I wouldn't."

He smiled.

"Yeah, that's right." He thought a moment. I could almost hear him telling himself that he had been a fool to rush out. It brought a smile to my face. Then he glanced at the clock on his desk. "We'd better get going," he said. "They might not let us in if we get there after the play has begun."

We completed our dressing in silence, moving safely around each other in his room, actually trying not to touch. It was as if we both believed that if we touched, we would lock in a passionate embrace and throw all caution out the window.

He looked very handsome in his blue blazer and tie. I fixed his hair for him and then we hurried out and down the stairs. As we rounded the turn in the lobby, I heard a door open and saw Leslie. She gave me a big wide smile, then laughed and stepped back into her room.

If only she knew, I thought, she'd wonder why we were bothering with the play.

Even a play by Shakespeare.

Giggling to myself, I clung to Randall's hand and hurried down the sidewalk with him into the warm evening, excited, never more alive and eager to see what lay ahead on this roller coaster Fate had decided I should ride.

7

The Hand of Fate

Unlike Randall, I had never seen professionally performed theater, but I didn't reveal that until after the play. Of course, I had read *Macbeth* in school, but seeing and hearing the actors, watching Lady Macbeth go mad and hearing the poetry was so overwhelming for me, I sat with my eyes glued to the stage, afraid to look away even for a moment. Throughout the production I sensed that Randall was gazing at me from time to time. If he tried to speak, I quickly shut him off. I didn't want to miss a word.

"That was wonderful," I announced when the actors took their last curtain call. Everyone in the audience was standing. My palms were red from clapping so hard. "I can't wait to see my next play!"

Randall laughed at my enthusiasm. That was when I confessed.

"Maybe you think I'm weird, but I've never been to one of these before."

"Never been to a play?"

"Nothing but school productions," I said.

"You're kidding?"

"No, I'm not kidding, Randall. You still don't understand what I've been telling you, where I came from, what my life was like. We didn't have enough money for food, let alone for plays, and my school in Washington, D.C., didn't arrange for us to go see any productions. Maybe they thought only a handful of us would go or those who would go would ruin the performance with our behavior. They were probably right."

"I did forget all that," he admitted as we walked from the theater.

"Well, it's all true, and now that I've seen how professionals perform, I really don't know what I'm doing here pretending I'm going to be an actress. I can't even begin to imagine myself up there, doing what they do."

"Oh, I'm sure you can do it, Rain. I'm sure you will," he said.

I gave him a side glance and smirked.

"I don't believe in the fairy godmother anymore, Randall. Some gang member in my old neighborhood mugged her," I told him.

"What?"

"Nothing. Let's just say I'm not making any plans to be disappointed, okay, and leave it at that."

He nodded.

"You want something to eat, right? We really didn't have any supper."

"I'm still too excited to eat, but if you're hungry, I'll eat something," I said.

He found a small place nearby called the Captain's Private Table where he ordered us fish and chips. When he asked for two pints of lager and lime, we exchanged quick glances, nervous as to whether we would be served without a check of identification. The waitress was overwhelmed with the noise and the crowd and just wrote our order down and brought it without question or comment.

"Now there's a successful performance," Randall told me. "We pulled it off together. Otherwise, it would have been embarrassing for me again. It's because you have that real sophisticated look."

"Getting by a distracted waitress is a little different from being on a stage in front of thousands of people, Randall Glenn."

I sipped my beer and gazed around. The restaurant looked like it was a local favorite, with no one but us appearing to be from out of town. At the table beside us, two young men spoke in what I thought was gibberish.

"I'll have Kate and Sydney," the taller of the two young men told the waitress.

"Me? I'll take the Lillian Gish with a pint of salmon and trout. Got a cigargette?" he asked his friend who quickly produced a cigarette and then stood up.

"Where ya off to?"

"Phone. Got to see if me wife is home."

"You mean your trouble and strife," his friend said and they both laughed.

I leaned toward Randall who had been listening with a smile on his face.

"What are they talking about?"

"They're speaking mockney. It's fashionable these days to use the odd phrase trying to sound like cockneys. They're having fun with rhyming cockney slang. The one guy ordered steak and kidney, Kate and Sydney, and the other ordered fish, which is Lillian Gish, with a pint of stout, salmon and trout. Understand?"

"No. Trouble and strife? What did he mean by that?"

"He went to call his wife, so the other guy said, oh, your trouble and strife."

"How do you know all this?" I asked, astounded and impressed.

"Like I told you, I read. I have this book back in my room. I'll lend it to you, if you want. It's like a dictionary of cockney slang."

"I have enough trouble with the English language here as it is," I said. "I'll skip it."

He sipped his beer and we talked about the play. Randall thought that Macbeth's life was predetermined by Fate and he really had no choice but to come to a bad end. I disagreed and pointed out that Fate merely tempted him. It was still his fault because he listened to his mad, ambitious wife and killed the king.

"Then you don't think your life is all predetermined for you?" he asked me.

"I hope not," I said. "Mine didn't get the best start, and if my future is anything like my past, I'm in for a worse Fate than Lady Macbeth."

He looked thoughtful.

"Sometimes," he said, "I feel that if I challenge things, do something I'm not supposed to be doing, I'm defying Fate and I'll suffer for it."

"Randall, if you don't want to be doing what you're doing, you should tell your parents and not let them design your life for you."

"I know. It's not that I don't want to do it. I love to sing. It's just that...sometimes, I think I'm missing so much, I won't have anything to sing about. Does that make sense?"

"Yes."

"Catherine and Leslie think so, too."

"Talk about temptation," I said, and he smiled.

The fish and chips came. I thought I wasn't hungry, but the aroma stirred my appetite and I fell in love with the fries. I know I ate too many of them. Later, on the way home, I heard my stomach complain about all the grease. It was as if big, thick bubbles were popping inside of me. I had to make our good night very short and just made it into the house in time. I expected my moans and groans would bring Boggs out of his room, but he didn't appear, and I couldn't wait to curl up in bed. I tossed and turned most of the night, waking up frequently with stomach cramps.

In the morning I felt like a hag and thought I didn't look much different. When Mrs. Chester asked me why I was so "buggered out," I told her what I had eaten. She laughed and said I probably had gone to a real dump. She made some concoction for me and it did make my stomach feel better. At least I didn't look like death warmed over when I stepped into the dining room to help serve breakfast. Only my great-uncle was there.

"So?" he asked as soon as I entered the dining room. "How was the play?"

"Oh, it was wonderful. Thank you for getting me the tickets."

"I've been hearing good things about the actress who plays Lady Macbeth," he said, nodding. "Did you take another student from the school?" he inquired.

"Yes," I said.

"Did she enjoy it as much?"

"It was a he," I said.

"Oh?"

His eyes widened a bit and he sipped his tea.

"His name is Randall Glenn and he's studying singing. He has a beautiful voice and will probably be an opera star," I said. "He's very nice. He's from Canada and he's been here before with his family, so he has been very helpful."

He looked at me with dark, almost angry eyes.

"You want to be careful about your relationships. One mistake can ruin your life," he advised. It sounded more like a threat. "The streets of London are full of girls your age who were tempted by far more sophisticated boys. Think of it this way," he continued, folding his paper and turning to me. Suddenly, he paused. Mary Margaret, who had been walking in and out of the dining room, lingered in the door a moment until he gazed at her furiously. Then she quickly disappeared into the kitchen.

"Think of it this way," he continued, as if he had been rudely interrupted. "Your hormones are like the engine of your vehicle. They run you and at this age, they are very powerful, so powerful, you can lose control of your vehicle and go off the road. You can crash and destroy yourself. Understand?" he asked.

He spoke to me as if he were speaking to a little girl, explaining the birds and the bees. I knew he was just trying to be helpful, but his tone of voice brought a small smile to my lips. He didn't like it.

"It's not a funny matter," he followed sharply.

"Oh, I know. Thank you for the advice. I appreciate it," I said.

"I hope so," he said. He went back to his paper, snapping it sharply.

"Is Mrs. Endfield all right?" I asked.

"She's just very tired this morning," he said. "Mrs. Chester has orders to send up her tea."

He didn't look at me. I could almost hear him say, "That will be all." I was dismissed.

When I returned to the kitchen, Mrs. Chester had my Great-aunt Leonora's tray all prepared.

"Ya can take this up ta 'er," she told me.

"Me?"

"And why not you, pray tell?"

I looked at Mary Margaret who turned away to get a dish of marmalade for my great-uncle.

"I've never been asked to do it before. That's all," I said.

"There's not much ta do, now is there?" Mrs. Chester chimed. "Jist don't drop it in 'er lap."

I took the tray and carried it up the steps to my great-aunt's room. I knocked and waited.

"Come in," she called.

She was sitting up in her bed. Without her makeup, her hair down, and still in her nightgown, she looked older, the lines in her face more vivid, her complexion more like thin parchment.

"Good morning, Mrs. Endfield," I said.

"Good morning. Please get that first, dear," she said, nodding toward a bed table resting on the floor by the wall.

I put the tray down on the vanity table, set up her bed table, and then brought the tray to it.

"Don't you feel well, Mrs. Endfield?" I asked.

"I'm just so tired this morning. The trip and the whole day yesterday was a little much. Don't go," she said when I started toward the door. "Stay a while and tell me about your day and the play."

I described our sightseeing and then the performance and what we did and ate afterward. When I told her how I had suffered a stomachache, she smiled and nodded.

"Heather was like that when it came to eating new things," she said and then she bit down on her lower lip so hard, it made the skin around it turn white. It was as if something forbidden had escaped her lips.

"Heather?" I said, stepping back. I knew who she meant because of what Grandmother Hudson had told me, but I didn't want her to know how much I had been told.

She shook her head, her eyes widening.

"I'm not supposed to mention her name," she whispered. "Don't you say a word."

"Who is Heather?" I asked.

"She was our daughter," she replied. Her eyes looked glazed over for a moment and then she batted her eyelids quickly as if she was clearing away mist and fog. "The Endfields suffered a horrible tragedy," she began like she was telling a story about some other people. "Heather was only seven when her little heart cracked and shattered as if it was some old glass window in the cathedral of her chest. She was a very sweet, precious little girl, full of smiles and love for her daddy. How her eyes would brighten when he appeared, two tiny lights flickering with her holiday laugh of joy as if every day was Christmas. Every day was special for her because she was given so few.

"Richard made every day festive for her. He never came home without a present in his briefcase or in his arms. He brought her dolls and doll's clothing, almost another doll every other day, and toy dishes and teacups, little furniture and clothes and jewelry. Whatever pretty thing crossed his eyes when he walked along the streets, he bought for her. She was never far from his thoughts no matter how big the case or important the client at the time.

"The morning she didn't wake up, he sat in her room and stared at her until it was nearly twilight. He refused to drink or eat a thing. He threw the doctor out, cursing the medical world for permitting it to happen. Nothing had helped, operations, medicines, nothing.

"Finally, his partners came from the firm and talked him into sending for the undertakers, but he would have nothing to do with it. Our solicitor made all the arrangements and when he went to the funeral, he moved and spoke like a man in a daze, hoping that any moment the nightmare would end. He looked at people and heard them, but he didn't believe they were there or they were really speaking.

"He's never once gone with me to her grave, you know. Heather's room is always kept locked. Mary Margaret is the only one who is permitted in it once a week to dust and clean. I don't see the point in that, do you, dear? If the door is always kept locked, why bother?

"You mustn't utter a word of any of this in front of him," she added quickly. "You mustn't. He can't even stand to hear someone mention her name now."

"Why don't you have any pictures of her anywhere in the house?" I asked.

"Richard won't permit it. Years and years ago, he removed any reminder of her that was in the house, anything that would force us to dwell on the sorrow."

"But don't you want to remember her?"

"Richard thinks it's better if we pretend we imagined her. He's right," she declared with a maddening smile. "It makes it so much less painful. When I think about her now, it's as if I'm dreaming about someone whom I wish I had as a daughter, but never did."

"You never tried to have any more children?" I asked.

She glanced up at me and stared so long, I thought she wasn't going to answer and I should just turn and walk out quickly for daring to ask such a personal question. Then she spoke.

"We were terrified that if we had another, the same sort of thing would happen. It was heredity, the heart problem. Richard's mother died when she was only in her thirties, you see.

"Oh, I know not having children has made us selfish," she continued with a slight nodding, "but there was nothing I could do. Richard wouldn't hear of adopting. A child wouldn't be loved properly in this house if he or she didn't have any Endfield blood, he told me, and I didn't argue. I suppose I was somewhat selfish too, and afraid.

"I'm not at all like Frances, you see. I pretend to be critical of her. It's a game we've always played, but I truly admire her for her strength. Sometimes, I think she wouldn't be rattled if the Queen herself came to visit. When our mother died, Frances was like a mother to me. She was even like a mother to her own husband sometimes," she added with a small laugh.

"Oh, but look at the time," she declared, gazing at the small marble-encased clock on her dresser. "You'll be late for school if I keep you here listening to my drivel."

"It's not drivel," I said.

She didn't seem to hear me. She sipped her tea and rocked herself slightly in the bed.

I started out of the room and then, gazing to my left, saw the rocker she had been sitting in the morning I had come up to speak with her. There was a blanket on it, but visible, just beneath it, was the tiny hand and arm of what looked like a doll.

It put a shiver in me and sped up my exit from her room and the house afterward when I had finished with my morning duties and could leave for school.

All during the week I went to my lessons and attended my classes with much more enthusiasm because of the play I had attended. Randall said I was inspired and I didn't deny it. When I sat and daydreamed, I did see myself on the stage. At the end of all my imaginary performances, the applause was deafening and someone always rushed up with an armful of roses for me. I envisioned my name in lights and saw myself featured in magazines. Back in Washington, D.C., those who had known me as just another poor black girl living in the projects were shocked to open newspapers and see my picture in the arts sections. I'm sure everyone around me in my classes wondered why I was sitting there with such a silly smile on my face, but they couldn't see into my fantasies.

Late in the week, my speech teacher pulled me aside to tell me I was making good progress improving my pronunciation and enunciation. On Thursday, I read for a dramatics presentation and as a result was awarded a role, the role Sarah Broadhurst had coveted. She was absolutely furious when she saw my name next to Ophelia from *Hamlet* on the assignment list the next day. Randall made such a big deal of it, I had to ask him to quiet down because he was embarrassing me in front of the others. He saw how Sarah was looking at me, her eyes green with envy.

"Don't mind her," he said. "If she doesn't get used to

disappointment, she'll never have a chance in the theater anyway. You're always auditioning and often being rejected until you're a big star and you can pick and choose what part you want to play."

The speeches I was given to deliver occurred in the play after Hamlet had killed Ophelia's father accidentally. It had turned her mad.

"I'll practice with you," Randall offered. "I've seen it a few times."

Everyone seemed impressed I was given the opportunity after so short a period at the school, especially Mr. MacWaine who said, "I'll include the news in a report I'm preparing for Mrs. Hudson. I'm sure she will be delighted to hear how well you are doing, Rain."

I was eager to tell Great-aunt Leonora and especially Great-uncle Richard that night when I helped serve dinner. As soon as I arrived, I hurried to my room to change. However, I was shocked to discover that someone had gone through my things. I could tell because clothing in drawers was disturbed and it was obvious that all my garments in the wardrobe had been shoved around. Boxes for my shoes had not been closed after someone had opened them, too. Whoever had done it had not been very subtle about it. Pockets of jackets were still inside out as well. I had nothing of great value for anyone to steal. Who could have done this? Why?

Furious, I marched down the hallway determined to complain to my great-aunt and great-uncle.

Boggs, who was my chief suspect, appeared just outside of my great uncle's den and office. Before I could get a word out, he growled, "Mr. Endfield just sent me to fetch you. He's waitin' to see you," he added and nodded toward the office.

"What's going on here? Who was in my room searching my things?" I demanded.

"Mr. Endfield's waitin'," Boggs replied, his eyes steely gray.

I might as well try to intimidate one of those statues in the park, I thought. I felt like kicking him where I knew it would hurt the most. Firing back my own gaze of fury, I stormed by him and into the office where my great-uncle sat behind his desk, his back to me. Before I could ask anything, he ordered me to close the door. I did so and then he turned his chair to face me. Before him, on his desk, was an opened envelope and a letter. He held it up.

"This letter came to my office today," he began. "It's from my wife's niece Victoria. Do you have any idea why she might have written this letter?" he asked, leaning forward and gazing like a prosecutor at my face.

"No," I said. "Why? What did she write? Is it about me?" I asked quickly, expecting that Victoria had defied Grandmother Hudson's wishes and revealed the truth.

Rather than reply, he sat back and made a cathedral with his fingers. He took a breath and straightened his shoulders as if he was about to address Parliament itself.

"You've been given some wonderful opportunities, not only here but in America, as I understand it. You attended a very expensive, prestigious school, were presented with a new wardrobe, had all your medical and dental needs provided for, were given luxurious living quarters and not asked to do anything in return but succeed and make something of yourself."

"I know all that," I said. "I'm grateful for it and I haven't taken anything for granted, so I don't need to be reminded, if that's what Victoria told you."

"No, that's not the problem," he replied.

"Is there something wrong with my work in the house? The other day you told me I was doing fine."

"I have no complaints about that."

"Then why are you talking to me as if I'm some sort of criminal? And who searched all my things?" I demanded. "My room looks like the FBI was in there!"

He remained calm, not even blinking an eyelid.

"Victoria has informed me that a very valuable family heirloom is missing from my sister-in-law's jewelry box," he said in a quiet voice. "It's a diamond brooch that once belonged to my mother-in-law." He picked up the letter. "She claims she saw it before you arrived to live with her mother and now when she went to look for it, it was gone. My sister-in-law is beside herself as well, but according to Victoria, she refuses to ask you about it," he concluded and put the letter down.

"Are you accusing me of stealing from Mrs. Hudson?" I asked, astonished.

"I'm not accusing you of anything. My niece thinks there is reason to be suspicious," he said.

"And so you had Boggs search my room?" I concluded.

"It's far better that if any investigation is conducted, it is conducted by the family and not by the police," he said. "It was for your own protection."

"My own protection? Treating me like a thief? Having that ogre go through my private things?"

"He is a trusted servant, a man of discretion. No one need know anything about this. Of course, that might be entirely up to you."

"I didn't take any diamond brooch, Mr. Endfield, and I would never steal from Mrs. Hudson," I said firmly. "You want to know what I think," I said, with hot tears in my eyes, "I think Victoria took it so she could blame me for it and now she is writing that hideous letter."

"Why would she do that?" he asked, more curious than astounded.

"She never liked me," I said. "She never wanted me to be there."

"Taking a diamond brooch and blaming it on you is quite extreme though, isn't it?" He thought a moment. "Why wouldn't she just voice her objections and leave it at that?"

"You'll have to ask Mrs. Hudson," I said. "Does she know about the letter Victoria has written?"

My heart felt like it would shatter if he said yes.

He gazed at the letter.

"Apparently, not. Victoria makes a point of asking me not to speak to Frances about it," he said.

"It doesn't surprise me," I said. "Mrs. Hudson would be even more enraged about it than I am. Excuse me for being logical, Mr. Endfield," I said, building my courage, "but what would I do with a big diamond jewel? Do you seriously believe I'm some sort of sophisticated thief who would know how to sell it? And where is all this money if I did do that? You and Mrs. Endfield know that the only money I have here came from Mrs. Hudson.

"Or, am I just to be considered some sort of kleptomaniac because I come from the ghetto and I happen to be a person of color?"

He looked at me and then at the letter.

"I don't know what to make of this," he said. "I'm only trying to do the right thing."

"What is the right thing? Making me feel like a criminal?" I pursued. "Doesn't a person have any rights here?

After the way you spoke, I thought everything was so much better than it was in America, everyone was more civilized. This isn't very civilized," I hammered home.

Now, he blinked.

"I'm sorry," he said. "Maybe I was wrong, but I felt I had an obligation and you *are* living in my house."

"What is that supposed to mean? Because of what Victoria has written, you think I might steal from you as well?"

Before he could reply, I straightened up and with my arms folded under my breasts followed with, "Do you want me to leave? I'll pack and be out of here within the hour. Just ask Mrs. Endfield to advance me the rest of my money."

"Of course not. That isn't necessary, but I assure you, if it turns out you are a thief…"

"You'll have Boggs flog me," I said. "I know."

He almost smiled.

"Please, accept my apologies for now. I will inform Victoria that there is no evidence of any sort of criminal activity and tell her to conduct her investigation in another direction," he concluded.

"That's fine, but now, everyone here is going to think I'm a thief," I moaned.

"I told you. I assure you, Mr. Boggs will not so much as breathe in the direction of those thoughts."

"Sure," I said smirking. I pulled back my shoulders and held up my head high again. "I would like a lock on my door. I think I should have at least the most minimum privacy."

"I'll see that it is done," he assured me. "You can prepare for your regular evening duties, and we will not discuss this matter again, unless there is some good reason," he said and turned around in his chair.

I glared at him a moment and then I marched out. Mr. Boggs was nowhere in sight, but I knew he wasn't far away. No matter where I went in this house, I felt his eyes on me. Sometimes, I imagined I could feel his breath on the back of my neck.

When I returned to my room, I sat on my bed and stared at the wall. Why did my Aunt Victoria hate me so much? Was it simply jealousy, jealousy of my mother, jealousy of the affection Grandmother Hudson had for me now? Or was viciousness just a natural part of her identity? I was frustrated. I longed to stand in front of her and dare her to make the nasty accusations then.

I was so depressed about it all that I almost forgot to mention anything at dinner about my winning the role of Ophelia. Then, while we served the afters, which this night were individual jam tarts filled with almond paste, something Mrs. Chester called Bakewell tarts, I announced it just to make my great-uncle feel a little more horrible about what he had done.

"I thought you'd like to know I was given a choice part in the upcoming dramatics presentation. Once a month the school has an evening of theater, singing, dancing and chamber music. This one is a week from Saturday and I was given the part of Ophelia from Shakespeare's *Hamlet*."

"Oh, that does sound impressive, dear. Congratulations," my great-aunt declared with a clap. "Don't you think that's impressive, Richard?" she asked him. "Maybe we'll be able to attend."

"Yes," he said. "Good show," he added, but he didn't look at me.

"I do hope you'll be able to attend," I said. "I'll be sure to get you tickets."

He didn't reply, but Great-aunt Leonora nodded and smiled widely. A moment later, she was moaning about her age spots. She had caught a glimpse of herself reflected in the silver dish and went on and on about the difficulties of growing old.

"The alternative," my Great-uncle Richard told her in a gruff voice, "is not very appealing."

She changed the subject and talked about a new restaurant Lord and Lady Batten had discovered. All Great-uncle Richard had to do was suggest his disapproval of a topic and she retreated. Was there ever any real love and passion between these two? I wondered, or had all of it died with their little girl years and years ago? Should I pity them or ignore them? I wondered.

Saturday afternoon, I went to Randall's dorm to work on my part with him. I had already memorized the lines and practiced reciting them in my room at Endfield Place. Our plan was to work for a few hours and then go to Piccadilly Circus.

"There's a great pedestrian area. We'll see all the shops, clubs, theaters, as well as the most visited museum, Guinness World of Records. I'll show you Her Majesty's Theatre and the Royal Haymarket Theatre. We can go to a production at one of them next weekend, if you like."

He talked so fast and so excitedly, rushing about his room to find magazines and brochures with pictures to show me. Suddenly, he paused and looked at me as if he just realized I was in the room, too.

"You look upset today. What's wrong?" he asked.

Beni used to tell me I was a poor liar because my face was like one of those one-way mirrors. Everyone could look in and see what I was thinking or what I felt and believed, and I never knew how much I was exposing to the world.

"You might as well walk around naked, Rain," she used to say.

"Maybe I'm not so good an actor after all, Randall," I said and flopped facedown on his bed.

"Is there anything I can do?" he asked.

I rested my forehead on my arms and closed my eyes. If I pressed them shut hard enough, could I lock out the world? Could I wish and wish and put myself back in time? How I missed Mama and Roy and even my troublesome sister, Beni.

Randall put his hand on my shoulder and sat beside me.

I thought hard about myself. Carrying lies was too burdensome. The weight of deception turned my heart into a lump of lead in my chest. How wonderful it must be to not have to worry about every word you said, not have to be terrified that you will reveal something, that you might accidentally speak the truth.

"The people I'm living with, Mr. Endfield in particular, had my room searched yesterday," I told Randall bitterly. "He had his man Boggs go through my clothing, my bags, even my undergarments!"

"Why?"

"He received a letter from his wife's niece accusing me of stealing a diamond brooch from her mother before I left for England," I said.

Randall didn't say anything. I turned over and looked up at him.

"I'm no thief, Randall."

"I know," he said. "I was just thinking how horrible it must be for you living with someone who thinks you might be," he said. He really looked like he was thinking that. In fact, he looked like he might cry for me. "Maybe, you should move into the dorm. There's another room available."

"No, there's no money for that, Randall. I'm all right. I let him know how I felt about it and I think he regrets it," I said.

"He should," he said angrily. His beautiful eyes grew even more striking when they filled with anger.

I smiled at him and he looked confused. Then he smiled back and lowered his face until his lips could reach mine. We kissed softly. He lifted his head and looked into my eyes.

"You're beautiful, Rain," he said. "You make me think of a rich, mocha sundae."

I started to laugh and he kissed me again, harder, longer. I reached up and put my hand on the back of his neck and held him. I felt his hand move up the right side of my body to my breast. He sprawled out next to me and moved his lips to my chin and my neck. When his fingers fumbled with the buttons of my blouse, I put my hand on his wrist and pulled back.

"This isn't helping me prepare for the dramatic recitation," I said smiling.

"Yes, it is," he insisted. "Like Catherine and Leslie say, you've got to experience it all to be a well-rounded performer."

"That sounds more like the argument for lovemaking a boy would use," I told him, but I kissed the tip of his nose and he kissed me again.

Maybe I was just tired of being sad and angry, or maybe

I felt stronger about Randall than I had anticipated, but suddenly, I wanted to give in, to abandon all defenses, to drop my arms and turn my head and moan and let him peel off my clothing, kissing every uncovered place until I was naked. He stood up and took off his own clothes quickly.

The taste of his lips on mine, the way he stirred me inside, the swirling in my head were all so wonderful, I did feel that for a few moments anyway, I was escaping all the darkness and deceit. I was someplace else where honest feelings were all that mattered, where words were molded by the rhythms in my heart and not by the workings of my mind.

"We've got to be careful," I whispered into his ear when I felt him shifting his hips to find a comfortable position so that he could bring us together as intimately as any two people could be. "Don't you have protection?"

"No," he said, "but don't worry. I promise I won't let anything happen, Rain. I promise," he said, he pleaded. I wanted to push him away. Everything told me I had to, but the passion that raged in me wasn't much less than what was driving him.

He entered me. I gasped.

"Randall!" I cried. "We'll get into trouble and I can't afford another bit of it!"

He moved quickly and then he pulled out and spent himself on the bed, between my legs, moaning. I waited for my heart to stop flailing about in my chest so that my blood would cool and slow its flow. Then I touched his hair and waited for him to catch his own breath.

"I'm sorry," he muttered. "I'm such an idiot. Leslie and Catherine wanted to give me some rubber Johnnies, but I was too embarrassed to take them. I should have gotten my own. I'm such an idiot."

"Rubber Johnnies?"

"That's what they call them here," he said and I started to laugh. I couldn't help it. I started to laugh harder and harder until tears spilled from my eyes.

He lifted his head and smiled at me.

"What?"

"Nothing," I said, sitting up and reaching for my clothes. Then I started to laugh again.

He laughed, too, although he didn't know why. He thought I was just laughing at the funny name for a condom.

I wasn't really laughing. I was crying with a smile on my face. I was so lost. Even when I was making love, I felt so lost.

Until I knew who I was, until I stood up proudly and said my name; until I could look into the mirror and see through the mask, I wouldn't be able to feel anything, I thought, not the way all this should be felt.

When I stopped laughing and just wiped tears from my cheeks, Randall stared at me, confused.

"Are you all right?" he asked.

"No," I said.

"I'm sorry. You're upset with me. I'm such an idiot."

"It's not you, Randall."

"Then what is it?" he asked.

"It's the big lie," I replied.

"What big lie?"

"Me," I said. "To be or not to be, remember?"

He shook his head. "I don't understand."

I hesitated and then I pulled the blanket over myself and began, and as I told him my story, my true story, it felt as if a weight was being lifted from my chest.

8

Disturbing Revelations

Randall lay back on a pillow with his hands behind his head listening attentively to my story. He didn't interrupt; he didn't ask a question; he didn't speak until I stopped talking, took a deep breath and closed my eyes for a moment. What drained me was not the length of time it took or even the revisiting of highly emotional moments. No, what sapped my spirit and energy was revealing to another person that my mother, my real mother, had given birth to me and then given me away as easily as she might have given away an old pair of shoes. If Mama Arnold hadn't contacted my real mother on my behalf last year, we might never have met. Her life wouldn't have changed an iota, not that I thought it had anyway. She claimed that she often thought of me, but I didn't really believe that and after all, she was still doing all she could to keep my existence top secret.

If anyone should suffer from a poor self-image and lack of self-confidence, I thought, it should be me, and those were two things you needed to have in tiptop condition if you were going to become an actress and perform before thousands of people judging you, measuring you along with critics who had microscopes for eyes.

"So," Randall finally said, "the people you are living with here are really your relatives, but they don't know it?"

"That's right. Mr. and Mrs. Endfield are my great-uncle and great-aunt, but Grandmother Hudson thought it would be better if they didn't know. The Endfields like being thought of as magnanimous and my Great-aunt Leonora won't be outdone by my grandmother when it comes to charitable acts, especially one as dramatic as this," I told him. "She brags to all her friends that she has an au pair from America."

"But wouldn't it be better for you if they knew? I mean, maybe you wouldn't have to be a servant," he said, "and you could spend all your time on your studies."

"To tell you the truth, Randall, I don't know if it would be better. I have the feeling Grandmother Hudson, who knows them a lot better than I do, believes they probably wouldn't let me live with them. They'd consider it all a big disgrace and ask me to leave. I'm surprised my Aunt Victoria hasn't told them the truth about me just so she could see that take place. She's probably torn between being happy I'm here and unhappy my grandmother cares so much about me and does so much for me."

"If she had never met you before and never even knew you existed, why does she hate you? Is it simply because she's prejudiced or..."

"I don't know if it's me or it's just that she hates her sister, my mother, and therefore anything or anyone connected with her. Except," I said thinking aloud, "I don't get the feeling she dislikes my mother's husband. It's complicated," I said, reaching for my clothing. "It gives me a headache just thinking about it all."

Randall continued to look deep in thought, and then his face suddenly brightened with an idea. I could practically see the lightbulb flash above his head.

"You said your mother told you that your real father came to London to write and to teach, right?"

"Yes." I clipped on my bra and slipped on my panties. Randall remained as he was, still thinking, his hands still behind his head, his gaze fixed on the ceiling.

"And your mother told you he was fond of Shakespeare and wanted to be a Shakespearean scholar and teacher? Isn't that what you said?"

"That's what she said, but I don't know whether to believe anything she told me," I said and finished dressing.

Randall lowered his gaze to me, his face even more animated and excited.

"Why don't we see if we can find him?"

"What? Find whom?"

"Your father. You said you knew his name, Larry Ward. It shouldn't be impossible to locate him. We can start with the greater London phonebook and call every Larry Ward listed," he said.

I shook my head. The very idea put icicles in my heart.

"And do what, ask each one if he's the man who had an affair with a Megan Hudson back when he was in college?"

"Maybe he succeeded and became an English teacher, a Shakespearean scholar, just like he had intended. That would pinpoint him, wouldn't it? How many black guys have come over from America to study Shakespeare, Rain? It's not going to be that hard to find him, if he's still here, that is. What do you say?"

I shook my head more emphatically.

"I don't think so."

"Why not? Don't you want to meet him? Don't you want him to meet you? I would, if it was me."

"What would I say to him if we did find him, Randall? Hi, I'm your daughter, the daughter you never hung around to see, you never cared about? No thanks. I don't need another devastating scene. I've been rejected once, and pretty firmly too, at birth. I couldn't take it again, especially face to face," I said.

"Maybe it wouldn't be like that. Come on, Rain, don't tell me you're not the least bit curious about him."

"I didn't say I wasn't, but…"

"So what harm can it do to find him? After we are sure it's your father, you can decide whether or not you want to meet him and tell him who you are, but first things first. I'd be glad to help you," he said.

"Why?" I smiled at him. "Why is this suddenly so important to you?"

"I don't know." He looked at me. "I want to do it for you. I want to do something…significant," he said.

"You are doing something significant, Randall. You're developing a great talent."

"I know, but I'd like to do this too."

"It's not just an amusing way for you to pass some time?" I asked.

"No. It's for you. I want to do something for you. Really, that's the truth," he said.

I took another deep breath and sat on the bed. He stared, waiting.

"Aren't you ever going to get dressed, Randall?"

"What? Oh, sure. I actually forgot I was undressed," he

said with a laugh. "So, will you let me help you find your father?" he asked.

"I don't know. I can't help being afraid, Randall. What if it causes more trouble?"

"How can it cause more trouble to find him?" He thought a moment and then he leaned forward and looked me in the eye. "You and I were just talking about taking control of our own destinies, Rain. Your mother decided to send you in one direction and even now other people are still deciding on where you go and how you go. This is your one big chance to take a little control of your life," he said.

I shook my head and smiled at him.

"Maybe you ought to go into law, too. You're getting good at making arguments. You can sing for your clients in court."

"I object," he sang in operatic tones.

I laughed.

"Well?"

"All right," I decided. "We'll try to locate him and if we do, then and only then, I'll decide whether or not I want to, or should, actually confront him."

"That's good," Randall said. He started to dress. "It'll be fun and you won't be sorry. You'll see."

"I hope you're right, but I'm not as confident about it as you are."

"And now, back to business. Start reciting while I get ready to go," he directed.

"Reciting?"

"The cut from *Hamlet,* Ophelia's big scene, remember? That's why you came, right?" he declared, amazed.

"Oh. I wonder what made me forget," I teased and he put on his little smirk.

Just the thought of attempting what Randall had suggested we do about my real father kept the butterflies swirling in mad circles in my stomach. I was so distracted, I kept forgetting lines and had to start over twice. Then, in the middle of my third presentation, there was a knock on Randall's door. He was still in bare feet and shirtless when he opened the door. It was Leslie, dressed in only her thin, cream silk robe, and from the way it lay open at her breasts, it was obvious she was naked beneath.

"Oh," she said, smiling at the sight of me and Randall still not completely dressed. *"Pardon moi.* I did not mean to interrupt."

"It's all right," Randall said quickly. "Rain was just practicing."

"I see, but I did not know it takes practice," she said with a laugh.

"I meant practicing her part for the presentation next weekend."

"Ah yes."

"What did you want?" he asked sharply.

"Just to see if you had left yet and if you were going to do anything interesting today? Catherine is just dressing. We slept late. You should have come with us last night. What a time we had. So, what do you do today? Anything of interest? Or do you stay all day in your room with this practicing?" she asked, looking at me with a suggestive smile smeared across her face.

"We're going to Piccadilly Circus," I said. "To walk and have some lunch. You're both welcome to join us."

"Ah, this is so?" she asked Randall.

"You heard it," he said.

She laughed.

"How soon?"

"Fifteen minutes or so," he replied.

"Then, we shall go along," she declared. As soon as she left, he closed the door and turned to me.

"I'm sorry. We don't have to have them come along."

"Actually," I said, "I like them. They're happy, never depressed and great fun to be with."

"Oh?"

"Not that you're not," I added with a smile.

"I'm glad of that," he said and finished dressing while I made another attempt to recite my speeches without mistakes. This time I did a lot better. Randall nodded.

"Good," he said. "I can see you're going to do well. Who knows?" he added with a wide, bright smile. "Maybe before then, we'll find your real father and if he is a Shakespearean scholar, he'll give you some pointers, too!"

I nearly threw my copy of *Hamlet* at him and he laughed. I wanted so to laugh about it all too, but those butterflies kept me tingling inside with just the thought of seeing him, much less meeting and speaking to him.

We took the tube to Piccadilly station. Although the day had begun overcast, the clouds were thinning out and breaking up, permitting sunlight to brighten the streets. Nevertheless, many of the places, especially the theaters, had lights on and there was a glitter and excitement in the air. Crowds of tourists had converged on the area that some called the Times Square of London. Everywhere I looked there was something or someone to capture my attention, especially the punk rockers in their leather and chains, the girls with multicolored hair, boys with heads shaved or carved into strange styles. Catherine and Leslie

V. C. ANDREWS

exchanged remarks and comments with some of them.

We browsed a flea market, window shopped and went in and out of unique stores, some reminding me of thrift shops back home, selling things from old shoes to used jeans and very old records and books. For lunch we had pizza and afterward, we walked and walked until we reached the river and then sauntered along, stopping to look at street artists and listen to street musicians. It was another fun day.

Neither Randall nor I mentioned our intention to play detective and locate my real father. It wasn't something I wanted Catherine and Leslie to know. We parted company late in the afternoon when they met two friends from school who were going to a rock show.

Randall thought we should return to the residence hall to do our research and then go for supper nearby. He located the phonebooks in the lobby and we sat copying out the numbers and addresses for all the Larry Wards. It turned out there were more than twenty, some called Lawrence, but most simply Larry. Then we went to Randall's room and used his phone. My fingers actually trembled with the first number I dialed.

Three out of the five people we called either didn't answer or had been disconnected. The other two were definitely not my father, one a man who sounded as if he was well into his eighties or even nineties. I had to repeat everything and shout half the time. I hung up, disgusted.

"Let's take a break and go grab some supper," Randall suggested, seeing the frustration and annoyance on my face.

"It's stupid," I muttered. "It's a stupid way to go searching for your real father. I feel uncomfortable doing it."

"Okay, okay," he said, "let's not push it. Come on. I'm hungry."

166

I grabbed my jacket and followed him out. We went to his favorite restaurant, what he called a Mom and Pop place run by a couple from Ireland. Their specialty of course was Irish stew and I had to admit it was the best stew I had ever eaten. Good food and a cozy atmosphere with friendly people put me back at ease. I listened more to Randall describing his life back in Canada, some of the happier moments, the fun things he was able to do. Whether it was part of his musical ability or whatever, he seemed to have boundless verbal energy, his face brightening with excitement, eyes twinkling like Christmas bulbs, his laughter melodic. He reached for my hand and held it while he talked about the first time he kissed a girl.

"It was very disappointing," he told me.

"Nicolette Sabon, your eleven-year-old?" I asked. He looked surprised that I had remembered.

"No. We never really kissed. It was someone else, someone I didn't tell you about."

"Oh? Why not?"

"She was my cousin," he said. "We were both about fourteen and it was more like an experiment. Her experiment," he emphasized.

"I don't understand."

"She told me she was doing a science project about kissing and kissing me would be part of the research," he said.

"You believed that?" I asked. He blanched at my accusing him of being naive.

"Well, I couldn't think of any other reason why she wanted to kiss me," he replied.

I raised an eyebrow.

"I couldn't!"

"Okay. So, then what happened?"

"We kissed and it felt like I had rubbed my lips against a stone. Nothing. She jotted down some notes in a small notepad and then said we had to do it again and touch the tips of our tongues at the same time."

I started to laugh.

"And?"

"The very idea made me nauseous and I ran out of the room," he confessed and we both laughed.

How much I enjoyed being with him, I thought. He was so uncomplicated, so fresh and new like a real discovery, making it easier to relax, to shut away my fears and tensions and lower my steel wall of defense. Once, I lived in a world where danger lurked in every shadow, where no one could be trusted to be who he claimed to be and more than likely, if someone was nice to you, he had some evil reason smoldering just beneath his candy-coated smile.

"You didn't run out of the room from me when my tongue touched yours," I said, teasing him again.

He turned a little crimson and looked back to see who was nearby. Satisfied he could speak even more freely, he leaned toward me and said, "I bought something while you were browsing with Catherine and Leslie today."

"What?"

He unfolded his hand.

"Some of these," he said showing me a condom.

Now it was my turn to look embarrassed and utter a small gasp.

"Randall. Put that away," I said, watching the waitress move toward us.

He laughed and did so quickly. The waitress cleared our dishes and asked if we wanted anything else. Neither of us did so she left the bill and walked away. He stared at me, still with that little tight smile on his lips.

"First of all," I began, "that's taking a lot for granted. Who said I would be doing it again with you?"

He looked devastated for a moment and then shrugged.

"It's better to be prepared, just in case," he replied in a matter-of-fact tone of voice. "I don't want to look like an idiot again." He looked up quickly as a new thought crossed his mind. "You're not insulted, are you?"

"I should be," I said, putting on an indignant face.

"Oh. I'm sorry. I..."

"But I'm not," I added.

He smiled.

"Which," I continued, "doesn't mean I agree to anything ahead of time."

"Oh, sure. Like I said..."

"I think I had better start for home," I said, catching a glimpse of the clock. "Breakfast is a ritual and a production at Endfield Place."

"Right." He paid the bill and we left the restaurant.

I told him I could get back myself, but he insisted that he escort me home.

"I'll tell you what I'm going to do," he said as we walked up to the house a little while later.

"What?"

"I'll make some of the calls to the Larry or Lawrence Wards myself. It'll make it easier for you, and if I discover anything important, I'll let you know, okay?" he asked.

I thought about it. Making those calls had splintered my nerves.

"I won't say a thing, of course. I'll just try to locate him for you."

"All right," I agreed quickly.

We kissed.

"Well?" I asked.

"What?"

"Did it feel like stone?"

He laughed.

"Hardly. It felt and tasted like candy cotton. I'll call you tomorrow, early in the afternoon," he said as he walked away. I waved and then turned and started toward the front door.

Suddenly, I thought I saw a shadow move on my right. I stopped and studied the darkness. My heart began to race when something did cross the lane of light that fell across the grass. The light came from an upstairs window.

"Is someone there?" I called.

All I heard was the soft breeze slipping in and out, under and above the leaves of the trees and around the roof of the house. Thicker clouds had moved in again and blocked what little moonlight there had been. The darkness felt heavier, deeper, rushing forward and coming up behind me like a tide of black water.

Everything sensible and cautious told me to go into the house and forget what I thought I had seen, but I didn't like being spied upon. It was enough to feel constantly under glass when I was in the house performing my duties, but not to ever have any privacy even out here was more than just annoying. It raised the temperature of my hot blood to near boiling. If that Mr. Boggs was lingering there to watch what I did and then report my kisses, I would give him a blast that would have even surprised and shocked Beni, I thought.

I took a step toward the corner of the house and then another, listening hard for footsteps and concentrating on the shadows, peering through the corridors of darkness in search of some silhouette. There seemed to be none. I was glad of that, happy to attribute it all to my overworked imagination, but before I turned back, I saw that there was a light on in the cottage.

For a long moment, I just stood there staring at the cottage. All the time I had been here, I hadn't been closer to it than this, I thought. What was the big deal about it anyway? I gazed up at the lighted window on the second floor of the estate. A heavy curtain had been drawn closed. No one appeared and it was very still, very quiet about the grounds. The light in the cottage flickered. It was a candle, I realized. Why would there be a candle lit inside?

Curiosity put magnets in my eyes and in my feet. I had to get closer. I had to know. Softly, almost as sleekly as a cat, I stepped through the shadows and the candlelight toward the small building. Every once in a while, I paused to listen, but I heard no one, saw no one. The candlelight flickered again. Shadows seemed to leap and fly across the grounds like dark spirits. A small glow burned through the darkness against the side of Endfield Place and then disappeared as would light from a match that had been blown out. The breeze picked up, whistled through some brush and small trees, spun a crown of cool air about my head and then lifted toward the ever darkening night sky, a sky without stars, blanketed in a shroud of silence.

I continued until I was about ten feet or so from the front window of the cottage. The candlelight came from this room, off to the right a bit. Still, I saw or heard no one. Inching forward, I leaned toward the window to gaze through the gauze-like white curtains. They were parted just enough to give me a view of the room. I lingered, confused for a moment at what I saw, and then I took two more steps toward the window and gaped.

It looked like a dollhouse inside. All the furniture was scaled down and sitting on the chairs and on the sofa were dolls. On top of the round center table was a set of teacups and a pot. One of the larger dolls was facing the window. Its bejeweled eyes caught the flicker of the candlelight and brightened at me. It took my breath away for a moment because the doll was large enough to be mistaken for a small girl. I looked more to my right and saw the candle in a holder placed on a side table. For a split second or two it looked like someone was sitting on the floor, but when I focused closer, I realized it was just some clothing, a skirt and a blouse and a pair of shoes.

Even more curious about it all now, I moved closer until I was right up against the window, but just as I was about to lean in and put my forehead to the glass, I felt a hand on my shoulder squeeze so hard it shot a jolt of pain down my spine. Another hand grasped me at the waist and I was bodily lifted and turned from the cottage as if I weighed no more than one of the dolls inside.

With the shadows and the candlelight distorting his features, making them even more grotesque and startling, Boggs stood there glaring at me.

"What'cha doin' back 'ere?" he demanded in a gruff voice.

"Nothing," I said. "I saw a light so I just wanted to see what it was."

"You was told not to come near 'ere, wasn't you? You was told," he said.

"Why? What's the big deal about this place anyway?"

"You was told to stay away. It ain't your business now, is it? You got to listen to what you're told, 'ear?"

He still had his fingers on my shoulder. I felt them tighten like a vise.

"All right," I said. "This is stupid anyway. Let me go," I snapped at him. It was a show of courage that didn't have much depth because my heart felt as if it had fallen into my stomach and my legs trembled so much, I didn't think I could get them to move forward when I wanted them to. Boggs kept his fingers lingering on my shoulder and brought his hard, cold eyes closer to me.

"Just remember what you was told," he said. "Now get to where you belong," he ordered and gave me a small push forward.

I kept walking, a part of me fuming, but a bigger part of me happy to get away. As I rounded the turn at the front of the house, I gazed back. He was gone and the candle had been put out.

The cottage was vaguely outlined in the shadows that eagerly closed around it as if night itself wanted to guard and protect all the secrets that lived within its walls.

It was another night of troubled sleep. After I had gone to bed, I couldn't help but listen for the heavy footsteps of Mr. Boggs as he made his way down the corridor to his room. He seemed to hesitate at my door and my heart stopped and started when I heard him continue. I still had no lock on my door, although my great-uncle had promised. I thought I would remind him in the morning.

Whether it was part of a dream or just my imagination, sometime during the night, I felt what seemed like a warm hand touch my cheek and brush my hair. I moaned and turned over and then realized what had happened. My eyes snapped open and slowly, my heart racing, I turned back, expecting someone to be standing there. It was very dark, of course, but I waited, my chest thumping.

"Is someone here?" I whispered loudly. I heard nothing but the wind scratching at my little window. Finally, I closed my eyes again and fell back to sleep, but later, I could have sworn I heard footsteps on the creaky wooden floor and my door open and close. I carried that impression with me to work in the morning.

"You promised me a lock on my door," I said to my Great-uncle Richard as soon as I began to bring out his and my Great-aunt's breakfast.

Great-uncle Richard glanced at his wife and then pulled himself up stiffly in his chair.

"One should greet someone properly before making demands," he declared.

"I'm sorry, but it's hard for me to be relaxed and sleep well without it," I said.

My Great-aunt Leonora's hand froze on the teacup handle as she waited for Great-uncle Richard's response. He cleared his throat and put down his cup.

"I'll see that it's taken care of today," he assured me.

"Thank you," I said and returned to the kitchen. Mrs. Chester and Mary Margaret worked in silence. Boggs came in and poured himself a cup of tea. He stood there sipping it and watching us, studying me mostly. I ignored him, but I gazed back at him once just to let him know he wasn't going to intimidate me. He was, of course, but I wouldn't let him know it.

Finally, he left. We finished serving breakfast and started to enjoy our own.

"Who keeps the cottage clean?" I blurted at the table in the kitchen.

Mrs. Chester looked at Mary Margaret and then at me.

"Ya mean the cottage in the back?"

"Yes. Mr. Boggs made it clear that it's off limits to me, but someone must look after it," I said. "Do you, Mary Margaret?"

She shook her head but kept her eyes down as usual. I watched her nibble on her toast and jam like a mouse and sip her tea. Her hand seemed to tremble.

"Someone lives in it, I think," I said.

"Ya'r balmy," Mrs. Chester said. "No one lives there."

"Have you ever been in it?" I asked her.

"No."

"So how do you know no one lives in it?" I pursued.

Suddenly, Mary Margaret rose, put her dishes in the sink and left the kitchen.

"Mrs. Chester?"

"What is it?" she snapped.

"So how do you know no one lives in it?"

"I don't know, but I never seen nobody and what difference does it make ta me? I ain't been asked to prepare fer another mouth, 'ave I?"

She rose and then paused to look down at me.

"Those who mind their own business do the best 'ere," she said. "So mind yer own business."

Afterward, as I was walking back to my room, I glanced out the windows of the office and saw Mr. Boggs talking to Mary Margaret. He looked like he was bawling her out for something. She kept shaking her head and then she walked away quickly. He stood there looking after her, and then, as if he could sense my eyes, turned and glared up at my window. It nailed my feet to the floor for a moment. I took a deep breath and continued on quickly.

I remained in my room for the remainder of the morning, completing some of my reading and studying my part for the school's arts presentation. Just before noon, a man arrived with the name *Lock Doctor* written across the front and the back of his shirt. He knocked on my door and advised me he had been asked to put in a lock.

"I don't usually come out on a Sunday," he remarked, "but someone wants this bad enough to pay time and a half. Never looked down on an extra bob or two," he said smiling.

Rather than look over his shoulder as he worked, I went out to the drawing room with my books. A little less than a half hour later, I heard him leave the house. I returned to my room and saw the lock had been installed, but where were the keys? As if he could hear my thoughts, Boggs appeared and held a pair of them out in his palm.

"He left these," he remarked.

I took them quickly.

"Are they the only ones?" I asked.

He glared at me and then gave me a smile so cold I felt ice slide down my back.

"No one wants ta go into that room." His smile widened. "Don't you know the story? Someone wants ta get out," he quipped with glee and walked away.

If he hopes to frighten me, I thought, he's doing a good job of it. Why would my great-aunt and great-uncle possibly want such a man to run their house? I tried the lock and was satisfied it worked. At least I'd have some sense of privacy, I thought, but

I couldn't help wondering about Boggs's comment.

Did some woman really die in this room? Was she really poisoned? And did her spirit linger, perhaps condemned to remain secreted in these walls, waiting for rescue? Sometimes, I felt as if there was a spirit present. Maybe she thought I had come to set her free.

Later, after I had just sat down to lunch in the kitchen, Leo appeared in the doorway.

"There's a young gentleman waitin' on you outside, miss," he said.

"Thank you, Leo," I said and hurried out to find Randall pacing excitedly in front of the house. As soon as I appeared he rushed to me.

"I think I've found him," he said. "I'm pretty sure I have."

I felt the blood drain from my face.

"How do you know?" I asked.

"First, let me tell you he was very nice. I asked if he was the Larry Ward who was an expert in Shakespeare. He laughed and said he didn't know if anyone was really an expert in Shakespeare, but he taught English at a community college and his specialty was Shakespeare. I heard what sounded like a boy and a girl laughing behind him, too. I couldn't tell their ages, but they must have been his kids," he added.

"What did you do then?"

"I didn't know what to do, so I pretended I had written a paper on *Henry V, Part I* and asked if I could send it to him to read. Of course, he wanted to know who I was and who told me about him. It started to get hairy, so I pretended I had to hang up but I would call him again soon. Before he could protest, I did."

"Oh, that sounds great," I said. "He probably thinks it was some kind of joke."

"Anyway, I have the address. I know where he lives. It's not far. It's in Hammersmith. We can be there in less than an hour," he added.

"Be there in less than an hour? You expect me to go there now?"

"Why not? We can just…wait outside to see him, if you like. I'm sure you want to look at him. Imagine," he said as if this was all happening to him and not me, "imagine looking at your father for the first time in your life."

"If he *is* my father," I said. "If he's not, I'll feel like a fool."

"Maybe he looks like you or you look like him and we'll know right away."

"Well, what are we going to do, stand outside his home and hope he steps out so I can study his face?" I asked.

"Exactly, unless you want to ring the bell and start a conversation."

"And say what? Oh, Randall, this is crazy. I told you I didn't want to do this. I'm sorry I let you make the calls," I moaned.

"It's him, Rain. I'm positive," Randall said. He was so excited about it, he couldn't stand still.

I stared at him and thought about it. Was he right?

"Let's just go look. What harm can it do? It was what you planned on doing, wasn't it?" he insisted.

"I don't know what I planned," I said. I was feeling so nervous, my body actually trembled. I embraced myself and looked down, thinking. "This is all happening too fast. I don't know what to do."

"It's just a short trip," he insisted. "What harm can it

do if we just wait for him to appear? You can go. You're off work now, right?"

I looked back at the house.

"Yes," I said.

"So? Come on." He looked up at the sky. "It's supposed to rain today. We should get going."

"All right," I said. "I'll go get my jacket and be right out."

"This is great," Randall said.

I had to laugh.

"I think you believe we're in the middle of some dramatic opera or something."

"That's what life is—'a stage, and all the men and women merely players.' Remember your Shakespeare so you can impress him when you do meet," he half-joked.

I shook my head and hurried into the house. On my way out, my great-aunt was descending the stairs.

"Oh, Rain, where are you heading today?"

I paused, not knowing what to say.

"Just a walk with a friend," I said. "More sightseeing," I added.

"How nice, you make friends so quickly," she said. "My sister will be pleased to hear it. May Boggs drop you off anywhere?" she added. She looked past me so I turned and saw him standing there. How he could appear and disappear without a sound amazed me. Maybe *he* was the ghost.

"No thank you," I said and muttered under my breath, "we'd rather walk."

Boggs smiled coldly.

I said good-bye and left the house like someone fleeing from one nightmare but terrified of entering another.

9

A Difficult Decision

From the moment we left Endfield Place until we arrived at the street in Hammersmith on which Randall believed my real father lived, my heart throbbed with a pulsation that echoed through my bones and kept my chest tight, my breath short. Randall, sensing that my nerves had been turned into sparking wicks of dynamite, talked incessantly, rambling on about sights we passed, people we saw, things he had eaten. He understood that silence fed my anxiety, which sat like some hungry monster at the base of my stomach and growled.

"How do we know he's even home now?" I asked, finally finding the strength to give voice to the storm of thoughts and questions that flashed and thundered across my brain.

"We don't. We could stop at a Dolly Malone and call," he suggested.

"A what?"

"Dolly Malone, a phone," he said smiling.

"Randall, I'm not in the mood to fool around with cockney slang at the moment."

"Okay, okay, I was just trying to get you to relax," he said.

"I can't relax," I said, slapping my closed fists against my thighs so hard even he flinched. "I don't even know why I'm doing this."

"Okay, okay. I'll call to see if he answers or if he's there and then I'll hang up. How's that?"

"Stupid," I said. "We might be tormenting some innocent man who just happens to have the same name."

"And just happens to teach Shakespeare? Don't you think that's too much of a coincidence?"

"Do you even know if he's black?" I asked.

"No," he admitted.

"Randall," I said, stopping on the sidewalk, "did he have an English accent? He might not even be an American!"

"Well, he had sort of an English accent. I mean it was very correct, resonant, but anyone who has lived here as long as he has would have picked up some British influences in his speech, don't you think?" he asked.

"I don't know. How would I know? Let's just turn around," I said.

"Turn around? We've come this far, Rain. That's silly. Come on. It's just another block," he said and my reluctant legs moved me forward. "That's it," he said, pointing, a few minutes later.

We stood across the street from a gray stone house that had a short picket fence. The window casing and the door were all painted a dull white. It looked old, but quaint. The street itself was very quiet, and I was sure that if we stood for a while where we were, we would attract some attention.

"Now that I'm here looking at the house, I really feel silly," I said. "I have no idea what to do."

"Why don't I just go to the door, ring the bell and pretend I'm looking for someone else," Randall suggested.

"No," I said taking a step back. I felt like just turning and running away.

"Why not? If he comes to the door, you'll get a good look at him. No harm done. I'll just apologize and that will be that," he said.

"I don't think so," I said, but not firmly enough.

"I'm doing it," he said and before I could stop him, he crossed the street.

"Randall…" I called. He didn't turn back until he went through the small gate and approached the door. He beckoned for me to come closer, but I couldn't move. I shook my head and then he sauntered up to the door and rang the bell. He looked back at me, smiled and waited. My heart seemed to shrink inside my chest when the door opened. Despite my fears, I couldn't help but be interested.

A dark-haired woman wearing jeans and a gray pullover stood in the doorway. She didn't look much older than her mid-to-late thirties at most. Her hair was straight and down to her shoulders. Her face was angular and very interesting even from where I stood. As Randall spoke, a young girl came up beside the woman. She wore a dark blue skirt and white blouse and had short, curly hair. The girl wasn't much more than twelve or thirteen, I thought, but she listened attentively, her pretty face full of interest in what Randall was saying. I couldn't imagine how he could go on and on like that.

Finally, he thanked them, turned and started toward me. The woman and the girl looked our way and then closed the door slowly. Randall waited until he crossed the street before speaking, a fat, cat-who-ate-the-canary smile on his face. He glanced back and then moved quickly to my side.

"He's coming out any moment," he whispered as if the woman could still hear him.

"How do you know?"

"I heard him tell someone named William to put on his jacket. It was time to go."

"What did that woman say to you? What did you say to her? Who was the little girl?" I fired at him.

He laughed.

"I acted like a very confused tourist looking for some relatives. She told me I was on the wrong block," he added. "She was very nice. The little girl has to be their daughter. I'm confident we have found the right Larry Ward," he concluded.

I saw the door open and turned quickly, seizing Randall's arm to move him along.

"Someone's coming out," I said between my clenched teeth.

He looked back as I walked, terrified of following his gaze. I was like Lot's wife in the Bible, feeling like if I looked back I would be turned into a pillar of salt. I kept walking, my head down.

"He's black," Randall announced. "I knew it. He's walking this way with a little boy."

I was relieved when we reached the corner and I hurried to cross the street.

"Wait a minute," Randall cried, seizing my arm. "Don't you even want to look at him?"

"I feel dumb," I said. "I don't want him to see me just in case it is him."

"We'll wait here," he said, tugging me toward a newspaper and magazine store.

I followed him in and Randall picked up a newspaper. He went to pay for it while I stood there gazing out the window. Moments later the man who could be my real father came into sight. He wore a tweed sports jacket and jeans. He was at least six feet tall and very good looking with a strong mouth. He was trim, too, his shoulders wide. He glanced at the store and I looked directly into his face, but he didn't look at me. Even so, I held my breath as he gazed at a newspaper headline, read it quickly and then continued on.

The little boy at his side clung tightly to his hand. I thought the child was cute, especially because of the proud way he held his shoulders back and his head straight. Every once in a while, he looked up at his father as if he wanted to be sure he was imitating him well. They crossed the street and continued toward the river. That little boy could very well be my half brother, I thought, and that young girl back at the house could be my half sister. I had come all these miles, all this distance, to look upon them and the man who could be my father. How strange I felt. It was as if I was caught up in a dream, floating through a sea of wishes and promises.

"Well?" Randall asked coming up beside me, "what do you think? I think there's some definite resemblance," he told me, nodding before I could reply.

"Oh, you can't tell that from a short glimpse, Randall," I said.

"Let's see where they go," he suggested. "Maybe we can get a better look at him."

"I don't want to, Randall."

"We'll just stay far enough behind to…"

"No," I said more emphatically. "I don't want to. I don't feel good about this. He's out for a walk with his little boy. It's just not right to spy on him."

"Not right? Why isn't it right considering who you are and who he might very well be?"

"I don't know," I said and left the store. I walked quickly in the opposite direction.

"Wait a minute. Where are you going?" Randall asked, running to catch up.

"I don't know. Back, I guess."

"Rain…"

"Leave me alone," I cried and walked faster. He lingered behind, following slowly, knowing enough to keep away. My heart was filled with so many raging emotions; so many contradictory feelings were battling inside me. Yes, I wanted to know him, to find out if he really was my father and then to talk to him, to learn about him and to make sure that he knew about me, but I was also still terrified that the moment I approached him and he discovered who I was, he would turn away from me and forbid me from coming near him or his family. What right did I have to walk in on him like this? How could I expect him to care about me, someone he has never known, he has never seen!

It almost made me feel dirty, like a voyeur, to have come here to spy on him and catch glimpses of him and his family. And yet, the image of his face, those bright black pearl eyes, that look of intelligence and that soft smile when he gazed at his little boy all flashed across my eyes again. What was his voice like? What if he looked at me with as much love and pride as he looked at his little boy?

I was still searching for that love and I was not at all sure that I would find it in this strange man's face, especially if I forced him to look at me, if I threw myself in his way and cried, "I'm here! I'm your daughter! You have to love me, too!"

Love, after all, wasn't something to be commanded or demanded. It came from that special place inside our hearts, blossoming like a flower properly nurtured. Real love took time.

"That's Chiswick Bridge ahead there," I heard Randall say. He had caught up to me slowly. "We're actually on one of the recommended London walks along the Thames. We could go to Kew Gardens."

I turned to him and shook my head.

"Always the tour guide, aren't you?"

"I just didn't want you to think you were wasting your time," he protested. Then he stepped in front of me and held out his arms. "This 'ere's all part of the package, ma'am. We aim to please all our customers, especially you Yanks with all the bob."

I had to laugh.

"That's better," he said. "You had me worried back there."

"I'm sorry I left you like that," I said, "but it was all too much too soon."

"Sure. You can come back anytime. I found out something else that might interest you," he said, digging into his pocket. He handed me a slip of paper.

"What's this?"

"The name of the school where he teaches and the address. I didn't want to give it to you unless there was a real possibility we were onto the right man. And I know he's the one."

"How did you find this out, Randall?"

He shrugged and smiled.

"I went over to the school. Mr. MacWaine's got these books on the schools in London and I looked up the faculty list, found Larry Ward and copied it down."

"Boswell Community College?"

"He's head of their English department," Randall said. He shrugged again. "Just trying to be helpful."

"Mr. MacWaine doesn't know you were looking into him, does he?"

"No, I was able to look up the information without his knowing. Don't worry about that."

"I can't believe you did all this."

"It was nothing, easy," he said.

I put the note in my pocket and gazed at the bridge. It hadn't rained although it still might, yet people didn't seem concerned as they walked along.

"Want to go into the Gardens?" Randall asked. "It's still early."

"No. I'm tired," I said. "I feel like I've been running and running for miles. I just want to go home."

"Okay," he said and we located the nearest tube station.

After we reached Endfield Place and parted, I went into the house quickly and then straight to my room. When I opened the door, I found a letter had been slipped under it. It was addressed to me and it had come from Germany. Roy had written, finally.

I turned it over and studied the envelope. It looked like it had been opened and then resealed, I thought. It just infuriated me that my mail had been read. However, at the moment I was more interested in what was inside the envelope, so I sat on my bed and slowly opened it.

Dear Rain,

When I got your letter, I kept it all closed up until I was ready for bed. Just seeing your handwriting put your face in my eyes. I read your letter over and over. Some of my buddies probably thought I was trying to memorize something important. Anyway, I'm glad you got to where you wanted and life there ain't so bad. I bet you already made loads of new friends and you're a big success in the school.

I plan on taking my first leave real soon and now that I know exactly where you're at, I'll be dropping by to see you. I hope you want to see me at least half as bad as I want to see you. I have your picture hanging by my bed. When anyone asks about you, I tell them you're my girl. I hope you don't mind that. You are my girl. You always were and you know it. Sometimes, I just lay back and remember and think about you growing up, especially the way you turned those eyes on me.

Of course, I remember one special afternoon when I told you what you really meant to me and, well, I can't even write it, but you know the afternoon I mean. Jeeze, I can't believe I wrote this much. It's probably more than I wrote all the time I was in school. I can see you smiling and laughing about that as you read this.

I don't want to keep saying the same things so I'll just sign off with love and hope you will keep a little room in your heart for me.

I was about to sign my name and seal it up, but I stopped and just thought about Mama and you and Beni and how all those days back then run together

*in my head. I miss them. If it weren't for you, I guess
I'd feel about as alone as anyone could. I wanted
you to know.*

   I'm running off at the mouth.
   Bye.
   Love.

                                         See ya,
                                         Roy

I folded the letter up carefully and put it back into the
envelope. Then I lay there with it beside me and thought
about Roy and Mama and Beni, too. My eyes flooded
with tears. I wanted to see Roy so much, but I knew he
was hoping I would tell him I loved him the way he loved
me, and I was so confused about that. For too long a time,
he was my big brother. It wasn't easy to just stop thinking
of him that way. I had tried to explain that to him, but he
had refused to accept it. There was no one in the world I
dreaded hurting more than I dreaded hurting Roy. I suppose I had been hoping that he would have found someone else by now and the problem would solve itself, but
that obviously had not happened.

   How strange it was, I thought, that there were people I
wanted to love but couldn't and there were people who
loved me and shouldn't. Fate was teasing me, dangling me
in front of all these mirrors so that as I twirled slowly, I
could see myself struggling at every turn. When would it
end? When would I stop spinning?

   I must have fallen asleep because of sheer emotional
exhaustion. Suddenly, I felt my body twitch and I opened
my eyes to darkness. For a moment I was confused about

the time and the day. Then I glanced at the clock and popped up like a jack-in-the-box. I had slept right through supper. How could that happen? Why hadn't Boggs come banging on my door? I had it locked now, but he still could have knocked until he woke me. He certainly wasn't bashful. Maybe he just wanted to have me do badly so that the Endfields would get rid of me.

I turned on my lamp and quickly straightened my hair and my clothes. Then I went to the bathroom, threw cold water on my face and hurried down the corridor to the kitchen to make my apologies. By the time I got there, the dishes had been cleaned up and everything was put away. Mrs. Chester and Mary Margaret were gone and the dining room was empty, the table set for breakfast. It was almost as if there hadn't been anyone here for dinner after all.

Now, very confused, I stepped out in the hallway and listened hard. Except for the usual creaks and moans in the house, I heard nothing, no footsteps, no voices, nothing. Slowly, I walked down the corridor and peered into the billiards room, the office and then the drawing room. They were all empty. There was only a small lamp lit in the drawing room. All the other rooms were dark. I listened again, heard nothing and returned to the kitchen.

Realizing I was a little hungry, I made myself some tea and had a crumpet with marmalade. As I ate, I expected to see Mr. Boggs come bursting in at any moment to chastise me for sleeping through my supper duties, but for once he didn't appear. I cleaned up and listened again to the silence in the house before starting back to my room.

I noticed that Boggs's door was closed and when I listened in the hallway, I heard no sound coming from his

room either. It must have been an early night for everyone, I thought with a shrug and prepared a hot bath for
myself. Afterward, I returned to my room where I thought
I would read a little before going to sleep. I had just
opened my collection of plays when a glow over the
grounds outside my window caught my attention.

Rising slowly, I went to the window and gazed out at the
small cottage. Tonight, it was lit more brightly and the flow
of that light on the grounds was what I had seen. As I stood
looking out the window I saw figures silhouetted behind the
curtains. Then, they disappeared. I opened my window a little more and brought my face closer to the opening. I
thought I could distinctly hear what sounded like the kind of
music you heard on a carousel. It was low, almost a tinkle.

No one lives there, everyone had insisted, almost angry
because I had asked. Who was *that,* then?

I was tired of the mysteries and the shadows, the fret-
ful side glances and the whispers. I didn't know what I
was risking exactly, but I knew I wouldn't be able to fall
asleep wondering. Except for the music that drifted over
the grounds, the house was still very quiet. Even the
creaks and groans in the walls and floor seemed to have
stopped. I reached for my robe and shoved my feet into
my slippers. Then, as softly as the famous ghost of Sir
Godfrey Rogers's mistress must move through this house,
I tiptoed down the hall to the back door and slipped out.

The night air was cooler than I had expected. I embraced myself and gazed at the cottage. Standing in the
darkness, I felt I could observe without being discovered.
I waited and watched, but saw no one. It looked safe for
me to cross the grounds and go to the cottage. I walked
slowly, gazing around. The music was definitely coming

from the cottage. I stopped about midway because I thought I heard someone else skulking through the shadows behind me, but I saw no one. After a moment more, I continued until I reached the first hedge in front of the cottage. Someone moved behind the curtain, hesitated and then disappeared. My heart had stopped and started and now was pounding under my chest like a jackhammer.

I crouched and inched forward to the window after I had checked the grounds behind and around me once more. Slowly, almost as if I didn't want to see, as if something inside me instinctively retreated, I brought my eye up to the corner of the window and peered into the room.

I had seen the small furniture before, of course, but tonight I noticed that there were more dolls, and the dolls I had seen before had been moved. The one doll that was as big as a small child was still on the miniature sofa facing me. It looked like it was laughing at me.

I realized the music wasn't coming from this room. It was coming from another room on the south side of the cottage. I retreated and then, keeping to the shadows, moved across the front of the cottage to the other side. Once again, I looked around before going forward and was confident there was no one else out there waiting to pounce.

The hedges on this side were somewhat closer to the cottage so I had to step very slowly in order not to catch myself on a branch. I reached these windows and crouched again, slowly lifting my head. Through the gauze-like curtains, I could see a figure in the bed and another, larger figure sitting on the edge. I moved my head very slowly toward the small opening in the curtains.

People often say that when they are frightened by something, their blood turns cold. It is as if ice cubes had formed in the base of your stomach and waves of freezing air crawled into your veins, chilling your blood so that when it reaches your heart, your heart feels like it has been coated with thin layers of frost. I understood that description now. It was happening to me.

It was my Great-uncle Richard sitting on the bed, holding a children's book in his hands. He was wearing a velvet robe over his pajamas. Dressed in a frilly little nightshirt with pigs and squirrels and rabbits embossed all over it was Mary Margaret. She was sucking on a fairly large round red lollipop. Her eyes were wide as if she was five years old and hearing the most fascinating tale. Beside her on the nightstand a music box played.

The room itself was unquestionably decorated for a little girl. There was pink and white wallpaper filled with cartoon characters, more dolls on shelves, a small mauve-colored desk and a chair, and a pink rug. All the pictures on the walls came from storybooks and children's movies. The vanity table had a small brush and comb on it as well as some little bottles of perfume.

The window was opened slightly so if I lowered my ear, I could hear what was being said.

Great-uncle Richard's voice rose and fell with exaggeration as he read the story of a little duck who had wandered into the woods too far from her mother and was trying desperately to find her way home.

"Her little quack quack echoed in the darkness around her," he read, "and she fluttered her feathers and ran faster, not knowing she was going in the wrong direction. Suddenly, she heard an owl and she stopped to look up.

"Who? the owl said. My name is Dolly and I'm lost,

Dolly said. She didn't know that owls only said who...
Isn't that funny, Heather?" he asked Mary Margaret.

I looked at her.

Mary Margaret nodded emphatically, pulling the lollipop from her mouth.

"Yes, Daddy," she said. She forced a giggle and then put the lollipop back into her mouth.

"Do you want to hear the rest or are you tired?" he asked.

She pulled out the lollipop.

"I want to hear the rest, Daddy," she said.

Great-uncle Richard smiled and continued.

"Who? the owl said. Dolly repeated her name and told him she was lost. She waited. The owl went who, who, who?

"Why don't you listen to me? Dolly said angrily. I told you who I was. All the owl said was who, so Dolly ran on until she heard a hiss. She stopped and looked into the darkness. Who's there? she asked. There was another hiss. She walked ahead slowly," Great-uncle Richard read and then he put his fingers on Mary Margaret's arm and pretended they were little feet inching up toward her shoulder. She giggled.

"Suddenly," Great-uncle Richard read, "a snake popped out from under a rock. He stuck out his tongue. That's pretty rude, Dolly told him. He hissed again and slithered toward her."

Great-uncle Richard's hand went under the blanket. Mary Margaret squealed and jumped in the bed. Then she looked like she was going to cry and Great-uncle Richard pulled his hand out and embraced her.

"There, there, don't be frightened, Heather. I was just pretending. Your mother will accuse me of giving you nightmares."

He stroked her hair and then he let her head return to the pillow. She looked up at him as he took the lollipop from her hand and put it on a dish on the night table.

"I think you're getting tired," he told her and she closed her eyes, opened them, fluttered her lids and closed them again. He leaned over and kissed her softly on the forehead.

"We'll finish this tomorrow. There's so much more, but don't worry. Dolly will be safe and get home to her mother after she has some more adventures. Okay?"

Mary Margaret barely nodded.

Great-uncle Richard stood up, fixed her blanket around her and then kissed her again, this time on the cheek. He turned off the music box and turned off the lamp. He stood there for a long moment looking down at her and then he left the room.

The rain that had been threatening all day suddenly began in a light drizzle, but I couldn't move. My legs felt frozen and cramped and my chest ached from holding my breath for so long. Just as I was about to work my way out from behind the hedges, the lamp went on again and Mary Margaret pushed the blanket away from her. She was wearing a nightdress that barely reached the top of her thighs. I was mesmerized. I couldn't move an inch even though the raindrops were thickening and falling faster.

She rose from the bed and went to the closet. I saw her pull off the nightdress and then put on her own clothes. After she was dressed, she turned off the lamp and left the bedroom. I hovered in the shadows, close to the cottage to keep out of the rain, and then I crouched even lower when I heard the cottage door open and close. Moments later, Mary Margaret crossed the grounds quickly. She had an umbrella and headed toward the front of the house. A few seconds later, I saw the Endfields' limousine pull away with Boggs driving.

I waited another thirty seconds or so and then I rose to leave, feeling as if my legs had turned to lead. With ponderous but quick steps, I hurried back to the rear entrance of the house and went inside. I could feel my blood settle, the chill ease up, but my heart was still racing and my throat felt as if there was a scream caught in it. After a deep breath, the feeling disappeared. I started down the hall toward my room.

My robe was soaked and so was my hair. I fetched a clean, dry nightgown, returned to the bathroom and dried myself with a towel. Gradually, the chill left me entirely and I went back to my bedroom. I gazed out the window. The cottage was completely dark now. The rain was falling harder and faster, beating a frantic tattoo on my small window. It matched the rhythm of my heart. I closed the curtain and retreated to my bed, anxious to get under the covers. Shivers came from thoughts now and not cold air.

How strange, sad and frightening it was. I could only imagine how long it had been going on. After what I had seen, could I ever look at my Great-uncle Richard the same way? Would he take one look at me and know that I had spied on him and Mary Margaret? And what about her? Would she know as well? Did he force her to do this or did she want to do it? Perhaps he paid her something extra.

The rain continued to lash against the house. Staccato beats on the walls and the roof were like drums marching me toward the nightmares that eagerly awaited entrance into my world of dreams as soon as I had closed my eyes. I was afraid to fall asleep.

What kind of place had I been sent to? Yes, these people were rich and highly respected. They socialized with royalty and dwelled in the corridors of power and prestige. They dressed correctly, spoke perfectly, and made it seem as if everything they did and was done for them had complete balance.

But they lived in a house with a dark history. They had restored and modernized it, yet they had brought their own ghosts to dwell alongside the ones that were supposedly trapped inside these walls. A river of pain flowed through these richly designed and decorated rooms.

Despite what they said and how they lived, my Great-uncle Richard and my Great-aunt Leonora had obviously been unable to accept their tragic loss. Now that I was in my warm bed and I could think, I was less and less frightened by it all. Pity and irony replaced the terror I had experienced in the shadows outside those cottage windows. Through their seemingly perfect English lives, they tried to build a wall around themselves to shut away their pain and lock away their secrets. It wasn't working; it probably never worked and never would.

Truth was as powerful and as insistent as water. It would seep in every small opening, and every attempt to plug up the holes in their hearts would fail, for another hole would simply form until all these castle walls would crumble and the truth would flood and wash away the false faces. There wasn't a false face in the world that could successfully hide what the false heart did know. Reading Shakespeare had taught me that.

All my great-aunt and great-uncle had to do was admit to their pain. Great-uncle Richard was trying desperately to ignore the pain with his secret cottage, but one day it would surely collapse around him and that would be even worse, so I did feel pity for them.

The irony came from realizing how desperately some parents held on to their children and the memories whereas mine had tried to deny my very existence. If Great-uncle Richard's daughter could appear before him now, how his heart would burst with joy. What would my father's heart do when I appeared? Would it squirm and shrink in his chest, close up like a fist?

Funny, I thought, how even though the scene in the cottage was terribly bizarre, I couldn't help but be jealous. I never had a father sit on my bed and read to me. I never had a father fix my blanket and kiss my cheek and wish me sweet dreams. I never had a father who gave me a feeling of security and love, who protected me from the demons that danced outside my windows. For a moment I almost wished I was Mary Margaret, pretending, but feeling the love I longed to feel.

What would be my first words to my real father? Should I ask him how he intended to make it up to me? Should I ask him to compensate for all those long and lonely nights, the deep holes of emptiness in which I dwelled? Should I hate him or should I love him?

Maybe I should drag him to the cottage of dreams and force him to read me a bedtime story. In my heart of hearts, I believed my Great-uncle Richard, perhaps more than anyone, would understand why I wanted to do that. He wouldn't laugh or condemn me for it. He might even send Boggs in that limousine to pick up my father and bring him here.

"You've got a daughter you denied all these years?" he would say in astonishment. "Why? Why were you given the opportunity to have her and deny her while I, who was thankful for my own daughter, was denied her? Why?"

Where were the answers to all these questions? Should I even bother to look for them or should I go on like so many people I knew now and pretend there were no questions? Did I even have a choice?

Some time ago, a beautiful young woman threw herself impulsively, recklessly into the arms of a handsome, intelligent black man who had somehow captured her heart. They were too passionate to care about anything but their own need to feel more alive. He planted his seed in her and she gave birth to me as much out of defiance as anything, I imagine. Their love was not the lasting kind. They parted because they weren't willing to make the bigger sacrifices and I, I was forgotten along with the passion.

Years later, I would appear before them and I would try to understand what it was that made me.

Was it Fate punishing them?

Was it love emerging despite them?

Was it some carefree, wandering spark of life that drifted into my name?

Today, I had looked at the man who made me and he was still a stranger.

Tomorrow, I would look at him again.

My ears were filled with the sound of that music box. I closed my eyes and imagined my father's lips on my cheek.

I heard him say, "I won't let you be afraid again."

And knowing I could dream that dream, I wasn't afraid of sleep.

10

Denied Again

It was performance night, yet my heart wasn't thumping as I had expected it would. Nervousness had turned into raw fear and that had dropped a sheet of thin ice over me, making me feel numb to the point where I couldn't feel my own heartbeat. It was being smothered by a pillow of tension. Philip Roder was finishing his dance selection taken from *The Nutcracker.* He looked so graceful and perfect. Why did I have to follow him? The distinction between someone who was well on his way to becoming a professional and me, a naked amateur, would never be as clear.

Sarah Broadhurst, whom I knew was green with envy because I had been chosen over her to perform the cut from *Hamlet,* made a point of coming up to me while I waited in the wings to tell me that the audiences who came to the school's showcase evenings were very sophisticated.

"These are the same people who frequent the London theater and there will be many agents and even some directors sitting out there looking for potential new talent.

It's far different from performing in some high school in America," she said with disdain. "It's not an audience clumped with doting relatives who refuse to see mistakes and mediocrity. These people have seen and heard *Hamlet* many, many times and will know immediately whether you are any good."

"Thanks," I said, refusing to show her how much she had unnerved me. "It's nice of you to care enough to want to help me."

"Help you?"

"I hope I can do the same for you someday, Sarah," I followed just as Philip's dance piece came to an end. The applause was deafening.

The school's theater was small, intimate. The audience was practically in the lap of the performers. Every sound resonated. I anticipated hearing my own voice reverberate, making me even more aware of every sour syllable I might utter.

Now that I was moments away from stepping onto that stage, my smothered heart burst out and pounded madly. The curtain was closed to give the audience the sense of a change of setting. One of the first things that had been taught in drama class was that an actor must establish an awareness of place, give the audience a feeling for the scene. One of the other drama students, Clarence Stoner, would read the lines of Laertes, Ophelia's brother, to help set up the situation. It was the point in the play after Hamlet has accidentally killed Ophelia's father and she has gone mad.

In a way it wasn't hard for me to understand her insanity. Her father had been taken from her and she felt lost and alone and terribly betrayed.

I waited in the wings. Clarence took his position. Sarah was right about one thing: the audience had that look of anticipation, clearly illustrating that they knew exactly what was to come.

The curtain opened and Clarence turned and said, "How now, what noise is that?"

I entered slowly, paused and looked up as if I had heard something. The audience was so still, I thought for a moment that they all might have left, including my Great-aunt Leonora and my Great-uncle Richard who were seated in the second row center.

Clarence finished Laertes's speech to express his shock at seeing his sister turned into a madwoman.

I smiled as insanely as I could at the audience. Caught in the spotlight, I could barely make out any of their faces, which was good.

"They bore him barefac'd on the bier," I began and sang, *"Hey non nonny, nonny, hey nonny.*

"And in his grave rain'd many a tear. Fare you well, my dove."

It didn't take more than five minutes or so to do the scene of madness. I crossed from one side of the stage to the other and when I entered the wing on the opposite side, I felt as if I had walked barefoot over a bed of nails.

The applause that followed was almost as loud as it had been for Philip Roder. Mr. MacWaine was waiting there to greet me.

"You're launched," he declared. "Hear that?" he asked referring to the ovation. "Remember it well. You'll hear it many, many more times, my dear," he promised.

Behind him, Randall was glowing. He was scheduled to sing his solo in a moment.

"Was I really all right?" I asked.

"You looked and sounded like you were born to be in the lights," Randall said. He gave me a quick peck on the cheek and strutted out onstage, looking buoyed by my performance. He sang beautifully. By the time all our performances were over, Mr. MacWaine was floating with such happiness, I didn't think his feet touched the ground.

"This was one of the best showcases the school has ever had," he declared.

Sarah Broadhurst grimaced so sharply, she looked like she was in pain.

Afterward, at our tea-and-cake reception, Mr. MacWaine's evaluation appeared to be justified. People were fawning over us, giving us so many compliments, I felt guilty of sinful pride. My great-aunt basked in the accolades I received, declaring at least a half dozen times that I was her au pair from America. My Great-uncle Richard was as reserved as ever, but I noticed he looked at me differently. Twice before the evening ended, I caught him staring at me. It was as if I had turned into Cinderella. There was a glint of respect, of appreciation in his eyes, although he never betrayed it in his voice or manner.

Afterward, in the car going home, he offered a more detailed review of my performance.

"The school is teaching you poise, control. I was impressed with your stage voice, your diction, and I thought you did rather well with your body. For an American youth performing an English classic, that is," he added.

"What a shame your parents aren't alive and here to see you," my Great-aunt Leonora added. "I'm sure their hearts would have burst with pride."

"She's too old for that sort of thing now, Leonora.

What she has to do is win over the minds and hearts of complete strangers if she is to go on with a stage career," Great-uncle Richard declared.

"Still, it's nice to have family around you at times like this," she said wistfully.

Great-uncle Richard seemed to be annoyed with her and turned away, growing silent. Still, from time to time before we arrived at Endfield Place, he stole what I thought were furtive glances at me. I could feel his gaze and when I looked at him, he always shifted his eyes and stared out the window. Once we arrived at the house, he quickly went to his den.

"I know you must be tired, dear," Great-aunt Leonora said. "These things are so emotionally exhausting. For the life of me, I don't know why anyone would want a career on the stage. Life is a stage enough."

"That's what Shakespeare said," I told her.

"Of course it is," she said even though I was positive she didn't know what I meant. "Why did you think I said it? Well, I'll be sure to write my sister and tell her of your great success," she added, laughed nervously and went to her room.

Randall had wanted me to go out with him after the reception, but I didn't think it was proper to leave the Endfields in light of their attending the performances. I retreated instead to my own small closet of a room, prepared for bed and then lay there, basking in my immediate memories: the applause, how I had felt on stage, the pleasure in Mr. MacWaine's face, Randall's glee and all the wonderful comments at the reception.

Maybe I could do this. Maybe it wasn't a pipe dream after all and Grandma Hudson was right in pressuring me to come here and study. What I couldn't help but wonder is what my real father would have thought of my performance. After all, he was a Shakespearean expert, wasn't he?

I imagined that he had come to our performance and sat in the back of the audience, undetected. Afterward, he was so impressed with me that he made a point of coming to the reception to tell me so, and all this without knowing that I was his daughter.

He would invite me to have coffee or tea with him to discuss my career and to talk about the great plays. And then, in the middle of all that, I would burst out with the truth and he would be so overwhelmed but so overjoyed that he would embrace me and be anxious to announce the news to everyone.

I felt a smile settle into my face as I lay there, staring into the darkness, dreaming. Suddenly I heard Boggs's loud footsteps in the hall. It sounded as if he was trying to poke holes in the floor with his heels. The door of my little room rattled when he passed by. I heard his door open and close and then all grew quiet. The small storm of noise shook me out of my reverie.

What was I doing anyway but pretending and dabbling in childish make-believe. Maybe I was not so different from my Great-uncle Richard participating in his illusions with Mary Margaret.

How long had she and my Great-uncle Richard been conducting this little drama? I wondered. Did she want to participate or was she forced to in order to keep her job? Who else knew beside Boggs? Did Great-aunt Leonora know but pretend not to? Was this why Mrs. Chester was so adamant that I mind my own business when I had asked about the cottage?

This is truly a house filled with ghosts, I thought, ghosts better left undisturbed. I would be like everyone else and pretend none of it was happening. Minding your own business seemed to be the credo for survival in this world. In a real sense it wasn't so different from the world I had been raised in when I lived in Washington. Hear no evil, see no evil and you'll get through it all was the lesson everyone learned as soon as she or he could hear, see and understand.

Maybe the stage was the safest place after all. It was like stepping through the looking glass into a wonderland where people could cry and laugh and touch each other and look at each other and worry about nothing at all except the sound of applause when the curtain came down.

Do anything you can, I told myself, to keep what my drama teacher called the invisible fourth wall between yourself and the real world. Then you'll always be safe. Then, you'll finally be safe.

There had been something magnetic about seeing my real father and his children. Try as I would, I couldn't keep the memory of it out of my mind. I didn't want to tell Randall how much I was thinking about my father because I was afraid he might rush out and do something even more dramatic. When he had forged ahead and crossed the street to knock on the Wards' door, I could hardly breathe. He was determined to bring me and my father face to face, but it wasn't his life to play with or his emotions to risk.

All the next week, whenever I could, I returned to the street on which my father lived and I stood around waiting across the street to catch a glimpse of him. I saw his wife twice, once by herself and once with their little boy. Seeing her again, I was able to appreciate her good looks more. She had a reddish tint to her brown hair. The first time I saw her she wore it down and loose around her shoulders, and the second time she had it woven into a French twist.

When I looked at her the second time, she wasn't much more than a dozen or so feet away. I kept my head down but looked up quickly when we were close to each other. Her face really was angular and interesting with almond-shaped brown eyes and tiny freckles peppered on the crests of her cheeks. She had a soft, perfect mouth that relaxed into a gentle, friendly smile when her eyes met mine, even for a split second. It sent a cold electric shock into my stomach because I felt like someone who had been discovered spying.

This time she was wearing a dark gray sweater and a long, flowing skirt. She looked no older than a first- or second-year college girl to me. Her little boy held tightly to her hand, but kept his head down as if he was counting cracks in the sidewalk. It was all over in seconds, but how my heart pounded.

I never saw my father the entire week. I was either there at the wrong times to catch him or he was away. It was frustrating. I told myself I was just tormenting myself more and more by going there. Why look at something or someone who could never be what you wanted him to be? I felt like a very poor girl standing in front of the windows of an expensive department store looking in on things I could never hope to own. Wasn't it better to simply pretend the store didn't exist, to walk right by and never look inside?

I recalled that was why Roy never liked to go to the fancier neighborhoods in Washington, D.C. He would rather make a wide detour, traveling farther and longer than necessary.

"But isn't it nice to look at beautiful things?" I would ask him.

"I don't want to see things I can't have," he'd reply. "All that does is make me bitter and unhappy. I have enough reason to be angry all the time. I don't have to go look for more," he said.

But if I really wanted to go, he would take me. There wasn't much in the way of pain and frustration that Roy wouldn't be willing to experience if it was for me, if it would make me happy. What would he say or think about all this? I wondered if I would ever tell him.

Randall didn't let up on the issue of Larry Ward. One of the first things he said the day after the showcase performance was, "Too bad we didn't invite your real father to come to see you. We should have just sent him an invitation. Maybe he would have come," he said.

"I'm sure he gets lots of those and it must be boring to attend each and every amateur performance of something from Shakespeare."

"Not if he had a special reason to come," Randall teased.

"We're not going to do that, Randall," I said, my eyes growing hot enough to singe his face with a look.

"I know; I know, but it might not be such a bad way to break the ice," he insisted.

"I don't want to break the ice. I told you. Now stop talking about it or I won't talk to you," I threatened. "I mean it."

"Okay, okay," he said. Then he smiled, looked down and added, "I wonder what his classes are like."

"Good-bye, Randall," I snapped and walked away from

him. He laughed, followed and swore up and down that he wouldn't talk about Larry Ward again. Of course, I didn't believe him.

I began to realize that there was something immature about Randall. All of this business about my real father was exciting to him but the same way some new game might be. This wasn't brought home to me until I found out he had told Leslie and Catherine.

I was sitting alone in the little cafeteria, sipping a cup of coffee, when they entered and quickly came to the table.

"Oh *chérie,*" Leslie said, "we have heard about your amazing discovery, but this is nothing to fear. You must go, boom, boom, right up to him and declare yourself."

"What discovery?" I asked, my heart doing a flip-flop.

"But your father, of course," Catherine said. "Randall has told us all about it."

"He has?"

"But of course," Leslie said. "He worries for you and thought maybe we should talk with you."

"Our father has another child, but he doesn't pretend she is not there," Catherine willingly admitted.

"Mama is always after him to make sure he provides for her, too."

"Well, that's very big of her. I'm glad it's all one big happy family for you, but my situation is quite different and Randall had no right to go and blab it all over the place," I said, my fury building.

"Oh, it's not blabbing. He says *entre nous,* just between us."

"As you Americans say," Leslie added, "on the Q-T. Eh?"

"We will help you, if you want," Catherine said.

"There's nothing to help me with. Just forget about it. Become D and D when it comes to me, if you please."

"D and D?" Catherine looked at Leslie. "This is one we do not know."

"Deaf and dumb," I said, rising. "My life isn't some French soap opera."

I spun around and marched out quickly, my tears of disappointment and betrayal mixing with my tears of fury. I felt as if a hive of bees were swarming around in my head. Without the slightest hesitation, I walked to the vocal suite, opened the door and looked in on Randall and Professor Wilheim. My abrupt entrance ripped them both from their discussion concerning the sheet music they were studying. They looked my way, the professor as shocked and surprised as Randall.

"You had no right to tell my secrets to Leslie and Catherine," I cried. "No right."

I backed out and slammed the door. Then I ran out of the school building, deciding I didn't want to, or maybe couldn't, attend my drama class. For a while I simply wandered the city streets, not really thinking about where I was going. I walked and walked until I ran down my anger and then found a bench in a small park where I watched a young couple walking hand in hand, their heads practically touching as they conversed. They, too, paused to sit on a bench. He embraced her and they just sat there watching the birds feed and flutter, neither of them speaking. For them it was just a moment, but for me it was again like looking through that expensive department store window.

Where is this place where some people go to find true love and trust? Where did they discover a way to invest their hearts and have faith in their relationship? What sort of a man would I eventually find? Who would love me more than he loves himself and begin his day by thinking, What can I do to make her happier and our lives more complete?

The way the couple sat so contentedly, so pleased with their moment, I was sure that some time in the future, each of them would think back to the peacefulness of this hour they shared and smile and think they were right, they were secure, they had made a good decision when they whispered their love and declared their intent to be one. No children would fall by the wayside. Was I living in an illusion again?

I rose and walked on. Maybe it was purely by accident; maybe I subconsciously knew where I was going. Maybe Fate herself decided to take a more direct and definitive role in my life, but I suddenly realized I was minutes away from my real father's school. The thought of going there titillated and excited me, but also filled me with fear.

Yet I needed to see him again and I wanted so to hear his voice. Randall had been right about that, at least.

Tossing caution to the wind, I continued in that direction and found myself standing in front of the building. Could I do this? *Should* I do this?

As if invisible hands had pressed themselves against my back to propel me forward, I stepped up to the entrance, took a deep breath and entered. He was, after all, my father. Maybe he could deny it and live as if I didn't exist, but I couldn't. I hated lies, but I hated being a child of lies even more. It made me feel dirty inside, contaminated, tainted with deceit. I longed to rid myself of all of it, regardless of the consequences. Only then, perhaps, could I look at anyone honestly and even dare to think I could love and be loved.

There was a directory in the lobby and an information desk with a girl who looked like a first-year college student sitting behind it, obviously taking the opportunity to do some homework.

She looked up after I reached the desk.

"May I help you," she said.

"Yes. I was wondering where Professor Ward's class was."

"You mean this hour?"

"Yes," I said.

"You know he has one this hour?"

"No," I said.

Her eyes blinked with confusion.

"Are you in his class?" she asked.

"No. I'm supposed to audit one," I said.

"Oh. Well, let's see then," she said and opened a large folder. She ran her forefinger down, glanced at her watch. "Oh, his class in Shakespeare's tragedies has already begun. Twenty-five minutes ago in Room 211," she said. "That's down the corridor, the second stairway and then to the immediate right."

"Thank you," I said and followed her directions.

Professor Ward's classroom was about three-quarters full. He paced in front of his students as he lectured and most of them were busy taking notes, their heads down, their pens scribbling. I opened the door as softly as I could and thought I had slipped in and sat in a seat in the rear completely undetected. How could he possibly notice me in this crowd? I thought confidently and sat back, listening to his lecture on *Othello*.

Twice he seemed to look my way, pause and then continue.

"The question I want you to ponder today is what was it in Othello's character that made him so vulnerable to Iago's evil plan?

"Shakespeare provides us with some answers," he continued as he started up the aisle. "However, this will take a closer reading, a reading between the lines, so to speak."

He paused, the moment of silence so long that heads were raised and pens stopped. Students looked at him, saw the direction of his gaze and turned to look at me.

He couldn't be looking at me, I thought. Why would he? My heart began to pound, and my throat suddenly became so dry, I couldn't swallow. He smiled.

"So," he said, "now some students are wandering into my classes to pass the time. Is that a compliment, I wonder, or should I consider myself to have become amusement rather than edification? What do you think, Miss Austin?" he asked the girl right beside him. "Am I entertaining or edifying?"

The girl shrugged.

"I don't know what you mean," she said.

"Oh, pity. Well then, perhaps we should ask our guest," he said, taking a step up the aisle toward me. "Miss Mystery Person?"

All eyes were on me.

"Why can't you be both?" I said and the classroom roared.

He smiled.

"Yes, indeed, why can't I? Now then," he said, turning back toward the front and permitting me to release the trapped hot air that threatened to make my lungs explode. "Let's return to Act I, Scene I."

When I felt my legs return from two wet noodles to flesh, bone and muscle again, I rose as quickly as I could and slipped quietly out of the classroom. What had gotten into me that I would do such a thing, have so much nerve? Now I could never permit him to see me accidentally. I could never spy on him and his family for fear that if I was discovered, he would surely connect me with this day in his class. Maybe this was good, I thought. Once and for all, I've brought it to an end. Let him live his life and let me try to do something worthwhile with mine.

The bell rang to end the class hour before I reached the stairway and doors to other classes were thrown open. The students burst out as if they had all been holding their breaths under water. It brought laughter to my lips. This was more like an American high school. I was actually jostled about as they streamed by me, their voices loud. Someone tapped me on the shoulder and I turned to face a tall, dark-haired boy with a twisted smile. Two other boys were beside him, both with similar grins.

"Excuse me," he said, "but haven't I seen you before in one of my dreams?"

"I doubt it," I said. "I'm not permitted to go to places like that."

His friends laughed as his confidence leaked out of his smug grin.

"Excuse me for talking to you," he shouted after me as I quickly started down the stairway.

I went back through the lobby, past the girl at the information booth and out the front entrance where I paused to get my bearings. I knew I had to get to the tube station and take a train. I had wandered so far, it would probably take me more than two hours to get home and I would miss my duties before dinner.

I stopped to ask a friendly-looking lady directions and then continued, now feeling rather stupid about missing my own classes and bursting in on my father's class. I had to stop to buy a ticket since I was traveling out of my zone. After I had done so, I turned to follow the directions to my platform and nearly fainted on the spot.

My father was standing there, a smile on his face.

"Well now, who's following whom?" he asked. "Do I have good reason to think it's you following me?"

Of course, I couldn't help wondering if he had spotted me near his home the past week as well.

All I could do was shake my head. His smile widened and deepened with interest and curiosity.

"You're not a student at the college, are you?" he asked me. That question I could answer.

"No," I said.

"Okay. You've got the advantage on me, Miss...?"

"Arnold, Rain Arnold," I said.

"Rain? Interesting name. How did you get it?"

"My adoptive mother named me," I said quickly.

"She wasn't a native American, was she?"

"No. Just an American," I said. He laughed.

"An American in London. Sounds like a movie." His eyes glittered with amusement. What beautiful, deep, dark eyes he has, I thought and tried to imagine the first time he turned them onto my mother and she got caught up in their power and beauty. "What brought you to my class today?"

"I, I'm in the Richard Burbage School for the Performing Arts and I've been doing some Shakespeare," I said. "I thought it might help me to know more."

"Don't they study the plays you're performing before handing you lines to memorize?" he asked.

"Yes, but not as detailed as you do," I said.

Skepticism tilted his head to the side.

"You discovered that with only ten or fifteen minutes of observation?"

"No. I had heard about you and your classes," I said.

"Oh?" His doubting smile lingered. "I'm flattered. However, maybe it's because I'm working on *Othello* at the moment, but I have a healthy skepticism for the obvious these days," he said. "Especially people's motives." He glanced at his watch. "Care to take a cup of tea with me? There's a little café I fancy right next door."

I hesitated.

"We could talk more about Shakespeare," he added with a different sort of smile now, one of glee. He was toying with me, but he was very interested in me, too.

"I don't have much time," I said. "I have to be back to help with my dinner chores."

"Oh? An American student in London working her way. Now you do have my interest, Miss Arnold. Indulge me a few minutes. After all, you owe me that much for all the free knowledge and insight you took from my class today," he said.

I couldn't help but smile.

"Okay," I said. "A few minutes."

"Right this way," he said and led me around to the café. We sat at a corner table near the front where we could look out at the hustle and bustle on the street.

"I imagine you would like coffee rather than tea," he said.

"No, English breakfast tea is fine. I've grown used to it," I said. He nodded and ordered for us. "I'm a mif," I added when the waitress left.

"Excuse me?"

"Milk in first."

"Oh." He laughed. "Yes. I do have some friends who are very serious about that." He leaned back and turned his head slightly so he was looking at me from an angle. "Seems you've learned a great deal about this country already. How long have you been here?"

"Not that long, but I've had good teachers, especially the cook at the house I'm at," I said.

"How did you come to this house?"

"My grandmother arranged it," I said. "Actually, she's primarily responsible for my being here at all and studying performing arts."

"I see. She must have quite a bit of faith in you."

"I don't know why she should," I said. "She hasn't known me all that long."

"Oh?"

The waitress brought our two teapots and I put my milk in first and poured a cup. He watched me before pouring his own.

"And why is it that your grandmother hasn't known you all that long?" he asked as he took his first sip of tea. He held the cup so that he peered over it at me. His eyes were full of interest, but the intensity of his stare suggested he was being more than curious. I started to get a little nervous.

"It's a long story," I said.

"And you don't have much time. I know. Well," he said, putting his cup down and gazing at it, "I have a confession to make." He looked up. "I've seen you before. Twice in fact, so that when I saw you in my class, I recognized you."

I felt my body freeze.

"I don't think you're a stalker or anything, but you have piqued my curiosity. I must confess, however, that you made my wife a little nervous. You've been in our neighborhood recently. She pointed you out to me one day and said you were there, across the street from our house the day before and the day before that. Is that so?" he asked.

I was shocked to know I had actually been discovered and yet he had never come out to see who I was.

"It's a very small, close neighborhood, easy to spot strangers, especially if they're repeat strangers," he added with a smile.

I wasn't just silent. I was fighting back tears. I had a great urge to jump up and run, but he didn't seem angry. He still had that impish smile around his lips, a smile of amusement.

"I'm not someone with a mad crush on you or anything," I finally said.

"Well, I'm happy to hear that. For your sake, I mean," he quickly added when I looked up at him. "Those sort of things are never good for either party, especially if one is an old married man with children."

"You're not that old," I said.

"You know my age?" he asked. I didn't answer. "You know more about me than I think, is that it?"

"Yes."

"This mystery is moving into melodrama, Miss

Arnold. Can't you give me a little more concrete information about it, another clue, perhaps?"

You want clues, I thought, all right. I'll give you clues.

"My grandmother's name is Hudson," I said sharply. "Frances Hudson, and her husband's name was Everett."

He stared, barely a movement in his face.

"The Hudsons of Virginia?" he finally asked.

"Yes."

"Frances Hudson is your grandmother?"

"Yes."

"Are you telling me you're Megan Hudson's daughter?" he finally asked.

"That's what I'm telling you."

Again, it was his turn to be silent. He sat back, his eyes growing larger and then growing smaller as he focused more closely on me and nodded.

"I can see the resemblances to Megan," he said softly. "How old are you?"

"Eighteen," I said.

He started to lift his teacup and then set it down. He shook his head and looked away.

"This can't be," he muttered. He turned back to me. "Did Megan send you here to find me?"

"No. She has no idea I've found you," I said. "She had told me your name and that you had gone to London to study Shakespeare and teach. A friend of mine at school made it almost a game to locate you for me. I didn't want him to do it, but he did and...I'm sorry," I said. "I won't bother you anymore." I started to get up and he reached across the table quickly to stop me.

"No, wait. Please," he said.

I sat.

"When Megan became pregnant, she left and I was of the understanding she was giving the child away for adoption. You are that child?"

"My grandfather paid someone to take me, if that's what you mean," I said. "His name was Ken Arnold and I was brought up as his daughter. Latisha Arnold was the only mother I knew until relatively recently. We lived in Washington, D.C. Ken Arnold was never much of a father to me or to his own children. He and his son Roy got into fights constantly. Roy is in the army now. Latisha died of cancer a few months ago. Before she did, she made sure I was taken care of by contacting my real mother, who arranged for me to live with my grandmother."

I recited my history quickly and took a breath. Despite his poise, he looked bowled over, speechless, and for a college professor, that was something.

"I see. Wow," he said, shaking his head, "what a difficult life you've had. This is very complicated." He thought a moment. "Megan must be married, I'm sure."

"Yes. To an important lawyer. She has a daughter and a son. None of them, except for Grandmother Hudson and her other daughter Victoria, know the truth about me. Yet," I added.

Once again, he simply stared at me.

"I didn't mean to worry your wife," I continued. "I just was curious, but don't worry about it. It won't happen again."

He shook his head.

"You're my daughter," he said as if the fact just had settled in. "My God, this is…"

"Terrible, I know."

"No, no. I didn't mean to imply that." He nodded and

smiled. "The fact is I've often fantasized about this. I mean, I knew you were going to be born and I couldn't help but wonder about you."

"Everyone couldn't help but wonder but no one cared to do anything about it," I said dryly. "Except my adoptive mother who turned out to be the only one who ever loved me."

"Yes," he said. "That's probably very true. What sort of relationship do you have with Frances Hudson? As I recall, the Hudsons were one of those old Southern aristocratic families."

"I have a very good relationship with her. She's even included me in her will."

"Is that right? Amazing. Well," he said. "You must be a remarkable young lady then. How long are you supposed to remain in London?"

"The school year," I said.

"Well…" He sipped his tea, which I imagined was quite cool by now. "Well…I'll have to see more of you. We'll have to get to know each other a bit."

"Why?" I asked coldly.

"Why? Why, simply because…we should know each other. Look," he said, putting his cup down quickly. "You have to understand. Megan and I were rebellious young people then. We had no sense of real responsibility. We were both infatuated with ourselves, our youth, our idealism. We wanted to be at the forefront of causes, fight for a new world. When she became pregnant, it was as if someone had thrown cold water in our faces and woken us to the reality of what we were doing.

"Even so, I volunteered to do right by her, but her parents were devastated, especially her father, and they swept her off. She disappeared from campus one night and I heard from her only once afterward. That's how I knew you had been born and given away for adoption."

"Sold away," I reminded him.

"Yes. I imagine that was the way Everett Hudson wanted to do it: just wipe the error off the record books and then pretend it never happened."

"Didn't you do the same thing?" I fired back at him.

He was silent a moment and then he nodded.

"Yes," he admitted. "I did. In fact, I'll confess to being grateful to Everett Hudson. I was in no condition to raise a child. I barely had enough for my own survival, and Everett wouldn't have permitted Megan to marry me or given us anything but his hate and anger if we had.

"Despite all our so-called intelligence and sophistication, we were mere children socially. Neither of us was old enough to do the right thing."

"You were just old enough to do the wrong thing," I said.

He blinked as if I had struck him.

"I can appreciate your anger," he said softly.

"Can you? You can read about such things in your precious collection of Shakespeare, I'm sure, but can you have any idea what it must be like for me to have no one, no real roots, no identity? Sometimes, I feel like I'm invisible, like I'm some sort of ghost who never had a body."

His eyes grew sharper, but rather than look offended, he seemed to become more appreciative, almost proud.

"You're a very articulate young lady. A good student, I bet."

"Yes. I worked hard at it because I saw how much it pleased my adoptive mother."

"That's good. But you're not exactly right about me

and my understanding your situation. Megan didn't tell you everything about me. I was something of an orphan myself. My parents split up shortly after I was born and I ended up living with my grandmother, too, only she was sickly and died after a little more than two years. I was then farmed out from one uncle to another and finally to an aunt, who, ironically enough, lived in Richmond, not all that far from where Megan was raised.

"There were many times when I wondered about myself, my identity. I concluded it's something you have to create for yourself anyway. You're not me or Megan or your adoptive mother and you shouldn't be. You should be yourself and from the looks of things, you're well on your way."

"Right," I said. "Nice rationalization. That way no one is responsible, no one's guilty, everyone can go on their merry little way."

He winced as if I had slapped him.

I glanced at my watch. "I have to go. I can't be late."

"Late for what? What do you do?"

"I help with the domestic chores in my great-aunt and great-uncle's home."

"And they don't know who you really are?"

"No."

"Will you ever tell them?"

"It's not up to me. It's up to Grandma Hudson. She says for now it's better that they don't know. They might be embarrassed and ask me to leave."

"I see. Can I see you again?" he asked quickly. "How about coming to my home on Sunday for tea?"

"You're going to tell your family about me?"

"Well, not exactly," he said. "Not right away. I hope you understand."

"Oh, I understand," I said. I rose and looked at him. "Better than you can imagine. Thanks for the tea." I turned and hurried away before he could respond and before he could see the tears streaming out of my eyes. I didn't look back. I charged into the tube station, panicked for a moment because I didn't know where I was going, and then caught my breath and found the correct platform. My train was just arriving. I got into it quickly and buried myself in a corner seat. The train filled with people and then the doors closed.

I closed my eyes. What did my real parents bestow on me?

Anger and fear, I thought. They were the twin sisters always haunting me now.

When would I be able to send them packing? When would I be what my father said I would be, my own person?

Would that ever happen? I wondered.

11

On Shaky Ground

The weather changed quickly before I reached my home station on the tube and once again I found myself scurrying with my head down, trying to take advantage of every overhang to keep myself from arriving at Endfield Place soaked to the skin. When would I learn that in England carrying an umbrella is almost as necessary as wearing shoes?

Suddenly everything about the country angered me. Why did they have to drive on the wrong side of the road? Why did they have to have all these silly expressions? Why didn't they just call a subway a subway? How could they want to be traveling in a tube anyway? Everyone around me looked just as displeased, rushing here and there with stern, grouchy looks on their faces. I felt like stopping on the next corner and screaming.

Just before the last two hundred yards or so, the rain grew heavier. It was as if God was dumping a pail of water over me to snap me out of my misery or maybe drive me deeper into it. Running didn't seem to help since

I was splashing in puddles and doing more damage anyway. I just stopped trying to avoid the rain and casually
strolled the remaining distance. Some people, well protected in their rainhats and raincoats and with their um-
brellas, gazed at me as if I were some lunatic loose on the
streets. Even drivers in passing automobiles slowed down
to look my way. I smiled back at all of them.

"You think it's raining?" I said to myself. "The sun is
out. It's a beautiful day. You're just too stuck in your English ways to see it."

By the time I reached the front entrance, my hair
looked like a mop and my clothing was thoroughly
soaked. Little streams of water ran down the sides of my
face, down the back of my neck and down the front of my
blouse. Leo stepped back and grimaced as if a wild creature had come through the door when he opened it.

"Blimey, miss," he said. "You'd better get into drier
clothing quickly or you'll catch the death."

"Nonsense, Leo. I was named Rain because I love to
be in it. I love it so much, you'd think I was English," I
added and his eyes widened. He looked like he didn't
know whether he should laugh or not but wanted to very
much.

As I started down the hallway, Boggs stepped out of
the sitting room and, after taking one good look at me,
shouted, "Stop."

I did and drew myself to military attention, too.

"May I help you?" I asked him.

"You're tracking a stream of water and making a mess.
Take off those wet shoes."

"Yes, Commander," I said and did so. My feet were
just as soaked. I shrugged. "Sorry."

"Get the fool a towel, Leo, and let her dry off a bit before she continues," Boggs ordered.

Leo hurried away as quickly as he could with his pronounced limp.

"Why don't you take an umbrella when you go out?"

"It slipped my mind," I said.

"Well, here on, don't let it slip," he snapped. "Get yourself presentable and ready for your work," he added, his words like little whips being snapped at me. Then he turned and walked off.

Leo returned with the towel and I dried my hair, my feet and brushed off some of the water from my clothing. I thanked him, gave him back the towel and hurried to my room. I could hear Mrs. Chester working in the kitchen. As I passed by, Mary Margaret stepped out and stopped when she saw me. For a moment I thought my eyes would tell her what I knew, what I had seen her doing with my Great-uncle Richard in the cottage, but as shy as ever, she looked away quickly, nodded and went into the dining room to finish setting the dinner table.

"I'll be right along," I said and continued down the hallway.

I got out of my wet clothing and dried myself off as quickly as I could. When I returned to the kitchen, Mrs. Chester glanced at the clock, which was her way of telling me I was a good ten minutes late, and then nodded at the hot potatoes.

"Peel 'em and mash 'em," she ordered.

"Sorry I'm late," I muttered.

"I'm not the one you need apologize to," she replied. "Got along well before you came. I'm sure we'll get along well after you're gone."

I knew she meant it as simply a statement of fact, but to me it sounded as if she was just another person telling me how insignificant I was to her life. If I disappeared off the face of the earth, who would even notice? Roy, I guess, but not for that long. Grandmother Hudson would, but she would also load that spine of hers with steel and continue on as if I'd never existed. Maybe Randall would miss me for a moment or two as well, but certainly not my real parents. I truly believed they would all recuperate quickly and in time probably even forget what I looked like.

"If you work at that pace, Mr. and Mrs. Endfield will be on their afters before we serve 'em those potatoes," Mrs. Chester commented.

I realized I was daydreaming and got back to my work. I finished everything I was supposed to do and then helped serve the dinner as usual. Only now, when I entered the dining room, my Great-aunt Leonora applauded and started to talk about the school's showcase night again.

"We have a budding new star in our home, truly another Vivien Leigh," she said.

Great-uncle Richard grunted.

"I think there are a number of more recent actresses she should emulate, Leonora. You and that *Gone with the Wind*. I can't tell you how many times I've been forced to watch it," he told me as I placed the bread on the table. I was surprised at how intently he stared at me and how long he watched me move about the dining room. He scarcely took note of Mary Margaret, who shuffled about with her eyes down, trying to be invisible.

"You must keep us up with your progress at the school, dear," my Great-aunt Leonora said. "And let us know when you will be performing again. Will that be soon?" she asked.

"I don't know, Mrs. Endfield. I intend to try out for the production of *Taming of the Shrew,* but I hardly think I'll get a significant part. Former students also audition and some of them have been in dozens of plays already, some professionally. It's the school's biggest production, a fund-raiser."

"Nonsense. You'll get a big part I'm sure," she insisted. "Won't she, Richard?" she asked as if he had the definitive opinion like some sort of theater god.

When I glanced his way, I saw he was still looking at me as if he was considering me for a part himself. He nodded.

"Absolutely," he said. "Absolutely."

I glanced at Mary Margaret, who had paused to watch me and listen for a moment. Great-uncle Richard felt her eyes on us and shifted his toward her angrily. She hurried away. He looked after her and then back at me. She was so afraid of him, I thought, and yet, she knew the most intimate secret about him. Why didn't she just tell him to treat her better or else?

"Thank you," I said and went back into the kitchen. I looked at Mary Margaret, who had begun to wash dishes and pots. Should I just walk up to her and tell her I knew what was going on in that cottage or would it put her in a panic? When she glanced back at me, I thought she appeared so fragile, so small and frightened, I decided it was better to let the skeletons in this house remain in their closets.

I had my own closets to think about now anyway and they were packed with hanging bones.

Think about them was what I did, too, almost all night. I was haunted by the question of whether I should or shouldn't go to my real father's home on Sunday for tea.

Wasn't it like torturing myself to sit there and pretend I was someone I wasn't? Or would he eventually see my pain and decide that he wanted me to be his daughter in every possible way, wanted it so much that he pulled his wife aside to tell her our story. I lay there, dreaming wishes, hearing him say the things I wanted him to say with all my heart.

"A long time ago, when I was an idealistic but reckless young man, I had an affair with a rich young woman and she became pregnant; maybe she did it to defy her family. Her father swept her off and they had her give birth secretly. They then put the baby up for adoption. I never had a chance to do the right thing, you see.

"Now, it's years and years later and here she is, a beautiful young woman. I'd like to lay claim to her. What do you think?"

His wife would take one look at me and say, "Of course you should, Larry. We'll make her part of the family immediately. She's seen far too much unhappiness."

Then the two of them would hug me and insist I move in with them right away.

I fell asleep dreaming this dream, but in the morning, the cold reality of where I was popped my fantasy like a soap bubble. Boggs thundered by my room as usual and I got up to wash, dress and help with breakfast. I knew I was moving about like a zombie, doing everything mechanically. Mrs. Chester and Mary Margaret both looked at me with curiosity.

Mary Margaret nervously folded and unfolded napkins for a moment before hurrying out. Now it was time for my suspicious little mind to lift my scrutinizing eyes and search the shadows through which Mary Margaret moved each and every day. I made a mental note to talk with her the first chance we had for some privacy. She needed someone to talk to more than I did, I thought.

I didn't eat much of a breakfast after my chores. Despite what I had thought was a good night's sleep, I still moved like someone carrying pails loaded with rocks on her shoulders. Yesterday's rain left a cool breeze behind and there were still dark, brooding clouds hovering around the city. I did take an umbrella this time, but it didn't rain at all before I reached the school.

Randall was waiting for me in the lobby and jumped up the moment I appeared.

"I tried to call you last night," he said, "but that grinch who runs the house answered the phone and said they don't take phone calls for you. I should contact you on your own time, whatever that meant. What happened? Why did you come bursting into my vocal lesson and where did you go?"

"I don't want to discuss it, Randall, other than to say you had no right to tell Leslie and Catherine about me. They think it's amusing and to tell you the truth, I'm very disappointed in you," I added.

"I just thought you needed female advice," he explained. "If anyone here could understand what happened to you, I thought it would be those two."

"You should have asked me first," I said, unrelenting.

He nodded.

"I'm sorry. I'll make sure they don't go blabbing it about the school."

"As my mama used to tell us, once the bell's rung, you don't unring it. I've got to get to class."

"Wait. Do you want to meet for lunch? We can talk some more and decide what to do," he suggested.

"Whatever I do from now on, Randall, should be something I've decided on my own. This isn't some little drama we can play out together."

"But…"

"Let me have some private time," I said. "I really need to be by myself for a while."

"Okay," he said reluctantly. "I'm sorry."

"You know," I said thinking a bit, "I bet I have the record for receiving apologies from people who should be kind and loving to me. My mother should have named me Sorry. Then, I could always reply, I'm sorry, too, and it would make some sense."

I hurried away from him, up the stairs and to my drama-speech class. Before class began, Leslie and Catherine tried to talk to me about it all again, and I told them in clear terms to mind their own business. Neither was offended, no matter how sharply I spoke. I began to wonder if anything would offend them.

At lunch hour, I left the building and had tea and a sandwich at a nearby café by myself. On my way back to the school, I saw a man about my father's age carrying his four- or five-year-old daughter as he and his wife crossed the street. They looked like tourists, both wearing cameras around their necks. The wife stopped to check a map to point out a direction. While they waited, their little girl had her arms wrapped about her father's neck, her cheek against his. She looked contented and safe.

The man I'd grown up thinking was my father never held me. I couldn't even recall him carrying me, even like a sack of potatoes, I thought. Of course, Mama had, and I did remember many, many times when Roy held my hand, but a little girl's relationship with her father was so spe-

232

cial. Only briefly glancing at this little girl's contented face, I knew that in her putaway heart of hearts, she had faith that her daddy could drive away demons, could smash nightmares with a growl, could lift her above any danger, keep her out of any fire or flood and help her defeat any pain. She'd wrap his power around herself like some suit of armor and never be afraid of the dark.

Perhaps the most delicious moments of her life would come much later when she was a young lady searching for a man to love her as much as her daddy did. Even when she found such a person, she would turn to her father to feel secure in her decision and when she looked at him, she would see that he saw her forever and ever as his little girl. Not a mountain of days, not a million ticks of the clock, not a string of birthdays could change it, and even if she would get him to say that she was no longer a baby, she would see a smile behind that agreement that said, "However, you'll always be my baby."

I want a daddy, too, even if it's just for an hour, I concluded and decided then and there that I would go to my father's house on Sunday. Before I went home, I stopped at a phone booth and called his house. His wife answered and said he wasn't at home yet.

"May I take a message for him?" she asked.

"Yes. Tell him Rain Arnold called and I will come to tea on Sunday."

"Rain Arnold?"

"Yes, ma'am."

"Okay," she said with a little laugh in her voice. "We'll see you on Sunday."

My heart was pounding again. Did I make some terrible mistake? He obviously had not mentioned me to her.

Had he expected never to hear from me or see me again? Was I disappointing him?

As soon as I got home, I sat in my little room because I still had some time to myself and wrote a letter to Grandma Hudson.

Dear Grandmother...

I began smiling to myself at how she would react to my addressing her so.

> *I have an important thing to tell you and ask your advice about. With a friend at school, I located my real father, using the little information my mother had given me about him. He did become an English professor specializing in Shakespeare. He's married and has two children, a daughter and a son. I spent some time spying on him. I couldn't help it. I wanted to see him, to learn more about him. I actually attended one of his lectures and to make a long story short, I've been discovered.*
>
> *We had tea together and I told him who I really am. He was shocked of course, and for now, like my real mother, he wants me to keep it all secret. He has invited me to his home, nevertheless, and I have decided to go.*
>
> *Am I making a terrible mistake? Should I permit him to make a decision about revealing me to his wife? Should I just walk away and try to forget him? What do you think my mother would say if she found out about all this? Of course, I don't want to upset you, but I don't have anyone I can trust here or anyone wise enough to give me advice.*

Please think about it all and let me know what you advise me to do.

I miss you and look forward to your coming here as you promised. I hope you're doing what the doctors tell you to do and you're not so stubborn as to prolong your recovery and make a trip to England impossible.

Please give my love to Jake.

P.S. Of course, your sister knows nothing of any of this, but I can't help wondering how long it will be before Victoria tells her something more.

Love,

Rain

I sealed the letter in an envelope, addressed it, and then hid it in my drama text to express mail the next day when I went to school.

Afterward, when I entered the kitchen to help with dinner, Mrs. Chester told me Mary Margaret wouldn't be working today.

"The poor girl's sick to her stomach and had to rush home. Got one of them flu bugs, I think," she told me. "So we got plenty to do. Mr. Endfield has invited a business associate and his wife to dinner tonight. I'm makin' poached salmon. Set the table for four," she ordered and I went to work.

With Mary Margaret absent, Boggs hovered over us even more. He made me nervous with his intimidating looks, inspecting every aspect of the dinner preparation to the point where he practically measured the spaces between pieces of silverware.

"When you bring out that food, don't let your fingers

touch any of it. I don't want to see you servin' them with your hands in their fish," he warned me.

"If you're so worried about it, why don't you serve the dinner yourself?" I shot back at him.

Mrs. Chester was so surprised at my remark and tone of voice, she gasped and brought her hand to the bottom of her throat, holding her breath as if she expected Boggs to explode like a stick of dynamite.

"Just do yer job," he muttered, his face red with fury.

"I'm trying to," I muttered, "and will if you leave me be."

He sucked in some air, blowing his shoulders up, bit down on his lower lip, and left the kitchen.

"Oh, dearie, you've gone and done it now. That man holds a grudge."

"So do I," I said, but I couldn't help being afraid. I had nightmares about him coming into my room and smothering me to death with a pillow.

After they had all arrived in the dining room and I entered, my Great-aunt Leonora introduced me to their guests, the Dorsets. Mr. Dorset was a banker. He was a man well into his sixties with thinning gray hair. His cheeks were robust and slightly crimson. They grew more and more so as he drank more wine. His wife was a fragile woman, bird-like with diminutive facial features and short, poorly dyed brown hair that was the color of rust with traces of gray at the roots and even along some strands.

"This is our au pair from America who is going to become a famous actress someday," my Great-aunt Leonora said. "Her name is Rain."

"Rain?" Mr. Dorset asked. "Where did you get that name?" he asked me with a wide grin.

"My mother gave it to me when I was born," I replied.

For a moment no one spoke, Mrs. Dorset looking as if her mouth had locked open, her little pink sliver of a tongue curled up, and then Mr. Dorset nodded and said, "Indeed."

The table was as silent as a funeral parlor, which made the sound of the dishes and silverware seem so loud. Great-uncle Richard watched me finish serving. I felt his gaze so close that I couldn't wait to return to the kitchen.

Boggs was standing right there. I nearly ran into him. He seemed to grow larger and wider in front of me, his eyes like two small drills at my forehead.

"Your insolent ways will get you tossed out on the street," he threatened.

Then he turned and left the kitchen.

Mrs. Chester glanced at me and then looked away, afraid to be drawn too close to an impending disaster. I completed my work without any further comment. No one addressed me in the dining room and I avoided Great-uncle Richard's eyes, not looking his way once. As soon as they all rose and left the dining room to go to the sitting room, I began to clear the table. With Mary Margaret not there, I had to help wash dishes, the pots and pans and put them all away.

"They all seemed to enjoy your dinner, Mrs. Chester," I said, noting the way the plates had been scraped clean.

She nodded.

"Will Mary Margaret be here tomorrow?" I asked.

"I hope so," she said. She kept looking at the door fearfully.

"You could probably get a job anywhere you wanted," I said. "With your talents in the kitchen, another family would feel very lucky."

She shook her head and turned to me.

"Without a recommendation, I'd be workin' in some hovel of a place and not make half as much. I do my work. I know my place and I get along," she said. "You oughta think about that."

"Maybe. The trouble is, Mrs. Chester, I don't know where my place is."

She looked at me very curiously, almost as if she was being sympathetic, and then she absorbed herself in her work and didn't say another word.

As I put away the last piece of silverware, Boggs came into the kitchen.

"Mr. Endfield wants a word with you," he said. "In his office. Now."

"Sent to the principal," I told Mrs. Chester, but she didn't understand. "I guess I'll be tossed out on the street."

I wiped my hands on a dishtowel and marched past Boggs. Whatever happens, happens, I thought. I'm tired of fighting with them all.

My Great-uncle Richard was seated behind his desk, his chair turned so he could gaze out the window. He was puffing on a cigar, the smoke twirling toward the ceiling where a ceiling fan seized it and spread it evenly throughout the room.

"You wanted to see me?" I asked.

He turned quickly and sat forward.

"Please close the door," he said.

I did so and he indicated the leather chair in front of his desk. I went to it and sat. He flicked his ash and then put the cigar down and clasped his hands over his stomach.

"When Leonora first told me she wanted to take you in, I wasn't wholly in favor of it," he began. "Our house runs like a Swiss timepiece, efficiently, successfully. It's a relief to know I don't have to worry about the domestic side of our lives. I have enough to do professionally and Leonora is not as strong as she was when she first came to England. That's why I'm glad we have Mr. Boggs."

"I'll leave tomorrow," I said.

He paused, blinked rapidly a moment and then shook his head.

"That's exactly why I wanted to see you. There you go speaking out of turn. Who told you I wanted you to leave?"

"I just thought…"

"You're probably right. I should want you to leave. You practically insulted my guest tonight with your sassy manner."

"Sassy?"

"You have good sense and poise when you're on the stage. Why can't you have it when you're off?"

"I am who I am," I said, tears burning at my eyes. I didn't know myself what that meant, except I liked the sound of it. After all, how many times a day could I be made to feel inferior?

"Nonsense," he replied. "You're nobody yet."

Now it was time for me to raise my eyebrows. Did he know it all? Had Victoria written that letter of spite?

"You're in the process of becoming someone, as are most young women your age, but you don't have any real identity yet. However, you still have the opportunity to shape yourself, your personality, your entire being.

"I'm not surprised at the way you behave and how you speak to people, especially older people. All the Americans I know have that same smugness, arrogance."

"Arrogance? Us? It seems to me it's the other way around. You think you've invented the wheel here, calling us the Colonies. America is the greatest country in the world."

He stared at me a moment and then he laughed.

"All right, all right. Let's not debate who has the best society and who has contributed the most to civilization. The fact is I called you here not to dispose of you and your services, but to offer to help you," he said in a much softer tone of voice.

"Help me?" I was surprised. "How?"

"You need, for the lack of another term, more refinement. I, like my wife, think you can become someone, but you've got to smooth out those rough edges. I understand you've had a hard time up until now and you have done remarkably well considering all that, but you've got to go a little further in other ways and I can help you with that, I think."

"I don't understand what you want to do," I said shaking my head. "How can you help me?"

"I'll teach you manners, give you the benefit of my upbringing, but you have to be cooperative and for now, for reasons I think best left unstated, I'd like it to remain something only known to you and me."

"Teach me manners?"

"How to conduct yourself in polite society. In short, behavioral etiquette."

"I know how to behave."

"Not for the world you're going to be in. Making a good impression is half the battle. Well?"

"I guess," I said, shrugging. I still didn't exactly understand what he was proposing.

"No, the proper thing to say is 'Thank you very much. I appreciate your willingness to work with me.' Now then," he continued, sitting back, "you might have noticed we have a guest cottage behind the house. It's not used for very much these days, but it's well kept."

"Yes," I said nearly breathless. Hadn't Boggs ever told him about finding me outside the cottage window?

"We'll make it our special classroom for a while. I have a few changes to make in it and then I'll advise you when we'll begin," he declared.

I stared at him. Classroom? What was he talking about?

"You still don't seem too appreciative of my offer," he said.

"I'm afraid I still don't understand it. What will we do exactly?"

"I will create social situations for you and explain how you should act, behave, what you should expect. As a student of the theater, you'll have no problem with a little pretending, I assure you," he said. "They'll be nothing all that difficult, but I know it will be of great benefit to you."

"Why do you want to do anything more for me? You said yourself you weren't all that happy about my coming here in the first place."

He looked down for a long moment and then raised his eyes slowly, the look on his face much less formal, much warmer.

"I don't talk about her anymore. It's too painful for Leonora, but we had a daughter who died when she was a little girl. Of course, I think about her often and I regret that I was never able to give her the things I dreamed of giving her, least of which is the benefit of my worldly and social knowledge.

"Had she lived, she might have been a talented young lady such as yourself. I can see her about your age in my mind. There is so much I would have wanted to tell her, show her. I have been frustrated, cheated by her untimely passing.

"What I might have given her, I can give to you. In all modesty, any girl would be quite flattered and appreciative, I expect." He took a deep breath and looked at me. "In short, I'm willing to be more of a father than an employer. Well?" he asked quickly.

"Thank you," I said, moved by his speech, but still a little frightened after what I had seen between him and Mary Margaret. Did he expect I would put on little girl's clothes and suck on a lollipop, too?

"Good." He picked up his cigar. "I'll let you know when everything is as I want it to be at the cottage. Until then, please keep those sassy horses in their stables."

He nodded and turned his chair as a way of saying "You can go now."

I got up slowly, paused at the doorway to look back at him staring out his window, and then left, my heart thumping like a parade drum all the way back to my little room.

Great-uncle Richard made no more mention of the cottage to me that week. I began to wonder if I hadn't imagined it all or if he had changed his mind. Mary Margaret returned to work the next day, but she looked pale and sickly to me. When I asked her how she was, she said, "Fine," quickly and left it at that. Any more questions seemed to make her paler, more frightened. She looked like she would burst into tears if I dared pursue her.

I suppose it was quite different between Randall and me at school: he looked like he would burst into tears every time he tried to talk to me. Some of my anger and reaction to him was caused by my own indecision concerning my father. If it weren't for Randall's insistent search for him, I wouldn't be faced with this emotional and psychological crisis, I thought. I blamed him and yet thanked him in my mind. He kept away, just off to the side, just behind me in the halls, waiting for a look or a word of forgiveness.

Finally, on Saturday morning, I decided I would forgive him and I would tell him about my father's invitation to high tea on Sunday. After breakfast chores, I decided I would surprise him and suggest we do something together that afternoon. Actually, all I wanted to do was take a nice walk in Kensington Gardens and talk. We could buy some sandwiches and something to drink and sit on a bench. It was a beautiful day with few clouds and lots of blue sky. There was a warmer breeze, too. I did love the fresh, clean smell that followed precipitation here.

Buoyed by the weather and my own willingness to be forgiving, I practically skipped along the streets. I knew Randall slept late on Saturday and would surely be just rising.

"They make us get up so early for class," he always complained. Sleeping late on the weekends was his way of getting revenge on the school.

The dormitory was very quiet, not a soul in sight. My own footsteps were the loudest noise, echoing off the walls and in the corridors. I conjured up Randall's look of surprise when I appeared in his room. I was looking forward to settling myself in the crook of his arm, my head on his shoulder, and just talking about my feelings, the events of the past week, and my fears, of course. It was hard talking to no one but yourself. After a while you grew tired of the sound of your own voice. Your head turned into an echo chamber and you knew every answer to every question before it was even asked.

Loneliness is a solitary bird lost in a northern wind flapping its wings desperately in search of its flock, its call to the other birds falling to earth. How cold and gray the world would look even on days without any clouds.

It was time to stop being such a lone bird, I thought. My anger had become a heavy chain around my ankles, slowing me down, keeping me from soaring alongside someone I needed.

I paused at Randall's door and listened. It was deadly quiet. For a moment I was afraid he had gotten up and left. It was that fear that stopped me from knocking. If I had, I might have been able to remain ignorant. Sometimes, ignorance can be bliss.

I reached for the knob and turned it, happy he had left his door unlocked. I opened it quickly and stepped into his room, hoping to find him curled up in his bed, still asleep. I'd wake him with a kiss of forgiveness and he would smile with happiness in his eyes.

Instead, my heart stopped and started. Leslie opened her eyes immediately. Randall was next to her, still asleep.

"Mon Dieu!" Leslie cried.

Randall opened his eyes and groaned.

"Huh?"

"Good morning, *chérie,*" Leslie said, sitting up. She had no inhibitions about revealing her nudity.

Randall rubbed his eyes and lifted his head. His mouth opened and closed without a sound emerging.

The sight had nailed my feet to the floor. I wanted to turn and run, but for a long moment, I couldn't move.

"Rain," he finally said, sitting up on his elbows.

"You must not be angry, *chérie*," Leslie said. "I am here only to cheer him up. He's been so sad because of you," she said, making a pouting, despondent face. "I felt pity for him."

"I see," I said. I glared at Randall. "Did she cheer you up, *chérie?*"

"Rain, you wouldn't talk to me all week and…"

"Looks like my instincts were right. Don't let me stop you, Leslie. Keep cheering him up. You can cheer him up to hell for all I care," I added, spun around and left, slamming the door behind me. The sound was like a bullet bouncing off the walls. I hurried down the steps before Randall or Leslie could follow. In seconds, I burst out of the dormitory and practically ran all the way to the park, nearly getting hit by a car twice on street corners. Even after all this time here, I still occasionally forgot on which side of the road they drove their cars.

I wasn't crying about Randall so much as I was crying about myself, about my innocence and faith, about my gullibility and my foolish blind hope. How many lessons in human nature did I need before I learned that trust was as rare as an unflawed diamond? Maybe that was why they named one of the biggest and best the Hope Diamond. From now on, I would confide in someone only as a last resort. Never again would I open my heart to anyone.

The tears that streaked my face were bitter tasting. I whipped them off my cheeks with flicks of my hands and dropped myself onto a park bench, folding my arms under my bosom and glaring ahead.

Who did I have here? A great-uncle and great-aunt who didn't even know I was related to them and who might pass out from the shock of it if they were ever told? Fellow servants in a house run by Frankenstein? Some nice teachers at the school who nevertheless maintained their professional aloofness, gazing down at me with judgmental eyes? And yes, of course, a father who learned practically yesterday that I existed and nearly turned inside out with the revelation.

Go home, Rain, I told myself. Get on the first plane you can and go home. If you're going to be a servant, be one for Grandmother Hudson. All of a sudden, I burst into hot tears, tears spilled for her and for Jake and for the memory of Mama.

"Are you all right, dear?" a small, elderly lady with a rather ridiculously wide brimmed hat asked. She had a pearl-handled cane.

"What? Oh. Yes," I said slapping my palms to my cheeks to smother the tears. "Thank you."

"How can anyone be sad on such a beautiful day?" she asked with a smile. "And someone so young, too? Whatever it is, my dear, it will pass. You know what time is? It's a big eraser on the end of a pencil. It will clear away your sadness. You'll see," she predicted.

I smiled at her.

"Thank you."

"Oh, see, when you smile, your face lights up. Such a beautiful face, too. I'm on my daily stroll," she continued. "I'm ninety years old and I have promised my children that when I can no longer walk in the park by myself, I'll let them put me in some old-age residency so they don't have to worry. Funny, isn't it? We spend all our lives trying to make our children happy and even at the end, that's what drives us to do things.

"But," she said, "it's hard to be selfish, even now, even when I should be.

"Yes," she said, nodding and starting away, "whatever is troubling you will pass. Someday, you won't even remember why you were crying." She paused and looked back. "Forgetting can be a blessing."

I watched her go on and then I sucked in my breath and stood up just as a solitary sparrow flew by desperately looking for its flock.

On Sunday I awoke trembling. Would I have the courage to go to my father's home to meet his family? Now that the day was here, I was sorry I had called to say I would come. We were still little more than strangers. How could I even begin to hope it would give me any pleasure or answer any questions?

I was nervous about leaving the house. I had anticipated Grandmother Hudson's receiving my letter on Friday or Saturday and assumed, or rather hoped, she would call over the weekend. She hadn't called yet, as far as I knew. Maybe she was waiting until today. If she had received the letter and was going to call, she would do so in the morning her time and even with the five-hour time difference, I would be speaking to her before I left for my father's home.

I sifted through my clothing to find the nicest outfit to wear. I had checked the weather report and there was no chance of rain, so I chose a light-blue cotton dress and my blue cardigan sweater. It would grow cooler later so I needed a jacket as well. After that I spent hours trying to decide if I should wear some lipstick and eye shadow or not. I couldn't decide about my hair either. Finally, I settled on tying it back with a ribbon to keep it neatly behind my neck. I put on some lipstick, but no eye shadow.

Endfield Place was quiet. My great-aunt and great-uncle had gone to the country and it was Mary Margaret's and Mrs. Chester's day off as well. Boggs had driven the Endfields so I had time to be by myself in the great house without feeling I was under constant observation.

I made myself some breakfast and sat eating in the kitchen. Even with no one here, I couldn't get myself to eat in their dining room. If I left a crumb, Boggs would find it and chastise me for daring to eat there.

I read for a while, pausing now and then to wonder about Grandmother Hudson calling. By now, I knew she was up and about back in Virginia. After having read my letter, she would surely call, I thought.

To pass the time, I thought about the house and my great-aunt and great-uncle. I recalled the time I had gone upstairs with a tray of breakfast for my aunt. That was the morning she told me about their daughter. On the way out of the room, I saw what looked like the arm of a large doll sticking out from under a blanket on her rocking chair. It was the only thing I saw that suggested a child had once lived in this house, that and what I had seen in the cottage, of course.

Curiosity grew stronger and stronger and finally beckoned me to the stairs. I looked up at the shadowy second floor and then I slowly ascended. The door to my great-aunt's bedroom was closed. I hesitated. I didn't like being a little snoop, but I couldn't help but open the door to peer in at that rocking chair. There it was, a nearly life-size doll, staring at me. It was so lifelike in fact that my heart skipped a beat. For a split second, I thought it was a real little girl. My great-aunt had dressed it in what looked like real clothes, too.

I continued to gaze around the bedroom. Everything was in place, the bed perfectly made. I glanced once more at the doll and then I closed the door and stood there for a moment thinking. Maybe the doll had been their daughter's. Maybe it was something Great-aunt Leonora couldn't put away or maybe she kept it there to remind her of her daughter. But why would a mother, any mother, need a reminder?

Yours would, I told myself.

I turned and looked at the door across the way. Great-aunt Leonora had shown me only her bedroom. Was that room once their daughter's? I went to the door and tried it, but it was locked. There was one more room down the hall. This door was not locked. When I peered in, I saw another bedroom, not quite as luxurious. Perhaps it was their guest bedroom, I thought, but it did have a lived-in look. I went into it farther and saw a man's clothing in the closet. There was a jacket on a hanger on the inside of the door, too. These were Great-uncle Richard's clothes. I recognized them. I never knew they slept in separate bedrooms.

The bathroom looked recently used, too. A tube of toothpaste was still open and on the tile counter by the sink. Next to it was a hairbrush and a razor.

Did they always sleep in separate bedrooms? There wasn't even an adjoining door. Was this common in English households? I wondered.

I heard a door close downstairs and froze for a moment. What if Boggs had returned and found me up here? It must be Leo, I thought. I hoped. I practically tiptoed my way out and down the stairs. Just as I reached the bottom,

Leo appeared, his head down, crossing from the living room toward the den. I stood so still he didn't notice me. When he was gone, I walked out of the house and released my hot, stifled breath.

Grandmother Hudson hadn't called, but I couldn't wait any longer. A moment later, I was hurrying down the street, fleeing from one house of strangers and heading for another.

12

A Father's Hope

"**I**'m so happy you could come," my father declared rather loudly when he opened the door. "Please." He stepped aside and I entered. Behind him, my half sister and half brother stood waiting politely to be introduced.

"This is Alexandra," he said. "Alexandra, this is Rain Arnold."

She extended her hand.

"Pleased to meet you," she said.

"And this is William," my father said.

He did the same. "Pleased to meet you."

His wife appeared in the entryway, wiping her hands on a lace apron and smiling at me.

"This must be Rain," she said softly. She did have beautiful eyes, I thought, so vibrant and intelligent.

"Yes. Rain, my wife Leanna."

"How do you do," she said. "Alexandra, would you show Rain to the sitting room. It's such a nice day," she told me, "I thought we'd have our tea in the garden."

"Yes, it is a nice day. I've learned to cherish them while in London," I said and both she and my father laughed.

"Getting used to English weather was the hardest thing for me, too," he said. "Even harder than the driving, not that I do all that much. We have a rather good public transportation system here, as I'm sure you've discovered. I'll be right along," he added. He looked to Alexandra who waited for me to follow her into the sitting room.

It was a cozy, yet elegant room with a rustic cottage feel. Fresh flowers were in vases on every table. The walls around the fireplace were covered with books, mostly leather bound, on built-in polished paneled shelves. All of the walls were painted coral with a group of china plates displayed on the wall to my left. The furniture was done in a floral chintz with a large butler's table in the center. There were two Oriental rugs adding a splash of color to the glossy wooden floor. A panel of lace curtains was drawn over the bay window which faced the street. I immediately thought to myself that this was where Leanna had spotted me watching the house.

I smiled at William, who stared at me intensely.

"Please, have a seat," Alexandra said, indicating the settee.

I did so and she sat in the chair across from me. William continued to stand and stare.

"Sit, William," Alexandra ordered. "And it's not polite to stare," she added.

He looked away quickly and sat. He was dressed in a pair of slacks and a crisp white shirt. His hair was neatly brushed back with a prominent part on the right. I thought he was very cute and well on his way toward being a handsome young man.

Alexandra took after her mother with the same small facial features, hair color and eye color. She wore a pink and white dress and had her hair woven in a tight French braid.

"How long have you been in England?" she asked me.

"A few months."

"I hope to go to America soon, especially New York City."

"You're not going soon," William corrected sharply.

"I hope to," she said. "Daddy says we will go before too much longer."

"He said in a few years."

"Well, that's not too much longer, is it? Our father has relatives in New York. Once a cousin came here. He was much older."

"And fatter," William added.

"William," she barked, glaring her chastisement at him. Then she turned to me and shook her head as if she was years and years older than he was. "My brother speaks before he thinks sometimes. Maybe, most of the time," she added, glaring at him once more. She turned again, her posture remarkably perfect.

"How old are you?" I asked her.

"I'm twelve and William is eight, although he often be-haves like a two-year-old," she fired in his direction. He screwed the corners of his mouth in tightly. She turned back to me. "Daddy says you're studying to be an actress."

"I'm in a school for the performing arts. I don't know if I will ever really be an actress."

"Daddy says you have to want something with all your

heart before you set out to do it or you'll never succeed," she replied.

"He's right about that."

"I'm going to be a big game hunter and live in Africa," William declared. "With relatives."

"We don't have relatives in Africa. I keep telling him that, but he insists that we do because some friend of his at school told him our daddy's family comes from Africa. They did come from Africa, but that was very, very long ago, William."

"What do you think?" he asked me.

"Well, there probably are relatives somewhere in Africa," I said. William looked redeemed. "However, your sister is right. Finding them would be nearly impossible."

Alexandra gave him a stern, sharp nod.

"Finding whom?" my father asked, entering.

"Relatives in Africa," Alexandra said.

"Oh?" He smiled and shook his head. "Our William is talking about that again?"

"Yes. He's being ridiculous, I'm afraid," Alexandra said. Maybe it was her beautiful speaking voice and accent, but she seemed so much older than a twelve-year-old.

"Wanting to find your relatives is not silly, Alexandra," my father said, glancing at me. "The problem would be not having much in common with them anymore, I'm afraid."

"They're probably good hunters," William insisted.

"Yes," my father said nodding. "I'm sure they are. Well now," he said sitting beside me on the settee, "tell me about your school. It's the one administered by Conor MacWaine, is it not?"

"Yes. He's a friend of my grandmother's, who…" I paused as Leanna appeared in the doorway.

"Oh, please, continue," she said. "I don't mean to interrupt."

"I was just saying Mr. MacWaine is a friend of my grandmother's and talked her into sending me to his school after he saw me perform in a high-school play."

"What play was that?" my father asked.

"Our Town," I said.

"And you were Emily Webb?"

"Yes."

"Quite a part. How many plays were you in before that?"

"None," I said.

"None? Well then, quite an accomplishment. No wonder Mr. MacWaine sought you for his school. He recognized natural talent."

"Your parents must be very proud," Leanna said.

"I've just my mother," I replied. "But I don't live with her. I live with my grandmother."

"Oh." She looked awkward, her eyes quickly shifting toward my father.

"Is it time for tea, dear?" my father quickly asked.

"Yes. Yes, please. Let's all go into the garden. Children," she said and they rose obediently.

"You have a very nice house," I told my father.

"It's all Leanna's doing. I'm afraid my head is in books and papers most of the time. As you will see, she is quite the gardener as well," he added, leading me to the rear of the house and their garden.

They had a patio with vines hanging through the latticed wooden overhang. Water trickled in a small, gray sculptured fountain and birdbath. The gardens themselves were impressive.

"Leanna will have to describe it all," my father explained.

"After tea, Larry," she said.

Set out on the table was a variety of tea sandwiches, including salmon and cucumber, shrimp and cream cheese and roast beef with watercress and horseradish sauce. There was also a big assortment of pastries and cakes. I recognized lemon shortbread, linzer biscuits, jam and lemon curd tarts and chocolate chip shortbread hearts, all things Mrs. Chester prepared for the Endfields' high teas.

"This is very nice," I said. Everyone sat and Leanna poured us each a cup of tea to start.

"Please, take whatever you wish," she said.

I did so and began to eat, remarking on how good it all was.

"My husband tells me you actually audited his classes to help give you insights into your acting. That's very ambitious of you," Leanna said.

I glanced at my father who ate silently. William and Alexandra watched me eat and listened to my conversation as if they were just as interested in my replies.

"My drama teacher always talks about knowing the character before you actually memorize lines. He believes in improvisation, too. I suppose you become the character more that way," I said.

"Exactly," my father said. "That's especially true for actors in a Shakespearean play because of all the nuances, subtleties of meaning, the imagery, poetry."

"What made you want to study Shakespeare more than anything else?" I asked him.

How odd it felt to speak to my own father this way, to ask the most basic things, to watch every movement in his face, his eyes, the way he held his tea sandwich, sipped his tea, smiled and laughed. Some of it was a search for myself, to see resemblances, to feel some linkage and be more positive about our relationship. What gestures did we share? Could anyone look at the two of us and see that I was his daughter? Would Leanna soon realize it?

If I had never known of him and Randall had never found him, would I have paused when passing him by in the street, or looked at him a second time somewhere, sometime? Was there something between a father and his daughter that couldn't be denied?

"I was always interested in that period, the Elizabethan Age, English history itself, I suppose. If I tried to analyze it deeply, I think I would conclude I was trying to escape from my own reality at the time. Being a lover of language and poetry, it was a natural marriage, Shakespeare and I," he said with a smile.

"My mother writes poetry," Alexandra revealed.

"Oh?"

"I just dabble," she said modestly.

"Hardly," my father said. "She's been published often in a number of prestigious literary periodicals; just this past week, matter of fact."

"Larry, don't make it sound like so much."

"It is to me. I'm very proud of her," he added and leaned over to kiss her on the cheek.

Both Alexandra and William smiled softly at their father's show of affection for their mother. They were properly behaved, I thought, but they didn't stuff away their need for love and their happiness and contentment. The pretty and elegant home, the magnificent garden, the warmth and love that put light in all their eyes and glitter in their smiles was wonderful to see and feel; and yet, it also made me feel lonelier than ever.

There was a time when Mama, Roy, Beni and I had something close to this, but that seemed so long ago, almost another life and maybe just a dream.

How could I ever become part of this life? I wondered. My father's world was truly as perfect as a valuable diamond. There was no room in it for someone like me, someone so lost and confused I could only bring trouble and pain. Why, the moment my half sister learned she had to share her daddy's precious love with me, this diamond would shatter.

"I'd like to hear one of your poems," I told Leanna.

"Read her the one about the clown, Mummy," Alexandra coaxed.

"Yes, do," William said.

"Maybe later," she said blushing a bit.

"What's your favorite subject, Alexandra?" I asked.

"I like music. I play the clarinet," she bragged.

"She sounds like a foghorn," William teased.

"I do not."

"Children," Leanna said softly.

Except for one final look of indignation, both William and Alexandra returned to their perfect posture and finished eating. I laughed to myself thinking how ineffective such a soft reprimand would be with most of the young children I knew back in D.C. Jake, Grandmother's driver, would say, It's like trying to hold back a wild colt with a bridle made of thread.

Leanna asked me more questions about the school for performing arts. She seemed to deliberately skirt any questions about my life back in America. From the occasional glances she gave my father when he spoke to me and from the way she stared at me when I replied, I had the sense she was wondering more and more about me and him. How much did she know? How had he explained my being around their house so often?

Maybe it was wishful thinking or maybe it was just raw paranoia, but there was a curiosity in her eyes that grew more and more prominent as the afternoon went on.

Afterward, my father offered to show me his rare book collection. Alexandra helped Leanna with the dishes and William trailed along behind us.

"I'm really very glad you decided to come," my father told me.

"I don't know exactly why I did," I said.

He laughed.

"Oh, I think it's probably natural. I know I would have done the same. I never did. I just accepted it all. I guess I was more stoic or fatalistic. You see why I'm drawn to Shakespearean tragedy?" he added with a laugh.

"Life's a stage," I quipped.

We stood there, staring at his books, neither of us really looking at them. William became bored with our conversation and wandered off to find his sister.

"Leanna doesn't know about me then?"

"Not yet."

"How did you explain my being around your house so often?" I asked.

"I told her you were very shy and just trying to build up the courage to approach me," he replied.

I looked at him askance.

"Somehow, I don't expect she would believe that."

"Probably not. I'm going to tell her all of it, you know. I wanted her to meet you this way, first."

"There's no point in your telling her. I certainly don't

want to be responsible for anyone else's unhappiness. I don't expect to stay in London after school ends anyway."

"But you'll come back here often until school does end," he said as if it was now a requirement.

"I don't know."

"Sure you will."

Alexandra entered the library with William in tow.

"Well now," my father said, speaking louder, "London is full of bookstores with very old and precious first editions. It's fun to go out on a weekend and scour the stacks, searching for a great find. This Dickens, for example," he said, plucking one from the shelf, "is really worth close to two thousand pounds. I bought it for twelve."

"Mummy says she'll be in the garden," Alexandra declared.

"Oh, certainly. We should go back out. It's so beautiful and Leanna wants to show you her garden. She's rather proud of it."

"I helped her plant the Bells of Ireland," William boasted.

My father laughed and brushed his son's hair.

"Mr. Green Thumbs himself," he declared. William beamed and took his hand. The love between them was practically palpable. How I envied my half sister and half brother.

Leanna took me through her garden, explaining the various flowers. She spoke about them as if they were her children, too, an extended family on which she lavished love and care.

"It's all so beautiful," I said.

"We have so much opportunity to bring beauty into the world if we just have the patience to nurture it," she told me. She looked back at my father, who sat with Alexandra at the table, watching us. "You've made quite an impression on my husband. He's been very selective about the students he invites to our home, and yet, if I understand what he tells me, you and he haven't known each other long."

"No," I said. Standing in her garden amidst so many natural and beautiful things, I felt deceitful and ugly. "But I really appreciated the invitation."

"You don't have much family, do you?"

"No. I have a brother who's in the army, stationed in Germany. He might come to see me."

"A brother? Does he live with your grandmother too?" she asked.

"No. Only I do. Now," I added. I smiled at her. "It's not a very happy story. I'd prefer to leave it for another time. I'm having such a good time today."

"Oh. Of course," she said. "I understand and I'm happy you're enjoying the day with us. You're a very pretty girl, Rain, and I just love your name. For me, a gardener, rain is very important. It's refreshing. It cleans and stimulates growth. I'm sure your name fits you well," she added.

"Thank you."

She laughed and put her arm around my shoulders to give me a quick hug.

When we returned to the patio, I reminded her I'd like to hear one of her poems and she brought out the most recent publication, which made William happy because it was the one entitled "The Clown." She sat and we all gathered around her at the table. My father beamed with pride.

She began, her voice soft, melodic.

He thinks the whole world is a circus
and God is the great Ring Master.
Chosen to bring smiles and laughter,
the clown pretends to stumble and fall.
He bumps into lampposts and trash cans.
He turns himself upside down
and crosses streets on his hands.
He makes sick children and frightened mothers forget.
He dances away depression and sadness
and turns gray skies blue.
He spends his days this way
and people passing toss him a coin or two.
When night falls he crawls back into his box,
a homeless jester born under a tent, content,
his stomach full of laughter and smiles.
Safely asleep, he dreams about tomorrow's show,
hearing the voices in the crowd chanting,
The clown, the clown, give us the clown.
As long as they want him, he'll never be alone.

"Look," William said, pointing at me. "She's crying."

"That's not polite, son," my father told him.

"It's a beautiful poem," I told Leanna, and she thanked me.

I looked at the clock and said I had better be going. I thanked her again for the tea. Then I said good-bye to William and Alexandra.

"Are you coming back?" William asked me.

"Of course she is," my father quickly said.

"Next time, I'll show you my animals," he promised.

"Animals?"

"He has a collection of toy animals. Some he had to

put together," Alexandra explained. "He's actually very good at it," she offered with a sister's pride.

"I'll look forward to seeing them," I told him. He lifted his shoulders and nodded, once again the little gentleman.

My father followed me out.

"Leanna is a very perceptive woman," he told me. "Before this day is over, she'll ask me the key questions about you, I'm sure. I hope you'll find a place for us in your life," he added.

I laughed.

"Me, find a place for you? I'm like an apartment building with no tenants," I said.

He laughed.

"Please call during the week. We'll do something next weekend perhaps. All of us," he emphasized.

"I'll see," I said.

I was truly like someone out in the cold so long, I was afraid of the warmth of a fire, afraid that if I got too close, I'd burn myself.

Everyone was home by the time I returned to Endfield Place. Almost as soon as I entered, Leo approached me immediately. He was more animated than I had ever seen him. Usually, he hobbled about with sleepy eyes, looking as though he would have to go and rest after opening the door.

"Oh, miss," he declared with raised eyebrows and arms lifting. "Mrs. Endfield's been asking for you ever since she and Mr. Endfield returned. She wanted me to send you right up as soon as I set eyes on you."

"What's wrong?" I asked.

Leo behaved as if he didn't hear my question. He closed the door, turned and muttered, "Right up."

I gazed down the corridor. All was quiet. Then I started up the stairs. When I reached my great-aunt's bedroom, I knocked and waited and then knocked again, a little harder.

"Please, come in," I heard her moan.

She was in bed with a damp cloth over her forehead. Her pillows were so large and fluffy, she looked like she was sinking into them and soon would be gone. The comforter was up to her neck.

"Oh," I said, "aren't you well?"

"Some bloody allergy, the doctor thinks. The country doctor, that is. I just suddenly started to sneeze and sneeze and sneeze. I sneezed so much, my legs gave out and they had to carry me into the house. They've got me stuffed with medicine, which is making my head spin, but at least I'm not sneezing."

"I'm sorry," I said. "Has this ever happened to you before?"

"No, but this isn't why I wanted to see you, dear. My sister called and was very, very insistent that you return the call, no matter what time, which I thought was quite unusual under the circumstances."

"What circumstances?" I asked.

"She's apparently back in hospital."

"Oh no. Why?"

"I couldn't make head or tail of what she was saying. Words were going into my head and then getting ground up like vegetables in a blender. Something about a blocked artery is all I do recall. That and her rather dramatic demand that you call as soon as possible.

"I must say Frances has become quite a mystery to me these days," she added, focusing on me. "You can use that phone right there," she said, nodding at the phone on her little secretary desk to the right of her bed. I knew she wanted me to use it so she could listen in on the conversation, but I couldn't think of any way to avoid it. "I've written the number and country codes out for you. She has a private room, of course."

"Thank you," I said and went to the phone.

"Mr. Endfield was so upset about my getting sick and ruining the day that he barely uttered a syllable our whole journey back," she muttered. "It's all made me feel so miserable, and now we have Frances back in the hospital. Oh dear, dear, dear. Whenever it pours, it rains," she said.

"I think you mean when it rains, it pours," I told her and she thought a moment.

"Oh, do I? Yes, I believe I do. You would know, of course, with a name like Rain." She closed her eyes and groaned.

I read the telephone number and then I dialed and waited. It rang only twice before I heard Grandmother Hudson say hello. I knew we were talking over a great distance, but her voice had sounded so much stronger the last time.

"It's Rain," I replied. "What's wrong, Mrs. Hudson?"

"This idiot I have for a doctor and his specialist have decided that there is more to my problem. They want to do some ridiculous thing involving a balloon, which is intended to open my artery. Something in the realm of science fiction, I'm sure, but they insist if I don't have it done, I'll topple over and die.

"I have your letter in hand," she added after a very short pause. "How far has this melodrama gone?"

"I've been to see him," I said.

"At his home?"

"Yes."

"And?"

"They're all very nice."

"And?" she sang.

"His family doesn't know about me yet," I revealed. "He says he wants to tell his wife, but I asked him not to."

"Very wise. You asked for my advice and it's simply let it be. What's done is done and too much time has passed. No one wants to be reminded of their mistakes, Rain."

"I don't think he sees me as that," I said.

"Nevertheless, when and if he does have to explain you to his wife, he will have to describe it that way. Once, he was young and careless, something like that," she said.

I recalled my first conversation with my father and his description of him and my mother being rebellious young people with no sense of responsibility. Grandmother Hudson was probably right. She had great wisdom.

"Eventually," she predicted, "you'll be resented no matter how nice they seem to you now, Rain. Don't invest too much hope in this situation. Concentrate on your purpose, on your own life now."

"Okay," I said, my throat closing. I wanted so much to say, "Okay, Grandmother," but I knew my great-aunt was hanging on every word and would be cross-examining me as it was.

"My sister is nearby?" she asked as if she could gaze through the phone line and see how sad I was and how tears had come to glaze over my eyes.

"Yes."

"I thought she was only moments from being swept away by the Grim Reaper," she quipped. I smiled. "I never heard such moaning and groaning and I'm in a hospital, too."

"She's in bed, treated for an allergy."

"Tell her it might be something more," my great-aunt prompted from behind, revealing that she was indeed plugged into my every syllable.

"She says to tell you it might be more than an allergy."

"Of course. She was always looking for attention. That's why I could never understand her marriage and her decision to live in a country where everyone is judged on how stiff their upper lip is."

I laughed again.

"What did she say? Rain?"

"She says she hopes you feel better quickly," I offered.

"Let me speak to that woman as soon as you're finished," she ordered.

"I've got to go, Mrs. Hudson. Please call to let us know how you are doing. Your sister would like a few words with you," I added. "Thank you for calling."

"I don't know if I have the strength to listen to her, but put her on or she'll make your life miserable," Grandmother Hudson said.

I handed my great-aunt the receiver and used the opportunity to slip out of the room before she could question me about my conversation with my grandmother. After I closed her bedroom door behind me, I took a deep breath and started down the stairs. When I had left my father's home and family, I started to hope that I could become part of his life, part of their lives. I even fantasized that I would eventually move in to live with them, continue my training, and eventually become a citizen of England as he had. Grandmother Hudson would come over frequently to see me in major theater productions and I would return to America to star in movies and on the stage. What dreams.

Are people like me more susceptible to dreams and fantasy? I wondered now. Are they like germs and viruses? Do we have less of an immune system when it comes to illusions? Surely people who are content with themselves, their identities and their lives don't spend as much time imagining another life, another identity. They don't need the avenues of escape. They're not trying to run from themselves.

Would I always be like this? Maybe it would drive me mad and I would lose all sense of what was real and what was not. Yes, Grandmother Hudson was giving me good advice. Brush away the fantasies and concentrate on what you're there to do, she'd advised. She was right. I would not return to my father's home. It was like visiting a dream, but I'm awake now, I thought, awake and ready to deal with cold reality.

Maybe that was a vain hope as well for at the bottom of the stairway, glaring up at me sternly, was Boggs, his hands behind his back.

"Mr. Endfield wants to see you immediately," he announced.

"Everyone wants me immediately today," I muttered and turned to go to my great-uncle's office.

"No," Boggs said. "Not that way. Follow me," he commanded and opened the front door.

"Where are we going?"

"Just step lively," he ordered and waited for me to go outside. I did so and he closed the door and led the way around the house toward the cottage. My heart felt as if it was made of ice and was sliding slowly down into my stomach. In daylight the cottage didn't look anywhere near as ominous and mysterious as it did in the evening with candles lit behind the translucent curtains, but I couldn't help thinking of myself as crossing from one world into another, perhaps into someone else's fantasies and dreams.

Boggs stopped at the door and knocked. He gazed at me disdainfully and rocked on his heels, but I refused to let him intimidate me with those cold gray eyes.

My great-uncle opened the door and smiled.

"Oh. Thank you, Boggs. Please come in, Rain," he said stepping back.

He was wearing a pair of dark, silk slacks, black leather slippers, a burgundy smoking jacket and held a white meerschaum pipe. It had either just gone out or hadn't yet been lit.

Boggs started away and I entered the cottage. I hadn't seen it all through the windows at night. The small sitting area had two beige oval rugs over the dark wood floor. There were two settees, a three-seater and a two-seater, a small butler's table and some antique lamps. The fireplace had white marble around it.

"I actually built this little cottage for my daughter. It was going to be her dollhouse," my Great-uncle Richard said sadly. Then he smiled. "As you'll see, I've improved it a bit over time."

He led me farther in. From the sitting room, a flagstone hallway led to the small kitchen and dining area with its timbered pine ceiling. The cottage had only the one bed-room with its wrought-iron double bed, a large mirror-fitted wardrobe and some small tables. I saw immediately that the bedroom had been changed. It still had the pink and white wallpaper with the cartoon characters, but gone were the dolls on shelves, the small mauve-colored desk and chair, and the storybook pictures. In their places were a much larger desk and chair, old theater and movie posters on the walls and some young-adult magazines on the desk and shelves. Some of the magazines looked years old, but there were a few that looked recent.

The vanity table had new brushes and combs, bottles of perfume and bath powders. There was also a tray of makeup with a variety of lipsticks, eye shadow and eyeliner. I noticed that the comforter and the pillowcases were different as well. In short, everything looked like it belonged to someone more mature, as if the little girl who had lived here had grown up overnight.

A flutter of panic made my heart skip when I turned and looked back at Great-uncle Richard. He had a strange, twisted smile on his lips and was staring at me madly.

"It's nice, isn't it? Sort of what I imagined her room would be if she was your age," he said in a soft, dreamy voice. "Well," he said, looking around and brushing back his hair, "I guess we can start."

"Start?"

"I thought I'd take advantage of the abrupt change in plans today, especially since everything is ready. I didn't expect Mrs. Endfield to get sick, but since she has why not make good use of the opportunity?" He crossed the bedroom and opened the closet. "I've chosen these dresses carefully," he explained, stepping back so I could see them all. "Each fits a different sort of social occasion, from casual to formal."

I crossed to the closet and looked at the dresses. The first had a faded department store tag and when I held out the dress and looked at it, I realized it was not a very recent purchase. It wasn't really my size, but a size too small.

"Are you saying you bought these dresses for me?"

"Of course," he said.

"But these would all be too tight on me," I said. "Why did you buy clothes without knowing my exact size?"

"Oh, don't worry about how it looks, my dear. The only one seeing you in any of this will be me, and yourself of course, but just consider them all to be costumes."

"Costumes?"

"Well, we are working on a performance of sorts," he said.

I looked at the shoes. None of them would fit me either.

"I couldn't get into these, costume or not," I said.

"Don't worry about that then. Go barefoot for now."

Some pairs looked old and faded.

"What kind of a store sold you this stuff?" I asked. "They look like thrift store clothes."

"I told you," he said a little sharply and sternly, "it's not important." The surprised look on my face brought a calming smile to his. "What's important is what we do, not what we look like. For now, that is," he added. "I tried to provide everything you might need," he said, nodding at the dresser.

I glanced at him and then slowly opened a dresser drawer. It was filled with undergarments, but the panties and the bras were too small as well.

"You bought all this for me?" I asked.

"I just had a package thrown together," he said quickly. "I wanted you to feel at home here, comfortable, as if this really was your room, your little dollhouse, too."

"I heard you say that, but it seems quite large for a toy," I said gazing around the cottage.

He laughed.

"As large as the love in my heart. That's what I used to

tell her every time she or someone else remarked about something I had given her being too extravagant. Well," he said, pausing and looking around with a smile that involved every part of his face, "here it is. Don't you just love it all?"

I followed his gaze, shaking my head, my thoughts rushing about in a maze of confusion.

"I still don't understand what I'm supposed to do, Mr. Endfield," I said.

"Let's begin with the simplest of things and work our way through," he said. "I'll create the scenario for you. Set the scene as it were. I think that's the term your stage directors use, is it not?"

"Yes," I said.

"Fine. This is your home or apartment. You are to imagine that you are now living on your own. Every child must leave the nest someday," he said, his expression darkening like someone who had to face an unpleasant truth. "The Bible even tells us so. But that doesn't mean we have to let our children go unaided or ill advised, does it?"

"No," I said, even though I still didn't understand where all this was leading.

"Of course not. Of course not," he muttered. He looked like he had forgotten his point himself and then he lifted his head, his eyes bright again. "Okay, now tonight you are going to entertain a producer who has shown interest in you. You're naturally excited about it. It's your first experience of this sort. I'm sure you've fantasized about such things, have you not?"

"Not really," I said. "I've just begun to study. It will be some time before I actually audition for something professionally."

"No, no, no," he said as if I were ruining the scenario. "Once you step on a stage, you're vulnerable to all this. You're exposed. They're all hovering out there, predators, swooping down on the young and the innocent such as yourself. You're not in my home anymore. You're not under my wing, you see."

"Not in your home?"

"Exactly," he said. "Why, tomorrow, someone like that could come up to you after school and say, 'Rain Arnold, I've been watching you and I think you might be perfect for a new production I'm beginning. I'd like you to audition and I would like to be personally involved in this.'

"Wouldn't you be flattered? Come on," he urged. "Be honest, my dear. Wouldn't you?"

"I suppose so," I admitted.

"Precisely. Now," he said, crossing back to the closet. "You have this occasion. What will you wear?"

"Nothing in there," I said, pointing to the closet. "Nothing fits."

He smirked and shook his head.

"If you don't, how do they say it, suspend disbelief, we won't be able to do this. I told you to ignore the sizes. Pick a garment," he practically ordered, his eyes darkening as his face tightened.

A tiny alarm bell went off in the pit of my stomach and rang its way up to my thumping heart. He looked like a lit firecracker, ready to explode if I said or did the wrong thing.

"All right," I said. I plucked a lavender dress out of the closet. "How about this one?"

He nodded.

"Yes, very good choice, not too formal and yet not too

273

casual. You have the right instincts. I knew it. All right. I'll step out and you put it on. Then, you will hear the doorbell ring. You come out to let me in and we'll begin the exercise," he said. "I'll give you a little time should you want to do something with makeup, hair. I imagine you would," he added, gazed around the room, sighed and then left.

I was standing there, holding the dress on its hanger, looking after him, my mouth still open. Never in my wildest imaginings after first meeting Great-uncle Richard could I envision this. Why would such a successful and respected man need these fantasies? I couldn't help being curious as to how far this make-believe would go, and yet I was also quite tempted to simply run out of the cottage and not look back.

"You want to make a good impression," he called from the other room, "but try not to be too obvious. Obvious women are usually not taken seriously. My mother used to tell me that understatement was the best statement, the most powerful statement. How are you doing?"

"All right," I called back and held the dress up against me. Should I really try to put this on? I suppose I have to, I thought.

I took off my skirt and blouse and stepped into it. As I suspected, it was snug at the hips and tight around my bosom. I could get the side zipper up only a little more than halfway. I thought I looked absolutely ridiculous. The moment he saw me, he would certainly realize it, laugh and put an end to all this, I hopefully concluded.

"It's just as I told you," I called.

"Don't tell me anything. We're beginning. Both of us have to step into character. I'll ring the doorbell," he added, opened the door, stepped out and did so.

Now what? I asked myself as I walked to the door. He rang the bell again. I felt like I was in the second grade playing with some of my friends. Nevertheless, I opened the door and he beamed as if he was looking in at the Queen of England.

"Oh my dear, you look absolutely radiant. Just as I expected," he said, winked and nodded. "Just as Constance does in the first act of my new play. I'd love you to read for the part. May I come in?"

"What? Oh, yes," I said. Couldn't he see the left side of the dress was hanging ridiculously over the unzipped portion and I was moving like someone in a straitjacket?

"What a quaint flat you have," he said looking around. "It's actually just as I pictured it would be."

I noticed he had some papers in his left hand.

"I've brought the script with me," he said. "I'd like you to read some of the dialogue, Constance's dialogue, of course. The lead," he added, widening his eyes and raising his brow into little folds.

He put his hand over his mouth and turned it so he could whisper out of the other side.

"Now you ask me if I'd like something to drink."

"Would you like something to drink?"

"Oh, just a glass of white wine if you'll join me," he said.

He leaned over, hand on his mouth again.

"Go into the kitchen. It's on the counter. You know how to open a bottle of wine, right?"

"Yes," I said. Was this pretend too? I expected so; however, when I went into the kitchen, there really was a bottle of wine, two glasses and a corkscrew.

"What a nice view you have. You're very lucky to have found this flat."

"Thank you," I said with a giggle. I couldn't help it. I thought I was only inches from falling into a pool of hysterical laughter. I opened the wine and poured two glasses, tasting it and smiling. It was good. Then I brought it out.

"You should bring some napkins with it," he whispered.

"Oh, right."

"You'll find them in the small closet on the left where they always are."

"Right," I said, returned to the kitchen, found them and brought them back. He was seated on the two-seater settee, sipping his wine. I handed him a napkin. He thanked me and asked me to sit beside him. I did so and he shook his head.

"Remember," he whispered, "you're alone with a man you really don't know. Don't be so quick to do everything he says or suggests."

"Okay," I said, my eyes almost as wide as his were. He sat back.

"Now then, I'll read Horace. I'd like you to be as relaxed and natural as possible, Rain. Read it as if I wasn't even here, understand?"

"Yes, I do," I said.

He handed me the script and I looked over the first page. It was a love scene.

"Anything wrong?" he asked when I hesitated.

"What? No."

"Good. Let's begin. Pretend we're seated just like this on the stage, in her living room, early evening." He sipped his wine, put the glass on the table, and sat forward. It was immediately obvious that he had memorized his part.

"What play is this?" I asked, quickly reading some of it to myself. I thought it was really bad.

"Love Undone," he replied. "The playwright is the rage of London these days. We're lucky to have the rights to it and anyone who gets a decent part will make an impression quickly on the theater community."

He paused and leaned toward me again, his hand over his mouth as if there were other people in the room from whom he was trying to hide his words.

"You have to decide how much of what he says is real and how much is hype. This takes experience," he added and sat back. "So, shall we start? Wait," he interrupted, "it's too bright in here. Not at all as it would be on the stage."

He got up and closed all the curtains tightly. Then he sat again and nodded.

"Any time you're ready," he said.

"Ready?"

"To read. Go on," he directed, flicking his right hand at me.

"Oh. All right." I began. "Horace, I wish you hadn't come here tonight. You know how I feel about our relationship."

"I know how you *think* you feel," he said, moving closer to me on the settee. Then, before I knew what to expect, he had his fingers under my chin and was looking deep into my eyes. It was strange to be so close to him.

"Our ages are just accidents of birth," he continued, still holding my chin. "We can't let time stand like a wall between us."

I pulled back a bit.

"But Horace, your daughter and I are best friends. It would break her heart."

"It's not her heart I'm concerned with now," he followed, inching closer to me again. "You're doing very well, Rain," he added sotto voce, "but try to look at me when you speak and show me how you are saying one thing, but feeling another. Go on, try it," he directed.

"I can't do this, Horace," I read, gazing up at him quickly. He stared at me.

"Your eyes tell me otherwise, Constance, and so do your lips," he said, seizing my shoulders and turning me so roughly, the pages flew from my hand. Then he slapped his lips against mine, pressing so hard, I lost my breath. With his mouth still on mine, he dropped his hand to lower the zipper on my dress even farther. Then he pulled back, taking the dress down with his small retreat.

I was too shocked and stunned to move, even utter a sound.

"You're beautiful, Rain. Just as I'd hoped. I'll make you a star. We'll blaze your name across the lights of London. Trust me," he said and leaned forward to kiss my neck.

I slipped out from under him and jumped up from the settee.

"What are you doing?" I cried, pulling the dress back up.

The lustful look in his eyes evaporated instantly and was quickly replaced with the stern, fatherly expression he had shown me before.

"Good," he said. "That's what I hoped you would do, but you're still in some danger here. We'll start again, and I'll show you another way this could begin. Repair yourself while I go back outside. I'll press the doorbell again," he said rising.

"No!" I cried the moment he opened the door. "I can't

do this. I don't want to do this," I said and charged by him when he turned with surprise.

I ran from the cottage.

"Heather!" I heard him cry. It was his dead daughter's name. I paused and looked back to see him standing in the cottage doorway. It put an even colder chill in my heart and I hurried along to the house. As I made the turn toward the front door, I saw Boggs off to my left, standing like a grim statue, watching me.

I practically charged through the front door and down the hallway to my room where I quickly stripped off the foolish dress and threw it on the floor. Then I sat on my bed and tried to catch my breath.

Was it great madness or great sorrow that makes him do these things? I wondered. I didn't have much of a chance to think about it. My door was thrust open so hard, it strained on its hinges. Boggs stood there, gaping in at me. I covered myself quickly with my hands.

"Don't go saying anything nasty about Mr. Endfield," he warned.

Then he closed the door.

"Oh, Mama," I moaned. "If you only knew the truth about what you hoped was my salvation. You might have left me to take my chances in the hell we at least understood."

13

Seize the Moment

Of course I was quite nervous about serving Great-uncle Richard and Great-aunt Leonora breakfast the following morning. I was emotionally exhausted and almost immediately fell into a comatose state the moment I lowered my head to the pillow, but very soon I began to toss and turn so much in anticipation of waking that my legs and arms actually ached when I woke. It felt like I had been swimming miles.

I don't think I really dreamed until shortly before waking. Just as the sun was coming up, I flitted in and out of nightmares, dreaming I was dressed like a baby in a giant crib. I wore only a diaper. Great-uncle Richard was a giant reaching in for me. His hands looked enormous and at the very ends of each finger, there were smaller versions of his head. I might have been screaming as I dreamed, but Boggs, if he heard it, didn't come to see what was wrong. I could hear myself crying and saw myself running in a forest in which tree after tree turned into Boggs, his arms stretched out toward me like great, thick branches.

After I rose and went to the bathroom, I gazed at myself in the mirror and saw eyes that looked glassy and still asleep, the lids drooping like flags on a day with no breeze. I didn't have the energy to make myself look much better and barely ran a brush through my hair. I let my legs carry me through the hallway to the kitchen as if the top half of me was yet not awake.

"Looks like I'm the only one chirpy this mornin'," Mrs. Chester commented the moment she set eyes on me. "Whatja do, get yourself good and sloshed yesterday?" she asked me.

"Sloshed? You mean, drunk?"

"Call it whatever yer want, the end's the same. You look like you turned yerself inside out and in again."

"No, I didn't get sloshed," I said sharply. "I don't *get* sloshed."

"Well, one gander at you tells me yer candle was burned on both ends, dearie," she insisted.

She could be so infuriating, making my stomach feel like I had swallowed a handful of straight pins. I decided to ignore her and do my work. Mary Margaret came in from the dining room where she had been setting the table. She looked pale, her eyes foggy. She threw a quick glance at me and then turned away. I could see Mrs. Chester watching her out of the corner of her eyes.

"Get a move on," she ordered. "They'll be down in a minute," she said.

I was surprised Great-aunt Leonora came to the dining room after the way she had been late yesterday. She said she had to get up and get presentable because she had an important social affair, a luncheon, that she insisted she had to attend. The proceeds were marked for a charity. However, she let us all know how much of a sacrifice it was for her. She complained about her nose and her throat and how heavy her head felt.

"I just hope I can manage all right. So many people are depending on me," she claimed.

Great-uncle Richard said nothing. He read his paper and except for one look he gave me when I first entered the dining room, he didn't so much as glance at me while I worked. However, that one look was enough to turn my heart into a drum with a skin too taut. Every beat sent a heavy thump to my head and seized my breath as if a great and powerful hand was squeezing at my throat. Great-uncle Richard's look was strange and haunted and then, just as quickly as it had come, the look was gone and he was back to being his formal, stiff self with certainly no mention made of the cottage or what he had done.

Great-aunt Leonora hated long silences and talked incessantly as she nibbled on her toast. In my mind her words bounced off the back of Great-uncle Richard's newspaper, which he held up like a shield. If she asked a question, she had to do so twice and then he would lower his paper to growl his reply, which was usually something like "If you don't know what you're talking about, Leonora, it's better to remain silent."

"Well, I'm just saying," she'd reply, but then grow quiet until another topic came to mind.

After they had left, I helped Mary Margaret clear the table. All through breakfast, she had been very quiet. She barely answered me when I asked her how she felt and she kept her eyes down as if she thought I could see the truth in them. I thought she looked more afraid and fragile than ever, and I was working up the courage to tell Mrs. Chester I thought there was something seriously wrong with Mary Margaret. But Mary Margaret did it for me in a most dramatic fashion.

She had just handed a bowl to Mrs. Chester at the sink when she looked up as if something had flown by her head, turned and then folded to the floor like a body whose bones had turned to jelly. Neither Mrs. Chester nor I moved or spoke for a moment, both of us thrown into utter shock.

"Mary Margaret!" she finally screamed. She looked up and yelled for Boggs.

I thought Boggs must have been standing right outside the kitchen door to come in as quickly as he did. I always felt he was nearby, eavesdropping on our conversations. For once, I was grateful. Mary Margaret still hadn't moved a muscle and her face looked as pasty and white as a faded lily.

Boggs stared down at her.

"What happened?" he demanded gruffly.

"She's upped and fainted," Mrs. Chester told him.

He glanced at her, at me, and then charged forward, kneeling at Mary Margaret's side.

"We'd better get the doc," Mrs. Chester said.

"I'll take care of 'er," Boggs replied, slipped his arms under Mary Margaret and lifted her as he stood up. He held her with little effort and walked out of the kitchen, her head against his chest. At the door he turned to us.

"Jist finish up in 'ere," he ordered and was gone.

"What's wrong with her?" I asked.

Mrs. Chester shook her head and returned to her work.

"What did he mean, he'll take care of her? What's he going to do? He's not a doctor, is he?"

" 'E'll take care of it," she replied stoically.

"I'll bet," I muttered. "He'll probably slap her awake and make her dust the piano."

Mrs. Chester said nothing more. I completed my work as quickly as I could. When I stepped out of the kitchen, the house was quiet. I went down the corridor, looking into rooms to see if Mary Margaret was resting on a sofa. Neither she nor Boggs was anywhere to be found.

"Where did he take her?" I muttered to myself.

I hurried back to my own room and went to his door to see if he had taken her to his room, but it was deadly quiet there, too. There was nothing else for me to do but get ready for school. With all that had happened, it was nearly impossible for me to concentrate on anything when I got there. I know I performed poorly in speech class and was so bad in dance, I could have been dancing with two left feet. I was probably the only uninspired student, too, because there was a great deal of excitement about the upcoming auditions for the school's production of *The Taming of the Shrew.*

There had been a rumor that one of London's most prestigious theater directors, Taylor Harrison, was going to do our production. Every year a prestigious director produced one of the school's shows. It was a clever way to give the school respect and draw attention to the production. Before the end of the day, Mr. MacWaine came around to announce that the rumor was indeed true.

"Auditions," he declared, "will be held this coming weekend. Anyone interested should stop by the office for cut sheets to prepare," he said.

Anyone interested? Who wasn't going to be interested?

The school quickly turned into a beehive. The excitement carried into drama class where Mrs. Winecoup asked us to perform some improvisations. Randall was in this class with me. Although we hadn't spoken since I'd found him with Leslie, I did stop glaring back at him with disgust. I think he took that for my forgiveness. In the scene we were to do, he ended up playing opposite me and suddenly turned it into a love scene. Before I could object, he rushed at me in front of the others and embraced me so tightly and so fervently kissed me that I pulled away, overwhelmed with his emotions.

"I can't live without you," he cried.

I saw Catherine and Leslie laughing.

"Well," Mrs. Winecoup said, "that was somewhat over-the-top, as we say. Drama is about restraint. I thought that was a lesson well understood, but apparently not."

"Sorry," Randall said. He looked at me. "Sorry."

"Stick to singing," I told him. That brought laughter and relieved the moment. Even Mrs. Winecoup looked grateful and continued the lesson about subtlety and dramatics.

After class Randall tried to start a conversation.

"You're going to the auditions this weekend, aren't you?" he asked.

"I don't know yet," I said. I really didn't. It was a major commitment and I wasn't sure I was ready for it yet.

"You should. You'd be a great Katherina."

"What's that supposed to mean, I'm a shrew?"

"No, no," he said quickly. "You'd just be great because you can act better than any of the girls here. Sorry about what I did in there. I guess I made a fool of myself."

"You made a fool of both of us," I replied coolly.

"There's no winning you back, huh?" he asked.

"I'm not anyone's prize, Randall."

"That's not what I meant."

"I know," I said, a little tired of being nasty myself. "Look, a great deal has happened and I'm very occupied at the moment."

"You've seen your father, haven't you?" he asked with a smile. "I know you have. I can see it in your face."

"I've seen the man who was responsible for my being born. I haven't yet seen my father," I told him. "I've got to go," I said and started away.

"Wait." He drew to my side. "Can't we meet and just talk? We had such great times together. I really don't like Leslie, not like I like you. She was just a distraction, a game. I can't take her seriously. I've said more serious things to you than I have to anyone," he declared. He looked so sincere, I had to smile.

"Maybe you are a good actor after all, Randall."

"I'm not. This is me, not some part I'm playing!" he insisted.

"I'll see," I said. "I have to get my head together by myself first."

"I want to be there for you, Rain. I mean it," he promised.

"Okay," I said. I started away.

"Don't be stupid. Go to the audition," he called after me. "You're the best in the school!"

I smiled to myself and continued on.

When I arrived at Endfield Place that afternoon, I went first to the kitchen to look for Mrs. Chester. She was preparing guinea hens for dinner.

"How's Mary Margaret?" I quickly asked.

"We've got a lot to do," she replied instead. "It's just the two of us tonight."

"But how is she? What was wrong with her?"

She kept working as if I hadn't asked the question. I stood, waiting.

"Mrs. Chester? Answer me," I demanded.

She turned slowly. She looked like she had been crying.

"Is she all right?"

"Yes," she said. "But she won't be back 'ere for a while; if ever," she added.

"Why not? What's wrong with her? Is it a bad disease? It's not cancer, is it?" I asked quickly, remembering Mama.

"No," she said, turning back to the food, "but for 'er it might just as well be."

"Why?"

"She's up the spout," she slammed at me.

"What? What's that mean?"

"It means 'er man, whoever 'e was, didn't use a Johnny."

"A Johnny?" I thought a moment. "You mean, she's pregnant?"

"Well there you go. You ain't a dumb Doris after all, are ya?"

"Pregnant?"

"It 'appens, yer know." She turned back to her preparations. "She 'ad me fooled, she did. All this time I thought she's like a girl in first school and needed someone to take 'er by the hand and show 'er where it's at. Mopin' about 'ere, 'er eyes explodin' every time I mentioned a tumble or havin' it off. Don't I look like the dumb one, eh?"

"Is that what bothers you? What you look like? What about her?"

"We all make the beds we sleep in," she muttered.

"That's not true. Sometimes, the beds are already made and we have no choice," I retorted.

She looked at me, eyebrows hoisted.

"Well there ain't much we can do about it then, is there? Mrs. Endfield's not goin' to permit a tart in the 'ouse, is she?"

"You know Mary Margaret is no tart, Mrs. Chester."

She turned away.

"If we don't help her, who will?"

"There's work ta be done and no sense in you and me workin' our jaws."

"No," I said. "No sense at all."

I turned and went to my room to change. No one made mention of Mary Margaret at dinner. I didn't hear Great-aunt Leonora say anything or Great-uncle Richard either. She was, as Mrs. Chester declared, persona non grata now. I couldn't help but feel sorry for her, however, and after dinner chores, I left the house and headed for Mary Margaret's home.

I got her address from Mrs. Chester and knew that it was close to Cromwell Hospital. Mary Margaret and her sick "Mum," as she called her, lived in a flat in what looked like the oldest building on the street. The doorway looked ready to fall off its rusted hinges, and the stairs were so narrow, I couldn't imagine someone coming down while someone else was going up. Mary Margaret and her mother lived on the third floor. The creaky steps ascended in six short flights. I was afraid to put too much weight on the rickety banister. I could see it was cracked and loose even though the lighting streaming down from weak, naked bulbs was barely adequate.

When I reached her door, I knocked and waited. I

heard what sounded like a radio commentator and then some music. I knocked again, louder, harder, and then heard the radio turned down and what sounded like someone shuffling along on a wooden floor. A chain lock was undone and the door opened a few inches. A short woman with thinning gray hair curled wildly like broken piano wires poked her face through the crack at me. She seemed to be looking directly at my chest. Her forehead gathered in small rolls and deep lines. I imagined she had to be Mary Margaret's mother.

"What is it?" she asked. Her nose twitched like a rabbit's. Was she trying to smell me, too? I wondered.

"I'm here to see Mary Margaret. My name is Rain Arnold. I work with her at Endfield Place."

She didn't respond. She continued to hold her head in the opening and twitch her nose at me as if she was deciding whether or not I was some sort of practical joker. Then she turned her head slightly so her ear was more visible.

"Who'd you say you were?"

"Rain Arnold. I work at Endfield Place with Mary Margaret," I told her slowly.

"Just a minute," she said and closed the door sharply on me. I heard her footsteps behind the door and some mumbling. These walls aren't very thick, I thought. If someone has a bellyache, the neighbors will know. Above me, I heard the sounds of laughter and to the right, just below, someone was playing rock music.

Mary Margaret's mother opened the door just a little wider this time. She stood farther back and looked away, her head slightly tilted to the right. I could see she wore a light-blue housecoat and well-worn leather slippers. There were bright red blotches on her ankles. She was stout and

heavy breasted with a short neck. It looked like her body
had simply stopped growing and her head had been
slapped on at the last possible moment. There was barely
any light in the room and her face was covered in shadows, but I could still see that she had thin lips and small
features like Mary Margaret.

"She says go away," she told me.

"I have to see her. Please," I said and stepped into the
flat.

The first thing that hit me was the oppressingly
heavy, stale air. It was as if the door or windows hadn't
been opened for years. Everything in the flat looked old
as well, but oddly the furniture was the ostentatious kind
found in rich houses, expensive pieces like a royal-
purple velvet lounging chaise with gold cording tar-
nished and falling off where it wasn't fastened by fancy
tassels. The blanket and pillow on it suggested it was
being used as a bed. The rest of the furniture was just as
eclectic, all of it looking like hand-me-downs. Most of
the furniture looked like antiques, and all of the pieces
were in some disrepair: cushions torn, springs hanging
out from beneath settees, wooden tables dull and
scratched. The one lit lamp had a torn shade and the
small area rugs were worn so thin, the wooden floor
peeked out beneath them.

The two windows in the living room faced onto an
alley and the building next door looked close enough to
touch. Off to the right was a small kitchen with a table
and chairs. The walls were painted pale yellow. The walls
of the living room were dark green, which with the dim
light, made it all the darker.

"Where is she, please?" I asked.

"She's in the bedroom," her mother said, "but she don't want no visitors. She ain't been well."

"I won't be long. Thank you."

I crossed the living room to the one bedroom. Again, there was only a single small lamp lit. The large, heavy-beamed bed took up most of the room. A dresser from a different bedroom set had been squeezed in on the right and another smaller one on the left. There was only a single nightstand and on that the one lamp. Mary Margaret was lying on her back, her head on a large pillow. She stared up at the ceiling and then turned when I entered. She was wearing only a slip.

"What'cha doin' here?" she asked me quickly.

"I came to see how you were and to be sure Mrs. Chester was telling me the truth," I replied.

"So no one sent you?"

"No."

"You'd better go," she quickly concluded.

"Maybe she'd like a cup of tea," I heard behind me and looked back at Mary Margaret's mother. She was standing in the middle of the room, her head tilted toward us. "I can make it, you know," she added.

"No," Mary Margaret called back. "She's not staying, Mum."

"What are you afraid of, Mary Margaret?" I asked, stepping farther into the bedroom.

"I'm not afraid. You'd better go."

"That's not very hospitable, Mary Margaret," her mother called.

"Mum, just be still."

"Is it true then, Mary Margaret?" I asked.

"What's true?" her mother asked. She was close to the

doorway, but she still had her head tilted as though she wanted to hear us better.

"Nothing, Mum, nothing. Go back to your radio."

I stood there staring and suddenly, Mary Margaret started to weep. I went to her and sat on the bed.

"It's all right," I said. "I came to help you."

"Are you crying in there, Mary Margaret?" her mother asked.

"No, Mum. No. Please."

"I'll make a pot of tea for you and your friend," she said and shuffled away.

"Is your mother all right?" I asked. "Should I go out there?"

"No, she's fine. She's blind, but she manages," she said.

"Blind?"

"She's what's known as legally blind. She can make out shapes and such, but she really doesn't see," Mary Margaret told me as she wiped the tears from her cheeks. She pulled herself up in the bed. "Why are you here?"

"I told you. I was worried about you."

"Why do you care about me?" she asked.

"We should all care about each other, don't you think?" I replied.

She stared at me suspiciously, as suspiciously as someone who knew there was more.

"Are you really pregnant?"

She nodded.

"Are you going to marry the man?" I asked.

"What man?"

"The man who made you pregnant. Is he going to do the right thing, take care of you and your baby?"

Or would the baby end up like me, I wondered, lost

and alone, forever looking for a home. I hoped Mary Margaret's lover was a responsible person.

She looked at me as if the idea was fantastic, not only the idea of a man taking care of her, but that a man had made her pregnant. Maybe she thought hers was an immaculate conception.

"You were with a man, weren't you? It wasn't more than one, was it? You know who the father is, don't you?" I asked all my questions in rapid fire, each one being born out of another fear.

"I don't want to talk about it," she said.

"What about the baby? Are you going to go through with it and have the baby?"

"I've got to," she said.

"What? Why?"

"I don't want to talk about it. Please, go away."

"Why do you have to have it? Is it because of your religious beliefs?"

"No," she said.

"Then what is it?"

"He's making me have it."

"Who?"

"Please, leave me alone," she said and started to cry again. She turned her head from me and I put my hand on her shoulder.

"Maybe I can help you," I said.

She looked back at me, with her small fists grinding the tears from her eyes.

"How can you help me? You're just an orphan girl from America. You can hardly help yourself. They sent you here because no one wanted you there."

"Who told you that?"

"It doesn't matter," she said. "Please, just leave me be. I can't get into any more trouble."

"It's not all your fault, Mary Margaret," I said. She shook her head and turned away again. "You shouldn't be thrown out on the street. They have no right to be so uppity. They're not so pure and good back there."

She kept her head turned away, her eyes down.

"I know what you've been doing in the cottage," I said softly.

This time her head whipped around so fast, I thought it might snap off her neck.

"What?"

"I saw you and Mr. Endfield through the window one night."

She shook her head, trying to deny it.

"I saw you dressed as a little girl and I saw and heard how he pretended you were his daughter."

"You mustn't tell anyone," she gasped, her hand on her throat.

"Don't worry, I won't. He's changed the cottage and he had me go there to pretend to be his daughter, too, only grown up."

Her eyes widened.

"He has?"

"Yes. So you see, he has no right to fire you and condemn you. He has plenty to hide and be ashamed of himself. You've got to stand up to him, not that working for the Endfields is any picnic," I added. She kept shaking her head. "You shouldn't be made to leave now anyway. You're not showing at all, as far as I can tell, and even when you do…"

"No, I can never go back there," she blurted. "Please."

"Why not?"

"Now here's a cup of tea for you both," her mother said, coming through the doorway. She held out the cups and saucers.

"Mum, I said no," Mary Margaret told her. Her mother stood there, arms extended.

I went to her quickly and took the cups.

"Thank you," I said and handed one to Mary Margaret. "Drink it. You'll feel better after a cup of tea."

She almost smiled.

"You sound like an English girl now," she said.

"It's catching."

She nodded and took a deep breath. Then she looked up at her mother who still stood there looking concerned.

"Go sit by your radio, Mum. Stop worrying about me," Mary Margaret told her mother. "I'll be all right. I swear."

"Okay, dearie," her mother said with a smile. "Call me if you need anything."

"What does she think is wrong with you?" I asked as soon as she was gone from the room.

"She thinks I just have a bad time of the month."

"What are you going to do, Mary Margaret?" I asked her. She sipped her tea and then shook her head.

"It'll be fine now," she said. "There's nothing to do."

"Why will it be fine? You've got a mother who's legally blind, you don't have a job and you're pregnant and not married; from the way you're talking, the man, whoever he is, won't be doing much to help you," I catalogued.

"He will," she said. After a moment she sipped her tea and then added, "He wants the baby, too."

"Then why doesn't he just marry you?" I asked. She

looked down at her cup. "He's married already, right?" She nodded. "Where did you meet him?"

"In his home," she said.

"In his home? A married man invited you to his house and you went?"

"I had to go," she said.

"Had to go? Why?"

She looked up at me. Her eyes told it all. I was the one who started to shake her head now. Now I was the one looking to deny the truth even when it slapped me in the face.

"What are you saying?"

"Please, just go and forget about it. Please."

"It's Mr. Endfield," I said, the weight on my chest making it almost impossible to get the words out. "He's the father of your child, isn't he?"

"Just go," she pleaded, putting the cup of tea on the nightstand. "Please, don't make any trouble for me."

"Trouble has already been made for you," I said. "I don't understand. He had you dress as his little girl. Surely when you were pretending to be her, he wouldn't...he couldn't..."

"I wasn't only dressed as his little girl," she said, the tears streaming down her cheeks and dropping from her chin now. "He had other things for me to wear, things them dancers in those clubs wear," she confessed.

"This is terrible. Who else knows?"

"Nobody," she said.

"Boggs," I said sharply. "He has to know. That was why he was always out there standing guard, wasn't it? Boggs knows it all, too, doesn't he? He knows you're pregnant. Doesn't he?"

She nodded.

"They both ought to be put in the Tower of London," I

muttered. "The next time that man even dares look hatefully at me, I'll…"

"You can't say anything to him," she moaned through her sobs. "Please, Rain, please. Go. Don't let him know you were here. Don't tell him anything."

"What can he do? I'll leave if I have to and he can't do any more to you. You can go to the police and turn them both in as perverts," I said. I was almost ready to tell her who Richard Endfield was to me, but I was afraid that might frighten her even more. "You should, in fact. If you want, I'll go with you."

She shook her head.

"No, please."

"Why not? Boggs is an ogre; he's a monster in a suit and tie. He's no better than Mr. Endfield. He's…"

I heard the apartment door open. Mary Margaret gasped and pressed her palms to her chest. She whimpered like a little mouse. I turned toward the doorway. The steps were heavy, familiar. A moment later he was standing there, his eyes blazing at the sight of me.

It was Boggs himself.

"What are you doing 'ere, eh?"

"I came to visit her," I said defiantly. "More to the point, what are *you* doing here?" I shot back. Slowly, I stood up to face him. "We'll call the police."

He smiled coldly and shook his head.

"Call the coppers on me? Ha! Lotta good that would do ya. This 'ere's my home," he said and lifted his heavy arm to point at Mary Margaret. "And that there's my daughter."

It was as if the floor had gone out from under me. A numb, cold feeling ran down the side of my face and my body to my toes. It took all the strength I had to keep myself straight and firm. If I was ever to be an actress, this was it.

Years in the projects taught me that sometimes it was better to go right on the offensive and not let your opponent know how afraid you were. It would surprise him or her and surprise was often the best and only weapon.

"She's your daughter and you let all this happen to her? What kind of a father are you?"

"Better than the one you 'ave," he said.

I winced, but stood my ground.

"I'd rather have no father at all than a father like you, a father who let a man do this to his daughter, who stood by and not only watched but protected the man."

"You don't know nothin' about it," he said, now wincing himself a bit. I had at least wounded him. I could see from the way he glanced at Mary Margaret.

"What is there to know? You let her be part of some sick fantasy. What's going to become of her now?"

"Damn you, girl. Don't upset 'er any more than she already is. Nothing bad's going to come of 'er. Besides, what else is there for her? She don't have no profession, no talents. She didn't even go far in school. Now, she'll 'ave money for the rest of 'er life, she will. He'll give 'er a better place to live and me wife will be with 'er. They'll be outta this rat trap."

He smiled and straightened his shoulders proudly.

"I saw to all this, yes. I knew what the guv was about and I says to myself, why not 'ave my family benefit, eh? Is your father lookin' out for you as well?"

He wagged his heavy right forefinger at me.

"Don't you go accusin' folks a bad things. You don't

know nothin'. Now get outta here and leave 'er be."

"How do you know she couldn't have a better life on her own? What right did you have to condemn her to this life?" I challenged, still holding my ground.

"Ah, go on with ya," he said, waving his hand at me. He looked at Mary Margaret and nodded. "She ain't complainin' none. Go on, ask 'er, ask 'er if she's unhappy about it."

I looked at Mary Margaret. She had embraced herself and was trembling so badly, I thought she might crack a rib.

"What do you expect her to say with you hovering over her like some monster?"

"Monster, am I? Monster." He lowered his shoulders as if he really was insulted. "We come from workin' stock. We 'ave no family wealth and no one's givin' us charity and opportunities. I've done the best I can for my family these years. I've driven the Endfields all over this city and listened to 'em talk about their teas and their fancy lunches where they waste more food than we 'ave all week. Whenever I could, I picked up what they tossed away and brought it to my family, and when there was an opportunity for Mary Margaret to 'ave steady, safe work, I made sure she got it.

"What'cha think 'appens to girls like Mary Margaret? It's not much different from what 'appens to poor girls where you're from," he said. "She mighta gotten 'erself up the spout with some good-for-nothin' and become just another ragtag woman scrounging for her supper.

"Now, she's going ta 'ave a decent house and always enough to eat and clothes on her back.

"Monster, am I? Go on, get your arse out of my 'ome and leave us be."

He lowered his head and turned away to go to his wife in the living room. I stood there, feeling so confused.

"Mary Margaret," I said softly. She shook her head. Her eyes were vacant, the eyes of someone who had already left the here and now and accepted her fate. She waved toward the door.

"Please, just go now," she said in a hoarse whisper and then lowered her chin to her chest.

"Okay," I said. "If you need me, you know where I am."

I walked out of the bedroom. Boggs was seated on the sofa, his hands clasped between his knees, his head down. His wife sat beside him staring ahead, her arm through his, holding on to him as if he was the anchor to keep her from floating into oblivion.

I had seen many a pathetic, sad family in the projects, people who looked like they had been struck in the head by life and were stunned forever. I had seen people without hope who dared to take out only a small moment of the day to wonder about their lives and themselves and why they were where they were. They inherently knew that if they spent too much time thinking about it, they would go mad or worse, they would do harm to themselves or others.

I wanted to hate Boggs. He was always so cruel to me, but I wanted to hate him more for what he had permitted to happen to Mary Margaret, but I could hear Mama whispering in my ear, telling me not to judge, asking me to understand.

"After all," she might ask, "the sort of anger and harshness you see in Boggs, you've seen in many men back in the projects, haven't you? Give him that same moment of pause you give the men struggling in the streets back home. You don't need to forgive him as much as you need to understand him and then move on, child. Move on."

"Okay, Mama," I whispered to myself. "Okay."
I walked out and closed the door softly behind me.

I don't even remember the trip back to Endfield Place. Somehow I found the tube station, rode the train and walked the streets, but all the while, my mind visited the store of memories from my childhood. Mama had done a good job of protecting each of us as long as she could. I don't think it was until I was seven or eight that I even had the inkling that we were living in such desperate conditions. In those days I never knew when Ken had stopped bringing in money or wasted what we had. I didn't understand how much extra work Mama had to do to make it possible for us to enjoy at least three meals a day and have warm clothing. I never heard about rent being past due or utilities coming close to being shut off.

And then suddenly, it seemed, my eyes opened and all that she had kept well hidden behind her wall of smiles and songs began to slip out before me. It was as if someone, some great power, had said, From this day forward you will understand the truth—you are *poor.*

Mama's simple dream was to get that word away from me.

Wasn't that the same dream Boggs had for Mary Margaret?

Mama went so far as to give me back to the people who had sold me. Someone who didn't understand, who wasn't there day in and day out to see her struggle and her tears and pain, might condemn her as easily as I condemned Boggs.

Why was it so hard for me to decide what was right and what was wrong? Should I spend much of my time trying to decide, or should I embrace the laissez-faire attitude, the *joie de vivre,* the laughter and the wind like Catherine and Leslie and just live, just be happy, just take every day as it came and stop being such a worrier?

Go and audition for the play. Be a success and seize the day, Rain, I told myself.

Seize the day.

With more energy than I had had since I left Mary Margaret's flat, I charged up the drive toward the front door of Endfield Place. I'll do my work and I'll have fun, I vowed. Whether I like it or not, I'll have fun.

The house was quiet when I entered, of course. I expected everyone was asleep, but I did hear someone in the kitchen and I went in to see who it was. It was Leo making himself a sandwich and having a cup of tea.

"Oh, Miss Rain," he said smiling. "I'm glad I caught you before you went off to sleep. You had two phone calls this evening and I took the messages for you," he said. He reached into his jacket pocket and produced a slip of paper. "The first was from a Mr. Ward."

"What did he say?"

"He said he wanted you to know he had told Leanna everything and he wanted you to call him the first chance you had."

"Oh," I said, wondering what kind of reaction his wife had to such a revelation. Maybe he wanted me to stay away from them now.

"You said I had two messages?"

"Yes, the second was from someone named Roy."

"Roy! Oh, that's my...my friend. What did he say?"

"He said he'd be in London tomorrow and would come

by about four in the afternoon. That's all he said," Leo added.

"That's okay. That's fine. That's plenty," I told him and hurried away. Those words had spread a magic shawl of comfort about my shoulders at just the right moment.

I couldn't wait to see him and throw my arms around him and tell him everything.

Almost everything.

There were things I needed to keep locked up in the vault of my own heart.

Much later, after I had fallen asleep, I woke to the sound of Boggs's heavy footsteps in the hallway. He had returned. His work kept him away from his family at night, I realized. Rarely would he be there to have breakfast with his wife. Rarely would he be there to hold her at night.

What a strange life, I thought, full of so many terrible sacrifices. What did he hope would be the end? Where did he see himself years and years from now?

I thought about the many, many nights Mama slept alone and not because Ken had to be away, but because he was either in a lockup somewhere or sleeping off a drunk someplace.

I made one vow to myself before I fell asleep again.

I won't fall asleep alone after I'm married. I'd wait for the man who would tell me that without me beside him, without his being able to hold me in his arms, he wouldn't sleep.

That was really love.

Or was it just another fantasy?

Another part to play?

"Raise the curtain, sunlight," I whispered.

"Bring on the day and the answers."

14

Bring on the Day

Anticipating Roy's arrival made me nervous and fidgety all day and I was expecting trouble from Boggs because of my visiting with Mary Margaret. However, just like Great-uncle Richard, Boggs barely glanced at me or did anything to suggest what had passed between us. This was a house of snails and turtles, I decided. Everyone living and working here creeps into his or her shell; avoid, ignore and pretend were the words that made up their credo. I laughed to myself thinking about the family crest the Endfields treated with such importance. Those words should be printed on it, I thought, and it should be hung over the front door.

When I arrived at school, I went to Mr. MacWaine's office and signed up for the auditions on Saturday. I took the cut sheets for Katherina, too. Randall was lingering outside the doorway of my speech class waiting to speak to me.

"Did you sign up for the auditions?" was his first question. I held up the cut sheets as a reply. "Good, good. I was wondering if we could spend some time together this

afternoon. We could go to the river and maybe even practice your lines."

"I can't today, Randall," I said. "I have a visitor."

"Oh?" He looked very disappointed.

"It's Roy," I told him. His face brightened a bit.

"Oh, you mean your brother in the army?"

"That's right," I said.

"Well, how about tomorrow then?" he asked.

"I'll let you know tomorrow," I said. "I don't mean to
be vague, but I don't know how much time Roy has here
and I do want to spend as much of it as I can with him," I
explained.

"Sure, sure. I understand. Well, I'd better get to my
vocal class or Professor Wilheim will have my tongue on
a platter," he joked. "See you later."

I went to class and tried to concentrate and to listen
well, but with thoughts of Roy behind them, my eyes were
continually drawn to the clock. I wished I had the power
to move the hands forward and rush the day along. I
couldn't wait to see Roy, see how he had changed and see
what he thought was different about me.

Before the school day ended, we had another rainstorm
and once again, I had forgotten my umbrella. I stood inside the school's front entrance, fuming. It was a little
after three. Roy would be at the house in under an hour
and I would look like a drowned rat.

"What's wrong?" I heard Randall ask from behind me.

"I forgot my umbrella again. I just can't get used to
treating it as if it was a hat."

He laughed and handed me his.

"But now you'll get wet," I said.

"I'll be fine. I'll lend it to you if you promise to bring it back to me personally the moment you have the opportunity," he added. "Yes," he said before I could utter a response. "It's a bribe."

I laughed and took it.

"Thanks, Randall."

He gave me that boyishly handsome smile. Roy was coming today. I couldn't harden my heart against anyone. The sky was gray and emptying its showers of tears over the city, but for me, there was the promise of sunshine and rainbows. Randall had his work and his wonderful talent, but I knew he was as alone as I was. I had been disappointed in him, but I had no right to condemn him. People who are left in the sea to be tossed and thrown about shouldn't look down on others like them swimming for the first available lifeboat. If anyone should understand loneliness, it should be me, I thought.

I leaned toward him and kissed him on the cheek. It was as if I had lit the small candles behind his eyes. How they glittered.

"Have a good visit," he wished me.

I watched him go, imagining that someday he would be a singing star. I wouldn't be beside him, but years and years from now, we might meet and smile and only for a brief moment, remember. For now, we were more like two comets passing close enough to linger in each other's magnetic fields for a few seconds of eternity before moving on toward other worlds, other suns, other destinies.

I stepped out, opened the umbrella, and hurried off, my heart beating faster and louder with every step I took. Even with the heavy rain, I was able to get home a little before four. Roy had not yet arrived. In an hour I had to begin helping Mrs. Chester with dinner. I changed into my uniform quickly and rushed back to the front of the house, hovering near the door. I had told Leo that I expected my brother. I knew Boggs would question him and I wanted him to understand that this wasn't just another visitor to be turned away or left standing outside for hours.

Finally, close to four-thirty, the doorbell sounded. I held my breath as Leo hobbled to it, far too slowly for me.

"Good afternoon," he said.

"I'm here to see Rain Arnold." The voice was so deep and commanding, I feared it wasn't Roy, but when I stepped up to the door, there was no doubt.

He did look taller, broader, and trimmer. His shoulders were back, his posture firm. A smile began in his lips and rippled through his face until it brightened his eyes.

"Roy!" I cried and ran into his waiting arms.

Leo stepped back, amazed, amused and a bit unsettled.

"You look all grown up," Roy said when I stepped back. He held me out with his hands on my shoulders. "Not that you didn't before," he added. "You just look older."

"And you. I wouldn't have recognized you. You look bigger and older and..."

He laughed.

"Can we go for a walk?"

"Don't stand there with the door open," I heard from behind and turned to see Boggs in the hallway.

"It's my brother," I said firmly.

Boggs stared a moment, his eyes locking with mine, then a slight warming slipped into his gaze. He surprised me by nodding and saying, "Then 'ave 'im in or 'ave 'im come back later."

"He'll come in," I said quickly and took Roy's hand to lead him into the house. "I've still got a little time before I help with dinner," I explained and led him down the hallway.

"Is that the owner?" he whispered.

"No. That's the owner's lackey."

"Huh?"

"I'll explain it all in a moment," I said.

"Where are we going?"

"To my closet of a room," I said.

Roy tried to look at everything he could as I dragged him through the house.

"These people must be even richer than I realized," he muttered.

"They've got money, Roy, but they're poor."

"Huh?"

He paused in my doorway when I showed him my room and just gazed for a moment, shaking his head.

"When I learned you were going to live in England with a rich family, I thought you'd be living a lot better than this, Rain. You were better off in our place in the projects," he said.

"I know, but I don't spend much time here between school and work."

He nodded and came in.

"We'll have to sit on the bed," I told him.

"That's fine."

"How long are you going to be in England?"

"Just two days," he said. "I managed to work it out with a buddy and get myself on an army transport." He continued to gaze about my small room as if there was so much to see. "I was worried you'd be spoiled by now, living with that rich grandma in Virginia and then here. They don't treat you like a relative here, I guess."

"They don't know who I really am, Roy."

"Why?"

"Grandmother Hudson thought it was best we keep that secret. These people are a lot more stuffy and worried about their family name and such."

"Thought so," he said, looking at the room and its pathetic furniture. "Treating you like some servant girl."

I laughed.

"It's not all so terrible. I'm enjoying the school and I've seen some wonderful things since I've been here."

"Sure," he said. He looked at me quickly and then down at the floor. It made me feel like it was painful for him to gaze at me too long.

"How have you been, Roy?"

"Me? Oh, fine. You know what they say," he added smiling, "you find a life in the army. I'm getting trained in electronics so when I get out, I'll be able to find a good job. I've got a lot of good buddies, too. Maybe it's the uniform, but everyone seems to treat everyone the same way most of the time. I mean, officers are still officers, but...well, you know what I mean," he muttered, frustrated with his struggle to express himself.

"Yes, Roy, I do," I said, touching his arm.

He looked at me for a long moment and smiled.

"I've been dreaming about this so long, I can't believe I'm actually here with you again. It's almost like we're back in D.C."

"Too much has happened since then, Roy. Neither of us will ever go back."

"That's the truth," he said, nodding. He looked down again and continued. "I heard more about Ken. He got in trouble in prison and he's going to serve eight years in total now for sure."

"Wow," I said. "I feel sorry for him."

"I don't," he said quickly, his eyes filling with that famil-iar look of rage I had known so well back in what I now thought of as my other life. "He had plenty of chances to be a man. Mama gave him lots of second chances. If she hadn't suffered so much, I bet she wouldn't have died like that."

"I don't know, Roy. Lots of rich, happy people get sick like that and die."

"That woman never had her head out of the water much on account of him. No sir, I don't feel a bit sorry for him. He didn't get enough time in lockup as far as I'm concerned."

"Okay, Roy."

"There's other bad news. Aunt Sylvia died."

"Oh, no. What happened?"

"Heart failure." He looked up. "Soon there'll only be you and me left in this whole family," he declared. "Not that it's much of a family anyhow."

"A family's a family, Roy."

"It just means there's people we can't deny," he de-clared. He looked at me harder. "You and me could do something about it, Rain. We can start this whole thing new and make our own family."

I nodded, but looked away.

"I guess that's a dumb idea, now that you're on your way to being a big star, huh?"

"Oh, I'm far from becoming a big star, Roy. All I've done is a couple of things on the stage and I'm still learn-ing. I have a great deal to learn yet."

"Yeah, but you will and then you won't want to know me."

"Oh stop that talk, Roy. That day will never come. You're all I have now, too," I said.

His eyes filled with some light again.

"You mean that?"

"Of course I mean that, Roy." I looked at the time. "I've got to get to the kitchen to help Mrs. Chester prepare dinner," I said.

"Oh. Yeah. Sorry."

"But I don't want you to leave," I said quickly. "I'll introduce her to you and you can watch us in the kitchen. She'll give you something to eat, too," I said. "Or I will. After I'm finished serving the dinner, we can visit longer if you want to."

"If I want to? Sure, I want to. It's the only reason I made this trip, Rain."

"Okay," I said, smiling.

On the way to the kitchen, I began to tell him about my life in England. Just before we reached the kitchen, I revealed how I had found my real father and how Grandma Hudson had advised me to let him be.

"Is that so?" he asked, eyes wide. "Are you going to live with him now?"

"No," I said. "It's too late for that. Grandmother Hudson was right. C'mon," I said, opening the door to the kitchen. "Meet Mrs. Chester."

She looked up from a bowl of lettuce she was chopping.

"Well, what's this now?" she asked quickly. "An invasion of Yanks?"

"This is my brother, Roy," I said. "Roy, this is Mrs. Chester."

"How do you do, ma'am," he said.

She looked at me and at him. I could see her measuring the differences in our looks.

"He's visiting from Germany," I explained. "He has a forty-eight-hour pass."

"That so?"

"I thought it would be all right for him to watch us work and maybe give him something to eat while he waits for me to finish," I continued.

"Sit yerself down over there," she said nodding at the small table and chairs in the corner. "We're 'avin' a fancy shepherd's pie."

Roy raised his eyebrows and looked at me quizzically.

"It's very good, Roy. Mrs. Chester is an excellent cook."

"I do what I got to do," she muttered. "There's lots better 'n me." She glanced at Roy. "How's the food in the Yank army?" she asked him.

Roy laughed.

"We don't refer to it as food, ma'am," he said.

She stared a moment and then she laughed.

"I know what that means. Yes I do," she said, wagging her head.

I smiled at Roy and began to set the table. Roy remained in the kitchen throughout the dinner, but when I served the afters, I announced his presence.

"Your brother?" Great-aunt Leonora asked, astonished. "In our kitchen?"

"Yes, ma'am."

"You should have told us earlier. We would have had him at the table," she added.

From the look on Great-uncle Richard's face, I could see he wouldn't have approved. I brought Roy out and introduced him. Great-uncle Richard continued to look displeased and uncomfortable, but Great-aunt Leonora rattled on and on about American servicemen in London and how one of her charity groups once held a dance for them.

"That was so long ago, it doesn't pay to bring it up, Leonora," Great-uncle Richard muttered.

"Where are you staying, Roy?" Great-aunt Leonora asked him, ignoring her husband.

"I have a room in a B and B."

"Bed and breakfast. How nice," she said. "If we had known, we might have made arrangements for you to stay with us," she added.

Great-uncle Richard's eyes nearly spun in his head. He cleared his throat and turned his back on Roy. I nodded at him and he told them he was pleased to meet them and returned to the kitchen.

"What a nice looking young man," Great-aunt Leonora said. "The uniform does so much, doesn't it? It makes them all so handsome."

"Nonsense, Leonora. If a uniform did that, you'd swoon at the sight of a bobby."

"Oh a policeman is something different, dear. He's...different," she insisted.

Great-uncle Richard raised his eyebrows and glanced at me. I looked away quickly and started to clear the table.

"Maybe we should give her the day off tomorrow, Richard," Great-aunt Leonora suggested just as I started out of the dining room.

"We're understaffed with Mary Margaret gone, and she's got school, anyway," he muttered.

I lingered in the kitchen until they were finished and then I went out and quickly finished clearing the table.

"You jist go off and visit with yer brother," Mrs. Chester said. "I can finish 'ere."

"But..."

"Don't work your gob. Just go on before I change me mind," she ordered.

I thanked her and left with Roy, returning to my room.

"We can go for a nice walk," I said. "Let me just wash up and fix my hair."

He waited and then we left and strolled toward Kensington. I told him more about my real father, about the school, my acting classes, the performance at the showcase, life with the Endfields, but not about the incident with Great–uncle Richard. I didn't want him to get upset and maybe furious about it. There was no telling what Roy would do if he learned about the cottage and what had gone on there. I didn't even mention Mary Margaret. Instead, I told him about things I found strange and amusing in London. I babbled on and on and he walked with his head down or gazed at me with a soft smile on his face.

Finally, we stopped at a bench and I gasped.

"I've talked your ear off without letting you get hardly a word in about yourself, I know," I said, "but it's so good to have someone who'll listen to me, someone I can trust."

"I'm glad you still feel that way about me, Rain."

"Of course I do. Why shouldn't I?"

"I was afraid I might have scared you off," he admitted.

We were both quiet for a long moment, just sitting there watching people pass and hearing someone playing a flute way off to our right. It sounded so melancholy my thoughts just naturally went to Mama. I just knew Roy was thinking of Mama, too. It was as if we could read each other's thoughts. Maybe that came from being so close, from living the lives of a brother and sister despite the different blood in our veins.

"She'd be surprised if she could see us both now, I bet," he simply blurted.

"Yes, she would, and I think happy, too, Roy. I hope so anyway."

"Seems a person like Mama should have happiness before she dies and not afterward though."

"Yes," I said.

He turned to me and reached for my hand.

"We should be happy, Rain. We can be. Time's gone by and we've been far apart, living different lives. Maybe you can think of me as someone different now, huh?"

I shook my head.

"Every time I think of you, Roy, I think about us back in D.C., about you holding my hand and taking me for walks and protecting me like an older brother. Maybe it was a sick joke pulled on us, but that's how we were brought up. It's not easy to erase those memories, those feelings, and replace them with something so different."

He stared, his eyes suddenly suspicious.

"Do you have a boyfriend here?" he asked.

"No," I said quickly.

"But you did meet someone, didn't you?" he asked.

"I thought so, but he's not what I expected him to be and maybe it's too soon for me anyway. I don't want to give my heart away easily, Roy. I don't want to make a mistake. If people were as extra careful about their love affairs as they are about their money or some of their other possessions, there would be less heartache in this world."

"I don't need to think to know how I feel about you, Rain, and why we're good together and why we would last forever and ever," he said.

I smiled at him and nodded.

"I know, Roy. I appreciate that."

"Think you'll ever feel the same about me?"

"I don't know. I don't know what I'll feel like tomorrow, much less in the future," I said.

He pressed his lips together and took a deep breath.

"I guess I should take you back. It's late and it's getting a little chilly," he said. I could see the disappointment darkening his eyes. Why couldn't I make his dreams come true?

We walked slowly back to Endfield Place, holding hands and barely speaking.

"Maybe you could come meet me at the school tomorrow," I suggested.

"Sure. Just tell me where it is," he said, "and I'll find out how to get there."

"Oh, I know London really well, Roy. Where is this bed and breakfast you're at?" I asked him. It took me only a split second to know he wasn't really staying anywhere. Roy's face was an open book when it came to his feelings. I could turn to any page and know if he was sad or happy, and especially if he was telling the truth or not.

"I haven't found one yet," he admitted. "I came directly here. I didn't want to waste any time I might be able to spend with you," he explained. "I'll find one now, I'm sure."

"It's late, Roy. Where are you going to look?"

"I've got some addresses my friends gave me," he said, patting his jacket pocket.

I stared at him and he started to laugh.

"You saw what my room was like, but you're welcome to sleep on the floor," I said.

"Really? You won't get into trouble?"

"I don't think so," I said. I couldn't imagine Great-uncle Richard taking me to task for anything anymore.

"Sure," he said. "It'd be almost like old times. The two of us under the same roof again."

"Okay, but let's be quiet. I'd rather not have Boggs on my case," I warned. "He'd be worse than your drill sergeant."

"Doubt that," Roy said.

"You haven't really met Boggs," I retorted.

The house was its usual dead quiet when we entered. As softly as we could, we walked down the corridor to my room. I told Roy where the bathroom was and then I got myself ready for bed. I fixed the best bed I could for him using an extra blanket and pillow. When he saw the makeshift bed, he smiled.

"I did the best I could," I said.

"I've slept in worse places, Rain," he assured me. "At least it's not damp and in the middle of a storm with all sorts of bugs and rats traveling over you."

I went to the bathroom. When I returned, he was lying in his bed, his hands behind his head, looking up at the ceiling and smiling as if he was lying in the softest king-size bed with silk sheets and pillowcases.

"I should tell you," I said when I got into my small bed, "that this room is haunted."

"Haunted? What do you mean?"

I told him the story of the original owner and his mistress. Roy listened with his eyes wide, especially when I described some of the noises, the breeze and the soft sound of weeping I either imagined or heard from time to time.

He sat up quickly.

"Damn, girl. Maybe this isn't better than some fox-hole. At least we've never had spirits along the march with us."

I laughed. How good it felt to have him near me, to know he was there once again to protect and watch over me. All the memories of him hovering nearby in the city when I thought I was alone, unprotected and vulnerable returned. Would I ever find anyone as dedicated to me? If only Mama had, I thought. How was it that Ken's seed could coproduce a man as good as Roy? Surely there were other ingredients that God himself threw in the mix from time to time. I hoped and prayed He had thrown something extra in for me, too.

"Now don't be afraid, Roy. I'm here to protect you," I said.

"Sure," he said laughing. He turned to look at me. "You mind if I just look at you awhile, watch you fall asleep?" he asked. "There were lots of times I did that back home and you didn't even know it."

"What? When?"

"Oh, different times. Beni would be fast asleep and I'd sneak into your room and just stare at you."

"You didn't."

"A-huh, I did."

"When?"

"Lots of times, Rain, especially during the last year we were all together. I worried about you, about things that were going on and about the trouble Beni might get you into. And…" he said after a moment, "I just wanted to look at you. You've always been the most beautiful girl to look at," he said.

I felt the heat crawl up my neck and into my face.

"There's lots and lots of beautiful girls in the world, Roy."

"Not for me," he said, shaking his head with a determination that made my heart heavy.

"Roy."

"Don't you ever get so angry you could just spit, Rain? Don't you ever just want to rip into anything and anyone around you?"

"I guess I do, but what good would come of it, Roy?"

"I don't know. Maybe it doesn't matter whether good comes from it or not. Maybe it's just a way of…of making yourself feel better. You were right before when you said something about a cruel joke being pulled on us, making us think we were brother and sister all this time when we weren't. It's like, like being tortured or something," he declared. "At least for me," he added looking away.

I reached out and touched his face and he looked up again. With just a slim shaft of moonlight at the one window, I could see the tears in his eyes, the pain.

"Can I just hold you?" he asked.

"Sure you can, Roy. I'd like that," I said and he slipped his arm behind my head and around my shoulders as he leaned on the bed and pulled me closer to him. For a long moment we remained like that, quiet, me listening to his steady, heavy breathing. My right arm was against his chest and I could feel his heart pounding. It made mine pound harder too.

He brushed my hair back and then he kissed my cheek.

"Look at us, cast out in this world like two lost fish dumped off a boat into a lake they never swam. Both of us, rushing about, trying to make some sense of it all and every once in a while, running across each other and wondering if the other knows anything new, found a new school or some new companion to help manage the mess."

"From what I can see, Roy, that about describes most people."

"Yeah," he said, "but it doesn't have to describe us." He kissed my cheek again. "Remember that day I looked at you and you didn't stop me?"

"Roy, let's not think about all that now."

"I never stop thinkin' about it, Rain. Whenever I was the loneliest, feeling about as low as a worm, I'd bring that picture up out of my treasure chest of memories and just fight to keep it there in my mind. After a while I didn't hear anything, smell anything or see anything else but you. That's the truth and I wouldn't tell it to anyone else but you, Rain. The other guys all think I'm some sort of dangerous, angry man, but if they knew how quickly a thought about you turned me into Mama's homemade jam, they'd probably jump me and pound the glory out of me just for the satisfaction."

"Oh Roy, don't say that."

"I have to say what I feel, don't I? You are about the only person I never lied to, Rain. Never, except when I thought we were brother and sister and I had to hide my feelings. I'd tell you I was watching you to protect you or make sure you didn't get into any trouble, but the real reason was my eyes wouldn't turn away from you. I just liked to watch you."

"You're torturing yourself, Roy. You're making the joke crueler on yourself."

"It doesn't have to be that way," he insisted.

I felt his hand on the side of my leg. It moved smoothly, softly up to my hip bone and then settled on my stomach. My heart was thumping louder and faster than his.

"Roy."

"If we did it once, Rain, just once, we wouldn't think again about who we were, only about who we are. That's the only way to know for sure if we could."

"I don't think I can, Roy."

"Sure you can. You just keep telling yourself we aren't blood relations. We are two different people. We had different mamas and papas and if we met someplace and never knew each other before, it would be fine. You just tell yourself that," he said. His hand moved down. I jerked myself away a little, but his hand stayed there and then he turned my face slowly and kissed me on the lips.

"What did you say your name was again? Rain? Wayne?"

I smiled.

"Where are you from, girl?" he followed, continuing his make-believe scene.

It seems that we all need our pretended lives, I thought.

"D.C.," I said. Maybe I shouldn't have. Maybe I should have just laughed and said I was tired and let's go to sleep now, but I closed my eyes and let myself drift into the fiction like someone who had been running frantically, full of terror, through a dark corridor, trying one door of escape and then another and finding them all locked, all except this one that let me out onto a cloud.

"D.C.? I was there once. Didn't like it, but if I knew you were there, I would have stayed longer," he said. He kissed me on the lips again and touched me gently, sending an electric warm sensation through my stomach and into my heart.

Then he peeled away the blanket and gracefully moved my nightgown up my legs, following along with his lips until he was at my breasts, kissing under them, around them and then touching each nipple with the tip of his tongue.

"I'm Roy," he whispered. "Roy Arnold. Pleased to meet you, Rain," he said.

When he kissed me this time, he moved himself onto the bed, slipping his legs between mine. The next kiss was longer, harder. I brought my arms around him and held on to him like someone clinging to a raft. When he entered me, I did feel like I was drowning, drowning in a swirl of unleashed, wild passion. I was a wild animal, collared and flinging itself, about to break free. I heaved myself in one direction and then another until he touched something inside me that shut down all my resistance.

I traveled over that sweet, soft pathway, out of the darkness, out of the fear, out of the loneliness. When it ended, I was like a kite that had lost all the wind and was drifting slowly back to earth, riding the warm air, coasting and then settling softly on a plush green, cool lawn.

Roy moaned his own contentment and then he lifted himself away and lay beside me on the bed, holding on to my hand. I didn't move. I didn't speak. I kept my eyes closed.

"You're a beautiful girl, Rain Arnold," he said. "I'm glad we met. I don't want to ever say good-bye to you. No, ma'am."

He still held on to my hand.

"You all right?" he finally asked.

"I don't know," I said.

"Just like two people who never knew each other before," he preached. "That's all it is. Two people, two strangers, getting to know each other and falling in love. Happens every day someplace," he told me.

Pretend, I thought.

Imagine.

Drive away the truth, shoo it out and slam the door on it.

Don't you come back here, you cruel joke, you. Don't you come knocking on this door, hear? You go plague some other poor soul or go back to hell where you were born, I told the darkness in my mind.

Roy and I held hands until we both grew too tired and then his fingers slipped from mine and fell away like the fingers of someone I was trying to keep from drowning, but in the end, didn't have the strength to hold on to.

Sleep closed over me. I thought I felt fingers in mine again, but this time, when I looked, it was Mama beside me, smiling, telling me not to worry.

"We'll do fine," she was saying. She was always saying. "We'll be all right. We've got each other and believe me, honey, that's a lot more than most folks have. Most folks, they've got only their poor selves."

She was so right about that. Mama, she was so right.

Morning broke through the window like a stone shattering the glass. I nearly jumped up. I had slept clear into breakfast. My heart did flip-flops just thinking about all the trouble I was about to be in. Not only would they complain about my oversleeping, but they'd find Roy was here. I looked down at him. He was on his stomach, his long, muscular arm around the pillow, his eyes still tightly shut.

As quietly as I could, I rose and went out to the bathroom. I rushed to get dressed and then I hurried down to the kitchen. Mrs. Chester was sitting at the small table sipping tea with Leo who sat across from her. They both looked up.

"You're the luckiest girl," she said. "I forgot myself that today they were goin' to the church breakfast."

"Oh," I said, releasing my trapped hot breath. My heart stopped pounding.

"What surprises me is Boggs didn't go poundin' yer door down."

Leo nodded his agreement.

"Lucky me. I'll get ready for school then," I said.

"Don't you want a cup of tea?" she called after me.

"No. I'm late," I shouted and hurried back to my room.

Roy had risen and gone to the bathroom. I quickly changed into clothes for school. When he returned, we just looked at each other.

"I overslept," I said. "I've got to hurry."

"Sure. I'll go with you to see where the place is," he said. He threw on his shirt and jacket.

"There's a side door," I said. "It might be better if you went out that way and met me out front."

He nodded, avoiding my eyes. Neither of us seemed to want to acknowledge what we had done. I took him to the door. Just as I opened it, Boggs stepped out of his room and looked at us. Our eyes met, but he didn't speak. He walked off.

"He doesn't seem that bad," Roy said.

"Everyone has his own problems here," I told him. "Be out in a minute."

Roy left and I went through the house, feeling silly about sending Roy out secretly now. The only ones I was hiding him from now were Mrs. Chester and Leo and they wouldn't have gone running to the Endfields with any stories.

I grabbed Randall's umbrella in the alcove and joined Roy in front of the house. We started for the Burbage School.

"It doesn't look like it's going to rain," Roy said, seeing the umbrella.

The sky was partly cloudy and the air was warm.

"You never know here and I've got to return this to a friend anyway," I said.

When we arrived at the school, I told him when I would be finished for the day, and he said he would meet me in front of the school.

"You okay?" he asked.

"I feel like someone still on a merry-go-round," I said. "When it stops, I'll know how I am."

He nodded.

"That's the way I've been feeling for a long time."

He gave me a quick peck on the cheek good-bye and I hurried into the school to class, my mind a maze full of confusion and turmoil. I was hoping it would all settle down before the day at school ended and Roy and I could have a sensible discussion about what had happened.

But Fate had other plans.

Fate was like someone in the wings watching us perform, smiling at us, knowing all along that what we thought was real was just an illusion. We thought we were the players, the actors, but we were really in the audience watching what we thought was ourselves.

When the lights came up, as they always would, we'd find there was no one there.

The curtains would close on just another dream.

15

CRO

Last Wishes

$\mathbf{M}$y mind was wandering like some satellite that had
fallen out of orbit and was drifting aimlessly through
space. Mrs. Winecoup's words seemed to become all one
continuous note falling farther and farther behind until it
was almost gone. In fact, I was in such a daze that it took
me a few seconds to realize I was being addressed.

"Rain!" she repeated.

I blinked and looked around. Everyone was staring at
me.

"Mr. MacWaine needs you," she said when she saw she
finally had my attention. She nodded at the doorway and I
turned to see him standing there, the expression on his face
so severe and dark, it made me tremble just to look at him.

"Please, come with me," he directed.

I rose slowly, picked up my books and left the classroom. When I stepped out, he closed the door.

"Your employers, the Endfields, have sent their car and
driver for you," he began.

"Why?"

"I'm afraid I have some rather bad news. Mrs. Hudson passed away this morning," he told me. "They'd like you to return to their house immediately."

It was as if my heart stopped and all the blood in my body drained down to my feet. He saw the paleness in my face and quickly seized my arm.

"Are you all right?"

I nodded but leaned back against the wall to catch my breath. It was just like being punched in the stomach without any warning. Grandmother Hudson, dead? No, *no,* I need her. I wanted to make her proud of me.

"What happened?" I barely managed to utter.

"I don't know any details, I'm afraid. I was just told she'd passed away and asked to send you to Endfield Place as soon as their car had arrived. I do hope it all turns out well for you," he said. "And I'm very upset myself about Mrs. Hudson's departure," he added as if Grandmother Hudson had merely decided to take an earlier train out of this world. "She was a very fine woman, a great lady," he said. "As I'm sure you were well aware."

He walked me to the front entrance. I saw the Rolls waiting with Boggs behind the steering wheel staring coldly ahead. The last place I wanted to go to now was Endfield Place. I just wanted to run far in any other direction. I certainly didn't want to get into that car with Boggs, but I had little choice. As I stepped out, I remembered I was meeting Roy. He would be coming here, looking and waiting for me at the end of the school day. I turned to ask Mr. MacWaine to tell Roy what had happened, but he was already on his way back to his office. There was no way to contact Roy. I was sure he was just wandering about the city. Maybe I could have someone call from the house and tell Mr. MacWaine later, I thought and continued toward the vehicle.

Boggs got out when he saw me and came around to open the door, which surprised me. Training was paramount, I imagined. A chauffeur was a chauffeur and a passenger a passenger, even if that passenger was someone like me.

"Thank you," I said and got in.

He said nothing, returned to the driver's seat and we started away. It wasn't until we were well along that I wondered why the Endfields would have sent for me immediately anyway. Why wouldn't they have waited for me to return from school? They didn't know about my real relationship to Grandmother Hudson and I would never have expected them to be so concerned for me.

The answer was obvious as soon as I had entered the house and Leo directed me to the drawing room. Great-aunt Leonora was on the settee, a handkerchief pressed to her face. Great-uncle Richard was seated in the chair across from her. He looked as stern and as formal as ever in his three-piece pinstriped suit, his face filled more with anger than sorrow.

"Have a seat," he commanded, nodding at the settee. I turned to Great-aunt Leonora as I crossed into the room. She lowered her handkerchief, revealing her bloodshot eyes and pale face, swallowed hard and watched me walk to the settee as if she was meeting me for the first time. I guess in a sense she really was.

"What happened to Mrs. Hudson?" I asked as I sat.

My Great-uncle Richard sat up straighter in his chair and glared at me.

"I'll be the one conducting this inquiry," he said.

"Inquiry?"

"Victoria called us a little over two hours ago with all the bad news," he said, stressing *all* and *bad*. "It appears that you have been living here under a deception," he said with stinging eyes of accusation. "Almost like some sort of spy planted in our home, disguised as a poor orphan girl who had to work her way through school as a mere domestic, when in reality, you are heir to Frances's fortune now and indeed a blood relative," he said.

Great-aunt Leonora let out a loud wail and sobbed hysterically for a few moments, her shoulders shaking so hard, I thought she might crack a bone. Great-uncle Richard just watched her disdainfully and then finally said, "That's enough, Leonora. Enough!" he commanded when she didn't stop instantly.

Her sobs diminished into gasps like a small engine running out of gas and so did her trembling. She covered her face with her handkerchief and glanced at me.

"There is sadness, tragedy and disgrace, almost in equal portions," he continued. "I don't know where to begin with this ugly mess."

"It wasn't my idea to keep everything secret," I said. "Grandmother Hudson thought that for now it would be best."

"Grandmother Hudson! Oh, dear, dear, dear," Great-aunt Leonora moaned.

"I'd appreciate it if you would refrain from calling her that while you are still here with us," Great-uncle Richard said. "We have been able to contain the embarrassment and keep it amongst ourselves in this house, however I must know immediately who else knows the truth about you. I mean, of course, who else in England? It's not as

329

important in America, but here reputation is more valuable than a large bank account."

I stared at him, trying to decide what Grandmother Hudson would want me to do: just get up and walk out or tell him everything? I decided it made little difference now. It was clear they didn't want me here and I couldn't want to leave any more than I did at the moment.

"My real father for one," I said, enjoying the look of shock on both their faces.

"What's that? Real father?" He grimaced. "I'm talking about here in England," he said condescendingly as if in England such a father would never exist.

"And I repeat, my real father. He lives here and has been living here for some time."

No one spoke. Great-uncle Richard looked lost for words for a moment and Great-aunt Leonora sat there with her mouth open, her tongue frozen.

"This man, this real father, this is the man with whom our niece Megan..." He waved his hand in the air to finish his thought. It was beneath him to do more than make some vague references to my mother's affair.

"That's how it works," I said. "How babies get born."

"Don't be impudent," he snapped, but looked away quickly. I began to wonder what bothered him the most about me now: the fact that I was a relative or that he had put a relative into one of his fantasies in the cottage? I was tempted to ask, to shoot hot, mean words back at him, but one glance at Great-aunt Leonora halted my fury. It would drive her into further hysterics and I had no reason to punish her.

"Well," he continued, suddenly buoyed by the news, "did this man offer to take you in?"

"No. He has his own family here."

"I see." He grimaced and nodded. "Actually, I expected to hear something like that."

"It's not what you're suggesting," I said. "He's a respected man, a college professor. I don't want to be the one to ruin his family," I said.

"No? You want to ruin this one instead, is that it?"

"I don't want to ruin any family. I didn't ask to be born like this and then to be sold off and returned this way," I said.

"Sold off?" Great-aunt Leonora looked at her husband. "I don't understand what she means, Richard."

"It's not of any importance now. Spare us those details," he said. "We have enough to deal with at the moment. I'm making arrangements as we speak for all of us to fly to Virginia for the funeral and for the aftermath. With you being a part of the legacy, you will have to be there, of course. I'm sure you won't mind leaving school for that."

"I'm going because I want to be there. Grandmother Hudson was very dear to me." I spun on Great-aunt Leonora before she could moan. "And I won't call her anything else anymore. The truth is finally out and that's it," I said firmly.

She looked like she would shatter into tiny pieces like some piece of china.

"You won't be coming back here," Great-uncle Richard said. "Take everything that belongs to you."

"That's fine with me," I said.

"Oh dear, dear," Great-aunt Leonora moaned. "What was Megan thinking of, to have a child with a black man?"

"She was always wild," Great-uncle Richard complained. "I warned your sister every time I set eyes on her that they were being too lenient, but that's the way Americans bring up their children," he lectured, "far too liberally. Once you surrender order, decorum, a sense of place and heritage, you . . ."

"Start pretending you're someone else?" I asked pointedly. "Participate in little illusions and games?"

He turned a little crimson, but held his posture and his gaze.

"There's no point in talking about it any further. We'll be leaving on the eight o'clock flight tonight. Get your things together. That's all I want to say about this right now," he added to tightly shut down the conversation.

"You don't want me to serve you dinner?" I asked, my voice thick with sarcasm.

"Hardly," he said.

"I don't want to eat anything," Great-aunt Leonora muttered. "My sister is gone. I have no family left," she wailed and rocked herself in her seat.

"You have two nieces and a great-niece and -nephew," her husband reminded her.

"Two great-nieces," I said.

She looked at me. The whole thing was finally settling into her mind and she didn't know what to say or what to feel. Finally, I thought, someone would know what I endured.

"What an incredible disaster," Great-uncle Richard muttered as he stood up. "What's that saying Americans love? You can choose your friends but not your relatives?"

"Exactly how I feel too," I said and walked out first, heading for my room and my private time to mourn Grandmother Hudson. Somehow, I knew when I had waved good-bye to her that day I left for England that I was waving good-bye forever. I think she knew it too. I think that was why there were tears in her eyes. She was too confident about herself and her future to cry at partings. She was that sad only because she knew she would never see me again.

I didn't have to call the school to ask Mr. MacWaine to meet Roy. As soon as I didn't appear, he went looking for me and found Mr. MacWaine himself and learned the news. Immediately thereafter, he appeared at the Endfields' doorway. I had completed my packing when I heard Leo's distinctive limp resounding in the hallway.

"Your brother is here," he told me when I peered out my door.

"Thank you, Leo. Why didn't you just send him back?"

"Mr. Endfield asked that I fetch you," he said. He looked embarrassed. "I'm sorry. The young man is waiting outside."

"He wouldn't let him in?"

Leo didn't respond. He didn't have to. I charged up the hallway to the front of the house. My great-uncle was in his office on the telephone continuing his preparations for a sudden departure. He glared at me and then turned his back as he continued talking on the phone.

Fuming, I practically lunged at the front door. Roy was standing in front, his hat in hand. He looked up expectantly when I appeared.

"I'm sorry, Roy. They pride themselves on being so polite and decent when the real truth is they're the cruelest, meanest . . ." I glared back at the house. If my eyes were cannons, the building would be blown away. "They're horrified now that they've learned I'm related to them. Grandmother Hudson was right about them. They're afraid their precious reputations might be damaged. They should know how terrible I feel about being related to them."

I folded my arms around myself and kicked a small stone down the driveway.

"What's this all mean?" he asked, obviously astounded by my display of raw rage.

"I'm going back to Virginia tonight for the funeral and everything. I didn't get a chance to tell you, but Grandmother Hudson put me in her will. I'm not sure yet what it all means, but one thing is for sure, my mother can't deny me anymore and pretend I don't exist. Her husband is going to want to know why I'm an heir and her sister will practically break her neck rushing to tell him and get him to help her get my rights denied."

"So your Mama's family still doesn't know anything about you?"

"Nothing real," I said.

He shook his head, his face full of concern.

"That's going to be some funeral, Rain, with a family feuding and arguing right in the middle of all of it. You sure you can handle all that yourself?"

"I've got no choice, Roy. If I don't, I'll be letting down Grandmother Hudson and giving them," I added, nodding at the house, "what they'd like. They'd like me to just go away, disappear, pretend I don't exist. My great-uncle is an expert when it comes to pretending," I added furiously. Roy didn't catch onto any innuendo or strange reference.

"Maybe you should just leave, Rain. You can forget them all and return with me to Germany. Lots of guys there are married. They do all right. It isn't a bad life for now and at least you won't have to be with a bunch of phonies," he said.

I looked down, kicking another stone, remaining silent.

"Not a good idea, huh?" he followed.

"I don't think so, Roy. I still have a few questions to answer about myself."

"Yeah," he said, looking off.

"I'll write you as soon as I know what's happening," I promised him.

"You coming back here?"

"Not here," I said, indicating the house.

"Back to England, though?"

"Maybe. I don't know yet. It's like I was riding on a magic carpet for a while and suddenly someone pulled it out from under me and I'm floating down, but down to what, I don't know."

"You sure are brave, Rain. I never knew how brave you could be. Someone else in your place would get the best deal and run," he said.

"I might still do that."

He stared at me a moment and shook his head.

"I doubt it," he said and I smiled.

"I'll miss you, Roy."

"Will you? Good. Miss me a lot," he said. "Miss me 'til it hurts."

I widened my smile and then he hugged me, kissed my hair and my cheek and put his hat on.

"Guess I'll just head back early then," he said. "It's hit and miss with a ride anyway."

"What do you mean? I thought you had your travel arrangements all set."

"I'm hitchhiking," he told me. "I've got to get on an army transport."

"What would happen if you didn't? It doesn't sound like you planned it all too well."

I fixed my gaze on his eyes and he shifted them away too quickly.

"You had a pass though, didn't you, Roy? You didn't just up and come to England now, did you?"

"Sure I had a pass."

I leered at him and he smiled.

"Maybe I stretched it a bit, but that's all right."

"Roy Arnold, you didn't?"

"I'll be okay," he said quickly. "You don't need anything more to worry about."

I shook my head.

"Someday, I'll stop getting everyone who comes into contact with me in trouble."

"Don't go blaming yourself for anything, Rain. I'm a big boy and I don't do what I don't want."

"I always knew that, Roy Arnold. Just promise me one thing," I said.

"What's that?"

"You won't follow in Ken's footsteps. No matter what happens, you'll never do that."

"You don't need to hear me promise, Rain. I'd rather be dead," he told me.

Neither of us sounded hopeful, however. It was as though a dark, brooding cloud, the one that had followed our family from the beginning, had lowered itself around us, and wave our arms as fast and as hard as we could, we couldn't move it away. It would always be there.

I rushed forward, kissed him quickly on the lips, and then turned back to the house. He watched me until I stepped inside and closed the door. I took a deep breath and started down the corridor. Great-uncle Richard stepped out of the drawing room as I started by.

"You and your brother must be very close, very close indeed to have such an intense good-bye," he remarked.

I glanced into the drawing room and realized he had probably been watching us out the front window. Before I could comment, he crossed behind me and headed up the stairs.

"We'll be leaving in an hour," he muttered.

"Not soon enough for me," I whispered back at him.

When I returned to my room, I sat on my bed and tried to catch my breath. It was all happening so fast. Some great force had taken the reins of my Destiny and was driving it headlong in another direction. Where? Why?

My thoughts went to my father and I quickly opened my notebook and began a letter.

Dear . . .

Should I call him who he is? No more lies, no more false faces, I thought.

Dear Daddy,

I'm sorry I haven't gotten back to you sooner. I really appreciated being with your family and meeting my half brother and half sister. They are lovely children, and I know they'll make you very proud. I was also so happy to meet Leanna. I like her a lot, and I'm sure we would get along just fine.

It was never my plan to rush into anything, even if you wanted me to. Now, all of it has to be placed on hold anyway. I have been given very bad news. Grandmother Hudson has passed away. You never knew her as I did, of course, so I don't expect you to understand why or how, but she and I did grow very close to each other and I will miss her. She had a great deal of faith in me and she helped me build my self-confidence.

As I told you, she has made me part of her will, and I am returning tonight with my great-aunt and great-uncle to attend the funeral. I don't know what will happen to me next, but I expect that I will return to England in due time, and I hope then we can get to know each other better and I can become a small part of your life.

Thank you for not denying me, for wanting to know me, for having the courage to acknowledge me. My mother hasn't yet, but I believe as I am writing this letter, she is probably breaking the news to her husband and children. She has little choice now, now that Grandmother Hudson's will is going to be read.

It makes me smile to think about that. I just know Grandmother Hudson is getting her final satisfaction in doing it.

I'll write you from America first chance I get. Please give my love to Leanna and the children. I'm so sorry so much time has gone by without us ever having met.

Love,
Rain

I folded the letter, addressed an envelope and went out to find Leo. He took it and promised to post it for me first thing in the morning. Mrs. Chester was in the kitchen working, despite the fact that no one was going to sit down to a formal meal. Habit was habit and she went through her motions no matter what occurred. She had no idea why I was leaving, but I wanted to say good-bye to her.

"I've come to say good-bye, Mrs. Chester. I haven't always understood everything you've said and done, but I appreciated your efforts to make things easier for me here."

She put away a bowl and wiped her hands on a dishtowel while she looked at me.

"They ain't makin' you go home account of anything I said," she told me. "Ya been a good worker and a good girl, ya have."

"No, it has nothing to do with you or this house or anyone," I said. "I have to go."

"I'm not one to snoop or tell anyone else what's ta do and what's not, but you be careful now."

"Thank you, Mrs. Chester." I gave her a hug and said, "And look in on Mary Margaret. She needs that."

Mrs. Chester nodded.

"We all do, dearie. We all do," she said and returned to her work.

I went back to my room to get my things. After I put on my jacket, I paused in the doorway and looked around the small room. Funny, how a person can get used to almost anything, I thought, even a jail cell like this. I thought about the ghost of Sir Godfrey Rogers's dead mistress.

"I never saw you or spoke to you," I said aloud, "but I feel sorry for you if you're stuck in this house."

I lifted one of my suitcases and struggled a bit with the other when suddenly Boggs appeared.

"I'll get that," he barked. "You go on ahead. There's a phone call for you."

"Phone call?"

He grunted and went for my suitcases. I returned to the main part of the house and lifted the receiver on the hallway table where Boggs apparently had left it for me.

"Hello?"

"Rain, it's Randall. I just heard from Leslie that you had some bad news today and had to leave school. I was looking everywhere for you. What happened?"

"I have to return to America, Randall," I said. "My grandmother has passed away."

"Oh. I'm sorry. When will you be back?"

"I don't know."

"Well, can I call you somewhere?"

"I'll write you a letter," I said, "and tell you more when I know more."

"Promise?"

"I don't like to make promises, Randall. Too many have been made and broken for me so I just say what I'll do and I do it," I told him.

"I believe you. I wish I could see you before you leave."

"I'm just about ready to go. We're on a night flight."

"Wow. That is fast. What about...you know who?" he asked.

"I've written him a letter."

"I'll be thinking about you," he said. "And that's not a promise; it's a fact."

"Okay, Randall. Thank you," I said, smiling.

"Rain. You're really the nicest girl I ever met. I'm sorry about what I did to ruin it."

"That's another thing I'm tired of, Randall, apologies. You don't have to make any. We didn't get involved enough to owe each other any promises or any apologies,"

I said. I was sorry I sounded so cold, but my emotions felt like they had been running on empty for hours and hours.

"I know," he said. "But I wish we had. Have a good trip, Rain."

"Thank you."

"Bye," he said. "I'll be thinking of you next song I sing."

"Bye," I said and placed the receiver in the cradle. I truly wondered if we would ever see each other again, or just be memories dwindling into shadows.

Boggs went by with my bags, glanced at me and continued on.

I could hear my great-aunt and great-uncle coming down the stairway. I took one final look at the big house. It was really never a home to me. Perhaps it could be a home only to ghosts, living and dead. I moved quickly to join my great-aunt and great-uncle at the door and we all walked out to the waiting Rolls. Boggs had already put their luggage in the boot. He held the door open for them and they got in quickly. I looked at him and then followed. No one spoke. Moments later, we were on our way to the airport.

We all slept for most of the trip across the Atlantic. When we arrived in Richmond, Jake was waiting for us at the gate. I felt like running into his arms so we could comfort each other. One look at his face told me of his great sorrow. His thick, bushy eyebrows were turned in toward each other as the ripples of deep sadness formed on his forehead. When he saw me, his eyes brightened and he smiled.

"Hello, Princess," he said before he greeted the End-fields. My Great-uncle Richard was obviously displeased about that.

"You can help us with our carry-ons," he told Jake.

"Oh, sure," Jake said. He pulled a cart around and filled it quickly with the smaller bags. Then he looked at Great-aunt Leonora and said, "Sorry for your trouble, Mrs. Endfield."

"Yes," she said in a dreamy, far-off voice, "yes, thank you, Jake. Do you know if she suffered any at the end?"

"How would he know, Leonora? He's not your sister's doctor. He's your sister's chauffeur."

"From what I understand, Mrs. Endfield," Jake replied ignoring Great-uncle Richard, "it happened so quickly, she didn't have time for pain. That would be like her," he added for me.

He leaned toward me as we continued toward the baggage carousels.

"You look all the lady now, Princess. She'd be damn proud," he whispered.

I smiled and squeezed his hand. He looked at me quickly, feeling how my own hand was trembling.

"How is my niece?" Great-aunt Leonora asked him.

"And which one would you mean, Mrs. Endfield?"

"Victoria, of course," Great-uncle Richard said sharply. It was as if they'd already plucked my mother out of their family tree.

"Oh. She's doing fine. She's at the house waiting on you all. Megan will be here with her family early in the afternoon," he added.

"It takes a funeral for us to see her," Great-aunt Leonora moaned.

"Humph," my Great-uncle Richard grunted.

Jake glanced back at him and then at me, winking.

I had one friend forever, I thought.

"How's Rain?" I asked him.

"Oh, boy, she's prime. Wait until you set eyes on her," he said.

"Who are you two talking about?" Great-aunt Leonora asked, overhearing.

"My racehorse, Mrs. Endfield."

"You named a horse after this girl?"

"A-huh. And the horse is mighty proud of it, too," he said.

If I wasn't coming home to a funeral, I would have laughed aloud. It would be a while until I could smile and giggle again.

"I always forget just how big this estate is," my Great-aunt Leonora said as we drove up the circular driveway.

It really was a big house, I thought. Endfield Place could fit inside of Grandmother Hudson's home.

"Ostentatious," Great-uncle Richard muttered at the four large, tall columns holding up a front-gabled roof. "I always thought so. Americans always think bigger means better quality."

"I did always like the front door, Richard," Great-aunt Leonora insisted. The large front door had four panels and was surrounded on the sides and top by a narrow band of rectangular panes of glass held in a delicate, decorative frame.

Of course, there was a great deal more land than they had back in England and there was the small lake as well.

"Ours has more class," Great-uncle Richard insisted.

"Yes, yes of course it does," Great-aunt Leonora was happy to agree.

Sibling rivalry, I thought, even reached across the ocean.

We all got out and went into the house where we found Victoria having a cup of coffee, her head bent over a pile of documents spread over the dining room table. She looked up when we appeared. She was pale, her eyes dull, but she always looked that way to me. If she was devastated by Grandmother Hudson's death, it was a well-kept secret, I thought.

"Victoria," my great-aunt cried and held out her arms.

Victoria rose slowly. She seemed even taller and thinner than I remembered, and not that much time had passed. She was dressed in a faded pink housecoat and wore no makeup, no lipstick. Her dull brown hair hung limply at her ears.

"Hello, Aunt Leonora," she said, She didn't move toward her to embrace her. "Uncle Richard."

"Hello, Victoria. We're sorry about all this," he said nodding slightly toward me.

"It's a mess," she said, gazing down at the papers. Then she finally took Great-aunt Leonora's hand and gave her a quick embrace. She kissed Great-uncle Richard on the cheek.

Jake made some noise coming through the front door with the luggage.

"Oh, Jake," Victoria said, stepping into the hallway. "Put my aunt and uncle's things in my mother's room and her things," she added, nodding at me, "in the maid's room downstairs."

"Not her own room?" Jake challenged.

"Alison will want to be in her room," she said. She turned to me. "I'm sure that's all right with you, isn't it?"

"Yes," I said. "I'm really not worried about which room I have at the moment."

"How sweet. Okay, Jake. Thanks," she told him and returned to the dining room table. "I've got some hot coffee if you'd like some," she told the Endfields. "Or I can put on some water for tea."

"What happened to Frances's maid?"

"Mother hasn't had a maid for some time now," Victoria replied, glancing at me. "There was a nurse here from time to time, but that didn't last either."

"Well, who's going to provide for us?" Great-aunt Leonora asked with a frantic tone in her voice.

"I've called a temp agency and they're sending some people over later today so we can do what is necessary for the funeral and after. I'm sure Rain might be of some assistance as well. You did help my mother with domestic work before you went off to become an actress, didn't you?"

"What I did for my grandmother, I did out of love," I said. "I don't mind sleeping in the maid's room, but I'm nobody's maid, especially nobody here," I added and headed for the maid's room. I was tired from the trip and instinctively knew that I better do what I could to conserve my strength and energy for what was soon to come.

After Jake took care of my great-uncle and great-aunt, he brought my bags to my room and we visited.

"You don't look worse for wear," he said, "but I can see you weren't exactly welcomed with open arms. Frances was worried about you, Rain. She tried her best to get herself over there to see how you were doing."

"I was all right, Jake, but they don't have what you would call a happy home," I said and laughed at the understatement. "I liked the school and I did well there."

345

"I bet. Well, maybe one day you can tell me all about it," he said. "If I'm still working here, that is."

"I don't know what I can say about it, but if I have anything to say about it, you will."

"Without Frances, there's not that much for me to do anyway, Princess." He checked his watch. "Megan and her family are taking a shuttle down so I'll be leaving to pick them up. I can't remember the last time they were all here together like this," he added. "When they were, it was Frances who kept them in line. Going to be some fireworks now, I suppose. Better than the Fourth of July."

"Maybe I'll be celebrating *my* independence," I said and he laughed.

"Bad reason to have you here, Rain, but I'm happy to see you."

"Thanks, Jake."

"You need anything, you don't hesitate to ask me," he said and left.

There was nothing left to do but rest and mark the time until my mother and her family arrived, all of them probably still reeling from the revelations.

How would they treat me now?

After napping for about an hour or so, I heard the temporary domestic employees arrive. Victoria had hired two maids to take care of the family and then contacted a catering company to provide service and food for the funeral. She and my mother had decided they would have the mourners at the house after the service and burial, which had been scheduled for tomorrow. How different even death was for the rich, I thought. Back in the projects, when someone close to us died, we would all gather

346

around and bring food and help. The work helped comfort the bereaved. It wasn't a formal party, planned and catered. It was only people doing things for other people to help them get over their sorrow.

I rose and went outside. The late summer day was a bit crisp with a cool breeze stirring the trees. I wandered down to the lake, recalling how I had stood here watching and listening to the birds just before I left for England. While I was sitting there staring out at the water, Jake arrived with my mother and her family. I watched them all get out and head toward the house. It was the first time I had seen my mother's husband Grant, and even from this distance with Brody beside him, I could see he was at least six feet two or three, slim with dark brown hair. He wore a suit and held my mother's hand as they all entered the house. Jake drove the car off toward the garage. I took a deep breath.

It begins, I thought, and made my way slowly back to the house. When I entered, I heard them all talking loudly, Victoria's voice competing with Great-uncle Richard's. They all turned and stopped speaking when I appeared in the doorway. It was the longest moment of my life, standing there and confronting each and every one of them.

My mother's husband was a handsome man. His hair was thick, neatly styled, and his hazel eyes were bright, intelligent, radiating self-confidence like two valuable jewels set in his evenly tanned face with his strong mouth and firm jaw. He looked the most relaxed, sitting with quiet elegance amidst the explosion of emotion and anger that raged around him. When he looked my way, his eyes grew small with studied curiosity while an almost indistinguishable smile softened his lips.

"Well?" Victoria finally said to my mother, shooting a

look of disgust and condemnation at my mother and then gazing at Grant.

My mother glanced at her husband, too, and he nodded ever so slightly, suggesting the two of them had done some planning for this moment.

Brody's eyes were fixed on me. He was smiling warmly, but Alison was practically snorting like a bull.

My mother rose and walked to me, smiling.

"Hello, Rain," she said. "Let's you and I go for a walk so that we can talk."

I glanced back at Grant who looked at me with even greater interest. He made me feel like he was waiting on my reaction, waiting to judge and conclude all sorts of things about me. All I did was turn and walk out of the house again.

My mother walked beside me, her arms folded under her breasts, her head down.

"This is all such a big mess," she began. "I always thought my mother was going to live forever. She had that air of immortality about her. I remember how well she dealt with my father's death. She was always everyone's pillar of strength. I can't help suspecting that she even plotted all this, deciding just when and how she would pass away and what would occur because of it."

She stopped and sighed deeply. Then she looked at me.

"How have you been? I'm sorry, I should have asked sooner."

"I survived," I replied. She lost her smile quickly. "The school was very good, but living with your uncle and aunt..."

"I know, I know. I was never very comfortable with them. Oh, Aunt Leonora is all right, just silly, I guess, but Uncle Richard makes you feel . . ."

"Inferior?"

"Yes," she said, nodding.

I considered telling her everything, just spewing it all out like some undigested meal, letting her know what I really had to endure, letting her know about the pain and the trouble her actions years and years ago were still causing, but this wasn't the time. We had Grandmother Hudson's funeral to think about first.

"I guess you've told them everything, right?" I asked.

She continued walking toward the lake, her head down, her arms folded.

"Well, not quite," she said.

"What do you mean?"

"Grant knows it all, yes, but I haven't told the children the truth about you. Both Grant and I hoped that maybe we could spare them that in the middle of all this," she added quickly. "I'm sure you can appreciate that."

"No, I can't," I said angrily. "There comes a time when all the lies have to stop."

"It's not lying so much as it's not telling the whole story."

"What did you finally tell them about me then?"

"Well, not much more than before," she said. "I just added that your father was a good friend of mine in college and I was doing all this for you because of that old friendship."

"But when they find out about the will…"

"They won't be at the reading of the will and we'll wait until they're a little older for the rest," she said. "Okay?" She looked like she was holding her breath.

What had she done: promised her husband she could convince me to play along with their plan?

"I don't care what they know or don't know," I said.

"Good. For now it's better this way. Grant will appreciate that, too."

"What did he say when you told him?" I asked.

"He wasn't very happy about it, but he's understanding. When he was younger, he sowed his wild oats, too," she said.

"I'm happy everyone's so understanding," I muttered bitterly. Then I paused and turned on her. "I should tell you that I met my real father in England."

"What?"

"Grandmother Hudson never told you?"

She shook her head.

"I found him with the help of a friend and I even visited him and his family."

"You found Larry Ward?"

"I prefer to call him my father."

She stared at me, astonished.

"It wasn't really all that difficult a thing to do. It was hard to get myself to have the courage to actually tell him who I was, but when I finally did . . ."

"What?" she asked eagerly.

"He turned out to be very, very nice, and later, when I met her, so did his wife."

She stared and then shook her head and smiled.

"What did he say when he found out? I mean, what did he want to do?"

"He wanted to get to know me more," I replied. "He told his wife all about me just before I left England and he said she was okay with it, too, but he didn't talk about sowing wild oats," I added. She ignored my sarcasm.

"How did he look?"

"Terrific," I said. "He's a very successful English professor, highly respected, and he has two beautiful children, a daughter and a son. Just like you, only his daughter is the older child and they are both very well behaved."

She nodded, her eyes distant. She looked like she really had been in love with him once and I had stirred up all those old memories. After a moment her eyes seemed to click back to the present. She took a deep breath.

"You're an amazing young woman," she said. "That's why I know we're all going to get through this. For some time Victoria has been in a rage about Mother including you in the estate, as you know. She has been trying to get Grant to do something about it, but he doesn't want to make a big legal issue. He rightly thinks that it will bring a great deal of unnecessary and unpleasant attention to our family."

"Is he still trying to become president of the United States?" I asked out of the side of my mouth.

"He's ambitious and I wouldn't put it past him to run for high office soon," she admitted.

I stopped and turned to her.

"All right, Mother," I said. "What do you want from me? Let's just get it out and over with, okay?"

"Well, we know that my mother . . ." She shook her head, smiling, "my mother created a situation that would make it all very difficult for us. She has apparently left you title to fifty-one percent of the house and property, the remaining forty-nine percent divided between Victoria and me. She left you fifty percent of the business, and she has left you what amounts to nearly two million dollars in investments that pay good dividends."

My breath caught in my throat. It would have taken Mama and anyone in her family twenty lifetimes to come

close to my fortune, a fortune I had inherited almost
overnight.

"Of course," my mother continued, "it's shocking. Victoria wants us to challenge the will and take it through
court to get a judge to invalidate it. She claims my mother
was not in her right mind at the time. Grant says there
could be a serious challenge to the will and while that was
going on, of course, your life would be in limbo, Rain.

"So what Grant wants to propose is we compromise.
We'll set aside a quarter of a million dollars for you in an
account and you could then be your own person and do
whatever you wanted with your life. Victoria would be
satisfied. Well, not really, but we could shut her up, and
everyone could go on with their life. What do you think?"

My eyes were so full of tears, I could barely see her.
Wasn't there even a tiny speck of a motherly instinct in
her for me? Was Grandmother Hudson's death and the aftermath only an opportunity to rid herself of me forever?

I should take this ugly deal, I thought, and turn my
back on this miserable family. I should just return to England immediately and make my own life there, maybe
close to my real father, who at least wasn't looking for
every opportunity possible to deny my existence.

"Rain?"

I turned and looked out over the lake. What would
Grandmother Hudson say to all this? What would she expect me to do?

I recalled the day I had left her. Every moment, every
second of that good-bye, lingered in my mind vividly. I
was so concerned then that it would be the last time we
would be together and I had been right. She had looked
into my face with such hope and said, "I was afraid there

was nobody in my family with a sense of propriety and the grit to do the right things. Don't disappoint me."

"Grandmother Hudson had a reason for what she did," I began and turned slowly to face my mother. "I made her certain promises, promises she will expect me to keep, even now, maybe even more now than ever. I wouldn't change a comma in her will," I said defiantly.

My mother looked shocked. Obviously she had been so confident she would convince me to do what Grant had wanted.

"But Rain, look at what will happen. Victoria won't give up easily and…"

"Somehow," I said smiling, "I think your husband will be able to convince her."

She just stared. I smiled and she shook her head.

"You really are like her," she said angrily.

"That, Mother, was the best compliment you could ever have given me."

She nodded, turned and started back toward the house.

I took a deep breath.

I was afraid.

My whole body trembled. I had no idea what I was going to do or how I would defend myself, but I was on Grandmother Hudson's land and I was in her house and her words still echoed inside me.

This wouldn't be easy, I thought as I started back, too.

"So?" I could hear Grandmother Hudson reply. "When has anything ever been easy for you, Rain?"

I smiled, closed my eyes and said, "I won't disappoint you, Grandmother."

Epilogue

N0 one bothered much with me before or during the funeral and its aftermath. Brody was the only one who really spoke to me, asking me questions about England and telling me about his school year and his achievements in sports. He was still a good prospect for a football scholarship. Alison avoided me constantly, which was just fine with me. She looked annoyed about having to attend her own grandmother's funeral. Most of the time, she stayed in her room, sulking.

It was really Jake who kept me informed about the time and place for everything. I rode to the funeral in the Rolls with my great-uncle and my great-aunt. Everyone else was in a hired limousine. Great-uncle Richard really didn't know all the details of the will yet and was simply anxious to get back to his precious England and his own work. Great-aunt Leonora played the deeply saddened sister, but she would brighten like a spotlight whenever some old friend approached her and she had an opportunity to describe and brag about her wonderful life in England. Very quickly, it all turned into more of a social event and I retreated to my own room to wait for the eventual outcome.

Grant paid me one final visit before the reading of the will. He came to my room, the maid's room, the day before to make one more attempt at what he called "a reasonable solution."

For any other man, I thought, this would be a very embarrassing and difficult meeting. After all, he was face to face with his wife's illegitimate daughter.

However, he handled it as if he were just the opposing party's attorney, keeping it formal, correct.

"I thought if we could have one sensible conversation, we could avoid anything unpleasant for all concerned," he began.

"It's too late," I said uncharitably. "I have had nothing but unpleasantness here."

"Which is my point. Why continue that? I could," he continued, "convince Victoria to agree to be more generous with the compromise. How does half a million dollars sound?"

"Disgusting," I said. I turned on him. "Whatever makes you think my relationship with my grandmother could have some price tag put on it? What right do you have to assume things about me? What do you know about my dreams, my sense of responsibility and love toward this woman who has given me so much? I'm not some sort of blemish you heave makeup over and forget."

He stared at me. Despite his purpose, he looked like he appreciated me.

"I'm just trying to make things right."

"For whom?"

"Everyone," he insisted.

"Grandmother Hudson," I replied, "has already done that."

He nodded, saw he could get no further, shrugged and left me.

Grandmother Hudson's attorney, Roger Sanger, a man in his late fifties, called me to personally tell me he would be conducting the reading of the will the next day. I told him about Victoria's objections and how she might be taking it all to court.

"I know all about it," he said. "I spent a lot of time with Mrs. Hudson, and Victoria knows I was a witness to the will. There was nothing wrong with Mrs. Hudson's mind and she knew exactly what she wanted to do. Victoria has spoken to me a number of times about this. I think she finally understands."

"We'll see," I said. I knew Victoria was not the sort of person you could read and then predict what she would do. To me, after what she had tried to do with the letter she had sent to my great-uncle, she was a viper.

Brody and Alison weren't at the lawyer's office, as my mother had said. She and Grant had sent them home. It was a very dry and official meeting. Victoria grimaced with pain every time my name was mentioned.

When it ended, my great-uncle and great-aunt were the most shocked. They had yet to be told all the details. Perhaps Grant still had hoped to clear it up beforehand. Except for their astonishment, very little was said and it felt like another funeral. Mr. Sanger spent time afterward with me, discussing some of the legal paperwork.

Great-uncle Richard and Great-aunt Leonora had

booked themselves on a flight back to London immediately afterward. They said good-bye to everyone and Jake took them to the airport. By this time Great-aunt Lenora seemed quite dazed and confused by all the events and every time she looked at me, her eyes widened. Before they left, she did come to me to say, "You're almost richer than we are."

"I always was," I told her. She had no idea what I meant. Great-uncle Richard didn't even try to say good-bye to me.

My mother came to see me before she and Grant started back home.

"I really don't know how all this will come out, Rain," she said. "What are you going to do now?"

"I'm going to stay here for a while," I said. "I will probably return to England for the next semester and continue pursuing my dramatics career."

"You want to stay in this big house by yourself?"

"It was home to you once, wasn't it?"

"Yes," she said, nodding. "Though it seems like that was another life now. I'll call you," she promised. She attempted to hug and kiss me. I stood like stone and she turned and left.

I went out front and watched Jake drive them off. The sky had become quite overcast. Low clouds rolled in from the east and the wind grew stronger and stronger. I could see how it made the water ripple on the lake. I wasn't chilled, however. It all smelled fresh and made me feel good. I was even looking forward to the downpour that the clouds promised. I expected it would wash away the sadness and the sorrow and make tomorrow look even brighter.

I was thinking I would return to the cemetery myself

when the weather cleared and say my own final good-bye to Grandmother Hudson.

Just then a door slammed on the side of the house and Victoria came around the corner, her arms full of folders. She stopped when she saw me.

"These are mine," she said. "They have to do with my business."

"Don't you mean our business?" I asked.

She glared at me and stepped closer.

"What do you think you will get out of all this defiance?" she demanded.

I looked away and smiled.

"My name," I said, turning back to her. "Nothing more and nothing less."

"We'll see," she said.

She walked away.

The two crows I had often seen before soared over the lake and toward the house, veering to the right, toward the sea.

They flew as if they believed the future always held promise for them, I thought.

I hoped and prayed I was right in thinking it did for me, too.